mean time

edited by

JERRY SYKES

BLOODLINES

First Published in Great Britain in 1998 by
The Do-Not Press
PO Box 4215
London SE23 2QD

A paperback original.

Collection copyright © 1998 by Jerry Sykes
All stories © 1998 respective Authors except
'The Names of the Missing' © 1998 Dennis Lehane, published by
arrangement with the Ann Rittenberg Literary Agency, Inc.

The rights of the Authors of this work have been asserted in
accordance with the Copyright, Designs & Patents Act 1988.

ISBN 1 899344 40 3

British Library Cataloguing in Publication Data. A catalogue
record for this book is available from the British Library.

h g f e d c b a

Printed and bound in Great Britain by The Guernsey Press Co Ltd.

Front cover photo credit: Lucienne Cole

Mean Time : **Contents**

NIPD BLUE

Colin Bateman

They're in the car, outside a video shop on the Antrim Road. *Planet of the Tapes.*

This has nothing to do with the video shop. Or the Antrim Road. It has to do with John Cooley standing there with his sunglasses and his confident smile and looking about him like he owns the world. They're going to take him down a peg or two.

Maybe even three if they feel like it.

Software. John Cooley's about to join the modern world.

It's an unmarked car, but they're in uniform. There's no mistaking them, really, but Cooley doesn't budge not even when they approach. He has a scar at the base of his scalp; when he raises an eyebrow, just one, as they walk up, the scar arches up like it's pointing to his brain. He's saying: I'm too smart for you boys with your fancy new uniforms and your fruity little hats. You're still RUC, you're still SS-RUC. A cease fire and a make-over isn't going to change that.

'John-boy, how are ye?' says Walsh.

'Fine and dandy,' says Cooley.

'Would ye mind comin' down to the station with us?' says Philpott.

'Not at all,' says Cooley, smiles and then pauses. He looks about him. Up to the sky. Back down and his eyes are all narrow and inquisitive. 'You don't think I've done something, do yees?'

They give him the supercilious smiles. 'Of course not, John-boy,' says Walsh, 'we just want a wee chat. About life in general.'

'Life?' says Cooley.

'We hope so,' says Philpott, 'unless they bring back the death penalty first, you evil fucker. Now get in the back of the car.'

'Fuck off.'

'Fuck off yourself.'

'Fuck the lot of yees.'

'Get in the fuckin' car. You fucker.'

'Fuck off.'

'Are we gonna have to make ye?'

'Fuckin' right you are.'

'C'mon John-boy,' says Walsh, 'we don't wanna have to call back-up.'

'Neither do I,' says Cooley, 'and my back-up's bigger than your back-up.

His back-up can cause rioting in north Belfast for weeks at a time. Or so he still likes to think. But the reality is, since the peace thing, since they gave up their guns, or at least buried them to use later, there isn't the same vandalistic malevolence; besides, since the Brits pulled out there aren't the same shops any more; all the nationals have sneaked off leaving just the crappy little locals. No point in lootin' those, it's like lootin' yourself.

They stand looking at each other. Then Philpott taps him on the arm and says, 'We have a new interrogator down at the station.'

'Big fuckin' deal.'

'He's the best in the business.'

'Big fuckin' deal.'

'Isn't a hood he hasn't cracked yet.'

'Big fuckin' deal.'

'He could reduce you to putty.'

'Big fuckin' deal.'

The video shop is closing for the night. The shutters are coming down. The owner looks suspiciously at them, but he doesn't say anything. Cooley nods across. The owner looks a little bit scared, and a little bit hopeful that the cops will drag Cooley off.

'Chicken,' says Philpott.

'What?'

'Big chicken leg. John Cooley.'

'Who're you callin' a fuckin' chicken?'

'You, ar-buck-buck-buck.'

'You fuckin' chicken bastard.'

'He'd crack you in no-time,' says Walsh.

'Like an egg, you fuckin' chicken bastard.'

'Fuck away off.'

'Chicken.'

'Chicken.'

'Chicken.'

'Chicken.'

'Right,' says John Cooley.

☐

They put him in the interview room. They remove his cigarettes and deprive him of coffee. There is no air conditioning. It's hot. They leave him for an hour. He starts to sweat, but it's just the heat, he's not worried. They've tried every combination before: good cop-bad cop; good cop-good cop; bad cop-bad cop; lady cop-lady cop: ugly lady cop-ugly lady cop; good looking lady cop-ugly lady cop; fuckin' fantastic looking lady cop-ugly lady cop; fuckin' fantastic looking lady cop-fuckin' fantastic looking lady cop. They've tried violence, they've tried abuse, they've tried common sense, they've tried reasoning, they've tried bribery, they've tried to turn him into a squealer. Thus far, he hasn't given them a single fucking thing. But now there's software.

Philpott says to him, as he's setting the gear up, 'You ever used a computer, John?'

'What's the fuckin' point?' Cooley sneers.

Philpott shrugs. 'Computer, it's the new thing.'

'Big fuckin' deal.'

'What you do,' Walsh says, 'is just sit there, and the computer asks you some questions. Simple as that.'

'Where's my solicitor?' Cooley asks.

'You're not entitled to a solicitor, John-boy,' says Walsh.

Cooley laughs. 'Course I fuckin' am. Go get him.'

Walsh laughs back. 'Sorry, old son, but you're not. You're only entitled to have a solicitor present if we're going to question you. And we're not going to question you.'

'Well what the fuck am I here for then?'

'*We're* not, *it* is.' He points at the computer. 'Legally it's a bit of a grey area. Doubtless it will be sorted out in due course. But for the mean time, you're not entitled to a solicitor.'

Cooley glances at the squat grey box on the table. 'So I'll just fuckin' ignore it then.'

'Ah, no, you can't do that, John. You have to respond to the questions. You know that. You know the government removed the right to silence a long time ago, you have to answer. Make any old shit up you want, but you have to answer.'

Cooley looks doubtfully at the computer. 'And what if I destroy the fuckin' thing?'

'Then we put you away for damaging police property.'

Cooley shrugs. 'Okay,' he smiles. 'Fuck away off and leave me to it then.' They turn to the door. Cooley calls them back. 'If you ask me,' he says, 'youse are fuckin' bonkers.'

'We're not askin', John-boy,' says Walsh.

❐

There is perhaps three minutes of silence. Just Cooley's steady breathing. There's a camera in the light-fitting, so they can see it all on the screen upstairs. They're placing bets.

'He's mine,' says Walsh.

'Not a chance,' says Philpott.

'Fear of the new,' says Walsh.

Philpott shrugs, and watches, and waits.

❐

The voice is plummy-English. He had expected something *electronic,* like that cripple Hawking or whatever on the box. But plummy-English. The most annoyingly plummy Colonel Mustard in the Conservatory English. It says: 'Did you murder Delores Watson?'

Cooley sits back. Like he's going to answer a fucking machine. And then he remembers what they said and he leans forward and hisses into what he presumes is a microphone, 'Yeah, I cut her fucking head *off*.' He cackles.

A light flashes. Cooley looks at it for a moment. Upstairs Philpott asks if the software can cope with sarcasm. Walsh shrugs. He didn't build the fucking thing. Just watch.

'Did you murder Delores Watson?'

'I answered that.'

'Did you murder Delores Watson?'

'I answered that.'

'Did you murder Delores Watson?'

'Fuck off.'

'Did you murder Delores Watson?'

'Fuck away off.'

'Did you murder Delores Watson?'

'Murdered her, fucked her, slit her throat.'

'Did you murder Delores Watson?'

'Yeah, I killed her.'

The light flashes. There is silence for forty seconds. Cooley leans closer, examining the machine. He looks to the door. Then he sits back. Folds his arms. Taps his foot. Reaches into his pocket for a fag, then remembers they took them off him. He pulls at his lip. He looks to the door. Then he leans forward and says, 'No, I didn't.'

The light flashes. 'Did you kill Delores Watson?'

'No, I didn't.'

'Did you kill Delores Watson?'

'No, I didn't, okay?'

'Did you kill Delores Watson?'

'I hardly fucking know her.'

'Did you kill Delores Watson?'

'Fuck off and die.'

'Did you kill Delores Watson?'

'I'm tellin' you, I didn't know her.'

'Past tense now.'

'What?'

'Past tense now.'

'What the…?'

'Did you kill Delores Watson?'

'What did you mean by …?'

'Did you kill Delores Watson?'

'No!'

'Did you kill Delores Watson?'

'I tellin' ye … !'

'Did you kill Delores Watson?'

'Of course I didn't kill her.'

'Did you kill Delores Watson?'

'Will you shut the fuck up?'

'Did you kill Delores Watson?'

'Fuck off!'

'Is your mother still alive?'

'What?'

'Did you kill Delores Watson?'

'What did you say?'

'Did you kill Delores Watson?'

'Not that … not that!'

'Did you kill Delores Watson?'

'Why did you mention my mum?'

'Did you kill Delores Watson?'

'Will you shut up about that stupid fuckin' whore … what about my mum? What about my mum?' He sits back. He looks to the machine. He's breathing hard. The machine isn't. 'What's my mum got to do with any of this?' There is no response. He sits forward. There is silence. He bites at a nail. He looks to the door. Back to the machine. A green light flashes.

He waits for something to happen. He peers at the machine. He leans into it and runs his fingers over it. The green light flashes. He jumps.

'What?' he says.

There is no response.

'I didn't kill her,' he says quietly.

There is no response.

'We were having a row. I mean, she was only a whore.'

There is no response.

'She took me back to her place. But then she didn't want to know. We had a fight. I hardly touched her.'

'Did you kill Delores Watson?'

'No, I didn't.'

'Did you kill Delores Watson?'

'She fell over! She cracked her head! What could I do?'

'Did you kill Delores Watson?'

'No!'

'Did you kill Delores Watson?'

'I don't know! I ran outta the fuckin' place as fast as I could!'

'What would your mother say?'

'*What?*'

'Did you kill Delores Watson?'

'No … no … what did … ?'

'Did you kill Delores Watson?'

'What is this obsession with … ?'

'Did you kill Delores Watson?'

' … my mother … ?'

'Did you kill Delores Watson?'

'I don't know! I don't fuckin' know! What do you want me to say?'

'Did you kill Delores Watson?'

'If she died, she died … I couldn't help … I didn't wait …'

'Tell mummy!'

'Stop it!'

'Tell your mummy!'

'Stop it, this isn't funny!'

'Did you kill Delores Watson?'

'Yes! Okay! Oh-fuckin -kay! I killed her! She was askin' for it! She tried to rip me off! I thumped her! She fell down! She cracked her head! If she died, she fuckin' died. I don't care. Just shut the fuck up …'

'Did you kill Delores Watson?'

'Yes, I killed Delores Watson.'

'Did you kill Delores Watson?'

'Yes!'

'On your mother's grave?'
'On my mother's grave.'

❐

The door opens. Cooley is crying, head on the table. 'Relax, John-boy,' says Walsh, crossing and switching off the machine.
'I didn't mean to ...' Cooley says.
'Didn't mean to what?' says Philpott, lighting a fag for him.
'Kill Delores Watson.'
'Relax,' says Walsh.
'You didn't kill anyone.'
'She's fine. She wants you done for assault.'
'We were just trying out the software.'
'Who's going to believe a hooker anyhow, a drunk one at that?'
'Relax. Do you want a coffee?'

❐

He is standing outside the video shop on the Antrim Road. *Planet of the Tapes*. This has nothing to do with the Antrim Road. Or the video shop. It has to do with John Cooley and his faded smile and the sunglasses he seems to hide behind.
They get out of their unmarked car. They approach from a different direction so that he doesn't see them. Walsh taps him on the shoulder.
Cooley jumps a foot in the air. 'What the ...' He turns, sees them. 'Aaaah ... fuck yees,' he says. He lights a cigarette. He looks at them, shakes his head. 'Fuckin' computers,' he says.
'Did you kill Delores Watson?' Walsh says, identical BBC plummy. He's laughing. 'Sucker,' he says, 'a microphone and a box with a little light on the front.'
'*Software*,' giggles Philpott.
'Hardware,' says Cooley, and lays him out flat with a left hook.

❐

He is led into an interview room. He is pale. The table is bare.

Walsh comes in with another officer and they sit opposite him. The tape machine is switched on and the cops make their introductions. Then Walsh says: 'Did you murder NIPD Detective Mark Philpott?'

SITTING PRETTY

Simon Conway and Peter Crowther

FOR KARI SULLIVAN

Fade far away, dissolve, and quite forget
What thou among the leaves has never known,
The weariness, the fever and the fret,
Here, where men sit and hear each other groan.
John Keats (1795-1821)

Jerusalem: January, 36 AD

*T*he hill is no longer green.

Many feet have worn away the grass and now all that is left is a well-trodden carpet of packed soil, rich and earthy red.

The night mist is still hugging the ground as two men move silently but with purpose up one of the hills overlooking Jerusalem, a mist that tastes sharp in their mouths... sharp and bitter.

Neither of them speaks. In fact, there is no sound at all: no bird-calls, no soughing winds... just a still silence.

The icy winter chill cutting into their bones, they have managed to leave the walled city under cover of darkness to begin their climb to the scene of yesterday's events. They reach their destination just as the first signs of light are showing across to the east.

Now, almost without realising, they are there. And there it is.

Or rather, there they are. Three of them, lying on the ground where they have been pushed over. One of them is still partly buried in the *soil, its transverse shaft splintered where the nails had been pounded in. Still without speaking, both of the men stare at those nails, crusted black now.*

The taller of the two men points to what they have come for and, like two well rehearsed dancers, each takes his end, lifting the heavy weight and now, in unison, the pair set off to the place they prepared the previous day.

It will be an arduous journey, but not a particularly long one.

Of course, the weight will make it seem to take much longer than it actually will, but at least they will be able to forget the cold that attacks them and concentrate on their task... although, by the time they reach their destination, their hands are numb.

Glancing around to ensure that nobody had seen them, they manoeuvre their burden inside the cave, a thin sheen of cold perspiration covering their bodies and their breath coming loud and forced.

After a short rest, they wash their prize very carefully, splashing it with the water they left in tubs specifically for this purpose. They work like mothers cleaning their new-born, almost caressing it with love and care.

And now that task has been completed, they bind it in muslinet, hide it in a very dark corner, and hurry away before they are missed.

London: Tuesday, 4th January, 2000, 8.05am

Adrian lifted the heavy sash window and looked out onto the Bayswater Road, breathing in the carbon monoxide and trying to discern lights across the city.

The lights Adrian was looking for were not electrically powered. They were human lights, lives blinking out or flicking on like LEDs on some colossal control panel, existences brief in cosmic terms, some coming to an end and some just starting out.

He had read somewhere that every minute of every day millions are born and millions die. He wondered which was the greater number. He also wondered if he was still hung over from toasting in the new millennium just three days earlier.

'Have you got that window open, Adie?' He heard a drawer or cupboard door slam. 'Christ, it's bloody freezing.'

Ellen sounded unusually fraught this morning. But Adrian knew why. It wasn't just that it was her first day back at work and it wasn't just that they seemed to have spent most of the past few days drinking and smoking – the latter being one of the reasons that Adrian had opened the window; it was due to the fact that Ellen was nearing that point in her menstrual cycle that just made her cranky.

'It's smoky,' he shouted over his shoulder and then leaned on the sill.

The sun was low and bright and the air carried that special crispness that only sunny winter days can bring. It had a fresh-ness about it which Adrian decided was very appropriate as he stared down onto the Bayswater Road and strained to look further into Hyde Park, but a slight ground mist prevented his gaze penetrating too far.

A steady stream of muttering from behind him in the flat suddenly grew in intensity and volume, accompanied by the clump of Ellen's shoes on the polished floorboards.

'Have you seen my hairbrush? Jesus, I can't find my hair-brush.'

Adrian had spotted some human movement in the park, something different to the cars and the pedestrians. It was a couple of joggers. He watched them running, marvelling at their concentration and determination. Maybe he should do that. After all, they were only a stone's throw from the Park ... and he did need to do something. Last night he had noticed the tell-tale signs of a rounded belly that was the product of too many lunches with his agent and publisher and too much alco-hol.

'A-*die*!' Ellen was standing in front of the Hopper print wear-ing only a sweater and tights over her pants, a cigarette in one hand and the other on her hip. 'My hairbrush?'

'I have no idea where your hairbrush is.' He looked point-edly at the cigarette. 'That's a cigarette.'

Ellen glanced at her hand and opened her eyes wide in mock horror. 'Hey, not bad, Sherlock.' She pointed to her wrist. 'And this is a watch. The watch says I'm going to be late.' She took a long pull on the cigarette and blew smoke up towards the ceiling. 'So, any ideas?'

Behind her, in the painting on the wall, one of Edward Hopper's eternally solitary women sat crunched up on a bed staring out of another sash window onto a long-ago Californian coastline.

'About what?'

'Planet Earth to Adrian ... come in, Adrian.' She took another pull on the cigarette and glanced around the room at the debris – channel changer, two empty wine bottles, one of them on its side, a big candle burned down to the plate it was planted on, piles of magazines and various heaps of crumpled clothing. 'About my fucking hairbrush.' She turned around muttering and flounced out of the room. 'And close that fucking window.'

Adrian turned back to the window. 'It's even smokier now,' he said quietly.

Across the road an attractive woman was leaving the park where she'd been walking her dog. Adrian watched her walk up to the side of the road and wait for a break in the traffic. The dog seemed to be more interested in sniffing the post alongside and the woman kept yanking him – he assumed it was a *him*: he always assumed dogs were *him*s – back beside her.

The woman looked stunning: long green coat, probably expensive, and a long brown scarf wrapped around her neck a couple of times, the tasselled ends hanging down over her breasts. Adrian wondered idly what her breasts looked like under all that clothing.

He leaned towards her almost imperceptibly and breathed in deeply. Of course, he had no chance of smelling her perfume, but he decided it was probably like a mix of spring flowers and sensuality. Why was it he could never meet women like this one? Just another age-old question that thousands of men before him had asked and would ask again.

And as he began to think about that particular poser, a large black Mercedes pulled up alongside her, the rear passenger side door opened and she got in and disappeared from his life forever. She hadn't been waiting for a break in the traffic after all. She had been waiting for a lift.

Ellen clumped back into the room.

'Got it. My hairbrush... I've got it.' There was a pause. 'You can stop looking now.'

'Okay. Good. I'm glad you've found it. My life is complete.'

Ellen muttered something. Then, 'My keys. Have you seen my keys?'

Adrian shook his head and considered – for the briefest of moments – throwing himself out of the window. But he decided they did not live high enough in the building. Knowing his luck, at only two floors to the ground, he would probably live... and be in a lot of pain for his trouble.

'Try the kitchen drawer. The big one.'

'*I didn't put them in there*,' she said over her shoulder as she left the room.

He heard the drawer grumble open and then slam shut. When Ellen came back in the room she was jingling the keys into her handbag. 'Did *you* put them in there?' Without waiting for a response, she added, 'Don't put *my* keys *anywhere* without telling me.'

'I did tell you.'

'What? I can't hear you when you speak to me out of the fucking window and with your back turned.'

Adrian turned from the window and slouched across to the sofa where he collapsed with a sigh. 'I said, I did tell you. Last night. After Jem and Cochise left.'

'Charise ... her name is *Charise*.'

Adrian shrugged and nodded.

'And she's my–'

'I know. She's your friend. I'm happy for you.' He lifted his arms wide beatifically. 'Ellen has a friend, everyone.' He dropped his arms to his side and gave her a cold smile. 'Given your current state of mind, I would say that was quite an achievement.'

'Fuck you.'

'Thank you.' He bowed. 'You have a good day, too.'

Listening to the cold finality of the door slamming, Adrian hoped that Ellen would remember where they had arranged to meet later. But he knew she would. After all, it was *her* kid brother.

Dover, England 607

The prize has been through many hands down the years, many hands and many countries. Now its grain has been fashioned and honed, its simple state converted into something more functional though equally simplistic… something more lasting albeit crude in appearance.

Now it sits upon a quay side overlooking the harbour.

There is sadness in the air. Melancholy. Loss.

Word will now have to be sent to Pope Gregory.

The emissary he sent in the closing years of the sixth century has now drawn his last breath, made his final benediction and forgiven all the sins he will ever forgive.

The body of Augustine, once a Roman monk and, more recently, as Archbishop of Canterbury, the man responsible for beginning the restoration of Christianity, so long buried after the Anglo-Saxon and Jute invasions, lies on a simple cot in Canterbury covered over with a threadbare linen blanket.

As the final passengers and crew board the creaking ship, the people gathered on the quay side watch silently. At their front, Aethelbert, King of Kent, newly baptised, wipes a solitary tear and wishes God's speed as the vessel lumbers its way towards the distant towers of Rome.

He turns back and faces into the gentle breeze that blows across the greensward overlooking the harbour. Then he walks to the chair and sits, staring out to sea at the swaying masts of the ship, running his hands along the polished wooden armrails.

Thor and Woden and Tiw can no longer claim a hold upon the English people. Now it is the one God, the only God.

Aethelbert smiles and, raising his hand, gives a single wave.

And now, returning that hand to the smooth wooden armrest, he looks down at the wooden seat gleaming at either side of his skirts and he wonders if this artifact could somehow be made more symbolic of the person who brought it. He will pass it on to his craftsmen for them to practise their skilled magic on it, dismantling it if necessary and then reassembling after chisel and scoring knife have worked their wonders.

But the King of Kent is himself nearing the end of his days and he will not see the finished article. Instead, it will pass on again to others who will be equally appreciative of its subtle charms.

London: Tuesday, 4th January, 2000, 10.43am
'Hello?'

'Adie?'

'Hi. You got there then?'

'Yes.'

Ellen sounded contrite. Against his better judgment, Adrian could not resist capitalising on it.

'*And* on time?'

'Yes,' she said tiredly, with just a hint of a smile tugging at her words. 'I got here on time.'

'Good.'

'Adie?'

He switched the phone to his other hand and flicked further through the book. 'Mm hmm?'

'Sorry.'

'Sorry? What for?'

'*You* know what for. I was a cow.'

'Well…'

'I *was*.'

'Okay, you were a cow.'

'You don't have to agree so vehemently!'

Adrian laughed.

'I've started.'

'Thank God for that.'

Her voice dropped to a whisper. 'Forgot my bloody Tampax though. Had to slip out as soon as I got in.' Ellen giggled. 'Feel better now.'

He pulled the book open and stared at the photograph.

'Adie?'

'Oh, sorry.'

'What are you doing? How's the story coming on?'

'The story? Oh, it's coming on fine.' Adrian always liked to write a few short stories between novels – to him it was like Pavarotti gargling before he went on stage to sing 'Nessun Dorma'.

'What are you doing now?' Ellen asked.

'I was just going through this book of architecture.' He jammed the phone between his shoulder and his chin and pulled his reading glasses off the shelf. 'You remember the one? The one we bought at Camden Lock? From the guy with the stutter and the wall-eyes?'

Ellen laughed out loud and then shushed him. 'Don't make me laugh when I'm at work,' she whispered.

'Okay. Sorry.' He slipped the glasses on. 'Hey, Elly… you'll never guess.'

'Try me.'

'You know that chair that Geoff and Margie had? The one you said you'd like for the spare bedroom?'

'The one Margie said they're wanting to get rid of? The one like the chair in the photos that Tim bought from that Godawful market in Lewes?'

Adrian nodded to the empty room. 'There's another picture of it – a photograph – here in my book.'

'Exactly the same one?'

He leaned for a closer look. 'Looks like it.'

'Hey, this is getting a little spooky.'

He was tempted to hum the opening bars of *The Twilight Zone* but Ellen spoke again.

'What time did you say you were going to pick me up?'

'Four. And I'm *not* going to try to park. I'll expect to see you on the street so make sure you get out in time.'

'Will do. Adie, I have to go. Ralph's coming.'

'Okay. Give him my love.'

Ellen laughed.

'See you at four.' He looked up from the darkness of the book and glanced out of the window. The day was brightening. 'You okay? About Johnny, I mean.'

'I'm fine. Really. Must go. Love me?'

'A little.'

'Bastard! Bye.' She blew a kiss down the phone. When Adrian responded with one of his own, the line was already dead.

Dover, England, 1254

If the prize could speak it would recall being here before.

Now its armrests are finely sculpted, exquisitely polished, delicately filigreed. Its straight back is scrolled with an overlay of intricately carved scenery, rolling fields, distant towers. If one were to spend much time staring into the wooden picture, one might almost imagine it to be real... might even fancy they could smell the breeze blowing across the meadowland or hear the distant call of bluejay and cuckoo.

Looking at it now, admiring its legs and its polished seat, Henry can recall feeling just that way when he first sat in the chair. He was nine years old and newly crowned the King of England, the third Henry to hold that exalted position, and the chair was deemed to be his throne.

In 1227, just 27 years ago, he came of age and inherited the permanent throne... but he has retained a special love for this seat. There is, quite simply, something about it.

Now he is partway through his reign and, though he does not know it – for few can foretell the future – he still has another eighteen years ahead of him. He is a good King, a good husband and a kind father.

He is here, on the dockside, watching the chair being hoisted onto the ship. His son, Edmund, stands by his side. Edmund has been offered the vacant throne of Sicily by the Pope. When Henry asked Edmund what special memento he wished to take with him, his son answered without a second's hesitation. The chair. And reluctant as he was to grant such a request, Henry agreed.

There will be difficult times ahead, for both Edmund and Henry. But they will rise to these difficulties and they will survive. And then the prize will move on again.

But for now, it is here. And it is going.

As the chair settles onto the deck, Henry nods sagely and puts an arm about his son's shoulder.

Edmund takes hold of his father's hand and squeezes it tightly.

London: Tuesday, 4 January, 2000, 12.02

It was almost warm but Adrian shivered and drew his full length sheepskin coat tighter around his body.

Underneath the coat he was wearing many layers. Next to his skin on the upper part of his body was a Budweiser T-shirt; on top of that he had an Atlanta Braves thick T and on top of that he was wearing a New York Yankees sweatshirt. Ellen was always asking why he didn't wear anything English – or, at least, British – and Adrian always responded with a shrug. What else could he do?

The whole ensemble was set off with a woollen hat pulled down tightly onto his head and over his ears and a very bright knitted woollen scarf, wrapped round his neck a couple of times.

On his legs he had thermal underwear, followed by heavy denim jeans. He was also wearing two pairs of woollen socks and had forced some old tennis shoes over them, although he had failed to tie the laces. He was, in the main, warm. Ellen always said he looked like Woody Allen in that movie where he tried to smuggle lots of clothes out of a prison workroom by wearing them all at the same time.

But Adrian didn't care. Wearing so much in the cold weather made him feel comfortable and secure, as well as warm. Usually. Right now, standing at the counter in Tower Records at Piccadilly Circus waiting for a girl with terrible posture to get Tim from the staff room, he felt distinctly uncomfortable. Nervous somehow, though he couldn't put his finger on why that was.

'Yo!' Tim announced as he appeared from the door behind the counter. In one hand he held a pencil and in the other a copy of *Music Week*. 'What gives, amigo?'

Adrian shrugged and waited until the girl moved across to serve a customer with a veritable pile of CDs. 'Not much,' he said.

'Don't tell me you want to *buy* something?'

Adrian shook his head. 'It's those photographs. The ones you bought in Lewes?'

Tim rolled his eyes. 'Lewes, gateway to God's waiting room.' He leaned on the counter. 'What about them.'

'Well, I don't know how to explain this,' Adrian began, letting his voice trail off. Then, 'Could you take a little time out to go home and get them?'

'What, *now*?'

Adrian grimaced and nodded apologetically.

'*Why*, for crissakes?'

The girl with the bad posture looked around and frowned.

'Why?' Tim asked again, lowering his voice.

'Let's say it's research.'

Tim pulled his head back and looked suspicious. 'Let's say "bullshit", amigo. Why not let's say *that*?'

'I know, it's a strange request. But humour me, okay?'

'Okay,' Tim said, holding up his hands. 'I'll humour you. But I can't get out of the shop now. I have to get this order in this afternoon.' He nodded to the copy of *Music Week* turned open to the charts page.

Adrian's shoulders slumped.

'But…'

'But what?'

'I don't need to.'

'Don't need to what?'

'Don't need to get out. I brought them with me this morning.'

Adrian shook his head in astonishment. 'Why?'

Tim frowned. 'Good question, amigo. Good question but no answer. Asked myself the same thing on the tube this morning. Put it down to wanting to buy some click frames… you know, the ones in Athena?'

'I know the ones.'

'But I could have bought them without bringing the damned photos. Hell, they're all the same size, for crissakes.'

'Serendipity.'

'How's that?'

Adrian laughed. 'Serendipity. You knew deep down they would be needed. Maybe you even knew I'd be calling in for them.'

Glancing around the shop, Tim leaned forward again. 'You doing anything? You know, like *smoking* anything?'

Another laugh. 'Uh uh. I'm working. On a story.'

Tim said, 'Right,' stretching the word out like soft toffee.

'So can you get them?'

For a second or two, Adrian thought that Tim was going to refuse or maybe ask him some more questions but then he straightened up and disappeared into the back room. A couple of minutes later he reappeared with a brown cardboard box, its lid held on by an elastic band. He handed the box across the counter and waited.

Adrian began to remove the rubber band.

'They're all there, officer,' Tim said. 'Honestly.'

'I only want one of them,' Adrian whispered as he flicked through the sepia photographs. About halfway through images of unsmiling Victorian poses and groups gathered in cobbled streets in front of shops which seemed to sell everything from coal to bread, there was the chair. And the girl sitting in it. He pulled it out and immediately felt the uncomfortable feeling fall away. 'It *is* the same one,' he said. 'Now I'm sure.'

'Same one?' Tim craned his neck. 'Nice looking girl,' he said. 'I think the word is "pretty". You know her from somewhere?'

Adrian flicked through the rest of the photographs and then, replacing the elastic band, he handed the box back. 'Thanks. You're a life saver. How much do I owe you?'

Tim shook his head and, just for a second, looked genuinely offended. 'I ... I can't take money for that,' he said.

'I'll buy you a beer,' Adrian said.

Tim shook his head again, so hard that Adrian thought it was going to come loose, and frowned. 'Not even a beer.' Then his face seemed to clear and he smiled. 'It's a gift, from me to you. Put it to good use.'

Adrian slipped the photo into his coat pocket and started away from the counter. 'I'll call you,' he said as he walked out of the shop.

'I'll wait by the phone,' Tim shouted. He watched Adrian shuffle by some people out onto the street and then saw him walking briskly in the direction of Shaftesbury Avenue, his arm waving frantically for a cab. 'Get better soon,' he said quietly.

London, England, 1644

Despite the fact that he is to die today, William Laud feels surprisingly calm.

He always feels calm sitting in his chair, running his hands along its arms and feeling… feeling a strange tranquillity filling his body. An acceptance.

He looks around at the stone walls of his solitary cell in the Tower and hears, far off but getting closer, the unmistakable sound of footsteps.

'They come for me,' he tells the silent cell, whispers to his beloved chair… the second Archbishop of Canterbury to treat it so.

He is here because of what he believes in. He is not the first person to sit in, or to lie against or to be nailed upon the wood from which the chair is constructed… and think these thoughts. Belief – even optimism – and the chair seem to go hand in hand. He can feel this, though he cannot explain it any more than he can explain its calming air.

The Church of England and the Roman Catholic Church are not unlike each other, despite the cries of heresy such an observation has received throughout his life.

The footsteps are close now, echoing through the corridors. He can hear the jingling of keys.

William Laud slips from his beloved chair into a kneeling position and begins to pray. He rests his clasped hands on the chair's seat and then his mouth and nose against the interlocked fingers. He will ask whoever or whatever listens to such arcane incantations to ensure the chair finds a new owner, though something deep inside him suspects that the chair needs no assistance in such a task.

The key turns in the lock.

He is ready.

'Our Father,' he begins.

London: Tuesday, 4 January, 2000, 13.17

'Okay, okay, I'm coming!'

The voice was accompanied by the sound of footsteps

descending stairs and then by the sound of locks being freed.

The door opened quickly and Margie stared out in surprise. 'Adrian!'

'Can I come in?' Adrian asked and immediately regretted his bluntness. 'Sorry, Margie. Are you busy with anything?'

Margie shrugged. 'Well, Geoff and I were considering going off to bed for an afternoon of wild sex and general debauchery polished off with a cup of Earl Grey but, quite frankly, with the amount of booze he's stuck away this past few days I doubt he could get his dick up even if his life depended on it.'

Adrian smiled.

Margie stepped back and waved an arm majestically. 'So you've probably saved him from a fate worse than death. Come in. I can offer you the Earl Grey but not the wild sex or debauchery.' She patted him on the shoulder as she closed the door. 'Not that I wouldn't like to, you understand, but I think Ellen might throw a wobbly. How is she, anyway?' She linked arms with Adrian and walked him along the corridor to the rear lounge.

'She's fine. Absolutely fine.'

Geoff's voice shouted hoarsely from somewhere upstairs. 'Who is it?'

'It's Adrian, light of my life,' Margie shouted back. To Adrian, she said, 'He's been on the pot four times this morning. We found an Indian in Knightsbridge – what will the locals say! – and Geoff, against my advice I hasten to add, insisted on a strong vindaloo on top of wine, real ale and a few joints. He's not as young as he once was,' she added, shaking her head as she filled the kettle. 'But then, none of us is.' She switched on the gas and lit it as Geoff's feet started down the stairs. 'Ah, here he comes now. I suppose we could have the toilet bricked up.'

'Now then,' Geoff announced striding into the room. He took hold of Adrian's proffered hand and shook it strongly. 'Feeling a tad delicate today.' He rubbed his stomach. 'The old belly's playing up and me arse feels like someone blow-torched it. I suppose Margie's mentioned it?'

Margie lit a cigarette and blew smoke out flamboyantly.

'Yes, I said you were a little under the weather, dear, but we needed your more graphic version to complete the picture.'

Geoff nodded and pushed his glasses up the bridge of his nose with one finger. 'You know the old joke I suppose?' Geoff continued without waiting for Adrian to respond. 'What's the difference between a manic depressive and someone who washed his vindaloo down with a crate of lager and a modestly-sized vineyard?'

Adrian shook his head and tried not to laugh at Margie's rolling eyes.

'One of 'em feels the bottom's falling out of his world and the other feels the world's falling out of his bottom.' Geoff laughed and pulled a face. He adjusted the seat of his trousers and shook his bottom. 'Christ, it stings.'

Geoff moved across to the sofa and sat down gingerly. 'Found a nice place out in Knightsbridge. Margie tell you?'

Adrian started to say something but Geoff carried on.

'Nice place. Kushi something-or-other. We'll have to get an expedition together... you and Ellen, maybe Nigel and—'

'I don't think Adrian came to make plans for destroying his sphincter, dearest,' Margie said as she poured water into a teapot covered with characters from *The Wind In The Willows*. 'Did you, Adrian?'

'Well, no,' Adrian agreed. 'Not really.'

'Mmm.' Geoff nodded. 'Quite. Well, why did you come? Not that you need a reason. Bugger me, no.'

'I doubt that buggery would be a good idea in your present state, my darling,' Margie observed.

As the ensuing chuckles died away, Adrian said, 'Actually, I came about the chair.'

'The chair?' Geoff accepted a cup from his wife and settled back on the sofa. 'What chair is that?'

Margie handed a cup to Adrian. 'He means the straight-backed job we bought in that lot in Plymouth. Am I right?' She took her own cup and sat at the table in front of the french windows.

Adrian nodded and took a sip of tea,

'Biscuit? I think it's too early for a joint.'

Adrian shook his head. 'No, the tea will be fine.'

'I think I may be missing something here,' Geoff began.

'Like a few million brain cells,' Margie interspersed.

Geoff continued without acknowledging the interruption. 'You want the chair we bought in Plymouth?'

Adrian set his cup down on the floor and leaned forward. 'I can't explain any of this,' he said. 'I was writing a story – still am, I suppose – and I came across this picture. It's in that big book of architecture? The one Elly and I bought in Camden Lock? You were with us.'

Geoff frowned.

'You were pissed, dearest,' she said. Then to Adrian, 'I remember it.'

'Go on, Adrian,' Geoff said.

Adrian lifted his hands and smiled at Geoff. 'Look, I have no idea why I'm doing this but I'd like to buy the chair.' He turned to Margie. 'You said you didn't want it, Margie.'

Margie stubbed her cigarette out in the ashtray on her knee and shook another out of the packet. 'I didn't say I didn't want it,' she said, 'or, at least, I didn't mean that if I did.'

Adrian lifted his cup and noticed that his hand was shaking slightly. 'I'm not sure that I follow you,' he said. 'I thought you said—'

Margie lit her cigarette and said around a cloud of smoke, 'I said I thought it should go to a *better home*, is what I said.'

'Well, isn't that the same—'

'No, Geoff, it's *not* the same thing. I can't explain it either.' She stood up and placed the ashtray on the table. 'I want to show you something.'

Margie left the room.

'"Curiouser and curiouser," said Alice,' Geoff said and took a sip of tea. 'God but that hits the spot.'

Margie had been gone for just a few minutes and Adrian felt the nervous tension rising within him. Where had she gone? And why? He didn't have much longer to find out.

Margie came back into the room carrying a large object

wrapped in brown paper and tied with green ribbon. She set it on the floor and stood back, hands on her hips.

'What's that?' Adrian asked, though he fancied he knew the answer.

'It's your chair.'

'*My* chair? You're going to sell it to me?'

Margie retrieved her cigarette and shook her head. 'I'm *giving* it to you. I don't think this thing should be sullied by money.' She turned to her husband and added, 'If you remember, the woman in Plymouth "threw it in" with the lot.'

'She *did*,' Geoff said. 'You're *right*. I'd forgotten that.'

'Well, *I* hadn't.' Margie looked at Adrian. 'I knew you were coming... knew *somebody* was coming, don't ask me how.'

'Serendipity,' Geoff said.

Adrian smiled. He didn't know what to say.

'You have a home for it, I take it?'

'I think so, yes.'

Margie pulled on the cigarette. 'Somewhere where it will do some good?'

Adrian nodded. He reached into his pocket and removed Tim's photo. He passed it across to Margie.

'Well, I'll be!'

'What is it?'

Margie handed the photograph to her husband.

'It looks like the same chair,' he said.

Margie said, 'No question about it.'

Geoff handed the photo back to Adrian. 'Who's the girl?'

Before Adrian could respond, Margie said, 'Emily Bronte.'

'I *thought* I knew that face,' Adrian said. He looked at the photograph. 'It is, much younger of course. But it *is* her.'

Geoff said, 'Will someone tell me what's going on?'

Adrian slipped the photo back into his pocket and got to his feet. He walked across to the chair and picked it up. 'I don't think any of us knows,' he said. Then he added, 'I don't suppose there's any chance of someone giving me a lift?'

'I'll do it,' Margie said, stubbing out her cigarette. 'Geoff might end up messing the car seat.'

Washington DC, 21 September, 1862

'And by virtue of the power and for the purpose aforesaid, I do order and declare that all slaves within these United States are and shall forever be, free; and that the Executive Government of the United States, including its military, will recognise the freedom of said persons.'

Abraham Lincoln replaced his pen in its holder, leaned back from his desk and started unconsciously to stroke the arms of his favourite chair as he read the words he had just written. Certainly the words conveyed his wishes in this dark hour for his country, but he felt them too hard-edged. Too blunt almost. Without hope or optimism.

The 16th President of the United States caught himself stroking his chair and smiled a knowing smile. He had taken it with him on every major journey ever since it had come into his possession – a gift from …who was it from? He couldn't remember now. But he always felt comfortable and at ease while he was sitting in it. Full of hope for his troubled nation.

He lent forward again and picked up his pen.

'And by virtue of the power and for the purpose aforesaid, I do order and declare that all persons held as slaves within said designated States and parts of States are, and henceforward shall be, free; and that the Executive Government of the United States, including the military and naval authorities thereof, will recognise and maintain the freedom of said persons. And I hereby enjoin upon the people so declared to be free to abstain from all violence, unless in necessary self-defence; and I recommend to them that, in all case when allowed, they labor faithfully for reasonable wages.'

He leaned back again and admired his own words. The words he would deliver the very next day to his nation in waiting. As he sipped the tea that had been brought to him, he felt he had just fulfilled his purpose.

London: Tuesday, 4 January, 2000, 15.58

'Are you okay?'

'That's a strange greeting, Adie,' Ellen said as she leaned across the car and kissed him tenderly on the cheek.

'Well, it's just that you're two minutes early,' Adrian responded with a grin.

Ellen punched his arm and stuck her tongue out simultaneously.

'Ouch!'

Nervous laughter and nervous smiles. The car was
suddenly full of them.

Ellen looked in the back of the car, saw the wrapped parcel
that lay across the folded seat, and faced back to the front.

'Don't tell me,' she said. 'Grapes?'

Without turning to her, Adrian said, 'It's the chair. Margie
wanted us to have it.'

Ellen nodded.

'She asked me if we had a home for it,' Adrian added.

Another nod.

Ellen reached out and touched the paper covering, feeling
the strength of the wood beneath. For once, even though Adrian
was driving, she felt very safe.

Adrian swerved to avoid a black cab that cut him up as he
headed towards St John's Wood and the private hospital where
Johnny had been for the last seven months.

'Damn cab drivers!'

She smiled, but said nothing.

They didn't have to queue for long to get round the Lords
roundabout and then just past the cricket ground Adrian
turned left into the hospital car park.

❐

Dorset, England, 1935
In this chair he has written many things and thought many thoughts.

*Now, pulling on protective clothing for what will be the last of
many great journeys, Thomas Edward Lawrence looks at his prize for
what will be one final time. He does not know this, of course, but something deep inside him senses a coming-together, a shift in the cosmic
scheme of things.*

*Pulling on his big gloves, he wonders what this chair – or the wood
from which the chair is constructed – has seen. Where it has been. He
only knows that it has been with him since the closing stages of the
Great War, when he was presented with it by a humble man in*

Damascus, a man with tears in his eyes. But he suspects it has been to many other places… seen many other things.

He lifts his helmet and looks around the room.

And then he leaves.

Outside, his motorcycle waits patiently.

Somewhere not far away, a group of children prepare to leave their school for an unexpected nature ramble.

Their teacher cannot think why she should suddenly decide to take the children out this afternoon.

In less than half an hour, when he swerves his motorcycle skilfully to avoid colliding with these children, Thomas Edward Lawrence will lose his life.

But it has been a full life. A job well done.

And that, too, is serendipity.

London: Tuesday, 4 January, 2000, 16.36

'I really don't care what the rules say, Sister, we're taking this into his room and that's final.' Adrian was angry now. Annoyed at the stupidity and certain of his rights. He would not be moved by a rule book or by Ellen's embarrassment.

'Maybe we should wait until he comes home, Adie,' she whispered into his ear, her warm breath having more effect than her words.

He smiled at her, but still he would not be moved.

'I'm sorry, sir, but that is not being brought onto my ward and if you don't remove it, I will have to call security.'

'Do it!'

'Is that going to be necessary?'

'Your choice, Sister.'

Ellen cleared her throat.

'What if we just took it in for this visit and then remove it when we go home?' she pleaded.

The ward sister turned and looked at Ellen with a quizzical stare.

She looked up, frowning slightly, and pulled her hand back, holding it with her other hand.

A minute of silence ensued as she pondered the request.

Then, hardly realising that she was doing it, Sister Joan Green placed a hand on the paper covered object.

She looked up, frowning slightly, and pulled her hand away, holding it with her other hand. 'Just this once,' she said, her tone softer. 'But you will not take him out of his bed.'

Adrian opened his mouth to speak, but Ellen interjected. 'That's fine, Sister.'

London: Tuesday, 4 January, 2000, 16.40

A feeling of well-being comes over Johnny as he lies in his hospital bed. The pain that had been his constant companion for these past seven months has eased slightly. Enough to make him more accepting of it, but not enough to make him totally comfortable. Not enough to make him think it isn't there anymore.

The pain is always there.

Silence was all that was in his room. It could have been the second day of his stay or, as was the reality, the 237th day.

He remembers back to the day – was there ever one single day? – that it started..

To the first dawning reality that something was seriously wrong. The unbelievable tiredness that the shortest movement could bring on.

*He thinks back beyond that, too. To the days of his childhood when he felt he should be **doing** something. A man trapped in a child's body and nobody taking him seriously.*

Johnny thinks a lot, thinks many things, but the thoughts are inter-rupted when the door to his room opens.

London: Tuesday, 4 January, 2000, 16.46

'Hi, sis.'

'You're awake? How's the pain, little brother?' Ellen said as she bent to kiss his forehead.

'A little easier today thanks. Hi, Adie,' Johnny said as he held out his hand. Adrian clasped it and squeezed, turning it flat so he could bring his other hand on top of the teenager's, making it the meat in his own hand sandwich. He didn't want to let go, but he felt the boy start to pull away and so he eased his grip.

Johnny lifted himself higher in his bed, the most movement he had achieved without assistance in weeks. Ellen hid her shock at his appearance as she again bent forward and plumped up his pillows for him.

'What's with the package, guys?'

'It's a chair.' Ellen pulled the wrapping clear in one sweep.

'We brought it for you, Johnny. We thought that you might like to try it when you were well enough. Build up your strength.'

Johnny sat even higher up and looked at the smooth wood. He wanted to touch it now.

He wanted to sit in it. To sit in it right now.

He began to move his weakened legs to the side of the bed. Ellen thought he was just trying to get comfortable until he was sat on the edge of the bed, with his stick legs dangling over the edge. Both she and Adrian almost rushed to help him, but he shooed them away.

'Let me do this,' he whispered, the pain returning to his voice.

It took a few minutes to travel the six feet from the bed to the chair, but when he reached it, he fell to his knees and started to stroke the smooth wooden arms.

His new chair.

It *was* his chair.

Of that he was certain.

London: Tuesday, 4 January, 2000, 16.52

This is crazy, he thinks. And yet this was his compulsion. How long has it been since he last got out of this damn bed under his own steam? Weeks at least.

He knows he has to do it. Just as the fifty or so people before him had known that they had to do it.

Had to get to it.

To touch it.

To possess it.

To sit in it.

*Not his birth. Not the first sliver of pain in his gut. **This** is the start of his destiny.*

'Crazy?' he whispers silently and to no-one in particular. 'But not

crazy.' This time he hears the voice in his head. It is his own voice, but it seems to come from a part of him that he hasn't known was there before.

His feet have been hanging over the edge of the bed for a while now and the voice is the final spur that pushes him towards the prize. He uses all the strength his arms can muster to ease him to the ground. His feet feel good to have something underneath them after all this time.

He reaches out in front of him as a blind person might and then he moves a leg...and then the other leg. It hurts, he is breathing that ragged breath that only the seriously ill seem able to produce, but he is moving.

Finally on his knees, looking for all the world as if in prayer, but in reality just exhausted, he feels the wood under his fingertips.

A minute passes before he pulls down hard on the chair arms and raises himself up. He turns and then flops into it. God it is so comfortable.

London: Tuesday, 4 January, 2000, 16.54

Adrian and Ellen watched in virtual amazement as Johnny manoeuvred himself into the chair. Neither of them spoke for fear of breaking the spell. Something truly magical had happened. Of that they were both certain.

As they watched him sit and his breath slowly come back to normal, they also noticed a serenity come over him. Of course, it could have been the fact that he was so near sleep, but it could have been something else, too.

'Something spiritual,' Adrian was to remark later when they discussed the day's events as they cuddled in their bed that night.

But for now, they just watched.

As Johnny fell into a contented sleep, Ellen tugged at Adrian's sleeve and motioned for them to leave. Ellen bent and kissed her brother's forehead and Adrian also felt the need to kiss him, and so he too bent and kissed the top of his young brother-in-law's head. The couple left the room and bumped straight into the ward sister.

'You can't go in there,' Ellen said to her, quickly following with, 'He's sleeping.'

The ward sister was about to say something, but instead she just looked into Ellen's eyes and nodded, heading off to another patient instead. Back in the car neither of them spoke as Adrian pressed on the clutch and slid the estate into gear, heading out into the traffic that had built up. He signalled and turned right, joining the slow parade of rush hour people heading off to homes or out for evenings of fun and frivolity. Living in the heart of London had its compensations.

'It's been a special day I think,' Ellen said as she moved across her seat to be nearer Adrian. She reached out and stroked his arm.

'It's been a bit of a *strange* day that's for sure.'

'He looked so peaceful sleeping like that.'

'Yes, I know.'

'Did you get any time to work on the new story with everything else that's happened today?'

'A little. I have a beginning on paper and I have the rest worked out in my head.'

'So tell me a little of what it's about,' Ellen said as Adrian got stuck behind a black cab on Baker Street, right in front of The Abbey National Bank's headquarters building which also happened to be the same address that Sherlock Holmes had when his fictional life was taking place in the London of old.

'Well, Sherlock,' Adrian said as he pointed to the plaque on the wall indicating the Holmes connection. 'It's about hope. Hope for a new era. A new beginning for the new millennium perhaps.'

'And you've written the beginning?'

'Yes. It starts in Jerusalem. I know it's a city of strife, but it also somehow seems to offer hope, too.'

'So what's the story called?'

'Sitting Pretty.'

MY LITTLE SUEDE SHOES – a Resnick Story

John Harvey

'So what do you think about it, Charlie?'

'What?'

'The Millennium.'

'Not a lot.'

What Resnick thought: I shall be two years older.

They were heading back from lunch at the house of some friends of Hannah's in Southwell, a former art teacher who'd jacked it all in to restore furniture and support his partner who made batik wall hangings. Resnick's stomach was still celebrating the collocation of tofu lasagna and home-made parsnip wine. Hannah was driving. Her friends, Dermot and Belinda, were convinced the Millennium would bring about a positive change in the way people felt about the world's ecology; they could already sense it in the atmosphere.

'I was talking to Trevor Lynton about it,' Hannah said. 'You know, from Leisure Services.'

Resnick didn't think he did.

'Seems there's all kinds of plans – fireworks in the Old Market Square, decorated barges on the Trent, lasers lighting up the sky from a dozen high points all around the county. The one I liked best, though, a giant hologram of Robin Hood across the top of Colwick Wood.'

'Lottery funding, all this then?' Resnick asked. 'Or straight out the Council Tax?'

Hannah, for whom the idea of celebration, almost any kind of celebration, was a positive thing, accelerated into the centre lane, rounding a maroon Rover towing a caravan and ducking back not so many feet short of a Ford Sierra heading in the opposite direction. Resnick managed not to say a thing.

'I wonder,' Hannah said, several miles closer to the city, 'what we'll be doing that New Year, Charlie? I wonder if we'll be seeing it in together.'

'Can see Colwick Wood, you know,' Resnick said, trying for a smile. 'Patch of waste ground at the end of the street.'

Hannah switched the wipers on to meet the first fall of rain. 'Trevor,' she said, 'he asked me to see it in with him.'

'Sherry party at the Council House, that'll be,' Resnick said.

'Condominium in the Virgin Islands.'

He turned his head to see if she were serious.

'Those competitions, on the back of frozen food packets, gourmet pickle, something like that. Seems he won first prize. A Millennium holiday for two.'

'And he asked you?'

'He's been onto me to go out with him the best part of three years.'

'Bit extreme for a first date, isn't it? The Virgin Islands.'

'The best he could come up with before was cocktails in the Penthouse Bar at the Royal, followed by a dinner dance at the Commodore. At least this time he's got me giving it some serious thought.'

Trevor Lynton, Resnick was thinking. Perhaps he did know him after all. Blue braces and spray-on stubble; waved his hands about like he'd just taken a course in semaphore. Not thirty-five if he was a day.

❐

As Freddy McGregor was fond of saying, any performer who doesn't work New Year's Eve might just as well be dead. And, as Freddy would have been the first to admit, there had been some close calls: the year he'd found himself stranded on the Isle of Man without his costume or the price of a ferry ticket to the mainland; the time the Pier Theatre in Hunstanton had burned down, taking his last chance to play Buttons along with it; worst of all, 1994, when he had lost his footing clambering over a greasy upper storey window ledge and broken one of his legs – the ward sister had finally agreed to let him sing 'O Solé Mio' from a makeshift stage on top of the linen cupboard, and Freddy had encored with 'Crying in the Chapel' and 'Auld Lang Syne', the nurses blubbing into their blue uniform sleeves.

Already it was late-October and he was getting decidedly edgy. Calls to his agent yielded half-formed promises or, increasingly, the blank charm of the answerphone; pubs and clubs which had previously welcomed Freddy with open arms and used tenners, slotting him in amongst their regular array of strippers and comedians, now simply didn't want to know. Plans for a fifty date Solid Silver Sixties revival tour broke down at the last moment, denying Freddy the chance to strut his stuff at the Flower Pot in Derby, the Regal Centre, Worksop, the Beaufort Theatre, Ebbw Vale. Even the landlord of the Old Vic, where Freddy had long been a regular star of Saturday Night Music Hall, took him to one side and wondered gently whether it wasn't time for him to find another line of work. 'Let's face it, Freddy, there's just so many times you can persuade the punters to shell out for a four-foot Elvis in a white satin suit, even if it is an exact replica of the one he wore in Las Vegas. Scaled down, of course.' And he slipped a crisp twenty into Freddy's top pocket and patted him on the head.

Patronising bastard, Freddy thought, crossing Fletcher Gate towards the car park. And besides, I've already got another line of work. Why else would I break a leg falling from a second-storey bathroom window?

□

Most times when Resnick and Hannah had been out together, one or the other, usually Hannah, would pose the traditional question, your place or mine? Once in a while, Hannah, especially if she were driving, would take Resnick's answer as read and head for her place in Lenton without bothering to ask the question. But this particular Sunday, again without asking, she took a left at Mapperley Top towards the Woodborough Road and Resnick's house.

Dizzy, the largest and the fiercest of Resnick's four cats, stared at them from the stone wall, flexing his claws. Hannah sat with one hand resting on the wheel, engine idling.

'You're not coming in?' Resnick said.

'No, I don't think so.'

'Quick cup of coffee? Tea?'

'I ought to be getting back.'

Clicking open the car door, Resnick suppressed a sigh. 'Are you okay?'

'I'm fine.'

Her cheek, when he kissed her, was marble against his mouth.

Dizzy wound between Resnick's legs as he walked towards the front door, pushed his head against Resnick's shin as he fidgeted for the key. Behind them, Hannah pulled away a little too fast, shifting through the gears as she turned the narrow corner and accelerated towards the main road.

When he woke it was a little after five, wind rattling the window frames. Bud, as usual, lay with his head close to the edge of Resnick's pillow, one paw folded across his eyes. Miles and Pepper were curled in a black and grey ball near the foot of the bed, impossible to tell at a glance where one began, the other ended. Dizzy, Resnick knew, would be within reach of the rear door, chewing over whatever prey the night had providentially provided.

In the depths of the house, he heard pipes rumble and stir as the central heating came awake. How far from winter, Resnick wondered? Black ice on the roads and mornings that defied the light; storm warnings on the shipping forecast, severe gales force nine, north-easterly winds becoming cyclonic all the way from Cromarty to German Bight.

He massaged lather deep into his hair, stood with head tilted back, letting the water spray across his face and chest. Quickly dressed, he fed the cats, depositing first Dizzy's ritual offering of rodent rump inside the bin. Buttering toast, he toyed with the idea of phoning Hannah before she left for work, but pleasantries aside, had no idea what to say. The first cup of coffee he drank standing up, the second he took into the living room, where the previous evening's *Post* remained unread.

A series of break-ins at late-night chemists in Aspley, Meden Vale and Selston; a children's playground vandalised in Keyworth; two Asian youths attacked on the last bus to Bestwood by a gang of more than twenty; several people injured, two seriously, when a fight broke out during an American Line Dancing evening at Tollerton Methodist Church Hall.

Resnick folded the paper and carried it through to join the ever-growing pile awaiting recycling in the hall. One of these days, he'd throw them in the back of the car, drop them off on his way to work but not today. The traffic was beginning to build up as he passed the roundabout where Gregory Boulevard met the Mansfield Road and Sherwood Rise. The station where his CID squad was based sat just east of the city centre, squarely between the affluence of the Park Estate and the down-at-heel terraces either side of the Alfreton Road. The kettle was boiling away in an empty CID room, Resnick's sergeant, Graham Millington, peering into the mirror in the Gents, counting the grey hairs in his moustache.

Resnick flipped open the folder the officer on first call had left on his desk and thumbed through the night's incident reports: sometimes it was easy to believe the houses on Tattershall Drive and around Lincoln Circus were as heavily targeted as Dresden or Hamburg during the last World War.

'Anything on this last batch of break-ins, Graham?' Resnick asked, hearing Millington's cheery rendition of 'Frosty the Snowman'. Millington whistling early for Christmas.

'Nothing as yet,' the sergeant said, adding one for the pot, 'Kev's down there now. Back entry, though, all accounts. Fire escape, drainpipe, neighbour's balcony, you know the kind of thing.'

On his return, an hour later, Kevin Naylor filled them in.

Eight burglaries in all, two neat batches of four, nicely professional. Cash, credit cards, cheque books, jewellery – a couple of Rolex watches worth a week of Ravanelli's wages, his and hers. Nothing that wouldn't fit into a set of well-lined pockets.

'Someone flying solo?' Resnick asked.

Naylor shook his head. 'Pair of them, sir. One to gain entry – bathroom window, that seems favourite – lets in his oppo, ten minutes later, fifteen tops, they're back out the front door.'

'These windows,' Resnick said, 'ground level?'

Another shake of the head. 'Not a one. And small with it. Any of us, not get our head and shoulders through, never mind the rest.'

'Kids, then?' Millington said.

'Don't think so, sarge. Too clean, no mess. Quiet, too. All but one, occupied. Slept right through.'

'What was that father and son team, Graham?' Resnick asked. 'Edwalton, Lady Bay – maybe shifted ground.'

'Used to boost the lad up on his shoulders, I know who you mean. Regular couple of acrobats. Rydale, some such name.'

'Risdale.'

'Risdale, that's it. Paul?'

'Peter.'

'Peter. Made his boy, Stephen, run five miles every morning, fed him fish and chicken. White meat. Leaner'n a whippet and about as fast.'

'Back on remand, is he? Youth detention?'

Millington stroked his moustache. 'Easy enough to check. Won't hurt to give Risdale a pull, any road. Nothing to say he's not been down the job centre, found himself a replacement.'

'Good.' Resnick was on his feet. 'Kevin, best get the details of those credit cards circulated; unlikely, but check if Scene of Crime fetched up anything by way of prints. And it might be worth a word with the home beat officer – might be time for another circular, see if we can't encourage a few more people to keep their windows locked nights.'

'Right.'

Resnick nodded and looked at his watch. After the meeting

with his DS, there was one line of enquiry he'd follow up on his own.

❐

Freddy had been busy since mid-morning, cold-calling bookers and agencies, club and pub managers within a fifty mile radius, anyone with a music licence and half a square metre of stage. Now it was scarcely short of one o'clock and all he'd to show was a kids' party at Snape Wood Road Community Centre and a silver wedding at the Salvation Army Citadel, Main Street, Bulwell. After fifteen minutes haggling, Freddy had promised the proprietor of a new burger bar in Ilkeston that he'd get back to him about performing on the pavement outside to mark the opening, one number every quarter hour, ten am till closing. And he was still waiting a call back himself from the events organiser at the Rotherham Transport Club, Masborough – we'd love to have you, Freddy, you know we would, but not all that old Elvis, you've got to come with something different, something new. An angle. Find a way to work the Spice Girls in somewhere and then we'd be talking...

Freddy lit the last of his king size and squeezed another half mug of tea from the same bag. It was all very well for someone stuck behind a desk to rattle on about trying something new. Over the years he'd tried them all – Laurie London, Little Jimmy Osmond, Michael Jackson with a full-out Afro and a kiddie voice singing that love song to a rat; once even Little Stevie Wonder, which had been fine until he'd fallen off the front of the stage doing 'Fingertips', unable to see where he was going through the dark glasses.

But no matter what anyone said, none of them worked as well as his Elvis Aaron Presley – the first of Freddy's pre-recorded tapes blaring out into the darkness and then the spot-light catching him from the waist down as his hips began to swivel, his little pelvis to gyrate, black leather trousers, blue suede shoes. A medley of 'Hound Dog', 'Jailhouse Rock' and 'Don't Be Cruel', slow things down with 'Heartbreak Hotel', whip them up again with 'King Creole'. A break then for the strip show or the bingo and Freddy would be back in his shiny white jump suit, perspiration, get some of that chest hair showing, 'Suspicious Minds', 'Burning Love', 'Are You Lonesome Tonight?' and the audience can't help but sing along, and for his encore what else but 'Blue Suede Shoes' itself?

How could it fail? How could he go wrong?

The phone rang and he lifted the receiver on the second ring. 'Derek, I knew you'd come round.'

'Fuck Derek, you short-arsed little cunt, it's Clayton. I'm in the back bar of the Portland Arms and if you're not here by the time I've downed this pint I'll take those excuses for legs of yours off at the knees.'

❐

Clayton Kanellopoulos was the thirty-nine year old son of a Scottish mother, a Greek Cypriot father; his family had happily owned a succession of greasy spoons and gentlemen's hairdressers, brother to brother, cousin to cousin, generation to generation: it had taken Clayton to break the mould. He had started out pimping for a string of scrawny girls in North London, got to know each nook and cranny of the Holloway Road, the Cali like the back of his proverbial hand. After that a spell of enforcing for a loan shark in Edmonton, till one razor stripe too many sent him scurrying north for safety. Leicester, Nottingham, Sheffield, Derby. Clayton settled down to an early middle-age of breaking and entering.

'Freddy, what kept you?'

'How d'you mean? I got here just as fast...'

'I know, fast as fat little midgets can go.'

'I'm not...'

'What?' One grasp of the hand, and Clayton had Freddy firmly by the balls. 'Not what?'

'It don't matter.'

'Fat? Not fat?'

'Yeah, that's right.' Freddy wincing with the pain.

With a laugh Clayton let go his hold and, tears blinking at the corners of his eyes, Freddy sat himself down.

'Not fancy a half?' Clayton asked, gesturing towards the bar. 'Maybe a short?'

Freddy shook his head.

All business now, Clayton leaned in close. 'I thought what you and me had was a deal?'

Knees clenched close together, not too close, Freddy's mind was racing into overdrive. 'We do, Clayton, so we do.'

'Then tell me it weren't you, who did all them places up the Park?'

'When?'

'You know all too fuckin' well when.'

The bone inside Freddy's left leg began to sing; the last time he'd gone in for a bit of B&E in the Park, he'd ended up on his back in Queen's. 'Not down to me, you got my word.'

'Who then?'

All Freddy could do was shrug.

Clayton stared him down a while longer before stretching back and lighting a small cigar with a match that he flicked against the front of Freddy's shirt. 'All right, this weekend coming. Sat'day night. I got a job.'

Freddy fingered anxiously the ring on the pinkie finger of his right hand. 'I can't.' The words only just carried across the small space between them.

'Sorry? I could've sworn you said…'

'Clayton, any other time, any other night. Even if you'd asked me – what? – an hour earlier, everything would have been fine. But I've got this booking, the Saturday, all agreed. No way I can let them down, you got to see that, no earthly way…' Freddy's voice fading now, words failing him as he watched the broad planes of Clayton's face break into a smile.

❐

Resnick had phoned Hannah mid-morning, knowing full-well that she would be out and leaving a message on her answerphone: hope everything's okay, maybe if you've got a minute when you get in, you'll give me a call.

Immediately after that paperwork claimed him, quarterly

crime figures to be checked and okayed before passing on to the Detective Chief Inspector of CID downtown. It was almost two before he crossed Canning Circus to the deli and bought a brace of brie and ham sandwiches and a large black coffee to go. The lunchtime traffic had thinned enough for him to be in the upper reaches of Carlton in time to catch Freddy McGregor just back from the Portland Arms and still looking a touch anxious around the gills.

'Mr Resnick…' Freddy thinking one shock was enough for one day, one unwelcome interview; though he had no reason to believe Resnick was the sort to use force – not like some of his compatriots – Freddy covered himself instinctively, both hands cupped in front of his crotch as if anticipating a Psycho Pearce free kick.

Without exactly being invited, Resnick found himself inside the living room of Freddy's ground floor flat: posters advertising *Freddy McGregor, the Miniature Elvis* vied for wall space with pictures of the man himself, snarling from the stage of the Mississippi-Alabama Fair in Tupelo in 1956; thoughtfully biting his thumbnail in an off-set still from *Loving You*. Underneath the latter, Freddy had neatly written out one of the lines Presley spoke in the film –

'That's how you're selling me, isn't it? A monkey in a zoo. Isn't that what you want?'

Freddy hovered nervously, watching Resnick's face.

'Working, Freddy?' Resnick eventually said.

'Oh, you know, bits and pieces here and there. Mustn't grumble, Mr Resnick, you know how it is.'

'Tell me.'

'Just fixed up a few things this morning, matter of fact. Small stuff, private parties, just while I'm putting a new act together. I…'

But Resnick was already shaking his head. 'Not the kind of work I mean.'

Freddy could feel himself starting to blush, guilty or innocent, the colour spreading up from his neck to brighten his cheeks.

'I was thinking more,' Resnick continued, 'the second storey kind.'

'Never, Mr Resnick.'

'Never?'

'Not any more. Not since, you know…'

Resnick nodded. 'Lost the nerve for it, that's what you're saying.'

'Absolutely.'

'Heights.'

'Giddy these days, Mr Resnick, climbing onto that table there, change a bulb in the lamp.'

'Vertigo, acrophobia.'

'If you say so.'

Resnick seemed to think for a while, then moved towards the door. 'All this, Freddy,' he swept his hand towards the wall, 'profession, a career. Show business. Something to be proud of. Shame to see it all fall by the by.'

Freddy nodded most emphatically. He knew; he knew.

Resnick hesitated, half in, half out of the room. 'Christmas on the way, New Year. Busy time for you, I dare say. Shame to be unavailable for work that festive season, shut away.'

For a long time after Resnick had gone, Freddy sat pondering over ways to avoid carrying through on what he'd promised – two twenty minute spots either side of a buffet supper at the silver wedding celebrations; gaining entry through the fourth floor skylight of a large detached house in Church Lane, Watnall Chaworth, its occupants booked into a banquet up in Buxton and due to stay the night.

❐

The first time the phone went that evening, it was a wrong number; the second heralded the membership secretary of the Polish Club, politely wondering if Resnick had received his second reminder. Promising he'd get the cheque in the post first thing, Resnick determined he would give Hannah till nine then try her again. Midway through dialling her number he thought better of it: she would have listened to his message; if she wanted to call him then she would. Just after ten he called Millington instead, television news just audible behind the sergeant's voice; the interview with Peter Risdale had been inconclusive. Lying, Millington thought, almost beyond question, but a man like that would lie to the police on principle, guilty or not. Either way, he'd an alibi that'd be hard to shake. His son, Stephen, was still in youth detention and there was nothing tangible to place Risdale himself at the scene or even close.

Resnick poured vodka over ice cubes in a chilled glass and closed his eyes as he listened to Johnny Griffin guesting with Thelonious Monk. 'Round Midnight', 'Misterioso', 'In Walked Bud'. Actually, the smallest of Resnick's litter was already making discreet snoring noises in his lap.

When the vodka was finished and the music at an end, he lifted the cat into the cradle of an arm and carried it up the stairs to bed.

Hannah called next morning, not so far after six. 'I didn't wake you?'

'No.'

'Charlie, I'm sorry I didn't get back to you last night.'

'That's fine.'

'This meeting after school became one quick drink, and then dinner and then, oh, it must have been nearly twelve.'

'Hannah, it's okay. It doesn't matter.'

There was a brief pause before she said, 'Sunday? Shall I see you Sunday? Maybe we could go for a walk, late breakfast somewhere, brunch, what'd you say?' Somehow she could sense Resnick was already smiling.

'Fine,' Resnick said. 'I'd like that a lot.'

❏

'What d'you mean, you're going?'

Freddy was half in, half out of his Ford van, still wearing his first-half costume, make-up, the whole bit. The anniversary couple's grandson, the one who'd booked him, standing there with both hands on the door. Aside from one slight glitch when the tape had got stuck at the intro to 'King Creole' it had not gone badly – if you glossed over Freddy transposing two of the verses in 'Heartbreak Hotel'. What was he doing? A song he'd sung how many hundred times?

He knew what he was doing. Not flustered he explained to the grandson that in his hurry to get there, he'd left his costume change, his white jump suit behind. Twenty minutes, thirty at most, he'd be back. No worries.

'Forget it,' the man said. 'You're okay as you are.'

But Freddy would have none of it: the whole show was what they were paying for and that's what they were going to get.

Clayton was waiting for him as planned, in a lay-by just past the motorway where they switched vehicles.

'There may be a problem,' Clayton said. They were heading east along the Watnall Road, keeping the speed below fifty, not wanting to attract attention.

'What?' In his anxiety, Freddy's voice little more than a squeak.

'Gave it a quick pass-by earlier, checking it out. Just in time to see him getting into a taxi, penguin suit, the whole bit.'

'So?'

'So she's standing in the doorway in this quilted dressing-gown, all she can do to wave him goodbye.'

'She's still there?'

'Sick, my guess. In bed sick.'

'Then what the hell we doing? For Christ's sake let's turn round and get...'

But Clayton's free hand was like a vice right above Freddy's knee. 'Easy, easy. Take it easy. What d'you think, she's in there wide awake, maybe doing a spot of housework? Soon as he's gone, she's back to bed. Nurofen, Paracetomol, it'll take more'n you to wake her, eh Freddy? You tip-toeing down the stairs like some fairy in your size four shoes.'

In the event, Freddy's shoes were in his hand. Gaining entry through the third floor bathroom window had been straightforward enough, the upper section easing back to admit his child-size body, Freddy pausing just long enough to adjust the way his black silk shirt tucked into his black leather trousers, sit on the side of the bath to slip off his blue suede shoes.

He was down as far as the lower landing when the dog started to bark. Fucking Clayton! Why the fuck hadn't he known about the fucking dog? Freddy jumped so hard his shoes jerked free of his fingers and went spiralling down towards the hall. By which time the aforementioned fucking dog, in addition to barking fit to raise the dead, was hurling itself against the door of the ground floor room it was shut in, a few more times and Freddy could see its nasty vicious snout breaking through the wood. An Alsatian, he imagined, some kind of mastiff, one of those slick and nasty Dobermans. Added to which, the lady of the house, far from being asleep, was standing somewhere above him, screaming fit to beat the band. Clayton hammering at the front door, wanting to know what the hell was going on, waiting to be let in.

Freddy slipped the bolts, unfastened the chain, turned both handles at once.

'What the fuck's going on?'

Freddy almost head-butted Clayton in the gut as he pushed past him, sprinting now towards the car, Clayton with nothing to do but follow in his wake.

'What... ?'

But Freddy was too angry, too wound-up, too scared to say a thing. It wasn't till Clayton dropped him off back at his van that he realised he was standing there in black nylon socks, a hole beginning to appear round the big toe of his right foot.

❐

'I don't think you're supposed to call them that any more,' Hannah said. 'Dwarf.' They were strolling round the long lake in Clumber Park, nice enough for a walk if you were well wrapped up.

'Not midget, surely?'

'Certainly not that.' She paused at the raucous clamour of

ducks, a small child lopsidedly hurling them bread.

'Vertically challenged,' Resnick suggested, only half in fun. 'Something like that.'

Doing her best not to smile, Hannah shook her head. 'I believe the correct term is person of restricted growth.'

'Person of restricted movement, certainly. That'll be Freddy McGregor for the next six months at least.'

'There isn't any doubt?'

Resnick laughed. 'One pair of little suede shoes, custom made. Better than fingerprints where Freddy's concerned. Even after the dog had got through with them.'

'I feel almost sorry for him in a way.'

'The good thing,' Resnick said, 'with Freddy's help there's a really nasty piece of work called Kanellopoulos we can put away for years.'

Uncertain about the efficacy of imprisonment, Hannah held her tongue.

They were in a corner of the lakeside café when Resnick showed her the reservations. A hotel in Matlock, five-course dinner and a jazz band ball.

'If you fancy it, that is.'

'Of course.' Lifting up the tickets, Hannah looked again at the date. 'Try-out for the Millennium, Charlie, that what this is?'

Just for a moment, Resnick squeezed her hand. 'One New Year at a time, eh? Happen that's best.'

ROOTS

Jerry Sykes

For over twenty years the house had been a part of the dark dreamscape of my life, but as I crested the hill it rose anew out of the mist, a burning red ember fanned by the wind of change that blew in my heart.

A pale sun hung low over the hills and the cool mist rolled down the valley, chasing a river that ran sepia from the iron ore in the soil. I could smell wet bracken and new grass through the open window.

I turned off the engine and let the car roll down the hill, tyres crunching on gravel the only sound in the still morning. I pulled up under a huge oak that buckled the road at its roots and watched the house through the rearview.

All the homes in the valley were made of stone, cottages built at the turn of the century for mill workers and their families.

Except the red brick house in my mirror.

The house had been built during the Second World War by a man named Thad Irwin, a foreman at the brickworks a mile further up the valley. Rumour was that he had stolen the bricks a wheelbarrow at a time right from under the owner's nose, the owner turning a blind eye due to the fact that Thad was the only regular worker left, all the others off fighting for their country. Any vengeful thoughts on the part of the owner were laid to rest when his heart exploded a month before VE day, spraying the inside of his eyes a deep red.

Thad eventually completed his task, but there were still piles of hot bricks in the yard thirty years later when I was a regular visitor of his grandson, Rob.

The yard may have held our attention on cold evenings, but it was the old quarry that lay beyond the brickworks that demanded our presence throughout the summer.

A gaping wound in the green hills that rippled through the valley, the quarry had been abandoned for as long as I could remember. With a huge pond of stagnant water that could only be navigated by rafts built from strapping twisted planks across oil drums, a dirt track worn smooth by daredevil circuitry, a junked Mini complete with four tyres, flowers of rust blooming on the cracked paintwork, the place was considered a death-trap by anyone over the age of thirty, but to us it was the surface of the Moon, Monument Valley, and Wembley Stadium all rolled into one.

But the one truth of childhood was that our parents knew best.

❏

Perspiration slicked my hair and ran down my neck, spooking a shiver that snaked along my spine. I climbed on, hands pushing down on my thighs, my ankles tearing through the tangled undergrowth. My lungs felt scorched and tiny black stars exploded before my eyes. I could see the stone wall that rode the hills above me and promised myself a cigarette on reaching it.

A few minutes later I placed my hands on the wall and rested my forehead on my arms. I couldn't breathe deeply enough and I felt nauseous.

Eventually I turned to look out over the valley.

A deep haze shimmered before my eyes, turning the view into a faded water colour. At the foot of the hill I could just make out the abandoned buildings of the old brickworks, the corrugated iron sheets covering the doors and windows booming in the wind like thunder. To the north of the brickworks I could see the old cemetery, the gravestones like broken teeth scattered on the ground, the spire of the church reaching upwards like a skeletal finger to scratch at the sky. To the south, armies of trees ran down the valley and circled the village.

I turned my attention to the sweep of hill before me. Where

the quarry had once been there was now only a sunken crater filled with scraggly brown grass, the dead land all that remained of the landfill site. Green grass crept up to the crater's edge and waved at its dead kin.

I wiped the rain from my eyes, felt the sting of tears.

❏

An invisible sun was burning in a clear blue sky as we snaked along the path that circled the brickworks and down towards the quarry. Beads of sweat bubbled on my forehead and I could feel my T-shirt sticking to my back. Rob walked a few paces ahead of me, kicking a football, red dust swirling around his ankles and sticking to his calves.

At the front of the building a group of men were standing on the loading dock. They were stripped to the waist and their torsos glowed red in the light from the kiln. Steam clouded above their shoulders and trousers heavy with sweat hung low on their hips. They looked like the newly dead at the gates of Hell.

As we reached the dirt track that led to the quarry itself, we saw Tom Dillon down by the water's edge. I couldn't see what he was doing, but he looked to be watching something in the water. Rob held his finger to his lips and gestured for me to follow him.

Tom Dillon was a weak child and consequently natural prey to anyone with muscles to flex. He was also well-off, and to someone like Rob, who never had anything of his own, well, that was like taking money out of Rob's own pocket. And Rob wasn't too subtle about hiding that resentment. One winter he had severed Tom's earlobe with a piece of shale hidden in a snowball, drops of blood bursting on the ground like brilliant red flowers. And the previous spring he had chased Tom through the cemetery with a fresh oak sapling torn from the ground, flicking it at his back until welts rose in the skin that looked like worms buried in his flesh.

I scrambled after Rob as he climbed the side of the quarry

and into the thick bracken that grew along its edge. We crawled further up the hill until we had a good view of Tom. I looked at the water, slick with oil; ripples carried rainbows to the shore. The raft that Rob and I had built the previous summer had been dragged onto the far bank, the dry warped planks the bleached bones of a giant skeleton.

'What's he doing?' said Rob.

Tom was sitting on his haunches and fiddling with something on the floor in front of him. He had his back to us. The ground by his feet was wet and there were footprints leading to the pond, as if he had been in the water.

'I dunno.' I shrugged. 'I can't see anything.'

'What is it?'

I shook my head.

Just then Tom shifted to the right and I caught sight of the object in his hands.

'Looks like a boat,' I said. 'A speedboat.'

'A what?' Rob looked at me with quizzical eyes.

'You know. Remote control.' I mimed the joystick.

'Hey,' he said slowly, 'let's go take a look.'

Rob climbed over the edge of the quarry and ran down the slope, digging his heels into the shale to keep from tumbling over. At the bottom he paused briefly, wiping his palms on the seat of his jeans, before crossing towards Tom. His shoulders were held artificially high and I sensed something nasty was about to happen.

I ran down the slope, fitting my footsteps to the grooves left by Rob, and walked towards them. But something held me back, an intruder in their private drama, and I pulled up short. I shielded my eyes against the sun.

Tom was explaining how the boat worked. It sounded simple enough – two-speed gearbox, forward/reverse switch, joystick – and Rob appeared to be listening. But after a moment I saw a change in the light in his eyes, the way a candle will flicker and then right itself when someone leaves the room, and I wanted to shout at Tom, tell him to run.

Lesson over, Tom took the boat over to the pond and carefully placed it in the water. Rob followed, eager to see the boat in action. I stayed put, a reluctant spectator, my heart thumping in my chest, the sound of blood swirling in my ears.

The boat kicked out a few bubbles and started to move away from the shore, but after a moment its movements didn't tie in with the way Tom was rattling the controls, his fingers knuckled white in frustration.

'It's jammed,' he said. His eyes flicked between the boat and the controls.

Rob reached out a hand. 'Here, let me,' he said.

Tom whipped the controls away and turned his back on Rob. 'No!' he snapped. 'It's mine.' He continued to work the controls frantically, his eyes off the boat.

'C'mon, it's gonna crash,' shouted Rob, pointing towards the boat.

Then, without warning, he snatched at the remote and knocked it to the ground. The boat responded to the violent command by cutting its engine. Within seconds it came to a halt.

Tom immediately picked up the remote and wiped it clean with the palm of his hand. He gave it a gentle shake; a muted rattle told us something was broken.

The boat drifted in a slow arc thirty feet from the shore.

Tom looked at the boat and then back at Rob. 'What did you do that for?' he said. His words sounded as if they were being squeezed out of his throat and tears welled up in his eyes. 'You've broken it … I only got it on Saturday.'

A sneer appeared on Rob's face. 'It's not broken you little fuckin' cry baby. Here, give it to me.' He held out his hand for the remote. 'Let me have a go.'

Tom put his hands behind his back.

Rob looked at his face, at the tears streaking the dusty cheeks. 'C'mon …' he said, trying to reach around Tom for the remote.

I couldn't watch it any more. I walked to the edge of the pond and picked up a couple of chunks of shale, thick plates about the size of my hand. I took a step forward and hefted one into the water. It landed with a slap about ten feet from the boat. Ripples shot out but the boat didn't move any closer.

'What are you doing?' squealed Tom. He ran over to me and slapped the other piece of shale out of my hand.

'Hey, we're trying to get your boat back. OK?' I said, holding up my hands.

'You'll break it.'

I dropped to my haunches and reached for another piece of shale. 'The waves'll push it to shore,' I explained.

Just then a loud splash echoed around the quarry. A drop of oily water hit me on the forehead. I saw Tom touch the back of his head and then quickly turn around, his eyes scanning the water.

Small waves lapped at the shore, the shale hissing as the water pulled back. Towards the centre, tiny bubbles broke on the surface.

'Where's my boat!' screamed Tom. He ran to the pool, the toes of his baseball boots in the water. 'Where's the fuckin' boat?' He turned to Rob. 'What've you done? Where is it?'

'It was only a fuckin' boat.' Rob was holding a piece of shale in his hands. He turned to walk away. 'No big deal. I'm sure Daddy'll buy you another.'

Tom grabbed his arm, pulled him back. 'You're mad. Fuckin' mad. Just because you never have anything–' He stopped abruptly, took a step closer. He struggled to keep his voice under control as he focused all his anger into his next words. 'Man, you even live in a stolen house!'

I saw Rob's eyes flare with a demonic iridescence. He lifted his arm to the side of his head, and then with a force that came from deep within, he brought his hand and the chunk of shale down on the side of Tom's head.

◻

I walked back down the hill, my boots dragging through the grass. The morning dew had yet to burn off and my feet felt damp and heavy. I reached the car and sat for a long while just staring out of the window, thinking of the cheap life I had lived, afraid to enter my imagination for fear of what I might find.

I put the car in gear and headed into the village. It had begun to cloud over and I could taste rain in the air.

I pulled into the gravel car park of the Beaumont Arms and went into the public bar. I climbed onto a stool and ordered a large scotch. There was one other customer in the place, some kid in dirty green overalls playing the fruit machine; a bottle of lager was on the table nearby, a cigarette feathering in the ashtray.

I looked at my watch. It was still not yet twelve. I rattled my empty glass on the wooden bar.

□

I helped Rob drag the body along the edge of the quarry. I held the right arm, my fingers sinking into the cold flesh, and watched Tom's baseball boots lay down a trail of broken plants and ragged grooves.

Rob had hold of the other arm. It was his idea that we throw Tom from the top of the quarry; the shoreline below was littered with large slabs of shale and other debris and the 'fall' would explain the wound above Tom's ear.

When we reached the spot where we had earlier spied on Tom, I let go of his arm. But instead of flopping to the ground, the arm moved slowly and for one mad moment I thought Tom might still be alive.

I looked over the edge, at the pool of dark blood that had formed around Tom's head as we had watched life drain out of his body. We would have to go back and bury it later.

I looked at Rob. 'We can't just throw him over the edge,' I said. 'It's Tom.'

He looked at me with hard eyes. 'He's dead, man. He ain't gonna feel nothin'.'

I looked at the stranger before me – even his voice had taken on a different texture – and for the first time I felt scared. 'We should go back, tell someone.' Then, 'It was an accident –'

'No,' said Rob calmly. 'Everyone knows that I never liked the spoilt fucker. Picked on him. They'll just think I took it too far this time.' He sounded like he had always known that he would kill him one day.

'But it was an accident.' I had to believe that, for it to have been anything else was beyond my comprehension.

I looked at Tom lying in the undergrowth. Most of the colour had drained from his body but I could see where I had held his skinny arms, the impressions of my fingers deep bruises in his flesh.

Rob grabbed Tom by the ankles and nodded at me. 'C'mon, get a hold of his arms.' I took hold. Rob counted to three and we hefted the body off the ground. He moved his arms to the left and grunted at me. I realised he meant for us to swing the body out over the edge. He started counting again, his voice a painful echo in my heart. 'One … two … three…'

The body seemed to hang in the air for ever. I didn't hear it hit the ground.

◻

Tom's body was found later that evening as the sun fell behind the hills above the quarry and turned the rain clouds a deep purple so that they looked like bruises floating in the sky. His father had got worried when he had not returned at dusk and, knowing that he had taken off with his new boat, had made straight for the quarry, assuming that Tom had just forgotten the time.

As he walked down the dirt track towards the pond, the spokes of the dying sun picking out the acid shapes that whorled around the breaks in the surface, he realised with mounting horror that the small figure lying in the shale, a twisted arm outstretched to the water in grotesque imitation of a dying man reaching an oasis, was the broken body of his only son. It was a realisation that was to tear his heart from his chest, again and again.

When I returned to the quarry later that evening it seemed like the whole of the village was there, etched into the landscape by a string of brilliant white arc lights that hovered in the darkness like giant fireflies. The sounds of whispered conversations drifted in the air and half-raised arms pointed to the spot where Tom's body had fallen.

I looked up at the edge of the quarry and saw disembodied faces staring back at me from the bracken. I wondered if the tracks made by Rob and I as we had dragged the body up the hill had been scrambled by these ghouls.

I looked over the faces of the people that were nearest the pond. Their eyes burned with a religious intensity, as if they awaited a spiritual cleansing in the murky waters before them.

On the far side of the pond I could see Rob standing next to Tom's father, tears burning on his cheeks like diamonds embedded in the skin.

The following morning both Rob and I were questioned by the police. I don't think that they ever really suspected us of having anything to do with Tom's death, but as we'd been the last ones to have seen him alive, we'd made sure that our stories were in sync just in case. In the event, the police didn't appear to be interested in finding out what had happened and were happy to absorb the tragic accident explanation that had passed silently through the crowd the previous night.

But far from being relieved at the turn of events, the wall of silence that had been erected around Tom's death served only to cast a dark shadow in my heart. Although I had not dealt the blow that had killed him, I was as guilty of his murder as Rob, and that guilt pumped through my veins with an intensity that would burst me awake at night in a cold sweat feeling that my head was about to explode.

Rob and I did not speak about the events of that day again, but when I saw him in school, his face open and bright, I immediately understood that it was me who would have to bear the burden of guilt for both of us.

The following November an opportunity for atonement presented itself in the shape of a school science project – a time capsule.

The idea was simple: between us the class would collect a selection of items that best represented the year – a newspaper, magazine, records, pages from a diary, photos – that would then be buried in a specially built chest in the school garden, to be exhumed in the year 2000 when a reunion party would be held.

My mind immediately locked into the possibilities and I volunteered to provide some photographs. On the way home that night I talked Rob into helping me out.

Following Tom's death the council had finally caved in to pressure from the parents in the village and decided to do something about the quarry, earmarking it as a landfill site. Work was due to start in the new year. It was my idea to take photos of the area for inclusion in the time capsule. One of my ideas, anyway – Rob would have to wait to hear the other. I arranged to meet him at eight the following Sunday morning.

As we walked down the dirt track the smell of stagnant water assaulted my nostrils. I turned to tell Rob that I had never noticed the smell before and caught him staring at the spot where he had felled Tom. His eyes seemed to be locked inside his head and his face was bleached of colour. I turned and followed his stare to the edge of the pond. I swore I could see the impression that Tom's body had left.

I swung my rucksack from my back and sat on the shale. I took out the cassette recorder and slotted in a fresh tape.

'What's that? I thought we were gonna take some photos,' said Rob. He had stopped several feet from the water's edge.

'Later,' I said. 'We've got something else to do first.' I pushed the jack of the microphone into the socket. I cleared my throat, but as I tried to speak my words seemed to spin in the air like dust and vanish before reaching the microphone.

I rewound the tape and started again.

'This is a confession,' I began. 'On the twenty-fifth of August, 1976, I, George Lowell, and Robert Irwin murdered Tom Willis –'

'What the fuck!'

I turned off the cassette recorder.

'Rob, we've gotta do something. I'm a nervous fuckin' wreck.'

'Shit. You didn't do anything.'

'I was there,' I said, the calmness of my voice betraying the drum roll of my heart. 'I'm as guilty as you are. Rob, we threw him from the top of the fucking quarry!'

Rob looked away, to the spot from where we had thrown the body.

After a moment he sat on the ground, leaning back on his hands. He stared into the water for a long time. 'No-one's ever going to hear this, right?'

'Not until the year 2000.'

'Yeah, right. Gimme the mike.' He flapped his hand at me and I leaned over and handed him the recorder.

Rob lit a cigarette and then spoke into the microphone. 'This is the confession of Rob Irwin. In August 1976 I killed Tom Willis. We got into an argument and I hit him on the head with a chunk of shale. Me and George here then dragged him up the side of the quarry and threw him over the edge …' He pulled on his cigarette. 'By the time you hear this I will be dead. Suicide. I can live with the guilt of Tom's murder, but I could not go to prison. So, by the time you get to hear this …' His voice broke and he hung his head.

My whole body felt cold, chips of ice floated in my veins.

❐

I ordered another drink and thought of that final day in the quarry. In many ways it haunted me far more than the day of the actual murder. My young heart, already cramped with guilt, was twisted beyond all recognition as we delivered our suicide notes on that day by the dead water of the pond.

As I grew older I began to feel more comfortable with myself, the twin demons of alcohol and guilt becoming the thuggish guardians of my soul, exuberant bouncers that kept the public at arms length.

My life had been an endless series of temporary postings to increasingly desperate locations, the only constant an expiry date handed to me one day in an abandoned quarry.

Rob had a different story to tell: he had escaped the past and made full use of his time on the planet. As well as successfully riding the software wave he had been married for over fifteen years and had two healthy children. I had not seen much of him over the years as he had moved to London immediately after leaving college, but we had always met up for a beer on his increasingly infrequent trips back home. It was over five years now since I had last seen him.

It was almost noon. The sun slanted through the dirty window to my left and lit the polished wood of the bar with a grainy light. The drink in my hand burned liquid gold. I looked at my reflection in the mirror behind the bar, at the eyes that were like dead candle wicks behind green glass, dead from lack of air. I thought about the murder and how both Rob and I had handled it, about how Rob had somehow transferred the whole stinking burden onto me. For a long time it had filled me with physical pain, a pain so deep that I could only communicate it through drunken threats and violence. But there was always something deeper inside me that not even physical violence could release, the simple need for revenge.

⌐

The call came on a bright morning in December.

I was sitting at my kitchen table watching the neighbours' cat chewing on a bird, my fingers knotted around a mug of coffee, when the phone started to ring. I was carrying a whisky hangover and thought about leaving it to ring and going back to bed, but there was an urgency in the tone, as if it may be bad news. I picked up on the fifth ring.

'Hello?' A woman's voice, familiar. I felt my heart step up a beat.

'Yes.' Hesitant. I reached across the table for a cigarette.

'Is that George? George Lowell?'

'Yeah, that's me,' I said with a note of finality in my voice, as if by guessing my name the caller had discovered my secret.

'I'm sorry. Have I called at an inconvenient time?' She sounded hurt.

'No, no. Now's fine. I'm just a little ...' I waved my cigarette in the air.

'OK. Well ...' She gave a nervous laugh. 'I'll start again, shall I?' Another laugh. 'Hi. I don't know if you remember me ... Claire Wish?'

My mind rewound furiously. Half remembered scenes.

'Sorry, I shouldn't have expected you –'

I sensed the faint echo of a missed heartbeat.

'Red hair and skinny legs?' I said.

I heard her laugh again, a gentle innocent sound this time. 'Well, not so skinny now … but, yeah, the hair's still red.'

I walked over to the cooker and lit my cigarette from the gas ring. 'What can I do for you?' I said. I looked out of the window and saw that the cat had gone, leaving the torn carcass of the bird in the middle of the lawn.

Suddenly I was gripped by panic.

'Well, do you remember the time capsule we buried –'

My blood ran cold.

'– in the fourth year? At school,' she added helpfully.

I couldn't speak; I nodded and hoped she could see me.

'They can't dig it up.'

Kaleidoscopic images of the murder flashed before my eyes, moving in and out of focus. Into focus – an iron fist breaking a face of stone.

'They …' I began to feel dizzy.

'You remember they planted it near that row of cherry trees?'

'Go on,' I managed. My voice was hoarse. I pulled out a chair and sat down, took a sip of coffee.

'Well, they buried it too near. Too near the trees. The roots have grown over the box.'

'They can't dig it up? The tree? They can't dig up the tree?'

'No.' A pause. Then, 'Well, they reckon nobody's gonna remember what was in the capsule anyway. Or exactly where it was buried …'

I felt my heart start to beat again. I struggled to bring everything under control. 'So they're not gonna dig it up, that's what you're saying? The whole thing's off?'

'Yes and no.'

'I don't understand.'

'We're gonna bury another capsule.'

'And dig that one up instead?'

'Brilliant, isn't it?'

'And where do I come into it?' I felt a smile break on my face.

'Well, I've been given the job of recreating the whole thing. I've had a new capsule made up, so now I'm just asking a few people – discreetly, mind you – if they've got anything I can use.'

'I don't know. I'd have to have a look around. Can I get back to you?'

'Sure.'

I took her number and promised to call back later.

◻

My mind was reeling. Was this a sick joke? Had they already dug up the capsule and found the tape? I headed for the loft.

I spent the next couple of hours choking on clouds of dust, cold sweat beading my face, until eventually I hauled a cardboard box down into the kitchen and hefted it onto the table. I had stuck things in the box as I came across them, but now I looked at them more carefully.

There were items from both before and after the murder.

- the *Mirfield Reporter* with a picture of the school cross country team on the front page, silver medallists in the Yorkshire Schools;

- a ticket stub from a Be Bop Deluxe concert at St George's Hall;

- my old school tie;

- a few singles, now scratched, covers torn, from punk bands long forgotten;

- a couple of music magazines, a local fanzine;

I felt a great weight lift from my chest as I realised that these innocent items were going to erase over twenty years of fear.

But as I began to put the things back in the box, I was filled with a deep sense of dread. Something drew my attention to the window. The wind was blowing the apple tree in the back garden around so that the branches seemed to be pointing at me, jabbing accusing fingers. A strong gust threw a branch against the window and as it scratched across the glass I heard the ghost of Tom Willis whisper to me.

❐

The bar was now full. A cloud of voices hung in the air, voices that spoke of emotions I had denied myself for so long. I heard laughter as if it was my native tongue and not the language of my neighbours.

The door opened and in the mirror I saw a man in a black leather car coat enter the bar. He moved his head as if looking around, but his eyes had the dark impenetrability of sunglasses. A spiderweb of burst veins was tattooed across his face and his belly pushed at his shirt.

I looked at the man for a couple of minutes before I realised it was Rob.

I leaned back on my stool and held up my arm. Rob weaved through the crowd and pushed into the bar beside me. 'Large scotch when you're ready,' he called to the barman.

Rob turned to face me and I saw nothing but darkness, dead eyes. He stepped back from the bar and pulled aside his jacket. Stuffed into the waistband of his jeans was a large black pistol.

'You remember that confession?' he asked, the words spilling out of his mouth.

I nodded slowly, unsure of what was happening.

'I meant every word of it.' His face looked as cold as marble, as if rigor had set in. He swirled the whisky around in his glass. 'Every single word.'

I looked at him closely. 'You remember Claire Wish?' I said, hesitant.

'Right after this drink …' He threw back the scotch and slammed the glass on the bar, wiped his mouth with the back of his hand. He pushed himself away from the bar and made to leave. 'Claire Wish? Yeah, sure. Course I remember her. What about her?'

I heard my heart beat deep in my chest, once … twice …

'Oh, nothing,' I said. 'It doesn't matter.'

OVER THE EDGE

Jason Starr

1

I had a lot to feel lousy about that night. My boss had been giving me hell because I didn't finish the payroll on time last week and a couple of freelancers had complained that their checks were late. I'd explained that it wasn't my fault, that I had been busy with other projects that he had assigned to me, but there was no reasoning with a mad man. He warned me that if this ever happened again he would 'terminate' me and when I tried to say something he told me he'd had enough of my shit and that he was sick of looking at my face.

I guess a lot of people get yelled at by their bosses, but when you're forty-six years old, working in what was supposedly your 'career', it can be pretty damn humiliating. I wanted to tell my boss to go fuck himself, but I couldn't afford to be unemployed with a wife, two kids and a mortgage. So whenever he yelled at me or treated me badly – which was pretty much every day – I always kept my mouth shut, telling myself that instead of getting angry, I should just try to feel sorry for him. After all, a guy who yells at his employees all the time couldn't be very happy, and in the long run he'd get what he deserved.

On my way home from work that night, I was feeling so miserable that I thought about stopping in at a bar on Sixth Avenue for a quick drink. But as I was about to go inside, I realised what I was doing and wisely turned around. I hadn't had a sip of alcohol in one year, five months, and eight days, and I knew that no matter what I couldn't fall back into that trap.

Instead, I went to the kiosk at the corner of Forty-seventh and Sixth and bought a pack of Wrigley's and a copy of the *Daily News*. The headline was MILLENNIMANIA. The big moment was just sixteen days away and lately all the newspaper headlines, and just about every article in every paper had something to do with the Millennium. I didn't know about anybody else, but I was getting sick of all the hype. It was only the people who didn't have any real problems who were going on and on about the end of the world. If they wanted to know real problems let them spend one day as Harold Pearlman.

Using my MetroCard, I went through the turnstile at the Forty-seventh Street, Rockefeller Center subway station, still feeling generally miserable and hopeless about my life. In other words, it was a normal weeknight. Or at least it was a normal weeknight until I stopped to tie my shoe.

I was at the top of the staircase that led to the subway platform. I guess I knelt down suddenly because I never saw the woman coming, but I felt her and I definitely heard her. She tripped over my outstretched leg, and tumbled down the staircase, screaming as her head banged against each stair. Her body seemed to gain momentum as she slammed hard against the metal railing, then there was a loud, horrifying crack as she landed head first on the concrete platform.

She lay still, purple blood leaking from her head in a slowly growing puddle. The whole fall had probably only taken two or three seconds, but to me it seemed like hours. The woman's screams, her crazed expressions, were still vivid in my mind. At first, people were standing around on the stairs and on the subway platform, staring at the woman in shock and horror, but then people rushed toward her.

It was obvious that the woman was seriously injured, if not dead. She wasn't moving. Although it was hard to tell from my position, about twenty yards away, she seemed to be about thirty years old, maybe older. She had short dyed blonde hair and she was wearing a black work suit. I hoped that she was all right, that somehow it wasn't as bad as it looked. Maybe she had just broken her nose or cut open a vein in her forehead. For several seconds, I stared down at the scene, probably still in shock, and then, as if awaking from a nightmare, I realised the trouble I could be in. What if someone had been watching and saw what happened? I'd be questioned by the police, maybe even arrested.

A few more seconds had passed and I realised that no one was looking at me. The crowd at the bottom of the stairs had grown, but all eyes were still focused on the woman. I stood up from my kneeling position and started walking slowly but steadily down the stairs. On the platform, I passed the crowd without pausing and then I started to walk faster. The end of the platform was almost empty because everyone had rushed to see what all the commotion was about near the stairs. No train was in sight and the whole station was quiet. I was ready for a police officer to appear at any moment. But seconds, maybe minutes passed, and no one was noticing me. Where was the fucking train? I leaned over the tracks anxiously, waiting for the rush of air. Finally, there was a roaring noise, then bright lights. I felt like I was stranded at the bottom of a pit and someone had dropped me a rope. It was a B and I needed a D, but I didn't care. The train doors opened and I got on.

2

I got out at the Fifty-fifth Street stop in Brooklyn. I lived a few miles away, on the D line near Avenue J, so I would have to take a bus or a car service home. Fifty-fifth Street was an elevated station and I walked toward the descending stairs at the end of the narrow platform, aware of the steady, ominous noise the heels of my shoes made against the concrete.

At the top of the steep staircase I thought I heard the woman's piercing scream again, and then I saw a glimpse of her frantic expression – those wide-open, horrified eyes. My legs wobbled and I had to grab onto the railing to steady myself. A man behind me asked if I was OK.

'Yeah, fine,' I said, not turning around to look at him. I let him pass, then I continued carefully down the stairs.

I waited about ten frustrating minutes for a bus. An empty

limo service car came by and I waved with my arms for it to stop. The driver said he would take me home for fifteen bucks, a rip-off price, but I wasn't going to haggle.

The car let me off in front of my two-family house on Fourteenth Street near Avenue K. As I walked up the steep staircase, I had the usual feeling of impending doom. All three of our TVs were always on full-blast, the kids were screaming, and there was always the odour of something burning. Tonight it was even worse because being on the stairs was giving me the same queasiness I'd felt when I'd descended from the subway and this, combined with all the noise in the house, was starting to give me a migraine.

When I came in the door, Carol, looking old, wearing a pink terry cloth robe, was leaning over Jonathan, screaming at him, loud enough to be heard over the TVs.

'I don't care who had it first – I said I want you to give it back to her!'

'No!' Jonathan screamed back.

'I want it!' Jennifer shouted.

'I want it!' Jonathan shouted.

'Give it to her!' Carol shouted above both of them.

'Fuck you!' Jonathan yelled back.

Carol slapped Jonathan on the top of his head and grabbed the stuffed animal he was holding. Jonathan ran down the hallway toward his room, crying. Jennifer took the stuffed animal from Carol, then chased after her brother.

Carol looked over at me, as if I had been home all day, and said, 'Can you believe that? What kind of ten-year-old says fuck you to his mother? He's been impossible – fighting with his sister all the time, taking her things. She's a girl, for Christ's sake. Doesn't he realise that?'

'I'll have a word with him later.'

'A lot of good that'll do,' Carol said, as if I were a worthless father, then she walked away into the living room.

The apartment was the usual pigsty. There were dishes piled high in the kitchen sink, toys strewn on the floor and on the table, and garbage was overflowing from the pail. I was starving and I realised that I hadn't eaten anything since a knish I'd bought from a cart on Sixth Avenue during my lunch hour. There were a couple of over-cooked hamburgers on the stove, covered with a thick layer of congealed lard. In a pot there was some spaghetti, soaking in a few inches of cold water. On another night I might have said to Carol, 'Couldn't you've at least heated this up for me?' and she'd have said, 'Because I'm stuck home with the kids all day. You can put it in the microwave just as easily as I can!' Then we'd have a few more heated exchanges, trading sarcastic, hurtful insults, and before we knew it we'd be screaming at each other, our voices soaring over the noise of the TVs and the kids. And if I got really angry and out of control, I might push Carol, or take a swing at her.

But tonight, strangely, I felt no anger or hostility toward my wife. I rinsed out a bowl, filled it with spaghetti and a hamburger and some Ragu from the fridge, then I heated the concoction in the microwave. To clear a space at the table, I pushed the toys away to one side, and then I sat down, blocking out the noise and the mess, and started to enjoy my dinner.

Midway through my meal, Carol sat down across from me. She was not a good-looking woman. Her brown hair was thin and greasy and she needed makeup to cover the acne scars on her cheeks, dark circles under her eyes, and deepening wrinkles.

Carol was telling me how she wanted to go shopping this weekend for new couches. It seemed like all she talked about lately were things that she wanted to 'get.' It was the same way with the kids – 'Get me this, daddy. Get me that, daddy.' Carol never asked me how my day had gone or how things were going at work. Of course the answer to both of these questions would've been, 'Don't ask,' but it might have been nice to know she cared.

In the middle of Carol's monologue, the kids stormed into the kitchen.

'He's a liar!'

'She's a liar!'

'He's a liar!'

'She's a liar!'

'Will both of you just go to your rooms and get to bed!' Carol screamed. 'You're driving us crazy!'

The kids chased each other around the table a few times, then Jennifer knocked over a glass and it shattered onto the floor. Normally, I would have gotten angry, maybe screamed at Jennifer or hit her with my belt, but I was starting to realise that tonight wasn't a normal night.

Calmly, I stood up, got the broom from the hall closet, and started sweeping up the glass.

'What's wrong with you?' Carol said. 'You just sit there and let them act like animals? Don't you care? I don't think you do. I think you just want to think about yourself. You're a selfish bastard, you know that?'

I had no idea why Carol was so upset and I didn't really care. I put my dishes away in the sink, then went into the bathroom to wash up. When I came out, I saw Carol's profile, on the living-room couch, watching TV. I went into the bedroom and closed the door behind me. Although my plan had been to try and forget about the incident on the subway, I couldn't resist turning on the TV news, just to find out what, if anything, was going on.

On New York 1, the local 24 hour-a-day TV news station, I had to sit through all the usual Millennium stories. The city was planning for the huge Times Square celebration, and there was the usual nightly report from the Vatican. Right-wing religious groups were planning a big march in Washington and there were demonstrations going on in just about every other major city in the world. When the Millennium reports were finally over, the anchorman recapped the top local story – the possible murder of a woman at the Rockefeller Center subway station. I watched the entire short report in disbelief. When it was over, I still couldn't believe it was true. The report said that the woman had died on her way to the hospital, but this wasn't what surprised me. While there was no way I could have known that she was going to die when I left the scene, I had somehow known all along that she wasn't going to make it. But what I couldn't believe was that I, Harold Pearlman, was the next news story after the Millennium. Arguably the most significant day in the history of the planet was less than three weeks away and my story was right there alongside it!

I watched the ten o'clock newscasts, switching back and forth between the local stations. Each channel reported the story, right after the Millennium reports, and the major new information was that the police were searching for 'a possible murder suspect.' They even had a description of me. It wasn't a clear description though, just that a witness had reported seeing 'a heavyset man in a beige trench coat' pushing the woman down the stairs, then 'fleeing the scene.' Of course the report was ridiculous. First of all, I didn't push the woman, she'd tripped, and second, 'fleeing the scene' made it sound as if I were a bank robber, but it was still incredible to see the story getting so much attention.

I started to watch the eleven o'clock news, but when I heard Carol's footsteps in the hallway I turned off the TV and shut out the light. When she came into the room I stayed still on my side with my eyes closed. When she lay down next to me, her weight shook the bed, but I remained still.

3

I left the house at a quarter to eight the next morning. Usually, I only bought the *Daily News*, but today I bought the *News*, the *Post*, and the *Times* at the newsstand near the subway. Of course the Millennium stories made the headlines. The *Times* only had a small mention of my murder story, but the *Post* and the *News* ran full-page articles. The woman's name was released for the first time – Mary-Beth Schaefer. The *Post* and the *News* printed the identical grainy photograph of her that seemed to be taken on a boat or a dock. She was very attractive – she definitely looked much better than she did lying at the bottom of the staircase. Wearing a black, one-piece bathing suit, she was smiling, squinting in the sun. The articles said that she was some bigshot real estate attorney for a prestigious law firm. One of the *Post* articles revealed that Ms. Schaefer had been on her way to the Village last evening to meet her fiance, who was an investment banker. A *News* article speculated that the 'killer' might have been mentally ill because witnesses described the man as acting 'erratically' in the subway station moments before the attack. I couldn't help laughing when I read that. The article went on to say that the police were working on a sketch of the suspect which would be released later today.

After reading all the articles that had to do with me, I just stared straight ahead, mindlessly reading a public service poster about child abuse that was above the seat across from me.

As the train headed over the Manhattan Bridge, bright rays of sunshine shone into the car, illuminating swarms of dust particles. I noticed how the old, Puerto Rican-looking woman sitting across from me and the Jamaican-looking man who was sitting next to her were both staring at me. At first I thought I was just being paranoid – people always stare at other people on the subway; there's nothing else to do after you're done reading the newspapers and the ads – but then I decided that they were staring at me differently. They were looking at me like they knew me, or thought they knew me, like they were trying to match my appearance with the description of the heavyset man in the beige trench coat they had read or heard about. I was wearing the same beige trench coat today that I had worn yesterday so I was probably an easy match to the description.

But I kept looking directly at the man and the woman, out-staring them until they looked away. A few seconds later, they looked at me again, with the same penetrating eyes, and again I returned their gazes, without showing any emotion, until they looked away. It was fun, making them think I was the killer, like I had my own private joke I was playing on the city.

I got out at Rockefeller Center. If I were worried about being spotted I would have gotten out at Forty-second Street and walked the rest of the way but, like I said, I was having fun being a murder suspect. Moving with the crowd, I looked across at the downtown platform and the stairs where the woman had fallen to her death. There were the usual streams of rush-hour commuters, swarming in straight lines, up and down the stairs. It was as if after the woman's body had been carried away and her blood cleaned up, the city had forgotten that she'd ever existed.

At the top of the stairs, I walked across the station, toward the turnstiles. As I was about to pass through, I noticed that I was heading right toward a police officer. He was standing by the token booth, looking straight ahead in my direction. I looked at him briefly as I passed. I was expecting him to say, 'Hey, you,' but I reached the stairs leading to the street and nothing happened. I was going to look back and see if he was following me, but I didn't want to give him the satisfaction of thinking I was afraid of him. At the top of the stairs, I glanced behind me and saw that the cop wasn't there. I realised how my heart was racing – not out of fear, out of excitement. It was exhilarating to walk right by that cop, to be so close to getting caught.

I had never felt so good on my way to work. I went into my office building on Forty-sixth Street feeling like I was Fred Astaire in one of those musicals from the 1940's. I imagined myself singing and dancing in the elevator, the entire building breaking out into a show-stopping number.

Reality set in when I got into my office. Papers were piled up on my desk and I remembered that today was payroll day again. The editors and managers of all the different departments would be inundating me with time sheets, plus I had my usual workload to do. I wished I had called in sick today.

I logged on to my computer and listened to my voice mail messages. Already, I felt like I needed to take a break. I killed some time going to the bathroom, then I poured a cup of coffee. I overheard two secretaries talking about the subway murder.

'It's so awful,' one was saying. 'I take that subway every day and I was there like ten minutes before that happened. That could've been me.'

'They think some mental patient pushed her,' the second secretary said.

'I don't doubt it,' the first secretary said. 'There're lunatics everywhere in this city.'

'I think it has to do with the Millennium,' the second secretary said. 'The whole world's going crazy.'

I had never been the topic of conversation before. Office gossip was always about *other* people. I was always just the guy who worked in Payroll who nobody paid much attention to. It was exhilarating to finally be getting some notice.

On my way back into the office, my boss called out my name. I turned around and saw him standing in the aisle between the cubicles where the editorial staff worked. He was wearing a tan wool vest over a white shirt and brown slacks. He looked like he was on his way to play golf at a whites-only country club. He must have been about my age, but he looked ten years younger, with his wavy blond hair and year-round tan. Rumour had it that his uncle was on the board of directors of the corporation that owned the magazine and had basically handed him the job as Managing Editor.

'How's it going?' I said, knowing that he was going to lash out at me again.

'How's it *going*?' he said mockingly. 'You stroll in late and miss the morning meeting, then you have the balls to ask me how's it going? You're lucky I don't throw you out on your ass right now.'

I'd forgotten all about the weekly staff meeting, but I wasn't upset about it.

'I can't stand this anymore – these lapses you have,' my boss continued. 'Unless you come in here one-hundred percent prepared to work, I don't want you in here anymore. Is that understood?'

My boss's voice had increased gradually during his tirade and when he said 'understood' he was screaming at the top of his lungs. People in the office had stopped what they were doing and were looking at us. Usually, this would have upset and embarrassed me. I would've imagined what they were thinking – *How could he let him scream at him that way?* My boss was much nicer to other people in the office than he was to me. For some reason, I was his personal scapegoat, the guy he could treat like shit as much as he wanted to because he knew I'd never fight back. But those days were over now because I knew something he didn't. I knew what it was like to kill. Tripping that woman had been so easy, and if I did it once I could do it again – to anyone. So now listening to my boss scream at me, thinking he had so much power over me, was hilarious. He was such a moron! *I* was the murderer, not him! I had the real power!

'I'm sorry,' I said, trying not to smile. 'I guess I've just had a lot on my mind lately.'

'Yeah, well make sure it doesn't happen again,' my boss said, still trying to project his voice like he was on stage, 'because I've about had it with you and all of your bullshit.' He started to walk away, then he turned back and shouted, 'And I want that payroll finished today too – on time!'

Instead of going to a pizza place for lunch, I went to the bar on Sixth Avenue that I had almost gone into last night. It was crowded with business people, but luckily I got a seat on a stool. I ordered a ginger ale, no ice, and asked the bartender to turn to New York 1. As I'd expected, the subway murder was still the top local news story, but there was no way I could have prepared for what the anchorman said. I'd expected him to say that the 'manhunt for the murderer was continuing,' or for the station to show the police sketch of me, but instead I heard the worst news possible – the investigation was over.

According to the report, the Medical Examiner had determined that the woman had almost certainly died from 'natural causes.' She'd had a life-long heart condition and there was evidence that she'd suffered a heart attack, probably before her fall. A police spokesman said that the witness who had reported seeing a man 'push' the woman down the stairs had a long psychiatric history, and the police were doubting 'the validity of his statement.' He added that the police were 'unofficially ceasing their investigation.'

I was the only one in the bar who was listening to the news item. Everyone else was laughing, mingling; in the background, music was playing, but all I could hear was the dull, pounding beat. I was devastated. I knew I was being irrational and I didn't care – I *wanted* to be responsible for that woman's death. I wanted to see my sketch in the newspapers and on TV; I wanted people to stare at me on the subway. But now it was all over; in a few days, it would all be forgotten, if it wasn't forgotten already.

Without really thinking, I ordered a Scotch on the rocks. I finished it in one gulp and ordered another. It was only when the bartender put down the third drink in front of me that it hit me what I was doing. But instead of feeling bad – like I probably should have – I felt like I was rediscovering how great drinking was. What the hell had I been doing all these years, avoiding the one thing in life that gave me pleasure? From now on I was going to do what I wanted, and I didn't give a fuck what anyone else said.

I lost count of how many scotches I had before I switched over to gin. Judging by the buzz I had going, I guessed I'd had about five. After my third gin, I looked at the blurry, wobbly clock above the bar and saw that it was after two o'clock and I realised that I'd been away from the office for more than two hours. I thought this was impossible because it felt like an hour had gone by, at most. Vaguely, I remembered how much work I had to do and I knew there was no way I was going to be able to do it like *this*.

My head felt numb and wobbly, as if it were attached to my body by a piece of wire. I left the bar and walked down Sixth Avenue, jostled by the crowds rushing by in each direction.

In the office, I went right to the bathroom and took a long, relieving piss. Afterwards, I splashed cold water against my face, trying to sober up. I looked in the mirror and, as often happened when I was drunk, I barely recognised myself. I had one of those anonymous, grim faces that sit across from me on the subway every day.

I wobbled back to my office and sat down at my computer. I had no idea how I would get any work done and, as it turned out, I didn't have a chance to try. My boss appeared and as soon as we made eye contact he said, 'Get the hell out of here, Harold! Right now!'

I stared at him for several seconds until I was aware of myself staring. Then I said, 'What's wrong?' hearing my slurred words.

'You're drunk, that's what's wrong,' my boss said. 'Who the hell do you think you are, going out and getting drunk on your lunch hour?'

You, I wanted to say. So maybe I'd had a drink or two too many, but what about all the times my boss came back to the office after his 'business lunches' with his eyes glazed and bloodshot?

But instead I said meekly, 'What makes you think I'm drunk?'

'Get out!' he screamed, louder than he had ever screamed at me before. He really sounded like an insane person and it felt good, knowing that he was making such a fool of himself.

'You can't fire me,' I slurred, trying to stand steadily. 'It's against the law!'

I had no idea whether or not this was true, but it seemed like the right thing to say. One thing for sure, it got my boss thinking, because he waited a few seconds then said, 'I'll have to talk that over with my lawyer. Meanwhile, just get the hell out of here and don't come back till you're sober.'

Everyone was standing up, looking out from above their cubicles, watching me leave the office.

Bright sunshine was stinging my eyes, sobering me up. I wished I had quit. All the usual reasons why I stayed at my job seemed absurd. Why was I working my ass off every day, taking all this abuse, to support my miserable, undeserving family? I should make Carol get a job, get back to work. Let her see what it's like in the real world.

In the subway station, I paused on the staircase where the woman had fallen last night. I was still a little drunk and I was so close to the edge of the stairs I almost started tumbling myself. But I regained my balance and walked slowly down toward the platform, wishing I was still a murder suspect. I wanted people to stare at me the way they had this morning, as if I were more than just another subway passenger.

It was well before rush hour so there were only a few people on the platform. I started staring at one guy who kept leaning over the track to see if a train was coming. I couldn't help thinking about how easily I could kill him. All I had to do was give him one push, just as the train was arriving, and he would almost certainly be crushed. And if I did it fast enough, I could probably get away with it too. What would the police and Medical Examiner say then? Would they say *he* had died of 'natural causes' too?

The man was less than a foot away from the edge of the platform now. He looked like somebody's boss. He was wearing a pin-striped suit and his thin grey hair was slicked back with grease. He kept checking his shiny gold watch that was probably a Rolex. Bosses were always obsessed with brand names. He probably drove a Porsche, the suit was probably an Armani. He had that 'boss look' to him, as if he never laughed at anyone's jokes but his own. You could tell he loved to control and torture people. No one would miss him if he was gone. His employees would probably celebrate, as if someone had murdered the prison guard.

As the rumbling of a train increased, I moved closer to the man. He was only a couple of feet from the edge so it would only take one quick push. I was going to do it – I was going to kill him.

The train entered the station. I was only about a foot behind him now and he had no idea I was there. I was wide awake and I wasn't dizzy anymore. If I pushed this stranger in front of the train I'd be back in the newspapers tomorrow, maybe even on the front page. Harold Pearlman would be bigger than the Millennium – all he had to do was stick out his arms and push this stranger, this boss, over the edge.

Harold put his hands against the man's back, already hearing the wonderful whoosh of the train's impact. At the same moment, another man tackled Harold from behind. He had no idea what was happening. He still saw himself on the front page of a newspaper, but people were on top of him, holding him down. With his face pressed against the concrete platform, using his arms and legs to try and get free, Harold was screaming about fucking bosses, Armani suits, Rolex watches, and the goddamn Millennium. In his mind, it all made perfect sense.

BLACK SHEEP

Ed Gorman

1

Good breasts are important, sure, as are a good face, nice ankles and wrists, and a tight bottom. Not to mention good breath and keeping herself clean and sweet-smelling down there and not wearing anything flashy or trashy. But you also have to be able to talk to them. A lot of guys forget that. Because, frankly, a lot of guys just aren't as sensitive as Bill Avery. You have to be able to talk to them and they have to be able to talk to you. Especially when your life takes a terrible turn all of a sudden. If you can't talk to the girl you're seeing on the side, you may as well just pay for it and get yourself a hooker...

Today, Bill needs to talk. God, how Bill needs to talk. The place for the conversation is Tiffany's bed in her apartment in the Windward Hills apartment complex. To Bill, who lives in a very nice new Tudor out in a very pricey new development, this place is sort of pathetic – toilets that won't flush the first time; water stains on the dining room walls; and not a single new car in the parking lot. But he's magnanimous about it. Tiffany is a small-town girl from Oskaloosa who came to Cedar Rapids and went to business school and then went to work for the law firm where Bill is about to become a full partner. He can identify with Tiffany because he came from the west side and went to all the wrong schools and instead of a degree from Yale or Princeton, which the senior partners always discuss proudly, he ended up at the U of Iowa. Nothing wrong with that, of course. A fine school. But still.

So they are in bed – this is after work and he's supposedly

working late, that's the word he gave his wife anyway – and it's snowing in the dusk and in the apartment above them somebody is playing Nat 'King' Cole Christmas songs and Bill Avery feels very, very sad. So sad in fact that he wasn't all that good in the sack tonight.

For which he apologises for the tenth time.

'Oh, gosh, Bill, I don't expect a stud service.'

'But I came and you didn't.'

'Well, I remember a night when I came and you didn't.'

'You do?'

'Yes. One night when you were drunk.'

'Oh.'

'So let's just say we're even.'

'Really?'

'Sure,' she says. 'But you really want to talk about your brother, don't you?'

'My brother?'

'Sure. Are you surprised I remembered he was getting out?'

'Yeah. Yeah, he is. The Governor wanted to let a bunch of model prisoners out right before the year 2000. Good public relations and all that bullshit.'

'You heard from him then?'

'No. But I can feel him here. You know that feeling? How you can feel somebody in the same town?'

'Oh, sure.'

She kissed him. She had warm, silken flesh. She was sweet in every sense.

'Who's really pissed is my wife.'

'Well, gee, he served his time. And it was just a robbery. Nothing violent, I mean. He served his time and she should give him another chance.'

'That's the bad part of marrying into a good family, I suppose.'

'What is?'

'Oh, you have to be so concerned what everybody thinks. Sharon's afraid everybody at the firm and all her friends at the country club will find out that I have a younger brother who just got out of prison. That I have a younger brother who's been stealing stuff all his life.'

'Oh, this wasn't the first time he stole stuff?'

'No; just the first time he went to prison.'

'Oh.'

'Kind of a career criminal, then, huh?' she says.

'Not, not a career criminal. He just – takes stuff. I mean, it's not like armed robbery or anything.' He thinks back. 'When we were in grade school, he took twenty dollars from the desk drawer of this teacher. And when we were in high school, he stole a hundred dollars from this cash box at a school dance. And then a year later, he took a couple of real expensive watches from gym lockers at school.' He sighed. 'Then he took that necklace at Mrs. Parker's. And that's the one that put him in jail.'

She held him. Tightly. 'God, you've had to go through so much with him. I mean, both your folks dying when you were only seventeen and you having to raise him and all. I just hope he appreciates it enough to stay out of trouble this time.'

He nods. 'God, so do I.'

'I had a cousin who went to prison once.'

'Really?'

'Uh-huh. He worked in a bank and embezzled. Over in Rock Island. It was funny.'

'What was?'

'Oh, he was this real straight-arrow when he was in Iowa but as soon as he started living on the other side of the Mississippi – he changed; changed completely. That's when he embezzled, when he moved I mean.'

He smiles. 'He just moved across the Mississippi and he changed?'

'I know it sounds weird but that's just what happened. Honest.'

'You're nuts, you know that?'

She kisses him again. 'Comes from not being very well educated.' And laughs. She's much smarter than she seems to realise; and it always makes him feel bad for her, how she's always putting herself down all the time.

She and Glen have the education thing in common. At least she went through high school and business college. Glen never even got through high school.

Suddenly, he feels claustrophobic. They're tangled up in covers, their body heat is searing him. He needs cool air. He needs to be alone. He disentangles himself and walks over to the window and looks down at the parking lot. All the clerks pulling in now, their cars heavy with snow on their roofs and trunks and hoods, big lumbering white bears in the cold Midwestern snow-blown darkness. That's who lives here, clerks. Shopping centre folks. When Bill was growing up on the west side – God, was it really thirty years ago now? – wearing a tie to work was a big deal. You wore a tie to work you were somebody special. Today, you wore a tie to work it didn't mean anything. Just ask one of the clerks. The lot is filling up. People are slipping cardboard windshield screens under the wipers. The swirling snow is getting heavy in the burning amber glow of the parking lot lights. All the clerks are hurrying to get inside. He isn't being very nice, thinking of them as clerks.

'You thinking about Glen?'

'Yeah.'

'You nervous about seeing him?'

'Yeah.'

'He loves you. Remember when you let me read those letters of his from prison that time? He really looks up to you.'

'Yeah, he does I guess.'

'Talking about how your Dad would be so proud of you and all. God, I was really crying when I read that, remember?'

'Yeah, I remember.'

'Maybe Sharon would like him if she gave him a chance.' That always surprises him, the way Tiffany talks about Sharon as if she's a good friend they have in common.

'Not Sharon.' That's the funny thing. He would have been much better off marrying somebody like Tiffany. Farm girl. No pretensions. Sweet. But what did marrying a Tiffany prove? Anybody could go out and marry himself a Tiffany. But marrying a Sharon… Marrying a Sharon meant getting accepted into the best law firm in the city, marrying a Sharon meant inheriting a substantial amount of money and property when her father died, marrying a Sharon meant that most people at the club feared you a little. And he liked that. He didn't exploit it – well, not often, anyway – but he liked it, a west side boy like himself watching these major players pay him a bit of fearful deference. You didn't get those kind of benefits when you married a Tiffany, no matter how sweet-natured she was.

He looked at his watch. 'Well, I'd better be going.'

'Oh, God.'

'What?'

'Just the thought of you going.' She held her thin white arms out to him, entreating, the way one of his own little daughters would. He found the gesture profoundly fetching, and oddly moving. She really wanted him. Sharon and he were long shut of wanting each other; long shut. They spend their last minutes just holding each other in the perfume-sweet heat of her bed; he closes his eyes and it is wonderful, the woman-smell of her, the tenderness of her, that odd fetching little laugh of hers. At moments like these, he can disappear inside her, just vanish utterly, no will or ego or memory of his own, and tonight he needs badly to vanish.

2

It is an alien planet he finds waiting for him. The snow is coming down harder than ever. In the streets giant yellow creatures with wild burning amber eyes scrape the snow off the streets. Growling trucks drop sifting sand. Here and there cars are stuck, obstinate little animals trying to fight their way out of the grip of huge snow drifts they skidded into.

There is beauty, too, of course, the moth-like way the large damp snowflakes flutter around the streetlights; the occasional pair of lovers, walking hand in hand in beatific harmony down the dark and snowy streets, their long scarves trailing behind them with perfect grace.

He keeps sliding around. He is not, in fact, an especially good driver and usually does the wrong thing in crisis situations. Such as slamming on the brakes when he's starting into a slide on an icy street. If he's not careful, he'll end up one of those cars buried in a snow drift. He should go home. This is upper-most in his mind: should-go-home. He's been spending far too much time lately with Tiffany. But the way he goes home from her place, he always comes very near the neighbourhood where he and Glen grew up. Usually, he resists the urge to drive past the old places but tonight – God, of all nights, the roads being what they are – tonight, inexplicably, he can't resist.

Snow shrouds everything, lends beauty even where there is none, gives the rusting cars parked along the street an antique rather than junky look. The snow does the same for all the houses. During daylight hours, these places are scars of smashed windows and tilting front porches and falling down garages and neon APT. FOR RENT signs on weather-rotted front porch columns.

But the snow softens all this for the eye, rounds all the edges, hides the cancer that daily devours wood and siding and paint and shingle and concrete. The snow even absorbs all the sounds that would normally be heard in this neighbourhood – kids crying, couples arguing, mean hungry watchdogs barking – so that a curiously dignified silence befalls the streets and alleys.

Then he sees it. Little square box on the corner of 1st Street and 8th Avenue. Fuzzy neon glow of beer signs somewhat diminished in the snow. When you grew up in this neighbour-hood, this was the place you always dreamed of. The tavern where the really cool guys hung out. They had neat cars and neater women and they knew how to fight and how to play pool and Briney, the guy who owns the place, even gave them their beers on credit. Even though Bill always wanted out of this neighbourhood Briney's tap was still a big deal for him. It was the place he bought his first legal beer. Drove back from Iowa City the night of his twenty-first birthday and went right to Briney's and Briney, which he did for anybody who was celebrating a twenty-first birthday, Briney gave him a free pitcher of beer. You were somebody when Briney gave you that free pitcher of beer – somebody in the neighbourhood anyway – and for all his success, Bill thinks back to his boyhood now not with his usual resentment and distaste... but with true pleasure. Memory is a con-artist, of course, but for this moment he allows himself to be conned... he is twenty-one and on the hardscrabble streets again and inside Briney's everybody whispers about him. That kid's gonna make it; smarter'n a god damned whip; too bad his brother Glen didn't get any brains. Poor little guy's dumb as a post. Bill was one of the real stars of Briney's for a year or so back then; and he enjoyed it, he really did...

The cars in the lot all wear snow-skins. Their drunken drivers will have to spend several butt-freezing minutes scraping off their windshields. And then they'll wiggle and waggle home, having to be careful, you slide into a parked car or something with liquor on your breath and a cop makes you take one of those breath test deals... in this state you can kiss your license goodbye for two, three years, especially if you have some kind of prior...

Briney's: clack of pool balls, cries of country western jukebox, revolving Bud clocks in the gloom above the bar, smells of cigarettes, beer, whiskey, disinfectant, urine. He remembers a night when two guys got into it over pool and one kept banging the head of the other against the edge of the pool table until half the people in here thought he might be dead. What he notices most is the lack of young women: in the old days, so long ago now it seems and he's not yet forty, in the old days going to Briney's was as big a thing for the girls as it was the boys, and this meant the sexiest most stuck-up girls in the neighbourhood, too. But not any more. The women are older now, sliding into middle-age, their bodies fighting the g forces of the grave that make them so unrecognisable. In the old days, the girls in Briney's had the faces of poetry; now they have the faces of bad, flat prose.

Briney himself is behind the bar, washing glasses. He watches Bill walk from the front door to the bar. A few other people start watching, too. 'Hey, Briney, how's it going?' Bill says. He's a little nervous, which he resents. It should be Briney who is nervous about seeing him. It's Bill who drives the BMW, it's Bill who belongs to the country club, it's Bill who went boating last summer with the mayor. But there's an obstinacy to the people in Briney's. A guy like Chucky O'Day, he starts making these tire gizmos in his home workshop, and pretty soon he's got his own business, the bank begging to loan him money, a nice house out where the yuppies are building on the far west side... Chucky O'Day tools in here in his new Firebird convertible, and he's still one of the boys. The clothes may be more expensive, he may not get in parking lot puking contests the way he did back then, but he's still Chucky, and they're always glad to see him, happy for his success. Bill, it's another matter. Bill, he was always a little stand-offish, anyway. Bill, he isn't one of them now – if he ever was.

Briney says, 'If you're looking for your brother, he ain't been in yet.'

'I just thought I might have a drink.'

'Slummin' tonight, huh?'

A couple of the guys along the bar, with long ears, they pick up on Briney's sarcasm and snicker like second-graders. For Bill, life will always be like the second grade playground, where he learned that he didn't fit. Too cool for the nerds; too nerdy for the cool ones. He doesn't fit here and, truth be told, he doesn't fit with Sharon's friends at the country club, either.

'You know I like this place, Briney,' Bill says, the sickening note of pleading still in his voice. How many of these people have ever even sat in a BMW, let alone owned one?

'Yeah, that's why you and your country club pals always come around.'

More snickers from the guys at the bar. 'Blue Christmas' by Elvis comes on the jukebox.

'You have Black & White Scotch? How about a shot and a glass of beer.'

Shot-and-a-beer. The bona fides in a place like this.

Briney goes to get his shot. Bill starts to look around. A few grudging Christmas decorations here and there in the gloom. He can hear Briney: why put all that bullshit up when you just have to take it right back down again?

Then he sees her and at first he doesn't think it's her, it's so dark in here, then he knows it's her and then he knows that Glen's going to be in here tonight for sure.

Briney sets his drink down and says, 'You seen her, huh? Susan Cramer. Sittin' over there.'

'Yeah.'

'She got in here a little before you did.' He smirks. 'Anybody woulda told me Susan Cramer ever woulda been sittin' in my place, I woulda laughed. Susan Cramer. She was always hangin' around the nuns. Surprised she didn't end up a nun herself.'

And it's true, back when they were at Catholic school, and everybody was doing drugs and sleeping with each other and getting into various kinds of trouble, back then little Susan Cramer, who stood maybe five-two and didn't weigh more than ninety pounds, and who was very pretty in a quiet, melancholy way, Susan Cramer was one of the few kids who didn't join in. Mass every day, good grades, always helping the nuns deliver food baskets to the poor and things like that, and then home to her parents who were much older and sick. Never went out much. But had this humongous crush on Glen ever since they were in grade school. She was one of the few people who believed in him, one of the few people who tried to turn him away from this thing he had about stealing things. Bill hasn't heard – or thought of her – in years.

'Maybe I'll go over and say hi.'

Briney smirks again. 'Yeah, and be sure and tell her about your BMW and that big-ass mansion of yours.'

The long ears are out again, the men along the bar snickering. Bill should be the one in charge here. It's a terrible thing to admit to – and Americans especially hate admitting to it – but there really is a social pecking order. Successful guy like Bill comes in, the other men should be intimidated by him. But that sure isn't the way it's working out.

'It isn't a mansion,' Bill says. Why does he always sound so desperate? He's that way around his partners at the law firm; a little bit sweaty all the time.

Briney says, 'It'll do till the real thing comes along.'

And gets another laugh.

3

He remembers that she always looked spooked, scared, like somebody was about to hit her or something. That's how she looks when she sees him walking toward the booth she's sitting in.

'Hi. Remember me?' he says.

She nods.

'All right if I sit down?'

She nods again.

She isn't exactly pretty but there's a wounded quality to the eyes and mouth that give her a vulnerability that some men – including himself – find erotic in a strange way. A child-woman, he supposes, that's her appeal. She never knew how to dress and she still doesn't, a rumpled brown sweater and blue eye shadow and blonde hair. She still doesn't weigh any more than she did in high school. Ninety pounds max.

He sits his beer-and-a-shot down and then follows it, sitting in the booth across from her.

'I shouldn't be drinking this,' she says, and tilts her head to her beer.

He smiles. 'I won't call the police. I promise.'

She doesn't smile. 'We have a lot of alcoholism in my family.'

'Oh.'

'My Dad and both his brothers.'

'I'm sorry.'

'So I get scared. Every time I have a beer, I mean.'

'You have many beers?'

'This is my first in maybe a year.'

He doesn't want to laugh and hurt her feelings. She's so sincere and ardent about everything. Has to be careful around her. She seems so skittish.

'Well, if all you drink is a beer a year, I don't think you have much to worry about.'

'I hope not.'

'You know who I was thinking about the other day?'

'Who?'

'Sister Mary Philomena. Remember her?'

'Yes.'

'I was remembering how she took a swing at Charlie O'Donnell one day and hit the wall instead. And broke her hand?' He laughs. 'God, Charlie never got tired of telling that story.'

'I liked her.'

'I sort of did, too. But it was funny. Her breaking her hand and all.'

'I suppose. But she was the one who helped me get in the convent.'

'Wow, I didn't know that. You were in the convent?'

She nods. 'Three years.'

'And you, what, dropped out?'

'Uh-huh. I decided I didn't have a true vocation.'

'Well, good thing you didn't go all the way and take your vows and stuff, then.'

'It was because I was writing Glen all the time. You know, your brother.'

'Oh.'

'That's what Mother Superior told me. Why I should drop out. Because of the letters.'

'How did she know about the letters?'

'You have to tell them who you're writing.'

'I see.'

'She said that I was in love with him and that I should take it as a sign.'

She'd followed Glen around since they were back in second grade. You saw Glen, Susan Cramer was never far behind.

'That I was in love with him, and that I didn't have a true vocation.'

Then, 'But by the time I actually got back to town here, my Dad was real sick – he had throat cancer – and my Mom wasn't able to take care of him by herself, so I never really got to see Glen all that much. And then I started seeing this guy who lived next door. You remember Denny Walsh?'

'Sort of.'

'Big comic book collector. That's a strange thing, you know, to say about somebody, I mean when that's the first thing that comes to mind and all. But that was his life. He collected comic books. He's got this good job out at Rockwell but what he's really about are his comic books. Anyway, I knew my Dad wanted to see me get married before he died so when Denny asked me – I said yes.' Then, 'We got divorced a couple of months after my Dad died. The whole thing didn't last more than ten months. Denny caught me calling Glen one night and then I told him, I mean I should've been honest with him to begin with, told him that I was in love with Glen and that I probably would be in love with him the rest of my life. I know that sounds corny but that's the truth. And then he said what my Dad always said, that Glen was just a thief. And right after that, Glen got caught in that house, and they sent him to prison. You know how many letters I wrote him in prison?'

'How many?'

'I kept count. 162. 162 letters. One every three days. Can you imagine that? And I saw him twice a month on top of it.'

'So now you're finally going to get together, you and Glen?'

'That's what I'm praying for. I pray for it every morning and every night. His last letter from prison, he wrote me that he loved me. He never said that before.' She smiled and it was a sad and nervous smile. 'I carry the letter right in my purse. Right with me all the time. You want to see it?'

'No, thanks. That's between you and Glen.'

Something changed in her face, then. 'There's just one thing I'd really like you to do for Glen.'

'What's that?'

'Ask your wife to be nice to him when he comes to see his little niece and nephew. He knows she hates him.'

'She doesn't hate him,' Bill says.

'Well, you know what I mean. A wealthy woman like that, she doesn't exactly like having an ex-convict for a brother-in-law.' Then, 'He loves you, Bill.'

'I know. And I love him. Don't think I don't.'

'That's why he went to prison for you.'

For a moment, his heart stops. Literally. Terror seizes him. He can't believe what he's just heard. Assimilating, that's what he's doing. He's assimilating what she told him. Then – rage. Slams his fist hard on the table. 'That's a goddamned lie!'

And even above the voices, even above the jukebox, even above the slamming of pool balls and the explosive flush of the toilet, even above all these things, they can hear his voice. And now they're looking at him, most of them, looking at him and wondering what he's so angry about, who could be so angry with pathetic little Susan Cramer, she was a goddamned nun for crissake.

She says, very quietly, leaning forward so she can speak in whispers, 'All those other times you stole stuff – that's why he always took the blame for you. Because he loves you. Your folks always expected you to be a success – Bill got the brains in the family, Glen always says – and he always looked up to you. He knew you couldn't help yourself, you know, about stealing stuff. So he took the blame every time you took something. Ever since you were little kids.'

'If he told you that, he's lying.' But the anger is gone now; there's just weariness. It's kind of funny, actually, little Susan Cramer – at this moment anyway – is in total control of the situation. What's even worse is that she's feeling sorry for him.

'Gee, Bill, calm down. I'm not going to tell anybody and neither is he. He loves you too much and I love him too much to do somethin' like that. He kind of lives through you – he's not the smartest guy in the world – you should hear him talk about you. That's why he had to make sure to return that diamond necklace you took from Mrs. Parker's when you were at her house for the party. He broke in the next night and was going to put the necklace under the couch. But they caught him.'

He checks his watch. 'I've got to get home.'

She reaches out and touches his hand. 'Bill, I pray for you every day. I really do. I pray you won't steal anything else so that you'll have a great life and so that Glen won't have to take the blame any more.'

Grey, the way this neighbourhood is grey; and worn beyond her years. The eroticism he once saw is gone now, at least in his eyes. Grey and worn is all she is.

He shakes his head. 'You don't know much about criminals, do you, Susan?'

'I know about Glen.'

'Criminals always blame somebody else for their troubles. Glen is blaming me.'

'He wouldn't lie to me, Bill. He really wouldn't.'

'He wouldn't, huh?'

He stands up. 'I really do have to run.'

'Bill. I really won't tell anybody. I really won't.'

'Good,' he says, throwing a twenty dollar bill on the table. 'Good, because you shouldn't go around spreading lies.'

As he passes the bar, Briney says, 'Bring the wife around some time, Bill. I'm sure she'd like to meet us.'

Another sure laugh with the grey and worn men along the bar.

4

The alien world again. But worse now. Cars stalled in snow-drifts all over the place. Even trucks spinning out of control on the icy snow-packed streets. He feels forlorn, isolated. He should've expected that someday Glen would tell somebody. Shouldn't be any big surprise. And certainly there was no threat in the way Susan spoke to him. God, she was understanding if anything. Glen always wanted to please the folks. He knew they were counting on older brother Bill to be the one who made it. He had all the poise and polish and brains. Glen, to be brutally honest, just isn't all that smart. They lived long enough to see Bill become a successful lawyer – and long enough to see Glen go to prison. That's probably what killed them (they both died within a year of each other; heart attack for mom, cancer for dad). Now, Glen is out.

Then he's home. Spectacular Christmas lights on his street. His very prosperous street. A huge sleigh parked on one roof top, a beautiful Nativity scene taking up an entire, sprawling lawn. The neighbourhood of a very successful man; the most prestigious area in all of Cedar Rapids.

Then he's turning into the long, winding drive that will take him to his Tudor-style house. Modest Christmas decorations here but the house looks gorgeous mantled with snow.

Needs to put Glen and Susan out of his mind. Enjoy himself. Everything is fine, under control. Next time he gets the urge to steal something – well, he'll just have to get the impulse under control, that's all.

He puts the car in the garage, next to Sharon's own BMW, and then walks up to the back door, snowflakes cold on his cheeks. He even opens his mouth, lets the snowflakes melt on his tongue the way he used to when he was a boy. But the air was cleaner back then. God only knows what kind of disease this snowflake is carrying.

He walks up into the kitchen. Sharon is lovely in a very nice, dark dress and a white apron. She is a very, very pretty lady.

'You look tired, honey,' she says.

'Long day, I guess.'

Then his two daughters burst into the kitchen. Three and four, they are, and even better looking than Sharon. 'Daddy, Mommy said that Uncle Glen is a criminal. Is that true?'

'Yeah, is he a criminal like on TV?'

He gives Sharon an angry look.

She is standing there with a small cooking pan filled with sauteed onions.

'I knew you wouldn't like me saying it, dear. But I wanted them to know the truth. I don't have anything against him – I'm a very open-minded person and I think you know that – but I just thought it would be a good thing if the girls knew the truth was all.'

The truth, he thinks all the time he's washing up for dinner.

The truth, he thinks all the time he's watching TV that night.

The truth, he thinks all the time he's lying there in the darkness tonight, unable to sleep.

The truth.

I WAS BARBARELLA

Lauren Henderson

*This story is dedicated to Kim, Symon, Rachael and Ewan, with love-
and thanks for all their help. It's also a blatant attempt to manoeuvre
them into throwing the Millennium party they've been mentioning
vaguely for a few years now...*

When you tell people that, at an end-of-the-Millennium
party, you happened to solve a mystery involving a
seventeenth-century ebony dagger – a family heir-
loom with a ruby set into its hilt – a pair of warring brothers, and
a blonde femme fatale, they tend to sit back in the old leather
armchair with the decanter of port at the elbow and the cigar in
the mouth, expecting a riproaring story. I'm sorry to disappoint
in advance. It was fun, but it wasn't sensational: neither the
party to end all parties nor the fling to end all flings. And nor
was what happened along the way the crime to end all crimes.

By way of undercutting expectations still further, I can say
that the blonde was myself – and you won't find a more
convincing brunette this side of Gina Lollobrigida – and the
femme fatale part was mainly due to the costume. It was a fancy
dress party: and I was Barbarella. I even won a prize.

❐

'We're MEN, we're men in TIGHTS, we roam around the
WOODS looking for FIGHTS,' piped a small voice from the
corridor. 'We're MEN, we're men in TIGHTS –' Through the
open kitchen door, a diminutive figure came into view, caper-

ing down the corridor, waving a plastic stick gleefully in front of him. He was clad simply, even minimally, in a green ra-ra skirt, his only accessory a pair of red woolly socks pulled up over the knees. Amber Valletta had been photographed in a not dissimilar outfit for *Vogue* quite recently. He disappeared from view, his voice fading gradually around the corner of the corridor.

'That *bloody* film,' said the small voice's father, pouring himself another glass of wine. 'If I hear that song one more time I'll throw the video out of the window.'

The small voice's mother looked guilty. 'I thought it was quite funny the first time, when we went to see it because all the other films at the multiplex were booked out,' she said defensively, turning to me. 'The witch was called Latrine. Well, *I* thought that was funny…'

'*Hilarious*,' contributed the small voice's father acidly.

'Lots of other people were laughing!'

'They were laughing at *you*, Rebecca, not at the film, because you went into hysterical spasms at what was probably the unfunniest joke ever written –'

'– we're men in TIGHTS – ooh, TIGHT tights!'

The small voice had completed a circuit; it came round for another lap and faded again. We were sitting in the cosy second-floor kitchen of Rebecca and Richard Mackenzie's house in Edinburgh – in Leith, to be precise, down by the old docks. The wave of tourists brought in the wake of *Trainspotting* had by now mercifully subsided and Leith was its old schizophrenic self again, a mixture of rundown shops and spit-and-sawdust pubs combined with smart restaurants and river-view loft-style conversions, all of which co-existed with surprising ease. Rebecca and Richard's house was on Great Junction Street, a converted Methodist chapel next to the funeral parlour, the entrance a forbidding iron grille over a steel door. The ground floor was equally unwelcoming, as it was just the well for a great echoing stone staircase, chilly and grey.

Things got better the further you climbed. The first floor was the old chapel itself, wood-floored, concrete-walled, the size of a tennis court, with a stage occupying the far wall. Since

Rebecca and Richard ran a theatre company together, the space was perfect for their uses. They rented out large tranches of it to artists and used the rest to build scenery and rehearse.

It was the first floor which, in a couple of hours' time, would host the Mackenzies' Millennium party (theme: Back to the Future). When Rebecca and Richard, already famous throughout Scotland and points south for their costume parties, had announced, some years ago, their intention to throw a turn-of-the-century bash, I had instantly reserved not only my invitation but also my bedroom. This had proved to be one of the most prudent steps I had ever taken. Edinburgh was bursting at the seams with tourists up for the Hogmanay celebrations; most hotels and bed-and-breakfasts had been fully booked for New Year's Eve 1999 at least two years now. Although I had been required to share my room with Rebecca's sister, Cathy, she was an insignificant airhead whose lack of assertiveness training had allowed me to bag the best bed, not to mention most of the wardrobe space, immediately on arrival.

We were all set to dance till dawn. I had very fond memories of the Heaven and Hell party (I was an imp), the Undersea party (an electric eel) and the Bad Taste one (don't ask), but tonight's Back to the Future looked ready to eclipse them all. I even had hopes of winning a costume prize, an accolade that had always eluded me in the past.

'I've hardly seen you since you got here,' Rebecca said rather wistfully, topping up my glass, 'and it looks like going on like that. I love having these parties, but the down side is that you never get a chance to talk to your friends, just wave at them across the dance floor –'

Steps thundered down the corridor and fell into the kitchen, panting heavily. They resolved into two small children, faces red with rage.

'He's got my FAIRY WAND!' yelled Catriona furiously. 'Make him GIVE IT BACK!'

Ian was mostly hidden by his older sister, who was practically smothering him. His voice piped up from somewhere underneath her tummy:

'It's not a wand! I'm Robin Hood and it's my sword –'

'Robin Hood hasn't got a sword, he's got a BOW AND ARROW!' yelled Catriona. 'Give me back my WAND!'

I looked at Rebecca and Richard, wondering how they would resolve this. Mothers and fathers have to be Solomons sitting in judgment ten times a day; it seemed to me that Catriona had something of a point, on purely logical grounds, but what did I know? I wasn't a parent.

Rebecca rose magisterially to the occasion.

'Since that is actually the handle to the sink plunger,' she announced, retrieving the apple of discord and putting it out of reach on the kitchen counter, 'it is neither a wand nor a sword and I will hereby reclaim it. It is, however, time to have a wee lie-down for an hour before you get changed into your costumes, and if there's any noise from either one of you during that time, you can both forget about dressing up as –'

'Mum!' Ian squeaked. 'You mustn't tell what we're going to be!'

'Then off to your room, the pair of you, before I get cross. And keep your voices down, you'll wake Geode.'

The bundle of limbs on the floor, impressed by this reference to Pip's baby, resolved itself into its two component parts and fled noisily. Nothing, fortunately, seemed capable of waking the bizarrely-named infant, but doubtless a baby whose mother was a set designer had been weaned to the sound of chainsaw blades. Pip had probably recorded a selection of industrial machines and played them to Geode while giving birth, just to emphasise the point. Unsurprisingly, the poor mite was eerily well-behaved; what would have been the point of screaming? No-one would hear him half the time.

'Jesus wept,' said a new arrival, entering the kitchen, 'could you no get the wains to signal before pulling out, Rebecca? Or perhaps install a system of traffic lights for the corridor? They nearly ran me doon. Oh good, I see you've got a bottle open.' His gaze, sweeping round the kitchen, took me in. 'Hello,' he said, with the friendliest of smiles, 'I'm James Grant. I take it you're Rebecca's sculptress pal up frae London. Nice to see something decorative in here for a change – my lovely hostess of course excluded.'

He flourished a bow at Rebecca and took the glass Richard was holding out to him. James Grant was not good-looking, with thinning sandy hair and a square stocky frame already carrying a little too much weight. He was heading for a solid middle age; but his good humour and air of being completely at home in his own body more than compensated for these deficiencies.

'I'm Sam Jones,' I said. 'You must be helping Pip with the decorations downstairs.'

'How d'ye know?'

'Sawdust in your hair.'

'I like a lassie with an observant eye. Aye, I've been skivvying for Pip. She reminds me more and more of that nurse in *One Flew Over The Cuckoo's Nest*.' He wiped imaginary sweat from his forehead. 'I've paid my dues to this party already, believe me.'

'She giving you a hard time?' Richard said sympathetically.

'She was,' James corrected. 'I'm no going back. I made the mistake of saying I liked those sort of space-age designs she's doing on the walls, and she fair bit my head off. Told me they were rubbish and I didn't know what I was on aboot.'

'Pip,' Rebecca sighed, 'is the sweetest thing in the world when things're going well...'

'Let's not exaggerate, Rebecca,' Richard said. 'She's not exactly Doris Day at the best of times.'

'Is there much more to do downstairs?' I asked.

'Well, apart from Pip's stuff, there's the lights to rig in the chill-out room. Won't take long.'

'I'll give you a hand,' I offered nobly.

Just then a cracked fizzing noise reverberated through the flat.

'Are we expecting someone?' Rebecca said, looking at her watch. 'It's only nine. No-one'll be here till ten-thirty at the earliest.'

'Might be a mistake. Buzz'em in and I'll go and have a look,' said Richard, standing up. I followed him out onto the landing, thinking he might need moral support; the intercom was broken, so there was no way of checking who the visitor might be.

The heavy front door banged shut and footsteps started climbing the stairs. Richard peered over the balustrade to see who it was, but was frustrated by the branches of the enormous Christmas tree installed in the stairwell, its branches hung so thickly with sparkling ornaments that we had to wait until the unsteady steps of the new arrival rounded the last turn of the staircase.

There was an awful pause. A youngish man, holding onto the railing, favoured us with an inebriated smile and swayed back and forth on one foot like a small boy caught out in mischief. He was dressed like the pictures in *Tatler* of Scottish Sloanes at Northern Meetings, what Richard would have called disparagingly a jock in a frock: velvet jacket, stock, kilt hung about with a great hairy sporran, polished brogues and castellated socks held just under the knee with elaborate flashes. From one of these protruded the *sgian dubh*, the traditional dagger, its hilt glinting as he moved.

'Robert,' Richard said eventually between clenched teeth.

'James shaid he wash going to a party,' Robert announced. 'Where'sh the party?'

For a moment I thought that Richard was going to deny all knowledge of a party. Then his better nature won out.

'Not started yet, pal.'

'Who is it?' Rebecca called from the kitchen

'Becca!' Robert headed along the corridor, pushing past us.

'James'll not be best pleased,' Richard murmured in my ear.

'Why not?'

'He's his brother. They don't get on. At all.'

In the kitchen James was confronting Robert, his eyes narrowed in anger.

'Shite!' he was saying as we came in. 'What the hell d'ye think you're playin' at, Robbie?'

'Come for the party!' Robert announced.

'And who bloody invited you?'

'Oh, fuck off, Jamie,' Robert said, 'alwaysh trying to spoil my fun. Miserable bashtard. Just because I make more money than you –'

'You say that again!' James started forward, fists clenched. Robert promptly evaded any consequences of his words by sliding slowly down the doorframe till he was sitting on the floor.

'Pissed as a newt,' Richard said, staring at him with considerable disfavour.

'Let's put him somewhere to sleep it off,' Rebecca suggested.

'Not in my room,' Cathy, Rebecca's sister, said fastidiously. She was sitting at the kitchen table, touching up her French manicure. 'He looks like he might be sick.'

Her tone of voice was rather too Little Miss Prim, but I approved of the sentiment; we were sharing a bedroom, after all.

James made a humphing noise. 'Toss him out and let him sleep it off on the pavement. If we're lucky the polis'll clear him away for us.' He caught my eye. 'I cannae stand him,' he said unnecessarily, nodding over at the happily smiling Robert. 'The family yuppie and tightfisted with it. Past master at crashing other people's parties –'

'Dressed about as appropriately as a clown at a funeral,' I finished.

'Oh aye. Shite,' he said again, looking more closely at Robert. 'Talking of which… I dinnae *believe* it. He's only gone and borrowed the old man's *sgian dubh,* the eejit. Dad'll dae his nut if he finds out. It's a family heirloom.'

Robert's legs were stuck out in front of him, his head now slumped on his chest. The *sgian dubh's* ebony hilt, inlaid with gold and set with something that looked very like a ruby, protruded from his sock.

James looked over at Richard. 'Shall we get him out the way, then? He cannae stay there.'

'I was OK with the idea of throwing him out,' Richard said dryly. 'You know we don't get on.'

'Right, let's do it,' James said. 'Roll him down the stairs...'

'Put him on the sofa,' Rebecca said wearily. 'God, just once I'd like *not* to be the voice of reason!'

James and Richard manhandled a dozing Robert into the living room and laid him out on the sofa. Rebecca looked at me, her brow creased with annoyance.

'They know I'm going to step in and sort things out,' she complained, 'so they can mess around pretending they're going to be naughty. Men, they're just like *children* – they *are* children–'

Fortunately for the good temper of our hostess, at this point she was distracted by Pip's entry into the kitchen, looking hassled. 'Glass of wine?' I suggested.

Pip stared at me blankly. 'No, I'm going to have a calming tea.' Putting the kettle on, she took up a position in the centre of the kitchen, arms folded, drawing all attention to herself. Pip had a tall, Amazonian build, square-shouldered and big-boned: under Penthisilea she would have sliced off her right breast and fought the Greeks, arrows slung at her hip. Ninety years ago she would have been perfect for the Edwardian music-halls, nearly six foot even without the plumes in her hair, her imposing bosom and neatly-turned ankle bringing her under siege by stage-door johnnies twirling their moustaches and calling her a fine figure of a woman. In this reincarnation she was a set designer who wrestled huge flats into place on a daily basis.

'Everything OK?' Rebecca said cheerfully, having known Pip since childhood and thus unintimidated by her. James strolled back into the kitchen and, seeing her, sat down as unobtrusively as he could.

'It's just not *working*,' Pip said fretfully. She turned to make her tea, her waist-length fair plait swinging heavily with the movement. I changed my mind; not an Amazon, a Valkyrie.

'How's Geode?' she said.

'Quiet as a mouse.'

'Good. *God*.' She sipped at her tea, steam rising around her face as she did so. Obviously she was immune to heat. Uninterested in the normal niceties of conversation, she threw out disconnected observations, pausing for reflection between each one:

'Did I tell you I didn't get that job at the National? We are so fucking skint I can't tell you... Hi, Sam, are you coming down to help?... This tea's quite nice, actually. Fennel and camomile. I must get some... God, it's so expensive having a baby. I wish you'd told me, Rebecca... Did you see the new Tarantino film? Very disappointing.' A longer pause than usual followed, during which she took a deep breath and rotated her head slowly in a circle.

'Did I hear someone coming up the stairs?' she said finally.

'My prodigal brother,' said James. 'Came to crash the party and passed out on the sofa.'

'Robert's here? Well, he'd better keep his hands to himself this time!' Pip said, her blue eyes flashing. 'If he tries to grope me once more I'll deck the bastard.'

'Wish you would,' James said wistfully. 'Crack him over your shoulders like the wrestlers used to do on afternoon TV.'

'Hmmph.' Pip put down her mug. 'Well, enough chat. I'd better start wrestling some more silver foil into shape. Keep an eye on Geode, will you?' she said to Rebecca. 'He should be good for another couple of hours yet.'

It was as if the room had been flooded and now was being drained again on her exit. James whistled slowly.

'Richard's gone downstairs to do the lights,' he said to me. 'He asked were you coming to give him a hand.'

I finished my wine and stood up. 'I'll be heading on down, then.'

'Brave woman,' James said. 'Don't get in her way, will you? Could be fatal.'

'Oh no, Pip'll be fine now that she's let off steam,' Rebecca said cheerfully. 'The good thing is she doesn't expect you to answer – she just needs an audience.'

I refilled my glass anyway and took it down with me.

'Just to be on the safe side,' I muttered.

Two hours later the stage was set, quite literally, for the party. Most of it was taken up by an enormous silver rocket, six feet around, which Rebecca had built some days ago. Cunningly, instead of the whole thing, she had made only the lower two-thirds, so that from the dance floor it looked as if the rocket went right through the ceiling. Richard, continuing this theme, had built two smaller rockets on either side of the bar, their transparent centres filled with slowly revolving lights in orange and pink like enormous lava lamps. Finally he had spray-painted silver the keg of beer and built a stand for it, a silver cone on its upper end making it a miniature version of the monster on the stage. Wide strips of plastic hung down the centre of the enormous room, separating the dance area from the chill-out zone; when he turned off the main lights they gleamed in the shards of light sent out by the mirror ball and the eerie reflections from Pip's Futuristic-inspired silver wall collages.

'It looks wonderful,' I said, smugly thinking how well the Sixties-inspired decor would set off my costume.

'Not bad, eh?' Richard said with considerable false modesty. 'Pip, those murals are fantastic.'

'I'm quite pleased with them myself,' Pip said, joining us by the door. The success of her work had calmed her down to the point that she could converse with relative normality. 'I'd better head upstairs. Geode'll want feeding.'

'Sam here brought a bottle of bubbly – what d'ye say to cracking that before everyone else turns up?' Richard suggested as we went upstairs to the flat. On cue, the doorbell promptly rang.

'Hell and damnation,' he muttered, 'it's started already.'

A rowdy group of people dressed as aliens surged up the stairs and into the flat, sweeping everyone along in their wake. In the confusion I took the opportunity to slip away and collar the shower. This kind of underhand guerrilla tactic is essential when the house is full of people.

'The hot water's practically finished now,' Cathy said fretfully, coming into our bedroom. 'It was *tepid*. I could catch a cold.'

'You will if that's all you're planning to wear,' I said, nodding at the filmy white costume laid out on the bed.

'I'm the princess from *Krull*,' Cathy said, perking up. 'Lots of people tell me I look like Lysette Anthony. Look at my wreath! I got it from a bridal shop. I like your wig,' she added thoughtfully, observing me as I painted on my eyeliner. 'I've often thought of going blonde, do you think it would suit me?'

'You should be careful,' I said, 'bleach can rot your brain.'

'Really?' Cathy looked shocked. 'That's awful!'

'Ah, I see you've been using it already.'

❐

Escaping from Cathy as soon as possible, I checked out my reflection in the living room mirror. In the dim light you could hardly see that I was preserving my decency with a flesh-coloured body under the fibreglass shell. I did up the white leather belt, adjusted the space guns at each hip, and flipped my head around to see if I'd pinned the wig on firmly enough. It seemed to hold.

'Aaah!' said Rebecca behind me. I swung round.

'My God, Sam, it's you! I thought you were a stranger. You look, um –'

'Fabulous?' I said hopefully.

'*Different.* I never thought I'd see you as a blonde! After all those jokes –'

'Well, if you can't change your look for the Millennium…'

'And white knee-length boots!'

'I'm going to spray them black afterwards.'

'Wherever did you get this from?' She tapped the fibreglass carapace. 'It fits you like it was made for you.'

'Lenny did it for free.'

'I bet he did, the old perve. What did he do, slap the clay all over you himself?'

'I see you know him almost as well as he now knows me.

You look wonderful, by the way. Like a sexy lizard from Planet Zog.' Rebecca struck a pose. She was wearing a black catsuit painted with weird green fluorescent markings, her limbs as long and slender as an Erte fashion sketch. Her hair was twisted up on top of her head and sprayed bright green.

'Wait till I put my contact lenses in. They're white. I can't see anything but everyone faints when I look at them.'

A loud grunt from the sofa signified that Robert was waking up.

'What we're going to do with him I don't know,' Rebecca said. 'God knows why he came – James and he are at daggers drawn and he had an awful fight with Richard at the Wilsons' party last week.'

'Politics?'

'He said the new parliament for Scotland was a disaster because we were only a second-string nation with delusions of grandeur. So Richard said that he should fuck off back to England since he'd taken so much trouble not to sound like a Scot anyway, and Robert put on this awful Morningside accent to piss Richard off, and then very fortunately about four people got between them before anything else could happen.'

'I'm going down!' said Cathy from the hallway.

'Just coming,' Rebecca called. 'She looks great, doesn't she?' she said fondly to me. 'My baby sister... You know she's got this great new job? She's an art consultant. She finds antiques to order for rich Americans. Probably marry one of them,' she added thoughtfully. 'Cathy's very big on money. Making it, marrying it, hoarding it... do you know, when we were little she used to take my toys and make me buy them back from her?'

I widened my eyes at the doting tones in which Rebecca told this distinctly unappealing little story. Rebecca adored Cathy; in her eyes she could do no wrong.

Robert made another noise, this one distinctly more ominous.

'I'll get a bucket,' I said, heading for the kitchen. 'I think Cathy might have been right.'

❐

The Millennium itself was an anticlimax, which was only to be expected from a glorified New Year's Eve. Huge quantities of silver balloons were released from the stage and pounced on with delight by the children, who, dressed as space monsters, batted them back and forth with their antennae. Richard, abetted by James, went over-the-top with the smoke machine and we spent the next half-hour coughing and fanning ourselves. The children, being at a lower level, escaped relatively unscathed. Finally they went to sleep in the chill-out room until Rebecca and Richard carried them up to bed.

Considered purely as a party, rather than a deeply significant event, it was a blast. The huge studio was packed with people, including a group of puppeteers who had been commissioned, for some reason which they had never understood, to make ten giant bumblebees for the Millennium Parade down Princes Street. They staggered in at one in the morning, the tattered remnants of their fifteen-foot-high puppets in tow, exhausted, half-crippled from the harnesses, and drunk as skunks, having been plied with whisky by enthusiastic spectators for the last three hours.

'Sam!' James tapped me on the shoulder. I was in the chill-out room, squashed up to an open window, trying, with my usual poise and sophistication, to fan some cool air down the front of my fibreglass corset. 'I'd be happy to help you with that,' he added optimistically.

'No thanks, it's hot enough in here all on my own. I like your brother's outfit, by the way.'

Robert, reviving, had made his entrance a couple of hours ago, clad only in a bin liner with holes cut for arms and neck, sporting a colander on his head. He had announced himself to be a Dalek and since then had been working his way round the room, making himself offensive to one attractive girl after another. No matter how red his face became, his freckles still stood out, a phenomenon I observed with interest.

'Look at that!' James said, as Robert, staggering up to Pip, tried to tweak her bra strap. She knocked his hand off with such a buffet that he nearly went flying and only saved himself by stumbling back against Cathy. For a moment I thought Pip was going to hit him again, but she held back, staring at him as he tottered away with such a vindictive look in her eyes that I wouldn't have been surprised if they had scorched twin holes in his bin liner.

'Jesus, I thought she was gonnae deck him,' James said, disappointed. 'Ah well, he'll get his sooner or later. Sooner is my guess.'

'You sound very sure,' I observed. He was watching his brother's progress, his eyes as cold as Pip's were hot.

'Oh aye,' he said lightly, turning to me. 'Karma, that's all I meant.' I had the feeling he was disguising the extent of his animosity. 'Hey!' he added, distracting me. 'Listen to that!'

Richard, a studiedly eclectic DJ, had put on the Waterboys' cover of 'The Raggle Taggle Gypsies'. James grabbed my hand and pulled me through the plastic curtains onto the dance floor. Reluctant at first to lose my cool, I realised quite soon that no-one was even noticing, and as we swung around the floor, linking arms with an endless series of whooping revellers, crashing from one body to another, I found myself roaring with laughter.

'It was almost like pogoing!' I yelled at James as the music finished and the dancers collapsed with exhaustion. We were near the door to the corridor, and I went out to get some air, James on my heels. Which was another thing – my boots were killing me. I hadn't worn them before. Somehow white leather knee-high boots with three-inch heels had never seemed to chime with any of my outfits.

I leaned back on the balcony rail, the Christmas tree behind me.

'Hold still,' James said. 'There's a wee bit of your wig tangled up on a branch.'

He started unweaving the strands, his face close to mine, completely absorbed in the task. This piqued me. I turned my head to look him in the face, his mouth only inches from mine.

His hands paused in suspended animation, then undid the last lock.

'There you go,' he said, without moving away, meeting my gaze. And then he gave a start and swung away to look down over the railing.

'What is it?' I said, even more piqued and now showing it.

'Thought I heard something downstairs –'

'So what?' I was cross.

'I've a fair idea who it was I heard –'

He tiptoed down the stairs. Puzzled, I followed him. Then I realised what he had meant. In the downstairs hallway, frozen to the spot, was Ian, who had obviously heard our approach. His face was pinched and tired, his eyes dark. His fragility was emphasised by contrast with the enormous tree, glittering like a Las Vegas showgirl and built on the same statuesque scale. Its bucket, the earth obscured by glittering confetti and fallen ornaments, was nearly to his shoulder.

'Ian! What are you doing down here?' I said. 'Rebecca put you to bed hours ago!'

Ian's face crumpled with misery, guilt and exhaustion. 'I wanted my Robin Hood cape,' he wailed, 'but I can't find it. Mum always hangs it on the peg for me, but it's not here –'

'Och, don't cry, there's a wee sojer. She'll have put it away for the party,' James said soothingly. 'We'll go and ask her, shall we? And then it's off to bed with you. Come here.'

He picked up Ian and carried him upstairs while I went ahead to find Rebecca. Ian was put back to bed with his Robin Hood cape found and draped over him; he had pretty much fallen asleep in James's arms, and needed only to have an edge of the cape clutched in one hot little hand before he passed out completely.

His sister Catriona, however, woke up at once and started protesting.

'Has Ian been at the party?' she complained from her bunk bed. 'It's not fair! What's the point of me being good if I don't get to go to the party again? I was all alone here, too! The monsters could have got me!'

Rebecca soothed her back to sleep at the expense of her own nerve-endings. Personally, I thought that Catriona was protesting a little bit too much for plausibility; I suspected her of having been up and about during Ian's absence.

'Let's have a drink up here,' Rebecca said finally, joining us in the kitchen. 'Host's privilege. Oh, hi, Pip. Did you come up to feed Geode?'

Pip was sitting at the table, the ubiquitous mug of herbal tea in front of her, looking sulky. She nodded.

'Can't wait to be able to drink properly again,' she said aggrievedly.

'Nice and private up here, isn't it?' James said, catching my eye and nodding in a let's-disappear-together way towards the living room.

'Ian left the door open,' Rebecca said ruefully. 'You didn't notice anyone coming in, did you, Pip?'

Richard and Rebecca followed the sound practice of locking their flat during parties and directing guests to the toilet on the downstairs landing. The latch key was hidden behind a brick near the door, but only guests staying in the flat were informed of its whereabouts.

Pip shook her head. 'I was feeding Geode in our room, it's just by the door. I'd have heard if anyone came in.'

Rebecca relaxed visibly. 'At least I don't have to check my bedroom for alien lifeforms getting off with one another.'

'Talking of which…' James said to me in a would-be casual tone. Someone started banging at the door.

'Leave it,' James said, 'they'll go away when they realise it's locked.'

But there came the sounds of a key being inserted in the door, and shortly afterwards Robert's voice, raised in song, punctuated by Cathy, giggling. They waved through the kitchen door at us and disappeared into the living room. Shortly afterwards there was a heavy dull thud.

'He's fallen over on top of her,' James said. 'Always an effective tactic.'

But just then Robert appeared in the doorway, so white with

shock that his freckles stood out like moles.

'What is it?' Rebecca said. 'Is Cathy all right?'

'Cathy?' Robert said blankly. 'No, she's fine. It's – it's – the *sgian dubh's* gone!'

'You *what?*' James thundered, rising to his feet. 'Did you no put it somewhere safe?'

Robert hung his head, the picture of shame. 'Not really. I just left it on the sofa with the rest of my gear.' He looked up at his brother beseechingly. 'The old man'll skin me alive if he knows it's gone, Jamie.'

'You dinnae need to tell me that! Get out of my road.'

He headed for the living room, Rebecca and I behind him. Cathy, still hiccuping with giggles, was lifting the sofa cushions in a desultory effort to search for the dagger. We joined in, but to no avail; half an hour later we had looked everywhere in the living room the dagger could possibly be. James was so angry he was almost beyond speech.

'Is it that valuable?' Cathy asked.

'Seventeenth-century,' James said shortly.

'*Really?*' Cathy said, sobering up quickly.

'After the Jacobite uprising had been put down, the only weapons the Scots were allowed to carry were daggers,' Rebecca said. 'For personal use. *Sgian dubh* means black dagger. I remember James and Robert's dad telling me that. This one dates right back to then. It's a real heirloom.'

'Not to mention the ruby in the hilt,' Cathy volunteered helpfully. 'I'll check to see if Pip or Richard moved it,' I offered.

Twenty minutes later we were all gathered in the living room, even the drunker members of the household shocked into temporary sobriety. Robert was whimpering on the sofa like a wounded animal which we were sadistically refusing to put out of its misery.

'You never should have taken it, Robbie,' James said in a quiet voice that was even more menacing than a shout would have been. 'This time you've gone too far. I should have taken it off you as soon as I saw you wi' it. The old man'll cut you into pieces.'

'About time too,' Richard muttered.

'Should we have a look round the flat?' Pip suggested. 'Robert might have forgotten where he left it. Or the kids might have taken it for a game.'

'That's right, blame it on the kids!' Rebecca said angrily.

'I didn't mean – '

'No, Pip's right,' Richard said. 'We'll look anywhere we can think of.'

Something in his tone made me look up sharply. It was the perfect excuse if the dagger should be found in someone's room; the children had been playing with it and had abandoned it there. A face-saving way to search through everyone's things. To me it seemed much more likely that the dagger had been taken to make Robert suffer, rather than actually stolen, but you never knew. Pip could testify that no-one had come in or out during the period that Ian had left the door open, so it could only have been taken by one of the people now present. Still, they might have used the key to come in and abstract the *sgian dubh* earlier, hiding it somewhere in the building. It would have to be well concealed, though, from the throng of people rampaging downstairs. Party guests are a mob of wild beasts with the morals of a fjord-full of drunken Vikings.

I looked round the circle of faces, images running through my mind. Pip, staring angrily after Robert, looking as if she wanted to kill him; James, saying with such certainty that Robert would get what was coming to him; Richard, who disliked Robert intensely – but surely Richard wouldn't do something like this at his own party. Then there was Cathy, the finder of antiques for rich Americans; Cathy might have seen the perfect opportunity to remove the dagger and sell it on for a fortune to some wealthy and sentimental buyer whose ancestors had come over from Scotland during the Clearances and didn't care how much he paid for a piece of history like the *sgian dubh* We split up into search parties. I went into the kitchen with Cathy and looked around me, half-blinded by these depressing thoughts. If it turned out to be one of these people who had taken the dagger, how awful it would be. My gaze fell on the kitchen counter, piled with clutter, bottles, bunches of keys, a hacksaw, bowls of food and miscellaneous items piled there by Rebecca – Rebecca, why did that make me remember something I had seen her do? For a moment, unable to identify the memory, a surge of depression ran through my veins – please, let it not be Rebecca – and suddenly I knew exactly where the dagger was. I could see it before me, its handle to my hand…

Slipping down the corridor, I left the door on the latch and ran down the two flights of stairs to the ground floor hall. When James and I had come down before, I had thought it was a fallen ornament I had seen in the bucket of the Christmas tree. Now I bent over, and, feeling like Arthur, pulled Excalibur out of its resting place. The earth was soft; the dagger had sunk in easily, right to the tip of the hilt. I blew off the soil. It was a beautiful piece of work, the carving as delicate as the gold filigree chasing on the hilt. The ruby flashed deep garnet under the lights of the tree as I turned the dagger in my hands. Personal defence only, Rebecca had said; I wondered how many people this lovely anachronistic piece of history, its blade now dull, had wounded when it was kept as sharp as a needle. I tested the point, and winced.

'Rejoice!' I announced, shutting the door quietly behind me and advancing down the corridor. 'Panic over! I've found it.'

'You have?' James blasted out of Pip's bedroom and shot towards me.

'She has, at that! No bad for a wee lassie!' He hugged me very thoroughly.

'I wouldn't have bothered if I knew that you were going to call me after a dog,' I said, extracting myself from his embrace rather slower than convention required. 'It was on the cistern. Robert must have taken it off when he went to be sick.'

It was a thinner story than I would have liked, but everyone fell on it with as much relief as James had on me. The dagger was put away safely and there was a general rush downstairs to rejoin the throbbing mass of the party. I said that I needed to go to the toilet and would follow everyone else down. Waiting a minute or so once the door had closed on the merrymakers, I went into the children's room instead. Tiptoeing over to the bunk beds, I looked into the top one where Catriona lay, fast asleep, eyelashes fluttering on her flushed cheeks. She was still in her party costume; I remembered Catriona earlier this evening, fighting over what she insisted on calling her magic wand…

'Ian? Are you awake?' I whispered.

'Auntie Sam?'

'Don't call me auntie, you little runt,' I hissed, kneeling by the bed. 'It's all right, I found the dagger and gave it back. No-one knows it was you.'

'I just wanted it for my Robin Hood costume,' Ian said in a very small voice. 'I know Robin's got a bow and arrow, but in the film he fights too. Wi' a sword. And Robert's was a real one, not pretend.'

'Better than the handle to the sink plunger.' Seeing the sink plunger on the kitchen counter where Rebecca had put it had been the trigger I had needed.

'Much better,' Ian said gratefully. 'I was scared when you and James came down, in case you'd be cross, so I hid it in the tree pot. And then I couldn't get it out again. I pretended to be asleep, and then I was going to run down and get it, but I didn't have time before Robert noticed it was gone.'

'Well, it's all sorted now. Go to sleep.'

'Thank you,' Ian whispered.

'You can thank me by never calling me Auntie Sam again as long as you live. OK?'

'Promise.'

I stood up to go.

'You're a funny kind of fairy,' Ian observed, staring at my costume. Clearly he had regained his spirits.

'I'm not a fairy, you little idiot,' I said, deeply offended. After all I had done for that boy! 'I am *Barbarella*.'

THE NAMES OF THE MISSING

Dennis Lehane

The fat guy in the yellow bowling shirt was missing the fingers on his left hand and half his tongue. He stood on a milk crate past midnight in Central Square and told anyone who'd listen that Americans had long ago forfeited their right to feel sorry for themselves. Looking at the guy, considering the source as it were, Ray had to agree.

The fat guy's five remaining fingers were covered in condoms, each a different colour, with the one on his index finger sporting a French tickler that wiggled whenever he made a particularly angry gesture. Because the guy had only half a tongue, it was hard to understand him unless you stopped and concentrated, listened real hard. But for a few minutes, Ray gave it a shot.

Rwandans, the fat guy said, they deserved pity. And food. Tibetans. Holocaust survivors. People from Chad. West Virginians. But not your average Americans. Then the fat guy started to waffle. He said, OK, West Virginians and crack babies and maybe, OK, homeless veterans. But not welfare mothers and junkies and certainly not self-absorbed yuppies and college students suffering malaise. Get a job where you have to chop bricks with a dull axe all day, you'll lose that malaise pretty goddamned quick. You can bet on that.

Ray left then because he still hadn't found Alana, and the fat guy had let him down the moment he made that first concession to West Virginians. Once extremists allowed for compromise, they became boring. You knew they'd never have the nerve to do something really loony like blow up a deli or shoot up a Stop-N-Shop. Then you could say, Yeah, I used to see that guy standing on a milk crate in Central Square with condoms on his fingers. Seemed a quiet guy, kept to himself...

Ray went back to walking his circuit around the square and back behind it, back in the dark of empty warehouses and dive-bars where he'd lost Alana and the short weird guy, the one whose name Ray kept forgetting, a friend of Ivan's he'd first met tonight. Alana and the short weird guy had wandered off while Ray and Ivan were looking for Ivan's car, before they faced up to the fact that it had been stolen. Now Ivan was back in the bar, telling his sob story to some waitress he wanted to pick up, trying to turn shit into salad, and Ray was being led in circles around one of the crappier sections of the city by a vague sense of duty to a beautiful alcoholic woman he wasn't even sure he liked.

It was Friday night – early Saturday morning, actually – and he knew he might have had a better chance of finding her, or not losing her in the first place, if they hadn't drunk so much. Actually, Ray had been comparatively good, sticking mostly to beer while the rest of them inhaled these violently blue concoctions from oversized daiquiri glasses. But he was still carrying a decent buzz, one which made him less afraid walking these pocked and cratered back streets than he would have been sober. But it seemed important to find Alana. Not to lose her like they'd lost the car.

He was at an age –twenty-five – where he'd begun to tire of the endless parade of alcohol and flesh and misplaced things – misplaced jackets and keys and wallets, misplaced people and cars. Sometimes you wouldn't have known you'd been out the night before if it weren't for the trail of things you'd left behind. It was all beginning to seem slovenly and predictable, their drifting from one forgotten good time to the next, their flippant self-awareness as they drained as much from a glass as possible before last call.

He'd checked each of the three bars in the area off the square twice, found only Ivan, who hadn't seen either his short friend or Ray's date. He'd come through the square another two times, the fat guy babbling away, a woman pacing the block punching the air with her fist. She caught Ray's eye and screamed, 'You're Bumblebee tuna! Little mermaids in a can. Get it?' A siren bleated somewhere behind him and the woman kept on going, still screaming, not looking at him anymore, her voice getting lost in the din: 'All those women you've slept with…'

Two cars crashed into one another right in front of the fat guy, and the fat guy grabbed his milk crate and ran down the avenue screaming about Bolsheviks, goddamned Bolsheviks, goddamnit and one of the local militia's cruisers pulled up to the curb, siren glare bouncing like strobe lights off faces in the crowd. Ray was crossing the avenue by the time the militiamen got out of their car and another cruiser skidded around the corner, lights streaking along the charcoal coffee shop windows, and it all seemed a bit much for a fender-bender. But it was that kind of night, the kind of night which was tight with something, an untaken breath, a barely perceptible ticking in the air.

He met the leper on his third circuit around the block, back by the forgotten depots and old rooming houses. He'd noticed the guy twice before, but hadn't been close enough to realise the guy's condition. The guy had been there, though, standing out back behind what Ray had first assumed was just another forgotten warehouse, until he noticed small yellow flowers growing out front in a fenced-in corner of flat grass. The leper hosed a pewter mist through the blue dark around him, and Ray didn't give it much thought – a guy watering his plants at one in the morning – until it occurred to him when he was heading back for his third circuit, that the water had been hitting the cement and cracked cobblestone in front of the guy with the hose, not the flowers off to the guy's left.

He'd been feeling pretty foolish by this point anyway, walking down the cracked deserted streets off the square, calling out the names of the missing. 'Alana,' he'd yell and hear his voice echo loudly off the empty loading docks, bounce along the deserted streets. He didn't feel so bad calling out, 'Alana,' as much as he felt really stupid yelling, 'Ivan's friend,' or 'Short little weird guy.'

Then he looked over and saw the guy with the hose staring at him. The hose hung limply by his side and water puddled around his shoes.

Ray crossed the street to him, 'Hi. I'm looking for a couple of friends.'

'I don't have any to spare. I'm a leper. Stay back.' He held up the hose, and a limpid stream of rusty water spilled out the end.

'No, really,' Ray said. 'I'm just looking for my friends.'

'No, really, I'm a leper,' the leper said. 'Got it?'

Ray stopped about ten feet away. The guy didn't look good. His face was covered in wet pink lesions and his nose was missing its tip.

'You have AIDS?' Ray said.

The guy rolled his eyes. 'I wish. AIDS. That's a good one. Whoo, boy. AIDS is a cakewalk compared to leprosy. Trust me on that.'

'Nobody gets leprosy anymore.'

'Except lepers,' the guy said. 'Lepers get it pretty bad, believe me.'

'It's an extinct disease,' Ray said. 'I'm sure of it.'

The leper shook his head slowly. 'This is a new strain. No known cure.

Soon there'll be *Newsweek* covers on it, lepers on talk shows, global medical symposiums, leper sitcoms. You name it. Five years from now some actor will win an Academy Award for his portrayal of a difficult, but ultimately kind and inspirational leper. Mark my words.'

Ray leaned back against the short fence that ran halfway around the leper's tiny yard of dead grass. 'There's got to be a cure. Right? There's always a cure.'

The leper shrugged. 'I've been to a lot of doctors. Some of the top leper-men in the country, and they just shake their heads and run more tests and wear rubber all over their bodies.'

Ray shook his head. 'That's too bad.'

The leper's eyes brightened. 'Not necessarily. I think,

leprosy, once it goes mainstream of course, will bring us back to basics, scare us into seeing existence the way we're meant to, shock us into a reality check.'

Ray nodded, but he doubted it. In his experience, people usually tired of tragedy after a while.

'So these friends,' the leper said, 'how'd you lose them?'

'It was just one of those things. The short little weird guy I don't mind about, but the other one, the woman, she's sort of my girlfriend, I think.'

The leper frowned at him, then walked over to the spigot beside his steps and turned off the hose. He sat down on the steps and gestured for Ray to take a seat beside him.

'Is it safe?' Ray asked.

'Oh, yes. Just don't touch me. Otherwise, I'm harmless.'

Ray looked at him.

The leper held up a hand. 'I swear.'

Ray took the seat, even though he knew he should continue looking for Alana.

She was missing after all. But then, she'd left on her own. It wasn't Ray's fault. People did things and then did other things and sometimes they ended up someplace else. It wasn't the responsibility of those they left behind to find them necessarily.

'How do you lose a sorta girlfriend?' the leper asked.

Ray smiled. 'It would seem to require a craft.'

'What I mean is – what's a personable young man such as yourself doing with a sorta girlfriend who disappears with another man?'

'She's okay. We work together,' Ray said as if that explained something.

'But are you in love with her?'

Ray laughed. 'No, no. No, I wouldn't say that.'

The tip of the leper's left pinky finger fell off and landed on the step below him. He sighed and picked it up, studied it for a moment. He looked at Ray and raised his eyebrow and sighed again then flicked it into a bucket by his feet.

Ray said, 'Is it painful?'

'Which?'

Ray nodded at the step where the fingertip had landed. 'You know.'

'The leprosy?' The leper leaned back on the step. 'Not really. I mean, it's not pleasant, but...' He turned toward Ray suddenly. 'Did you ever see that video footage taken in the aftermath of the Tulsa Incident?'

'Of course.'

Everyone had. Meteorologists, scientists, and top data statisticians had said the chain reaction of events which had caused the Tulsa Incident was so unlikely as to be unquantifiable. A freak occurrence one could liken in statistical probability only to the Big Bang.

In August of '99 an Air Force C-130 carrying fourteen tons of Assault Vapor 1 6K9 en route to central Nevada for 'infinite containment,' according to an Air Force spokesperson, rode into the path of a Level Four tornado. The subsequent crash a mile east of Tulsa city limits dropped the fuselage and half the plane's payload into the reservoir. The tornado carried the rest of the wreckage into the city. Among the dead, someone had discovered an amateur videotape of downtown Tulsa's dying populace taken minutes after the crash.

'Remember the clown?' the leper said.

Bright blue and green hair, vibrant red coat, pink bow-tie with white polka dots, a sherbet array of balloons tied to his waist as he dropped to his knees on the sidewalk in front of Sears, hands to his throat, red lips twisted, ropes of black vomit dribbling down his elongated rubber chin.

'I remember the clown,' Ray said.

'That was painful. And the triplets in the carriage,' the leper said.

'The triplets, too,' Ray said.

'But you know what's terrible?' the leper said.

'What's terrible?' Ray said, trying to feel the weight of the word, the horror of it, but failing as always.

'As much as I remember that footage, I remember the movie more.'

'Me, too. It was a hell of a movie.'

'Oh, it was.' The leper turned on the steps, nudging Ray's knee with his own, rubbing his maimed hands together vigorously. 'When that clown went down in the movie, gasping and clutching, that picture of his estranged daughter falling in slow motion from his white vest, all his clown dreams of owning that coffee shop getting blown away in that toxic vapor as he locked eyes with one of the triplets – My God, that was drama.'

Ray cleared his throat and blinked his eyes against the tide of emotions welling up in the wake of the leper's recollections of a superior television mini-series. For a few minutes, he realised, he'd forgotten why he was here. He'd forgotten his worry and Alana's possible distress and the leper's pain. He'd been swept up, he supposed, in the sharing of emotion over a national tragedy. Isn't that what happened in the wake of good movies, a key sentence was added to the paragraph of our national mythology? We were then that much closer to a unification of some kind.

'You were looking for someone,' the leper said.

'Yes,' Ray said. 'A woman.'

'For whom you feel no love.'

'I'm not *in* love with her.'

'Semantics.'

'No,' Ray said, a bit desperately. 'See –'

'Why are you sleeping with a woman you don't love?' the leper asked.

Ray thought about Alana in the club earlier. She'd surprised him, the way she'd suddenly looked at him in the full power of her beauty and said, 'What do you see?'

They were so drunk.

'Where?'

'In me? Do you see anything besides the beauty?' Her lower lip trembled. 'Is there anything besides that? Or am I, like, a hole or something?'

He didn't know. She was beautiful. She was polite. She seemed nice. She could hang out with people and have a good time, not make anyone uncomfortable.

She was a hostess in the restaurant he managed, the best

French restaurant in the city. She had a degree in hospitality from some tiny Midwestern college and he'd heard her mumble, 'Don't,' over and over one night while she slept in his bed. She had no ambitions or opinions that he knew of, other than the same vague want he'd seen in several of his friends – to be happy and feel valued. She was a vacuum.

But so was he. So was almost everyone he knew.

So, he'd lied. He'd said, 'I see plenty in you, Alana.'

'Like what? I don't.' She'd slapped her chest hard. 'What do you see, Ray? What do you see?'

He'd kissed her. 'The intangibles. Okay?'

He looked at the leper, his shoulders frozen midway through a shrug that had started when he considered Alana. 'I end up with a lot of women I don't necessarily care for. Soulless women in good suits, alcoholics, women who talk about real estate or pet causes they probably only half-believe in.'

'Why?' The leper leaned forward.

'Why what?'

'Why do you end up with these women?'

'They're very beautiful to look at.'

'But if they're not beautiful internally. . .'

'I'm a very shallow guy,' Ray said.

The leper smiled and his lips made a cracking noise when they split. 'Aren't we all?'

'You're not,' Ray said.

'Sure, I am,' the leper said. 'It's just that my disease and impending death give me the appearance of depth. I think if I'll miss anything, I'll miss beer commercials.' When he looked at Ray, his eyes were wet. 'You watch a beer commercial and you can pretty much believe anything is attainable.'

'The good ones, yeah.'

'I've never been in love,' the leper said. 'Have you?'

Ray remembered a woman in college and a small cramped bed and short fat candles and running barefoot through a hail storm and the way her eyes crinkled to slits when she laughed. How after they'd made love one afternoon she'd held him so tightly he'd felt tremors in her blood snapping against his bones and she'd said she'd never, never been so happy. And the last time they'd seen each other, how she'd held her smile as the pain filled her pupils and the rest of her face crumbled around her lips. How the engine of the jet taking off on the runway had sounded like a scream in his ears.

'Yeah, I have. She left,' he told the leper. 'I left, too. We just sort of separated and went different places. We decided we were too young.' He saw her face for a moment, streaked with rain. 'I miss her sometimes.'

The leper moved his arm as if he were going to pat Ray's back, but then he placed the hand on his own knee. 'I've never been in love and I've never really known myself, and I'm not sure those things are bad necessarily, but sometimes they make me cry when I'm alone.'

'I know a couple,' Ray said, 'they met, they fell in love. He's a great guy, she's a great woman. They're married now.'

'Yeah?'

'Yeah.'

'And that's it?' the leper said. 'I mean, the world just worked out in their case?'

'Yup.'

'God, that makes me sad.'

'Me, too.'

They sat there for a bit, and Ray noticed a spot on the cracked cobblestone that the leper had missed with his hose, a dull spot the colour of rust beginning to stand out now that the ground was drying.

'So,' he said, 'you're sure you didn't see my friend. The blonde woman?'

The leper nodded. 'You said she was beautiful.'

'Yes.'

'I always remember beauty,' the leper said.

'Because I don't care about the short little weird guy, but –'

'But what?' the leper said. 'Do you really care about some alcoholic mannequin you're sorta dating?'

'Well,' Ray said, 'I wouldn't want anything bad to happen to her.'

'Why not?'

Ray looked at his own hands for a moment, at the lines in the palms, the profusion of fingers attached uniformly and perfectly to the knuckles. 'Because bad things should happen to bad people, and she's not bad, she's just kind of, well, gone like the rest of us.'

The leper nodded. 'She's passed out in my kitchen.'

Ray stood. 'No kidding?'

The leper opened the screen door. 'She's in there all right.'

Ray considered the open doorway and dimly lit hallway beyond it. 'What about the short weird guy?'

The leper shrugged. 'I ate him.'

'Really?'

'Would I lie to you?'

❒

She was in the kitchen, her arms on the table, head on her arms, snoring very softly.

'I need you to understand something before you go,' the leper said. He opened his fridge and removed two cans of beer, handed one to Ray and cracked open his own. 'I'm not a bad man.'

Ray looked around the kitchen, into the darkened living room. It was a very well-kept house. Bright wallpaper, baseboards free of dust, a clean sparkling oven top.

You'd never know a leper lived here.

He sipped his beer. 'I know you're not.'

'I'm not a bad man,' the leper repeated. 'I'm just not a very happy one. I've been so lonely. So lonely. And my therapist says I sublimated too much aggression as a child, but I'm not evil.'

'You're one of the nicest people I've met in weeks,' Ray said.

'Yeah?'

'Definitely. The restaurant I work at? You wouldn't believe all the shitheads I have to deal with. Leper or not, you're okay. And thanks for taking care of my girlfriend.'

'When she sobers up, you might want to get her into detox, show her you care. An act of hard kindness, as it were.'

Ray nodded. 'Maybe I'll go with her. Or I might join The Peace Corps.'

'The Peace Corps?'

'Yeah,' he said, warming to the idea. He could see himself wiping the brow of a starving woman, the air humid and smelling sickly sweet like overripe bananas, the tall grass bowing under the heat outside the tent, the film crews. 'Maybe I'll go to Chad, save starving children. Or parts of Oklahoma. I hear the Tulsa side-effects are spreading.'

'Well, maybe Chad's a possibility,' the leper said. 'There's always some misery there. It's, well, Chad, after all. But Oklahoma?' He shook his head.

'What?' Ray said, determined suddenly to go to Oklahoma if only because the leper was indicating he couldn't. Screw Chad. Chad was Chad. Like the leper said, it would always be there. He could go anytime. But Oklahoma was now.

'They've quarantined the whole state. It was on the news this evening. They have a fence, supposedly it was in storage for the Tex-Mex crisis. Electrified.

They threw the whole thing up last night. Hundreds of miles of it. A combined effort by all standing U.S. armed forces.'

'The whole state?'

'The whole state.'

'Shit.' Now Ray wanted to sit down. He didn't want to go Oklahoma or Chad or anywhere. He just wanted to sit and not think about things.

'Noble thought, though,' the leper reminded him.

'Yeah, I guess.'

Alana looked up at them, her eyes bleary. 'Where am I?'

'In a leper's house,' Ray said.

'Bullshit.'

'True shit,' the leper said.

'Time for us to go.' Ray held out his hand.

She looked at it, looked at the leper. The leper smiled and gave her a small wave.

She took Ray's hand. He pulled her to her feet and she fell into him.

'Bars closed?'

'Yes.'

'Oh, I love you,' she mumbled through her hair.

'I know you do, honey.'

'No, really.'

He looked over at the leper. 'The short little weird guy, he…?'

'Tasted like chicken,' the leper said.

'No, I meant –'

'Go home,' the leper said.

Ray nodded and held out his hand.

'I'm sorry,' the leper said, 'but I can't shake that. No matter what the doctors say, we can't be too careful.'

'Of course,' Ray said. 'You can never be too careful.'

'Be well,' the leper said as he closed the screen door behind them.

Ray and Alana stumbled out of the yard, Alana so sluggish against him that he was beginning to worry she'd passed out again. He stopped out on the road, looked down and saw that the bar they'd been in and where he'd last seen Ivan was definitely closed, the windows black and the bulbs of neon clear and translucent and still. Within the hour, curfew and the militias would descend in force, and safety would be imposed.

How odd, he thought, that this is my life these days. How unplanned. And he wondered what had become of Gail, if she still cried sometimes after making love, her blood shaking with tremors. We should have worked harder, Gail. I think we should have.

'Where's Ivan?' Alana mumbled.

'Gone I guess.' He kissed her forehead. 'Come on. We're cabbing it.'

Ivan, he decided, must have either hopped a cab home too or gotten lucky with that waitress he'd been trying out his sob story on, telling her all about his derailed dreams and stolen cars and withered longings. You'd be amazed, Ivan once said, how many people get turned on by the piteous.

UNKNOWN PLEASURES

Ian Rankin

Nelly sat with his head in his hands. He could feel the sweat, except it was more viscous than sweat, more like a sheen of cooking oil. The tenement stairwell smelt of deep-fried tomcat, and the cold step beneath him was stained and scuffed. Over the years, thousands of pairs of feet must have pulled themselves up here, tired or drunk or ailing. But no one in the whole history of the tenement had ever come near to feeling as bad as he did right now. Eleven o'clock, an hour shy of the Millennium, and the only way he was going to make it was if he got some stuff. Hunter was mean at the best of times, doubly mean at this festive period. 'Reverse goodwill' he called it. Chimes outside. Nelly counted eleven. The crowds would be gathering in Princes Street, laser shows and live bands promised, then the fireworks. He could have some fireworks of his own, here on the stairwell, but only if he got some stuff. Which was why he'd climbed the three flights to Mrs McIver's flat. He knew she was out: Cormack's Bar every night, eight till eleven. She was in her seventies, wouldn't swop her eyrie for a retirement home with a lift and ramp. In her seventies and well pickled. Rum and black. When she laughed, her tongue was an inky tentacle. He'd nothing against her, only he'd figured her door would be easiest, so he'd shouldered it and kicked it and shouldered it again. Nothing. She'd morticed it, even though she was only round the corner.

So now he sat with his head in his hands. Soon as the pain got to him, he'd top himself, couldn't see any other way. He'd leave a note grassing up Hunter: revenge from the grave and all that. There was nothing in his flat worth hawking, and nobody to hawk it to at this time of night, this night of all nights. Everyone was on the outside. Hunter and Sheila and Dickie and his mum and gran, part of the party that was Edinburgh, kissing strangers and wishing Happy New Years less than an hour from now. Should auld acquaintance be forgot. His acquaintance was the big H, and no way was it letting him forget it.

Methadone was a joke. He sold his. Some chemists had started taking the junkies in ten at a time, shutting up shop while each dose was dispensed. Standing in a line like cub scouts or something. One wee plastic cup… With jellies hard to come by, what was the alternative? There is no alternative, that's what heroin would have said. It wasn't true it would kill you. It was the crap they cut it with did that. Anybody who could afford a good, big habit of the nice stuff, they could go on forever. Look at Keef. Learned to ski, used to whip Jagger at tennis, made *Exile on Main Street* – skagged out the whole time. Skagged out and playing *tennis*. Nelly started to laugh. He was still laughing when the sound of the tenement door closing came crashing up the stairwell. Slow steady steps. He rubbed tears from his eyes. His shoulder hurt where it had connected with Mrs McIver's door. And here she was now, climbing towards him.

'What's the joke, Nelly?'

He stood up to let her past. She was getting her keys out of her bag. Big canvas bag with Las Vegas painted on the side in loopy red writing. Looked like big red veins to Nelly. He could see a newspaper and a library book and a purse.

'Nothing really, Mrs McIver.' A purse.

'What're you doing up here anyway?'

'Thought I heard something. Wanted to check you were all right.'

'You must be hearing things. I thought you'd be out on the town, night like this.'

'I was just heading out.' He stepped onto her landing. She had her key in the door. 'Eh, Mrs McIver…?'

As she turned her head, his fist caught her on the cheek.

❐

Johnny Hunter was holding court in his local. He was in his favourite corner seat, both arms draped round the necks of the blondes he'd chatted up at Chapters on Boxing Day evening. He'd given them champagne, driven them around in his Saab convertible, keeping the top down even though it was cold. He'd told them they needed fur coats, said he'd measure them up. They'd laughed. The littler one, Margo, he'd told her that was the name of an expensive wine. The other one, Juliet, was quieter. A bit stuck-up maybe, but not about to duck out, not with The Hunter throwing his money and his weight around. He'd done a few deals tonight, nothing cataclysmic. The punters wanted speed to keep them going, coke to lend an air of celebration to the new beginning. He'd steered a couple of them towards smack instead. Fashion was cyclical, whether it was hem-lines or recreational drugs. Heroin was back in style. That was his pitch.

'And it's safe,' he'd tell them. 'Just follow the instructions on the box.' And with a wink he'd be off, rearranging the lines of his Armani jacket, eyes open to the possibilities around him. Margo seemed to be cosying into him, maybe to get away from Panda, who was seated next to her. Panda was the scariest thing in the pub, which was the whole point of him. He was paid to be a deterrent, and also did the deals outside. The Hunter didn't touch the goods if he could help it. The cops had come after him three times already this year, never enough for a prosecution. And now he had a pair of ears in the Drugs Squad: a hundred a week just for the odd phone call. Cheap insurance, Caldwell had agreed when Hunter had told him about it. Cheap for Caldwell, at any rate. Hunter didn't know how much Caldwell was making. Ten, fifteen grand a week, had to be. House down in the Borders apparently, more a castle than a house. Six cars, each one better than the Saab. Hunter wanted to be Caldwell. He knew he *could* be Caldwell. He was good enough. But

Caldwell had the contacts... and the money... and the muscle. Caldwell had made people disappear. And if Hunter didn't keep business moving, he might find himself on the wrong end of his boss. There were other dealers out there: younger, just as hungry, and edging on the desperate, which meant reckless. All of them would like Hunter's power, and his clothes and car, his women and money. They all wanted his money. And now Nelly of all runts was giving him grief – just by his very existence. Caldwell's goons making sure Hunter knew what had to be done, making him acknowledge just how low he was on the ladder.

'It'll be you takes the fall,' one of them had said. 'You or him, so make it clean.'

Oh, he'd make it clean, if that's what it took. He knew he'd no choice, much as he liked Nelly.

'Are we clubbing or what?'

Billy Bones talking: skinny as a wisp of smoke, seated the other side of Juliet, whose legs he'd been staring at for the past half hour.

'One more,' Hunter said. The pub was heaving, table service impossible. There were a dozen empty glasses on the table. Hunter reached out an arm and swept them onto the floor.

❐

Patrick Caldwell examined himself in his bathroom's full-length mirror. He was casually dressed: brogues, chinos, yellow shirt, and a Ralph Lauren red v-necked sweater. Nearing fifty, he was pleased that he still possessed a good head of hair, and that the only grey was provided by touches at either temple. His face was tanned, and his eyes sparkled with self-satisfaction. It had, in the words of the song, been a very good year: less merchandise apprehended by the authorities; demand steady in some areas, increasing in others. A very satisfactory year. But still something niggled him. The more money he made, the more contented he should be: wasn't that the dream? But the things he really wanted seemed still intangible. Seemed further away than ever, yet so close he could almost taste them…

He turned out the light and headed back downstairs, where his guests were waiting. The cheeseboard was being placed on the table. A huge log fire crackled and spat in the hearth. The room was wood-panelled and fifty feet long, a devil to heat. But nobody looked uncomfortable. The whiskies and champagnes and wines had done their trick. Armagnac still to come, and the best champagne kept for midnight itself. On his way to his chair, he leaned down and kissed his wife's head, which drew smiles from the guests. Eight of them, all but two staying the night. His driver would take these two home – that way they could both drink.

'I'll have no sobersides tonight,' he'd told them.

His guests were all professional people, wealthy in their own right, and as far as they were concerned Caldwell made his pile in a variety of property deals, security transactions, and foreign investments. The Tomkinsons – Ben and Alicia – were seated nearest Caldwell. Ben had made his money early in life, a communications company in the City. He'd been a lowly BT engineer before founding his company, taking his one big risk in life. Now, twenty years on, he had homes in Kent, Scotland, and Barbados, and liked to talk too readily about fishing. But Caldwell's wife got on well with Alicia, ten years younger than Ben and a real beauty.

Jonathan Trent had been an MP for two years, resigning finally (and famously) because the hours were too long, the pay laughable. He'd returned to his merchant bank, and was these days one of Caldwell's many advisors. Trent didn't mind where Caldwell's money came from, didn't ask too many questions. His first piece of advice to his client: get the best accountants money can buy. These days Caldwell was shielded as much by his small army of legal people and moneymen as by his hulking Mercedes and bodyguard. Even tonight Crispin was on duty, somewhere on the property, revealing himself only to any unwelcome visitors.

Caldwell glanced at Trent's wife, who was as usual putting away double the drinks her husband was. Not that she couldn't hold the stuff, but it was always quantity over quality with Stella, and this irked Caldwell. Put the finest Burgundy in front of her and she slugged it like it was off the bottom shelf at Thresher's. He'd seated Parnell Wilson next to her, in the hope that the racing driver's tanned good looks would take Stella's mind off grain and grape. But Wilson was too obviously besotted with his girlfriend, Fran, who sat directly opposite him. From their looks, Caldwell knew they were playing some provocative game of footsie under the table. And why not? Fran was like all Wilson's conquests: tiny and gorgeous and leaping out of what dress there was, naked skin the only cloth that would really suit her.

Caldwell had a large share in the syndicate which owned Wilson's racing team. Not that Caldwell enjoyed the sport: frankly, he could see no point to it. But he did enjoy the travelling – Italy, Brazil, Monte Carlo – and he always met interesting people, some of whom turned into useful contacts.

Final guests: Sir Arthur Lorimer and his museum-piece of a wife. Lorimer was a judge and near-neighbour, and it pleased Caldwell to have the old soak here. Cultivate the establishment: Trent's second piece of advice. His reasoning: if you're ever found out, it reflects badly on them, and as a result they'll try to ignore what misdemeanours they can. Caldwell hoped he'd never have to put this to the test. But that might be up to Hunter.

There'd been a phone call earlier from Franz in Dortmund, just to wish him a happy and prosperous New Year.

'With your help, Franz,' Caldwell had said. They never said very much on the phone. You never knew who was listening, even at Hogmanay. It was all codes and intermediaries.

'Your party's tonight?'

'In full flow. I'm sorry you couldn't make it.'

'Business so often interrupts my pleasures. But I'm sending a little token, Patrick. A gift for the Millennium.'

'Franz, you needn't have.'

'Oh, but it's nothing really. I look forward to seeing you soon, my friend. And enjoy what's left of your party.'

Enjoy what's left.

They were on dessert when the doorbell rang. Caldwell decided to answer it himself, thinking of Franz's gift.

A man was standing on the porch. He was dressed all in black, smiling, pointing a gun directly at Caldwell's heart.

❐

Franz knew he was going to have to head up to Denmark. Those damned Hell's Angels and their little squabbles. All that tribalism was so bad for business. Not that they cared much about business, all they cared about was themselves. They reminded him of nothing so much as feuding families in some American cartoon book, a face-off between two mountain shacks. It had started as a question of territory – almost always his business disputes were to do with encroachment. That was why meetings were so important, so lines of demarcation could be drawn. But these bikers... put them in a room together and the hate was like some fug in the air, sucking out oxygen and replacing it with toxic gas.

He needed couriers in Denmark, and the Angels were good at their job. But they lacked *dedication*. And he definitely didn't need a war starting up between rival chapters. He needed that like he needed a hole in the head.

He thought of Caldwell's gift and allowed himself a smile.

No visitors to Franz's home this night. Few visitors on any day of the year. He conducted business from an office in the city, and travelled often. But here, in this fortress he had constructed, spending the best part of Dm300,000 on security alone, here he felt safe, felt a certain tranquillity at times. These were the moments when his thinking was at its best, when he could plan and debate. Beloved Mozart on the stereo, and tonight not the *Requiem* – not on a night that should be a blossoming of hope and fresh intentions. His second fresh intention: after the diplomatic trip to Denmark, a further trip to Afghanistan. He'd heard worrying reports of depleted harvests, and of crops and fields being burned by suddenly efficient soldiers. He'd asked an associate in Chicago what the hell they thought was going on.

'Blame our fucking dick-dipping President. He's trying the same shit he pulled in South America. "Be my friend," he tells them. "Let me loan you money, billions of dollars of clean government money. Use it to rebuild your infrastructure or line your private Zurich bank vault. But just get rid of all the shit you grow." It's all politics, as usual.'

The voice from Chicago was distorted – a side-effect of the scrambler. At least no one would be listening in.

'I don't understand,' Franz had said – though he did. 'I thought we had arranged for friends to be placed where they could help us.'

'What can they do? CBS go prime-time on a field of burning poppies, then up pops the Prez to say he did it. His ratings jump a couple of points. Franz, this guy would do his dear departed grandma in the ass for a couple of points.'

End of conversation.

Sad really, to think that decisions taken a continent away could affect one so much, but thrilling too. Because Franz saw himself as part of a network which embraced the globe, and felt his importance, his *place* in the scheme of things. If they ever set up colonies in space, *he* wanted to be supplying them. Dealer to the universe, by appointment to infinity...

Mozart silent now. He hadn't realised, but midnight had come and gone. Then a buzzer sounding: the guard-room, one of his men informing him of intruders entering the compound.

❐

It was not yet quite dawn, and Kejan lay in the darkness, as he had for the preceding five hours, his eyes staring, ears attuned to his wife's light breathing. Three of their children slept in the room with them. Hama, the youngest, coughed and turned, made a slight moan before relaxing again. Kejan didn't know if he'd ever relax again in his life, ever sleep again on this Earth. Would the soldiers fulfil their promise and return to torch the shacks by the side of what had once been fields full of crops? Those fields had been Kejan's future. Not that he'd owned them: the owner was a brutal man, a slave-driver. But Kejan had mouths to feed, and what other work was there? Now, with the fields reduced to cinder, he could only wait and wonder: would the soldiers drive the families away? Or would the Bossman chase them off his land, now that there was no work for them?

It was a matter of time. It was for the future.

He tried to envisage a future for his wife, his three children. He had more than once caught the Bossman staring at his wife, running his tongue over his bottom lip. And talking to her once, too, though she would not even admit it, kept her eyes on the ground as she denied and denied.

Kejan had slapped her then, the bruise a lasting smudge against her cheekbone. It didn't seem to want to go away.

There were so many things Kejan didn't understand.

The soldiers, lighted torches passed around. Their commander, arguing with the Bossman. The Bossman saying that he always paid, that he always kept everyone sweet. The commander not listening, the Bossman persistent. Soldiers fingering their weapons, noting that the Bossman's men were better armed with newer, gleaming automatics.

'Orders,' the commander kept saying. And: 'Just let us get on with it for now.'

'For now': meaning things might be okay later, that this had some deeper meaning which the commander felt unable to share.

But later... later there would be other workers, willing workers. New people could always be found later. *Now* was what mattered to Kejan. He lived from moment to moment in this dark, overcrowded room. He waited for the moment he knew was coming, when the future would become the present and he would be consigned to the road with his family.

Or perhaps – please, no – without them. He had hit his wife. The Bossman had smiled at her. The Bossman would take her, and Kejan couldn't be sure she wouldn't go. Would she take his children? Would the Bossman want them? Would he treat them right?

His wife's breathing, so shallow. The room a little lighter

now, so he could see the outline of her neck, the way it was angled against the stem-filled sack she used as a pillow.

Slender neck. Brittle neck. Kejan touched it with the tips of his fingers, heard a child cough and pulled his fingers away like they'd been too close to a torch. He sat up then, looked down on the dark, curved shape. Twisted his own body around so that it was easier to reach down with both hands.

And heard the sound of lorries on the rough track outside, coming closer.

❑

An aggrieved Hell's Angel sat in Franz's study, and it was all Franz could do not to reach into his desk drawer for the pistol and blow the man's brains all over the walls. Defilement: that's what it felt like. Engine oil and cigarette smoke had invaded his most private space, and even when the man had gone, those taints would remain.

The rest of the gang was outside. One on one: Franz had demanded it, and the leader had agreed. A dozen of them. They'd scaled the perimeter wall. A dozen of them armed, and Franz with only three guards on duty. But now more were on their way: calls had been made. And meantime the three guards faced off the leather-clad bandits, while their leader and Franz sat with only the antique rosewood desk between them.

'Nice place,' the Angel said. His name was Lars. Well over six feet tall, hair stretched back into a thin ponytail. Denim waistcoat – his all-important 'colours' – worn over leather jacket. And his jackboots up on Franz's desk.

He'd grinned when Franz had stopped short of telling him to take his feet off the desk. But Franz was biding his time, waiting for his other men to arrive, and wanting to rise above all this, to be the diplomat. So he'd offered Lars a drink, and Lars now rested a bottle of beer against his crotch, and looked relaxed.

'You're financing our rivals,' the gang leader said, getting down to business.

'In what way?'

'We're in a war, no room for neutrals. And you're funding their side of things.'

'I pay them to act as my couriers, that's all. I'm not financing any conflict.'

'But it's *your* money they're using when they buy guns and ammo.'

Franz shrugged. 'And whose money are *you* using, my friend? Are your mortal enemies at this very moment confronting *your* employer?' He smiled. 'Do you see the absurdity of the situation? I'm not happy, because here you are invading my privacy, and I don't suppose your employer will be feeling any different. I'm a businessman. I *am* neutral: business always is. What you're doing, right this second, is fucking with my business. My instinct naturally is to get out, which is what you want, yes?'

He had lost the biker, who nodded slowly.

'Exactly. But what if the same thought is going through *your* employer's mind? Where does that leave you? With no money, no prospects.' Franz shook his head. 'My friend, the best thing you can do for all our sakes is to begin discussions with your rivals, settle this thing, then we can all get back to what we want to be doing: making money.'

Franz reached into a drawer, held one hand up to let Lars know nothing tricky was coming. He produced a fat bundle of deutschmarks and tossed it to the gang-leader.

'See?' he said. 'Now I'm funding both of you. Does that make me neutral?'

Lars studied the notes, stuffed them into a zippered pocket.

'Let me set up a meeting,' Franz went on blandly, 'get all sides together, anyone who has an interest. That's the way business works.'

'You're full of bullshit,' the biker said, but he was grinning.

'Should your employer ever wish to dispense with your services,' Franz continued, 'you may wish to contact me.' He wrote a number on a sheet of paper, ripped it from the pad. 'This is my private line. Maybe next time you're thinking of coming to see me, we could arrange an appointment?'

A nice big smile. Lars slid his feet from the corner of the desk. His heels had left marks on the woodwork. As he reached for the paper, Franz snatched it back.

'One thing, my friend. Try something like this again *without* an appointment, and I'll destroy you. Is that clear between us?'

Lars laughed and took the number, stuck it in the same pocket as the money. Franz's mobile phone rang. It was in the desk drawer, and he opened the drawer again, shrugging, telling Lars there was no rest for the wicked.

'Hello?'

A hushed voice, one he knew. 'We've got every one of those dirty fuckers in our sights.'

'Fine,' Franz said, making to replace the phone in its drawer, bringing out the pistol in its place. Lars was already reaching across the desk. He'd pulled a combat knife from one boot. Franz was leaning back to take aim when the gunfire started outside.

❐

Caldwell was in the library. He'd locked the door, and when his wife had come knocking, saying the judge and his wife were thinking of leaving, he'd hissed at her to fuck off. He sat in a burgundy leather chair, hands on his knees, while his visitor stood four feet away, the gun steady in his left hand.

'My bodyguard?' Caldwell asked.

'Tied up outside. Let's hope someone releases him before hypothermia sets in. It's a bitter night. We wouldn't want any unnecessary deaths.'

'You've come from Franz?'

The man nodded. His accent was English. He had a heavy body, thick at the neck, and cropped grey hair. Ex-forces, Caldwell presumed.

'With a message,' the man said.

A typical gesture by Franz: he always had to show his *puissance*. Caldwell thought he knew now what this was about, and felt a mixture of emotions: the thrill of fear; fury at Franz's little game; embarrassment that his guests would be wondering what the hell was going on.

'Everything's set,' Caldwell told the man.

'Really?'

'Does Franz have any reason to doubt me?'

'That's what I'm here to find out. It's nearly midnight. Everything was supposed to be finalised by midnight.'

'Everything *is*.' Caldwell made to rise from his chair, but the gun waved him back down again.

'Links in a chain, Mr Caldwell. That's all we are. The weakest links have to be taken out, the strong ones reconnected.'

'You think I'd put myself on the line for a little turd like that?'

'I think you like to operate at a distance.'

'And Franz doesn't?'

'He always uses the best people. I'm not sure Hunter falls into that category.'

'Hunter'll do as he's told.'

'Will he? I've heard he might have a personal stake in all of this.'

Caldwell frowned. 'How do you mean?' His wife knocked at the door again, her voice artificially bright.

'Darling, Sir Arthur and Lady Lorimer are leaving. I've asked Foster to bring the Bentley round.'

Her voice grated. It always had. The way she spoke now, like she'd been to elocution classes, like she'd been saying 'Darling' and 'Sir This' and 'Lady That' all her life. And all she was was a piece of crumpet he'd picked up early on in his travels through life. Too early on. He could have done better for himself. Still could, given the chance. Send her off with a settlement, or bring some mistress into the equation. It seemed to Caldwell that he hadn't really started living yet.

'Apologise, will you?' he called. 'I'm on the phone. Important business.' He lowered his voice again, mind half on his life to come, half on the gun in front of him. 'How do you mean?' he repeated.

'You see,' the man said, 'that's the difference between my

employer and you. *He* takes the trouble to know things, to know *people*. He's a thousand miles away, and he knows more about your operation here than you do.'

'What does he know?' There was a slight tremble in Caldwell's hands. Why would Franz be so interested in Caldwell's territory? Unless he was planning some incursion, or to move in some new operator. Unless he thought Caldwell wasn't his best bet any more…

'Hunter,' the gunman was saying. 'He's tough, but just how tough? I mean, that's what we'll find out tonight, isn't it? If things go the way they're supposed to.'

'Nelly's just a runt. Hunter won't have any trouble with him.'

'No?' The man got right into Caldwell's face. 'What if I tell you something about Nelly?'

'Such as?' Caldwell's voice nearly failed him.

'His surname's Hunter, you fucking idiot. He's Johnny Hunter's kid brother.'

❐

Hunter was in the club, chain-smoking, eyes everywhere. He didn't feel like dancing. The bass was like God's heartbeat, the lights His eyes shining down across this little world. Hunter's right knee was pounding, speed working its way to his fingertips and toes. He sat alone at the table, Panda not six feet away, just standing there so nobody'd bother his boss unless the boss wanted to be bothered. He hadn't much left to sell. Not much at all.

His friends were whooping on the dance-floor, waving to him occasionally. They probably thought he was cool, sitting the dances out, smoking his smokes. He rattled a cube of ice into his mouth and crunched down on it. Another drink replaced the empty glass. Fast service in the club, because he owned thirty percent. Thirty percent of all of it. But he knew that fifty-one was the only percentage that mattered.

Fifty-one meant control.

He was waiting for Nelly, hoping not to see him, knowing

he'd come here eventually. Hunter could have gone elsewhere, but what did it matter? Nelly would always find him. It was like the guy had a homing instinct.

Nelly: young and whacked out and terminally stupid.

Hunter had always tried to keep things between them strictly business. He could have refused to deal with Nelly, but then Nelly would have gone elsewhere, maybe gotten into worse trouble. But Hunter had never done him any favours. No dope better than anyone else was getting; no discounts for family.

Strictly business.

Only tonight, Nelly was going to get better dope. He was going to get the best stuff going. Caldwell's orders.

'Hey, Hunter!' A girl he knew: short skirt, any tighter and you'd have to call it skin. Waving him onto the floor. He waved back in the negative. She blew him a kiss anyway. Margo and Juliet were off somewhere: maybe at the ladies', or whisked away by other raptors. They were meat, the window-dressing in a butcher's shop. Hunter didn't give a fuck about them.

He didn't give a fuck about anyone but himself. Number One. Looking out for.

Ah, shit, Nelly…

Hunter punched the table with his fist. It was all about the future, about Nelly's versus his. No contest, was it? Nelly all fucked over anyway, while Hunter was just starting out. There was never going to be any contest. But all the same, he hoped the crowds outside, the swoop and swirl of this millennial midnight, would keep Nelly away. Maybe the tide would wash him down onto Princes Street, and he'd score there. Or maybe the cops would grab him, spot him at last for the one they wanted. Which was just what Caldwell didn't want. No telling who Nelly would grass up. No telling where the trail would lead. So instead there was to be a deal. There was to be the purest heroin going, stuff that would stop your heart dead.

Caldwell's orders. And Caldwell was acting on orders, too. And the person *above* Caldwell – Hunter had the idea it was some German or Dutch guy – *that* was who Hunter had to impress. Because he had to make a name for himself pronto, had to get ahead of the game, had to stake his place as Caldwell's replacement.

Had to make contact.

Had to make good.

'Yo!'

His chest tightened. Lanky and dripping sweat, unlikely ever to be let in by the bouncers if they didn't know he was Hunter's brother, here came Nelly, nodding towards Panda, sliding into the booth and tipping the remains of someone's lager down his neck.

'Thought I was never going to find you, man.'

Hunter gazed at his brother, couldn't find any words.

'Happy New Year, 'n' 'at,' Nelly said.

'It's not midnight yet. Another couple of minutes.'

'Oh, right.' Nelly nodding, not really giving a toss about any of this conversation, or any emotions his brother might be feeling. Only needing a taste.

'Dosh,' Nelly said, sliding the money across.

'You know the score, Nelly. Panda takes care of that.'

Panda: standing there with one packet in his pocket exclusively for Nelly. Hunter's orders. And when Nelly OD'd, Panda would know Hunter had balls.

Everyone would know. Nobody'd ever try to screw him. The word would be made flesh. Suicide a small price to pay for that big bright future.

Nelly was already thinking of getting to his feet. He had no business now with Hunter. His business, his most urgent and necessary business, was with Panda. But he had to make a bit more conversation, pretend he'd a bit more respect for Hunter than was the case.

'Eh, man, just to say... ' Nelly twitched. 'Like, sorry about the kid.'

'Are you?'

'Christ, man, how was I to know he'd take the whole shot? I didn't know he was a virgin.'

'But you sold him your methadone, right?'

'Needed the dosh, man.'

'And he was fourteen?'

Nelly twitched again. 'It's going to be cool though? I mean, the police and the newspapers are going apeshit looking for –'

'I've got friends, Nelly. They'll take care of it.'

Nelly's face brightened. 'You're the best, Johnny.' On his feet now. 'Don't let any of the bastards tell you different.'

Hunter got up. They hugged, wished one another Happy New Year as the siren in the club sounded, releasing balloons. The DJ put on 'Auld Lang Syne', and it was like they were kids again, getting to stay up late this one night of the year, ginger cordial and madeira cake. Sneaking into the kitchen for swigs of whisky and brandy, giggling at each new pleasure revealed to them.

And when Hunter let his brother go, and watched him put an arm around Panda, and saw them vanish into the haze in front of his eyes, he felt a stab of terror for what he would have to become in this new Millennium, and for all the things he would do, and the pleasures he would of necessity forego.

HALF AMERICAN

Nicholas Blincoe

She was talking at international rates, keeping him tied up when he wanted to go out. Her latest question: 'So how many people from Manchester live out there?'

Freddie lifted the corner of his net curtains and looked down to the street. It was a reflex fidget; like he was trying to take his mad sister seriously even though she couldn't see him. Anyway, to the best of his knowledge, there was no-one from Manchester on the sidewalk. He said, 'Do you mean here in America or here in Florida?'

'Where you are, Freddie. How many people from Manchester are there where you live?'

'Well, seeing you ask, there's a couple of Bee Gees here. Maurice, I think, and one other. So there you go: the most successful disco group in the world, the Bee Gees, and they're not only not black, they're from Chorlton. I remember they started their careers as flower powerers but, you know, after Saturday Night Fever they never looked back.'

She said, 'What the hell you chunnering on about?'

'The Bee Gees. A couple of them live out here in Miami, on one of those islands under the MacArthur causeway. I think Maurice and maybe Barry.'

'I'm not talking about pop stars. I'm talking about people you know. People who understand you and care about you. You know you're still not right in the head, Freddie. You need help.'

He could have told her, there was no rule that said you would feel happier if you were surrounded by familiar people.

But there was no talking to his sister when she was on this kind of logic. He said, 'How long have I lived here? I tell you, twenty years, almost as long as I lived in Manchester. So don't you think I might have got familiarised with the people by now? I'm already half-American.'

'Listen to yourself!'

'We're all half-American. It's the end of America's century and we're all half-American. Mickey Mouse, Big Mac, Elvis, Ol' Blue Eyes and Jordan Airs. We're all half-American... even you.'

'Well, it's better than American.'

'*Exactly*.'

She was on the phone for another five minutes but they really didn't say anything else. Except wish each other Happy New Year. She was on Greenwich Mean Time so she celebrated 2000 AD five hours ahead of him. She was his older sister, she did everything first.

Freddie turned round and took a look in his mini Fridgidair. He thought his sister sounded mildly drunk and he tried to imagine what she was drinking. When he left England in '79, she liked Cherry B's but he doubted she still drank them. Freddie took out a bottle of Bass and poured himself a perfect half pint.

One thing he didn't mention to his sister was his girlfriend, Janeanne pronounced *Janine*. But he couldn't be doing with sis nosing into his affairs, it was bad enough having her prodding into his mental health. As he lifted his Bass to his lips he caught sight of the wall clock over his kitchenette counter. He couldn't believe how long she kept him talking about nothing, just bugging him. You'd think she would have better things to do, considering the date. Freddie definitely had plans. He was supposed to meet Janeanne at eight o'clock and if he didn't get a move on he'd be keeping her waiting. He never liked to do that.

Freddie's sister worried but he really couldn't blame her. The day he disappeared, he was suicidal. It was a fact. Even if he wanted to deny it, he would have to explain the note: *Gone To*

US To Kill Self. He found out much later, about five years, that no-one had been sure what the note meant. They thought, in his fragile emotional state, he had been driven to illiteracy and meant *Gone To Us House* or *Gone to Ours*, meaning: *Gone home to kill myself*. His sister alerted the fire brigade, police and ambulance and the whole of his street was sealed off. The betting, apparently, was on gassing: the head and oven option. While they staked out his terrace in Urmston, he was moving into a wooden-sided house in Queens, New York. At the time, heroin was a big problem in the States and Freddie's chosen method of suicide was barging into the middle of drug deals, acting like a knob-end.

◻

There were two major factors, basically accounting for his lack of success.

Queens was not a rich suburb, not by a long chalk, but it wasn't a violently druggy area either. At least, not on Freddie's block. He had to walk quite a way to find a potential life-threatening situation. His other problem, when he found it, everyone thought he was funny. Phrases like 'knob-end', especially, seemed to go down big on the mean streets. Freddie probably brightened the lives of more New York junkies than anyone except *Hannah-Barbera*. The oddest thing – Hong Kong Phooey was a big favourite with smack heads.

The fact that he walked around everywhere also kept him alive. He got to know all the main faces in his neighborhood; waved to them when he saw them sat out on their porches (read *neighbourhood* and *stoop*); let their kids play basketball on his drive using the hoop that the previous tenant had fitted to the garage. He was a popular figure, no-one was going to off him. And no-one thought he was particularly unstable or unhappy. In Queens, a lot of people liked to sit in the dark, watching television in their underwear.

Freddie stepped onto the wide, white Miami sidewalk and turned right, down 21st Street towards Collins Avenue.

Between his apartment block and Wolfie's Delicatessen Diner on the corner, he said *Hello* and *Happy New Year* to about ten people. It wasn't even busy. That was his problem, he might be crying inside but everyone thought he was great: a real jolly *bloke*. You know English Freddie, *what a guy!* It took someone like his sister to get beneath the surface, recognise the tears of the knob.

The next person he saw was Mrs Grodman, yelling, 'Freddie! Every time I see you, you get better looking. So where you going this night of nights?'

Freddie bent down, let her pinch a great wad of his cheek between her surprisingly strong fingers. 'Just boulevarding, Mrs Grodman. I got a table booked at the Raleigh later to celebrate the bells with my baby.'

'Where is Janeanne?'

'Waiting for me, I got to get a move on.'

Mrs Grodman let him go, shouting after him, 'You know, I never seen you drive. You're like me, if it ain't walking distance then you gotta think: do I really need to go?'

He nodded over his shoulder, 'You're on the money, there, Mrs Grodman.'

She lived in the apartment below and to the left of him. Their block was currently in limbo because it was Art Deco but not in the Deco area. The owners couldn't decide if they were sitting on a goldmine, the developers couldn't decide what to offer. In the meantime, Freddie paid his rent cheques and stayed on. There was time enough to buy a bigger apartment. For the moment, he felt settled. He liked having a few elderly Jewish neighbours. Over the past twenty years, he kept hearing they were an endangered species, even semi-extinct, but they were proving resilient. They certainly out-lasted the Marielitos.

❑

Freddie moved to South Beach on Monday, May 19, 1980. He knew the exact date because it was two days after an all-white jury acquitted the cops accused of beating Arthur MacDuffie to death. It was five thirty, Freddie was watching the early evening news report, washing down a box of popcorn with a bottle of cough syrup. He heard the news anchor describe MacDuffie as a black professional, stopped while driving his motorcycle in a place called Liberty City. After the jury came back with their verdict, half of Miami erupted into riots. Freddie put on some clothes and went straight out to buy a plane ticket, one-way New York to Florida. Looking at the TV pictures, Miami really sounded like the place to get yourself killed.

The reason he ended up in South Beach was down to the police sealing off the whole of Liberty City and the next-door Overtown (read *Coloredtown)* and he couldn't find a way in. On top of which, there was a city-wide curfew so once he took a hotel room in South Beach he had barely any time to go apartment hunting in a more dangerous area. Another thing he didn't know, Miami Beach was a different place to Miami and without a car he was stranded miles away from the riot strip. Understandably, he had problems persuading cab drivers to take him anywhere dicey.

He remembered sitting out on the front porch of his hotel on Ocean Drive, looking at the sea, sun, sand. Thinking: I'm depressed as fuck, if I have to look at this much longer I'll be loony as well as depressed and still too chicken to kill myself. As far as he could tell, everyone in South Beach was a nice Jewish dear ... he'd already been asked, did he know how to play Mah Jong? ... Checkers? ... Poker? This town was way safer even than Queens; the only risk, he might get hustled by a card-sharp in a mauve rinse, housecoat and sling back pumps. Then Freddie saw the car, one of those huge American-style refrigerators on its back, like an *Olds* or a *Caddie*. It pulled a handbrake turn in front of him, two Latinos jumped out the back and started shooting with these guns that sounded like Tommy Guns but looked like plastic toys. Freddie though they were firing in his direction, ducked instinctively, then remembered why he was out here in America so bobbed up again, looking for a stray bullet.

The man they were actually killing was an Italian businessman who liked to watch his asthmatic Peke take a dump on the beach every evening at six-thirty. As the Italian was a connected-businessman, he should have followed a less predictable routine. The killers were two Marielitos and this was Miami's first positive evidence that perhaps some of the guys involved in the boat lift earlier that month weren't such deserving cases. There were maybe a few psycho killers in the mix. Freddie watched, open-mouthed, unable to believe his luck. As the Marielitos drove off in their car, he chased them down the street shouting, 'I know who you are. When the cops ask, I'll ID your arses, see if I don't.'

He even threw a zimmer-frame at the back of the car then had to go and pick it up, straighten it out and give it back to the woman it belonged to. She had fallen over during the shooting and was so old and shrunken, Freddie didn't see her at first.

Within a week, Freddie was on the way to being a major South Beach drug player. The way he saw it, there couldn't be a riskier job in the whole of America. What he didn't allow for, when he came to his great realisation: he would be so good at his job.

◗

Freddie waited at the corner of 21st and Collins. The lights were with the pedestrians and he was one foot off the sidewalk, one foot in the road, when he remembered he didn't have any gum. Ever since he gave up smoking, he had to carry a packet. This was another of the ways Janeanne had changed his life. She laid it out so even he could understand, if he'd changed his mind about dying, why the hell was he still going through two/three packs a day. What was his problem? He wanted her to grow old alone, like Mrs Grodman? He told her, 'No, honey.' Though he thought that was unfair on Mrs Grodman, the woman lived life at her own pace, investing life with an unmistakable Grodmanesque savour. That was something. It was a lot more than most people had. It was a kind of dignity most schmucks could never aspire to. Believe it.

There was a newsagents right behind him, next to Wolfie's. Freddie walked in, immediately surprised he didn't see Hector standing behind the counter. That guy could pull a 23 hour shift, seven days a week, but tonight his younger brother, Bam Bam, was waiting there. A great big smile on his face.

'Mr Freddie, it's been a long time. Happy New Year.'

'Bam Bam. I haven't seen you in… what?'

'Seven to ten. Actually worked out closer to eight years. Though I been in circulation for the past three months. You din' hear?'

Freddie shook his head. Bam Bam never took the smile off his face. Finally Freddie had to say, 'What is the fucking problem?'

'I got to say, I never seen you looking so cheerful, man. I mean, you always a friendly guy but still, there's something different. What is that?'

Freddie shrugged. If he stood on tiptoes, he could crane upwards and take a look at himself in the mirror shelves where the cigarette packets were stacked. 'You think I look happier?'

'For you, yeah. I'm saying that's a happy look.'

All Freddie saw was a moon-faced Manchester guy, going bald but nowhere near as pasty as he once looked, all those years ago when he arrived in the States.

'I don't know, Bam Bam. Maybe I'm in a party mood, ready for New Year.'

'That's it, man. Anyone looks at you, they see a man who's looking forward to something.'

Freddie took another look. Maybe Bam Bam was right. Still, forget it: conversation over, Freddie had to get moving. He said, 'You're bozz-eyed. That's all I can say, Bam Bam. You're one bozz-eyed clown.'

'Bozz-eye? What's that… Inglese?'

Freddie nodded, pulled a funny face at himself in the mirror and said, 'Just gimme a pack of gum, sugar-free.'

He didn't pay. Bam Bam just waved him away. Freddie was left walking down the road, wondering if it was true. Could he be emanating a more positive aura? He found love and happiness with Janeanne and now he was radiating an affirmative life-force?

He snapped his eyes forward, looked where he was walking. His first bit of gangster work, after he arrived at his decision to kill himself by inviting violent Hispanic retribution, happened close by here. While he was still living in that same hotel on Ocean Drive, he took to eating his breakfast in Wolfie's Diner. So, everyday he strolled from his hotel up along Collins, walking the exact opposite direction he was walking in now. What he noticed, there was an old Hotel on the left hand side and its verandah was always full of Marielitos. They liked to sit back from the road, hidden by a screen of bougainvillea. Of course, there was no reason to think they were criminals, except they all dressed like the Bee Gees and, unless you actually were the Bee Gees, that had to be suspicious. They wore Panamas, colourful shirts and white suits, everything in a kind of Disco-take on the Planter's style. The way Freddie saw it, if you were dressed for a disco but it was only 10.05 in the morning, you were saying, *Me? No, I don 't work.* You were saying, *I have an alternative source of funding.* And none of these guys were responsible for writing Stayin' Alive or Night Fever. There was one other clue: Freddie recognised the two men who pulled the execution the week before, over on the beach, so it wasn't all superficial bigotry on his part.

❐

Freddie was surprised how easy it was to buy a gun. It was one of those cliches you heard from all foreigners in America. How many times Freddie heard someone say, *I can 't believe it, I just showed them my driving licence.* As Freddie didn't have a driving licence he had a little more trouble. The man at the counter said, 'You want it for protection?'

Freddie said, 'No. I want to cross the street, rob those Cubans sat over there.' He pointed out of the window, over to the hotel. You couldn't actually see any of the Marielitos, the verandah faced the front and the gun shop was on the side street. Still, the gun-man knew who he was talking about.

'Okay, take the gun. You get killed, I'll say you held me up first. If you don't, gimme twenty per cent of the take. How's it sound?'

Freddie stuck out his hand: 'Brill. You got a deal.'

He trotted over to the hotel, jogging up the steps with a newspaper in his hand. Passing into the shadow of the verandah, he was thinking, I can't believe America. Everywhere he went, he seemed to hit it off with everyone. They were so friendly. Once he was through the screen of bougainvillea plants, in the shadows where the Cubans liked to sit, he looked around, wondering what kind of *recepcione* he was going to find here.

A man looked up, said: 'You looking for service, man, the coffee shop closed. This a private hotel, anyway.'

'No, no coffee thanks. It makes me jittery.' Freddie swung his gun hand up, letting the newspaper slip to the floor and expose his new Beretta. 'Better keep my head together, just til I robbed you.'

The man fixed on him with eyes that showed all of the white around the pupil, like a fried egg with a brown velvet yolk. Freddie moved around quickly, so he was now behind the guy. That way he could see the rest of the verandah and decide on a strategy.

One Cuban at this table, three at the other side of the verandah. All of them getting to their feet and pulling out guns. Freddie thought, Bloody hell. He started firing.

The noise was the most surprising thing. That and the distinctive sound bullets make: exactly like in the cinema but somehow more focused, more frightening when they're cracking around you. All Freddie could do was tell himself, I'm not afraid to die. He wasn't, he still wanted it. He stood there, his gun arm outstretched and shot three men. If not exactly in cold blood, his blood was cool enough. When the shooting stopped, he cast his eyes upwards. Maybe at heaven, though all he saw was a flash of blood across the ceiling, like someone had flicked a dollop off the end of a loaded paintbrush.

He looked down, the man with the big eggy eyes was dead

too. Accidentally shot by one of his friends. Freddie turned, stepped over the hotel threshold and down the corridor that led away from the reception desk. Before his eyes were fully accustomed to the relative dark, he managed to shoot another two men. Then he saw a fire door open at the end of a corridor. Bright light from outside, flooding in from the carpark. Freddie stepped through. He found the gunshop guy waiting for him on the other side.

'This way.' The man hauled on Freddie's arm. 'Down the alley by the side of my shop. Drop the pistol in one of my neighbour's plant pots and come in the back way. I'll leave the door open for you.'

Freddie followed the instructions the best he could, still feeling a little dazed. When he reached the store front, the man was waiting at his counter with a big fat grin, a kilo of cocaine and a thick wad of cash.

He said, 'Those guys have been there a month, playing poker half the night. They think no-one knows which room they use as their club room? I just walked in and stole all this while you distracted them out front.' He riffled the edge of the money stack. 'What about a new deal, fifty-fifty, and I find a client for the drugs?'

Freddie said, 'Maybe I should shoot you.'

The man started, 'I told you to get rid of that.'

Freddie changed his grip, lay the gun on the shop counter and slid it along to the man. 'I forgot.'

The man was clutching his chest now, making out that he was having a heart attack but not exactly joking… at least not one hundred per cent.

'I tell you what it is, what your edge is. Anyone who sees you, they like you. You make them feel relaxed and that's their fucking downfall.' A pause, now. 'I'm Barney, by the way. Barney The Bullet.'

Freddie took the guy's hand. 'Pleased to meet you, Mr The Bullet.'

'Ha ha. You mind if I continue? Finish my analysis?'

'Not me.'

'Okay.' The man dropped his head slightly, giving Freddie the kind of quizzical, under-the-eye-brow look that Robert De Niro liked to use. 'Well, what it is, you find yourself in certain situations you gonna find, as a matter of course, anyone you meet is ready to shoot first, ask questions later. I'm talking about drug deals, criminal get-togethers, anywhere where there's no time for niceties or conversational gambits, that crap. These guys know the occupational risks so they always gonna pull a piece on a stranger. They figure, You got an itchy trigger finger, at least you don't got your finger up your ass when it counts. And then they meet you and it's like someone pressed the pause button.' Barney pointed at a water cooler, over by the wall. 'You like, there's a pint of bourbon hidden behind that.'

Freddie said, 'I wouldn't mind a beer, Barney.'

'Well, okay. Let me lock up, we'll go finish this conversation in a genuine Irish biker bar. You Irish, right?'

'English.'

'Yeah? The fuck's with the weird accent, no offence.'

Back in 1980, no Americans could identify a Lancashire accent. But since *Frasier* got his own show with a Lancashire nursemaid, everything had changed. Americans could not only identify the accent, most of them could do an impersonation. More than once, Freddie was walking down the street, he thought he heard his Aunty Julie, Aunty Connie, whoever, yelling at him. He almost had a heart attack. But when he turned around, he'd find a couple of pre-teens having a laugh. The woman on the Frasier show, Daphne, did an accent that was comic because it was so hokey and out-of-date. But it scared the shit out of a man with a gaggle of geriatric, deep-Lancashire Aunties.

❐

Freddie finally crossed the road opposite the Raleigh Hotel. There was a table booked for the whole party, Janeanne, Barney the Bullet and his wife, as well as a few other guys, Swordsteak Jake, Doc Spots, The Hog, Fingal and Hyram and all their wives.

Freddie knew he was late, he expected everyone was there ahead of him. But as he walked in the Exit side of the circular drive he saw Barney getting out of his car. Barney had put on a whole lot of weight in the last twenty years and was doing a car-door 'n' belly dance with a kid from the valet-parking crew. In the end, Barney slapped the kid upside the head and sent him sprawling.

Barney said, 'You believe this fucking prannock?'

Freddie shook his head, 'Belief nil, mate.' He opened the passenger side door for Mrs B and asked her how she was doing. 'You know you better mark your dance card now, because I'm not letting you get away.'

Mrs B stepped out saying, 'Okay Okay.' Then she mouthed, '*Prannock?* The hell he heard that, another of your stoopid words?'

'Guilty, Mrs B. Guilty as all get-out.'

The car swished away, the valet kid finally behind the wheel. Freddie and Mrs B followed Barney the Bullet up the steps into the portico of the hotel and through to the lobby. Freddie had to say, he was impressed. Outside, there were huge swathes of cloth. Maybe silk. The way they filled and billowed, though, they looked like sails. You'd think the Raleigh was a great white ship, about to sail out into the Atlantic. Then inside, there was the deep rosy glow of the wooden floor. The brass fittings. Everything, again, ship-shape and perfect. As a special decoration touch for New Year, 2000, the hotel had removed all of the authentic deco light fittings and replaced them with more frivolous plastic and glass lights on a sea-creature theme. An octopus for a chandelier, for instance. Starfish on the walls. It looked great. Like, it wasn't something you would want to see every day but it was perfect for the occasion. It was cheerful, it made you smile. Freddie was feeling good. As he stepped through into the dining room, everyone he met said as much. *Fuck, you looking good, man.*

Everyone except Janeanne who said, 'Hey, slow coach. You overshot your siesta?' She wasn't mad, she was just remarking.

'Sorry, love. My sister called from Manchester. She's had her

New Year, so she called me up.'

'She's celebrated already? You Brits, you're so impetuous.'

Freddie was about to say it was past midnight in Britain. But when he looked at Janeanne, she was wearing her mind-reader look and Freddie realised that not only was she making a deliberate joke, but she already knew it would sail right by him. He pulled an apologetic shrug. 'I love you, babe.'

She pinched him in the ribs, just at the spot where he was ticklish. 'Love you, too.'

A waitress passed through with a tray of drinks, explaining they were Bellinis. Freddie had to throw Janeanne a look: Do I like these? She nodded.

About 11.45, they were through eating, beginning to think about another dance. Basically, in that uncomfortable time when the only thing anyone is thinking is, *What's the time? Is it New Year yet?*

Freddie turned to Barney and said, 'You remember Bam Bam? I saw him tonight.'

'Bam Bam?' Then in another voice, 'Bam Bam?' Finally, third time lucky, 'Oh, Bam Bam. Yeah. What is it… eight years?'

'On the nose.'

'So you saw Bam Bam?'

'In his brother Hector's store.'

'Yeah? Old Hector let that bum hold the store? You should of checked out back, you probably find Hector head-first in a dumper, his fucking throat slit from ear-to-ear. Bam Bam's a bum, you know it.'

'Maybe he's reformed.'

'Reformed! Ask anyone, they'll tell you there's only two things for sure in this world. A bum's a bum. And that guy Freddie Taylor is the most gullible son-of-a-bitch walking. I tell you, if Satan came in now, horns on his head and an arrowhead on the end of his tail, yeah?'

A pause while he waited for Freddie to fix the image.

'And then, say, he was holding Janeanne's dripping bloody head in his fucking horny Satan-hand, what the fuck you think you'd say?'

'Nothing. I'd have fainted dead on the floor, man.'

'Fainted! Not my fucking Ice Fredo. You'd say, Give him the benefit of the doubt. That's what you'd fucking say. Give Satan an even break. Yeah?'

Freddie nodded. 'Yeah.'

'So what Bam Bam the bum say to you?'

'He said I was looking cheerful.'

Barney took a step back, giving Freddie a look. 'He said that, huh?'

Freddie didn't get it. 'Why you sounding so surprised? Everyone always says I look cheerful.'

'No, they don't'

Freddie wasn't sure what to say. 'You having me on? Everyone says I'm cheerful. I don't know why they do because I'm a miserable fucking dog but everyone says it anyway.'

'Maybe they do. I mean, looking at you, I'd say you look cheerful at this very moment. But I'm hoping it's a passing phase.'

'What is this shit, Barney? The first day I met you, I was trying to commit suicide and you told me it was never going to work. People take one look at me, they immediately like me. You said, that was my edge. I would always get to shoot first because no-one would ever want to shoot me.'

'I remember saying that. But I never said you were cheerful. What you had was a poignancy. Like, you were *Mr Reality-Check*. What you had, people wanted to relate to.'

'So I looked miserable?'

'You looked like one fucking miserable son-of-a-bitch. What do you think, you were trying to commit suicide.'

'Well I don't want to anymore.'

'I know. I know. I just hope the organisation can survive your change of heart.'

❐

The big hand was finally ready to check out what the little hand was up to. Welcome to the Millennium. Janeanne came up behind Freddie and told him to waltz her away, out onto the terrace.

The swimming pool was covered to make an outdoor dance floor but – dig this – it was covered in perspex and there were powerful purplish-blue lamps sitting under the water. Beyond the pool and the Hotel's Italian-style garden, the beach swung down to the sea. There was going to be a firework display out there, only two minutes away.

Janeanne swung him out into what she called her Two-Thousand-Tango. The last fortnight, they'd been having dance classes for just this moment.

'Happy, darling?'

Freddie didn't know. Maybe, he felt, his life was running away with him. He said, 'No-one controls one hundred per cent of their life, do they?'

She gave him a little look, just a flash because they were about to move cheek-to-cheek for one of their Tango-trots across the pool.

Out the corner of her mouth, she said: 'You having one of your *funny turns?*'

She couldn't help but give that phrase something of a Manchester spin, swapping the American *u* for a fruitier *oo*, almost the way he said it.

'I'm fine, love.' They did the cheek-to-cheek switch and tangoed back across the floor.

'You got the Millennium blues, honey. Sad to see the end of the American Century?'

'Maybe that's it.' He thought about it, maybe it was. 'After all, I'm half-American.'

'And I'm your better half, aren't I, honey?'

She was right. She was his better half, his reason for living. The only question was, would they live happily ever after? Suppose he lost his career as a consequence of losing his melancholic edge. Could he support her? Could he even count on stayin' alive, once his lugubriousness faded? He might not even want to stick around, once he lost the only thing he ever managed to stamp on his life. Maybe he was half-American, but his sadness was all his own.

He said, 'I feel like I'm losing the better part of me.'

She didn't hear him. She didn't hear anything over the prerecorded Millennium bells ringing out the hotel PA; the party-poppers firing streamers around the garden; the fire-works exploding off the beach. But she felt the jolt of his Beretta as he timed his moment to the New Year.

Barney shouting, 'Happy New Millennium... what's the matter witchoo two?'

'Just me,' said Freddie. 'Feeling sad again.'

Y2K

Molly Brown

Martin sat motionless, barely breathing, watching the digital display on the clock above his desk.

23:51

Nine minutes to go.

Four *years* he'd spent at this desk, in this office. Four years of keeping his head down, being a quiet little cipher. Four years of scrolling through figures in a cramped little room on the first floor of a suburban bank branch.

23:52

Eight minutes.

Martin was only 26 but his mouse-coloured hairline was already receding. He had a thin pale face and watery eyes. He'd tried to grow a moustache once – three years ago – but Lisa had laughed at him. He'd come into work on a Tuesday morning after a Bank Holiday, not having shaved his upper lip since the previous Thursday. He'd spent the night before in front of the mirror in his room, admiring the new growth on his face. It made him look mature and rugged. Or it would, given time. All it needed was a few more days. Ten hours later, he'd walked past Lisa's desk and she'd laughed.

By lunchtime, the moustache was gone. He never spoke to Lisa again.

23:53

He saw her standing outside the building after work sometimes, waiting for a man with thick black hair and a supercilious expression. Once he'd walked out of the front door as she was getting into a car with the man. It was a nasty looking little car with a noisy engine that spewed black smoke.

'Planning a wild evening, Martin?' Lisa asked. She didn't seem to realise that he no longer spoke to her.

23:54

He'd heard Lisa and the man laughing as he walked away.

His mother had dinner waiting when he got home. He ate from a tray in front of the television while his mother talked to someone on the phone. 'Yes, Martin's doing very well. He's got a job in a bank, you know.'

She was still on the phone when he went up to his room and switched on the computer.

23:55

He remembered one afternoon when he was thirteen. He'd just got home from school and opened the front door to hear voices coming from the lounge.

'The woman I spoke to at the school says Martin's a very clever boy,' his mother was telling someone, 'but he's not got much in the way of social skills.'

'Well,' the other voice murmured. 'You know how it is.'

'Exactly,' said his mother. 'So he's never been much of a mixer, has Martin. So what? At least he isn't getting into trouble, like so many boys his age. And that's what I told her. I mean, really…'

'Well, yes,' said the other.

Martin slammed the door behind him as he ran up the stairs to his room.

'Martin? Is that you?' His mother turned back to her friend. 'He spends all his time up in his room with that computer of his, doesn't he? What he finds so fascinating up there, I'll never know.'

23:56

From the day Martin started at the bank, he never missed a day of work. He was conscientious and thorough, which meant he often worked late. When he stayed on after hours, he was more or less locked in. There were two thick doors between him and the main part of the bank, both alarmed and on time locks. The door down to the vault was on another time lock. The only way out was down the back stairs to a door leading out into the alley. You had to press a code into a little keypad next to the door to open it, and once you were out, you couldn't get back in.

'They're working you too hard,' his mother would complain when he finally got home. 'I just hope they appreciate you.'

23:57

He was so engrossed in the text on the screen, he didn't hear his mother knocking. He turned around, startled, as the door behind him opened.

'I've brought you a nice cup of tea,' his mother said. She put the cup down on the desk, beside his elbow.

'Ta,' he said, blinking. He realised she was looking at the web page on his computer. He leaned forward to block her view, but it was too late.

'Here, what's that?'

'What?'

'That,' she said, pointing to the heading at the top of the screen: *COUNTDOWN TO Y2K*. 'What does it mean?'

He decided it couldn't hurt to tell her. She'd never guess what he was doing, what he was planning. She didn't have a clue.

'It means countdown to the Millennium. Y2K is an abbreviation.'

He could see by her face she still didn't understand. 'Look, the "Y" stands for year, so it's 'Year 2K'... get it? Year two thousand?'

'Don't stay up too late, dear.'

He went back to his reading: 'Most computers use a two-digit shorthand for the year, so that 1997 is 97, and when 1999 becomes 2000, computers will read it as 00. Some computers will interpret this as a malfunction and shut down; others will assume it is 1900. Either way, the end result is chaos...' He skipped ahead to the part that interested him, the part about banks. 'Your bank account may be credited with a hundred years of extra interest, or it may be wiped out completely. Unable to recognise the correct date, time locks on buildings will lock out staff and open vaults...'

23:58

Two minutes to total shutdown.

The bank had tried to stop it happening. They'd spent a fortune on programmers to come in and fix the system, back in 1998.

What they didn't know was that Martin had spent most of 1996 and '97 making back-up copies of the old system, which he gradually reinstalled throughout 1999.

He'd heard some of the freelance programmers talking about how stupid this 'Millennium Bomb' business was, how it was a problem so obvious that any idiot could have seen it coming, yet all these highly intelligent people had either failed to spot it or decided to ignore it in the hope it would go away.

Highly intelligent people? Martin wanted to laugh, but he didn't dare let them know he'd heard. He didn't dare show any interest.

23:59

Martin was alone in the building, completely alone. He was always the last to leave, so when he stayed behind on New Year's Eve to finish up some paperwork, no one took any notice. It was typical of sad little Martin, who just sat in his corner, never saying a word.

A woman from another department had actually invited him to a Millennium Eve party at her house. He knew at once she didn't really want him there, she was just asking because she felt sorry for him. He couldn't believe it. She was his mother's age, with flaps of wrinkled skin hanging from her upper arms, and *she* felt sorry for *him*.

He told himself he didn't care. Soon no one would ever feel sorry for him again. They'd envy him, they'd want to *be* him.

His only regret was that Lisa wouldn't be around to see what he'd done. She'd married that moron with the sneer and was off on maternity leave.

He didn't care about her anymore; he'd never cared about her, really. But he wanted her to *know*.

It would be in all the papers and on TV. They'd interview his boss and his mum, maybe even the woman with the flabby arms.

Martin would be long gone by then, of course. He'd be someplace hot and sunny, with no extradition, and Lisa would be sorry.

He opened his briefcase, removing a torch, a couple of large folding suitcases and a backpack.

He looked up at the clock, holding his breath.

00:00

Nothing happened for nearly a second. And then the lights went out.

He breathed a sigh of relief as the first of the time-locked doors opened easily, with no flashing lights or sound of sirens.

Down in the basement, the vault door stood open and waiting. He placed his torch on a shelf while he crammed stacks of notes into his backpack, his suitcases and his pockets.

What he took now was going to have to last him the rest of his life. He didn't want to work again and he never wanted to commit another crime. He was smart enough to know that repeat criminals always got caught eventually, and he had no intention of going to jail.

Besides, there would never be a crime as perfect as this one, with no noise or obvious disruption. The building looked fine from the outside, with everything locked tight. No one would notice a thing until next week, when the malfunctioning front door wouldn't open.

He'd thought everything through in advance; he had a car parked in the street outside and a boat waiting on the coast. He'd be out of the country long before it occurred to anyone to look for him.

When his pockets would hold no more, he stuffed as much as he could into the waistband of his trousers, then his shoes and his socks and even his shirt collar.

He glanced at his watch. Twenty past midnight and he was rich, rich, rich.

He picked up the torch and struggled back upstairs, weighed down with more money than most people would ever dream of. He paused a moment in his old office, having one last look around in the dark. Everything was still and silent. Even the clock on the wall had stopped.

He ran a finger along the edge of Lisa's old desk, where she used to sit before she got married.

Four years of life in this room.

He shook his head and carried on walking. He headed down another flight of stairs, to the rear of the building and the start of a new life.

He put down his bags, punched in the code on the keypad beside the door and turned the handle.

Nothing happened.

He keyed in the numbers again. Then again and again. The door wouldn't budge. Like everything else in the building, it was controlled by a computer.

REAPER

John Foster

He vowed long ago that Richard Maidment would not
see in the Millennium. The man had to die before the
year 2000 dawned, now under sixteen hours away.

Alan had waited a decade, preparing this murder for the
Millennium. There was a satisfying unity to killing Maidment
at the turn of the century, on its eve. Almost ten years since
Emma and the children had died, not quite to the day, but close
enough. It was neat. Tidy. Soon the pain and ugliness of the past
would be efficiently filed away. Then Alan Shaw could change
his identity again and start afresh. The reaper reborn.

It was his practice to rise early and watch the prison lying
opposite his top-floor flat for two hours each morning, staring
out through the misty greyness until he heard the purr of the
milk float in the street below and the bottles rattling in their
crates. Standing at the lounge window, which directly overlooked the prison, his dispassionate eyes would graze over the
battleship-grey walls as they gleamed in the morning light.

He had waited several months for the flat to fall vacant,
paying extra to secure the tenancy of its cheerlessly unadorned
rooms. He felt secure here, inside the square prism of the
lounge. It was a good place to hide in, to watch from. The landlord was not in residence and the other tenants kept to themselves. Rarely was he disturbed by noisy neighbours. He never
watched television or listened to the radio. There was no longer
any music he wanted to play. He preferred silence and the
sounds of the street.

For years Alan had haunted the gaunt facades of the various

custodial institutions holding Maidment, trying to fathom a covert route to the man he had charged himself with killing. Finally, he had devised a Trojan Horse of infiltration. Today Alan would access the prison's high-security wing and murder Richard Maidment in his cell. He knew exactly how to take the man's life and had practised the technique to perfection. Yet it was imperative that he complete the business before the dead-line midnight of the dying century, or Maidment's demise wouldn't occur. Without this pressure point, Alan knew that he would be incapable of murder.

Uncertain if retribution was deeply important to him anymore, it remained an irrevocable commitment sworn over the willow-leafed graves of his kin. He had systematically suppressed his intensity by turning revenge into a routine, knowing that uncontrolled his emotions would betray him. Now he felt like a puppeteer, as if it was not him who would murder Maidment, but this punctilious, po-faced impostor in his mid-forties called Alan Douglas Shaw, long dead and buried in a Bedfordshire graveyard, whose identity he had borrowed.

The depersonalised culture of the avenger had become an antidote to his rage, stilling the vehemence now incapable of being roused. So Alan needed an artificial dynamic, a closing gate of time. To kill Maidment by twelve that night. One second past the hour would be one second too late, the moment lost. Maidment's survival would also mean that Alan could not shed his counterfeit persona, with all the baggage of yesteryear continuing to claim him. Richard Maidment and Alan Shaw both had to die before midnight chimed.

He conducted his two-hour reconnaissance for the final time that last December morning. It had been a ritual Alan had main-tained for nine months, since Maidment had been transferred to this particular jail – a hi-tech, 21st century bastille set down in a crumbling, coastal city. The sound of the milk float was like an alarm-call for Alan and foreclosed the watch. He would break-fast frugally and ready himself for work. Although he knew the exact location of Maidment's cell, he would sometimes carry his mug of black coffee into his shoebox study and, tasting the unsugared caffeine, contemplate the plans of the prison he had surreptitiously procured now sellotaped across the wall above his desk.

Most of Alan's spare time was spent in the study, a back-bedroom with a dour outlook across huddled, dead-end terraces. He would peruse his thick files of newspaper cuttings concerning the triple murder, Maidment's arrest, trial and conviction. There were the yellowing, faded news photos of the killer, his victims and the bereaved, the police detectives with their glum, press conference faces, the sad crime scene with its bullet-ridden family saloon, the whole circus of murder.

He always left the photograph albums until last. The priest-like dome of his bald head shone under the anglepoise as he turned the pages, staring down at the faces. Occasionally he paused longer over the photographs of Emma and the children, without permitting himself to dawdle too long. It did no good. The dead faces which smiled impishly out at him stimulated no feeling other than pensive sentimentality. He preferred the clear-eyed recall of when, called to the mortuary to identify them, he last saw his wife and two daughters. Their bodies lay on the slabs like waxworks under the cold white lights. Parodies of their living selves, perfectly formed, except for the neat bullet holes struck into the centre of each forehead, livid flaws in the precious porcelain of their scrubbed skin.

Emma, her wedding ring glinting under the fluorescent glare. Rose and Debbie, aged fourteen and twelve. Now strangely small and still. Alan wanted to snap his fingers, wake them from their hypnosis and hear their laughter and their bick-ering again. The shock was etched deeply in the pupils of their eyes, lingering on the surfaces of their pallid, plasticine faces. The cops waited tensely, standing behind Alan to catch him mid-fall if he fainted. He smiled with thin-mouthed incredulity before he nodded and simply said, 'Yes,' his monotone voice echoing off the tiled walls as vomit broke between his lips.

Emma. Rose. Debbie. Strangers picked at random and killed in casual malice on a lonely country road. Three summary executions dedicated to the lost cause of exhuming Richard Maidment's imploded ego.

He longed to cry some nights, to weep in a great exorcism, and often walked with swift determination down to the midnight sea, stood by the solitary shore and screamed with simulated venom out across the belly-dancing waves. The pretence quickly evaporated. Back in his study, he would make a prosaically mundane diary entry onto his database, and review the video playback of the camcorder footage he had filmed of the prison he knew so intimately, but still reacquainted himself with. He would check the handgun strategically placed in the top drawer of his bedside table and, mindful of security, lock himself firmly into the flat with the brusque efficiency of a jailer.

For fifteen minutes each night he would practice the fast chopping action with his right hand which he intended to employ when breaking Maidment's neck. Then there was his uniform. His prison warder's uniform.

He would iron the freshly laundered uniform, getting it ready for the morning. Guiding the steam iron across the thick, black linen with patient thoroughness, he ensured that the leg creases were properly centred, sharp and smart looking. Next the uniform would be fitted onto a wooden hanger and suspended from the picture-rail high against his bedroom wall, hovering there above him, waiting to be worn. With this final chore complete, Alan would go to bed, where his sleep was shallow and dreamless.

◻

He always imagined that on the day of Maidment's death the weather would be overcast and rainy, but instead Alan looked out upon a morning of sharp winter sunlight. Friday, December 31st, a national holiday to mark the Millennium. Few people were about and there was a Sunday atmosphere. The hungover streets looked ragged with debris from days of street parties. Tattered buntings draped lazily from camel-necked streetlights.

Alan shaved, enjoying the feel of the hot blade against his skin. Today he was to become a killer. By the time champagne frothed to the cries of 'Happy New Century!' he would have murdered. He told himself it would be so. He willed his frayed enthusiasm to make it be.

He flannelled his face and regarded his tightly-shaven, taciturn features. Maybe tomorrow he would start a beard and grow his hair, and look as he once did, when he was the ebulliently gregarious Ben Edwards, maths teacher, weekend rugby player, family man. He had sported a bushy beard and a thick head of hair in the days before Maidment imposed his rabid impulses upon a contented provincial lifestyle of small ambition. Ben disappeared shortly after Maidment had started serving three life sentences, resurfacing three years later as Alan Douglas Shaw, holding a birth certificate, national insurance number, an electoral registration listing, and a passport all recorded in that name.

His hicksville accent smoothed out, now an experienced security company operative, he applied for recruitment to the prison service. His curriculum vitae, indicating that he had been living abroad for many years, was impeccably falsified and he was accepted for training. Once a bona fide prison officer, he diligently networked his way through the system, expediently gauging his applications for transfers until he inconspicuously arrived at Maidment's prison.

Sometimes he wondered if his mother was still alive. What had happened to his sisters. The kids he taught. The mates he drank with. Who lived in the cottage now, or if superstition had allowed dereliction to overrun it. Whether the hilltop graves were properly tended. How the vicissitude endowed by Richard Maidment had affected the lives of those in his Somerset home-town Ben Edwards had left behind.

❏

He lifted his uniform down from the picture-rail, removed the tunic and trousers from the hanger, and dressed into them for the last time. Removing a piece of fluff from a cuff, he swept a clothes brush briskly over the shoulders, arms and lapels. Alan pulled on his boots, running a duster over them to enhance their dark shine. He smoothed his palm over the bald contours of his head and eased on his cap. Yes, he looked good. Neat, clean, well-advised. He wanted to appear his best today, the day.

Pulling on his raincoat, he looked around the rooms without nostalgia. Everything was left in its properly accorded place. Soon the Marie Celeste interiors would be invaded by cops nonplussed by the amassed intelligence of this backroom zealot. Their search would disclose the loaded handgun in the bedside table. Lodged there as a precaution, Alan had rejected it as a murder weapon since the prison's X-ray surveillance system would have detected it. Like all his possessions, the handgun was now obsolete.

Alan slipped out deftly, like a cat through an ajar door, and stepped softly down the five flights of stairs. Sunlight bladed as he reached the passageway leading onto the vestibule, and turned to the back door. Since the house faced onto the prison, Alan always left by the rear entrance. He wanted no-one at the jail to know he lived there, especially since his personnel records detailed a different address.

Outside, Alan glanced at his wristwatch – his rota began in 35 minutes. He ducked under a clothesline and crossed the backyard. The street ahead was vacant and the houses looked washed-out, drained of colour. The darkly austere silhouette of the prison perched predaciously over the slate rooftops.

He paused, ill-at-ease, eyes raking. Sun-sheened windows stared back. An overhanging branch drummed lightly upon the glass of a greenhouse. He walked down the street, unable to dismiss the niggling suspicion of being watched, a gut feeling which frequently visited him. Maybe it was the voyeur's inherent paranoia, the side-effect of constant surveillance. Yet, wherever he went, he sensed this presence, conscious of eyes. Cold, harsh eyes, laughing at him. Even inside the prison he felt vulnerable. A face behind a newspaper, an eye behind a lens.

Derisive, ridiculing, sneering. As if, for all his intricate plotting, Alan's pathetic scheme would come to nothing.

He turned down a tarmac lane leading onto the main drag. The unkempt stretch of mangy municipal parkland fringing the prison was newly pockmarked by bonfire craters, scars of the Millennium jollifications. A few embers smouldered from the previous night, thin wisps of smoke snaking. Fireworks display mounts stood blackened like burnt-at-the-stake scarecrows. Barbecue apparatus lay dormant, glistening with cobwebbed white dew. Disco lights hung from fish-skeleton winter trees. Seagulls scavenged upon trestle tables littered with party left-overs.

Christmas and New Year had merged into a week of boorish exuberance, a non-stop carnival of tedious revelry. That night the park would pound with raucously false bonhomie, escalating into crazed hysteria as the bogus celebrations reached their heady summit. Alan wondered how many people would get killed in drunken accidents and brawls during the fervour of the ruthlessly commercialised festivities. If Maidment was to die on the eve of the Millennium, so would others.

He eyed the jail's high-walled portals. Some nights he woke in fright, convinced that Maidment had escaped. He climbed the cascade of concrete steps leading up to the looming, fortress-shaped enclave. It stood there, bearing down, waiting for him.

At the staff entry point, Alan slid his access pass into the computerised check-in booth and punched in his identity number. The processing seemed to take longer than usual, but maybe he imagined it. Rooftop searchlights beamed down, interweaving magisterially as Alan passed unintercepted through the security gate. He walked tautly towards the main entrance, whilst surveillance cameras with narrow, greyhound heads swivelled on tripod necks, their bloodshot eyes winking at him. The barred windows studded along the jail's inner walls each concealed for Alan a watching face.

Waiting for the steel doors of the entrance foyer to open, his spine tingled as he again felt menaced by mordant eyes. Carved in large stone lettering and boxed in an oblong frame above the double doors was the prison's name, in dedication to an illustrious now deceased local dignitary. But to Alan the prison had come to symbolise Maidment. He always thought of it as Maidment, the name which tolled through his mind.

◻

He braced himself as he paced the cellblock, convinced that those in charge would soon rumble his hapless conspiracy. Alan waited for something to go wrong, an unpredictable vagary which would derail him. Two hours of his shift had elapsed in numbing anxiety, where even commonplace procedures had assumed ominous overtones.

As the tinny chimes of midday sounded from a nearby church tower clock, the remainder of Millennium Eve stretched out in tortuous uncertainty. Those unseen eyes seemed to bore into him with greater vindictiveness than ever, relishing his prospective downfall. He felt completely out of sync with the festive mood of the jail, its regimentation today relaxed and low-key. Workrooms were decked out for the 'New Century's Eve' parties for the inmates, who had made the Millennium decorations brightening the dismal rows of cells and soulless walkways.

A substantial number of warders had taken leave over the Millennium weekend and only a skeleton staff was on duty, a context ideal for Alan's purposes. He nevertheless scrutinised fellow officers, searching for some telltale facial expression or inflection of voice that indicated they had been briefed concerning him. Their easy-going demeanour he interpreted as a front, luring him into a false sense of security.

Instinct pummelled him. They know about you. Get out of here. Do it now. But he knew he would see this through, whatever. Alan wasn't about to kiss-off ten years of meticulous masterminding. If he had been blown, arrest was inevitable and attempts at escape futile.

The morning snailed along incident free, yet everything

seemed too normal. Visitors invaded at lunchtime, bringing Millennium gifts and cards. The chaplain conducted a service of new century prayers in the chapel. A police escort delivered a new prisoner. Alan was aware that no transfers of current inmates to other jails were scheduled. He made it his business to know, especially about transfers.

He sat alone in the refectory at his usual corner table, picking at a 'Millennium Special' of roast duck and new potatoes. A toe-curling Millennium version of 'Auld Lang Syne' muzakked. He glanced at the well-bonded warders at nearby tables. They all ignored Alan, regarding him as a non-joiner. Outside, the streets had come to life. Traffic cruised and pedestrians were out on their last-minute shopping, or making for the pub in cheery camaraderie. People were in the park, preparing for the eve's mammoth junket.

He glanced across at the rooming house opposite, his attention suddenly galvanised, staring in disbelief at the lounge light shining in the dusk, the shadeless bulb hanging from frayed flex. Alan never left windows open, doors unlocked, or lights on.

Trying to sight intruders, he saw drifting shadows. He caught a movement, only for it to unfurl as a reflection. Convinced that he had turned the light out, the more he scoured the murky rooms so silhouettes rippled across his eyes, imagined figures stared back at him from behind windows. He stood abruptly, the chair scraping. Shutting his eyes, he cleared his mind. Alan looked back out. All appeared normal now, just the single bulb burning in the late December twilight.

His head biffed as he took up his position on the high-security wing which housed Maidment. Alan had known for several weeks that he was on the afternoon shift designated to patrol the cellblock. A temporary rota over the Millennium involving additional duties for warders not taking leave, it ideally facilitated Alan. His roll call could have fallen anywhere over the weekend, but it was that afternoon. Alan had a remaining time-frame of four hours to kill Richard Maidment.

Walking the hushed corridors insulated from the

Millennium celebrations, he surveyed the monitor bank screening surveillance images from each cell. Maidment was sitting at the table in his cell, writing, his hand moving with limp-wristed ungainliness across the page. Left-handed, his script was large and childlike, with expansive loops and curls. Books and papers sat piled on the table. The interior resembled an office rather than a cell. Legal tomes lined shelves and files were stacked on the floor. A computer workstation stood in a corner.

Careful not to signal his interest in Maidment to the guard minding the monitor bank, Alan resumed his patrol. He mused upon whether Maidment was ever aware of being shadowed, if some sixth sense told him that Alan was there, in the prison, invariably on duty outside his cell as he was that afternoon, or one of the officers detailed to accompany him during exercise periods. Maidment showed no sign of recognition, apparently oblivious to the vengeful mole amongst his guards.

Alan had spoken to Maidment just the once, when delivering some stationary he had requested. An inconsequential exchange, Maidment was stammering and inarticulate, speaking in a soft, obsequious voice. The same voice that Alan had heard plead 'not guilty' in court ten years before.

Maidment wanted the stationary for yet more letters to the Home Office, his long-suffering lawyers, the media, prisoner support charities, rough justice watchdogs. To anyone remotely likely to listen. He had never accepted responsibility for his crimes, claiming a miscarriage of justice. Maidment had been a semi-literate farm worker, living with his mother. Following an anonymous tip-off, police found the murder weapon in Maidment's garden shed. There were no fingerprints on the handgun, but Polaroids of the dead victims were hidden in the shed where Maidment would while away the hours, carving wooden models of farm animals.

In prison, Maidment educated himself with formidable application, and engaged in a complex correspondence with lawyers, trying to prove that he was at home with his mother, his only defence witness, on the afternoon of the murders. Few doubted the validity of Maidment's conviction. Apart from his mother, no-one trusted him. There was something creepy about the guy. He looked guilty, behaved guilty. His evasive eyes and unctuous manner condemned him.

There he was now, on his afternoon exercise, taking the air with apologetic gratitude. Resembling a shuffling country vicar, a short, self-effacing man with a portulant figure and moon-shaped face, his 47th birthday only a few days away and now unlikely to be reached, he was the archetypal mild little man who turned out to be a murderer.

Twenty minutes after Maidment had been returned to his cell, Alan relieved the guard overseeing the monitor bank. He quickly disabled the monitor transmitting the surveillance pictures of Maidment's cell and waited for the guard to return from his tea-break. When eventually he did, Alan explained that the monitor was dysfunctional and that he had reported the fault to the technical resources department.

He stood outside Maidment's cell door, listening. Intuiting the cops invisibly concealed at both ends of the corridor ready to rush him, Alan was immune to their threat, hoping to kill Maidment before they reached him.

There was nothing left to do. No more preparing, research-ing, blueprinting. An end to watching and waiting, living a double-life out of suitcases in anonymous rooms. All that remained was Maidment.

Alan tapped a four-figured computer code into the panel embossed upon Maidment's cell door. The door pinged open. Sitting at his table, Maidment looked up from his writing. He put down his pen and looked wanly at Alan. 'I've been waiting for you,' Maidment quietly said.

Hovering on the threshold, Alan watched for the cops to swarm towards him. There were none. He stepped inside. The cell door closed.

Alan stared at the man who had hijacked the family saloon and shot dead his wife and daughters when Emma drove the girls home from school at the end of an ordinary day nearly ten years ago. His overwhelming impulse was to go immediately for the kill, yet he could hardly move and pressed back against the cell door, feeling the perspiration break upon his forehead and rivulet down between his shoulder-blades.

'Please... don't hurt me,' Maidment stammered asthmatically, his balled fists pressed down upon the dove-grey steel table.

'You know me.' Alan heard the tremor in his flat voice.

'Mr Edwards.' Maidment's eyes glistened. 'Don't harm me. I'm... glad, though. Yes. Glad you're here.'

'I don't understand,' Alan murmured.

'I feel... so really sorry,' Maidment's voice salivated, as tears sluiced down his face. 'I recognised you from the start. I'm very sorry about it all.'

Alan stepped warily away from the door. 'You've shopped me.'

'Of course not.' Maidment sounded almost affronted. He shook his head, his chubby face creased in a disconcerted frown. 'All the weeks and months. You a prison officer with your duties. I couldn't find a way to talk to you. The right moment. The words. I wanted you to know. I wanted you to be clear. But I had to wait... wait for you.'

Dizziness hurtled across Alan's eyes and he swayed. His hair was damp and he shivered. He wiped away the sweat running down his nostrils onto his upper lip. Tasting blood, he saw it stained on his fingertips. A nosebleed. 'Would you like a tissue?' Maidment dolefully asked.

Alan looked at him coldly. He felt manipulated, his malevolent priority sidelined by Maidment's slippery ploys. 'You know why I'm here,' Alan said with deliberate softness. 'I'm here to kill you.'

Maidment started trembling, craning back-and-forth in his chair. He passed wind, the reek of the odour filling the air. Watching Maidment squirm in raw fear brought Alan a surge of satisfaction. He stepped toward Maidment, who tried to stand and then reeled back. Alan felt a warm, physical glow swell up as he watched Maidment wriggle and contort.

'I don't want to die,' wailed Maidment. 'I don't want to die.'

'I'm going to break your neck,' Alan told Maidment and

struck him harshly across his face. Maidment cried out pitiably.

Bemused by his involuntary violence, Alan nevertheless savoured its impact. The adrenaline pumped as his energy and confidence intensified. He was swept by the febrile power he commanded, fascinated by the unbridled terror he was able to instil in Maidment who, his hands cupped together in prayer, began to beg with pathetic indignity.

'Please don't kill me,' he moaned breathlessly. 'I ask you. Let me be.'

'Stop,' Alan said suddenly. 'Stop this.'

Shame enveloped him. Maidment's humiliation had not been part of his design, and he had no stomach for it. He wanted his revenge to be simple and clean, a straightforward and unvarnished reckoning. The unedifying state to which he had reduced Maidment disgusted him. He wanted to shake Maidment, return him to some semblance of self-respect. A high-pitched whine drilled through Alan's head as Maidment began speaking in a crazed half-whisper, his lips puckering. He heard Maidment's timorous, simpering voice as if from behind a wall. Despising himself, urgently wishing to absent himself from the cell, Alan realised that, despite everything he had striven so tirelessly toward, he would not murder Richard Maidment.

As familiar as he was with Maidment's diminutive personality, the impetus to destroy disintegrated. Maidment was too flawed, his frailty and instability no equal to Alan's veracity. He was an invalid, an abject casualty of his own dark side. It was impossible to execute such a sorry, broken man.

Alan needed someone worthy of murder, whose unambiguous callousness would justify his exhaustive endeavours. The monster he wanted to confront was confirmed as the loveless guy Maidment had always seemed, overweight and bumbling, surrounded by his law books and files, writing letters to the disbelieving. No hidden ogre waited to be uncovered. Maidment was just incredibly sad.

Maidment stood nervously. Arms flailing, he knocked over a Millennium greeting card from his mother propped on the table. His crotch was stained with urine. Alan watched with distaste as Maidment moved awkwardly out from behind the table and crossed towards him. 'Sit down!' Alan tried to put edge into his voice, unsuccessfully. Revulsion filled him and then, as Maidment continued to approach, an apprehension teetering upon alarm. He felt a sharp fear well up, an inexplicable gut terror.

'I wanted to say... ' began Maidment in a blotting-paper voice.

'Get back,' Alan heaved, wiping spittle from his lips. 'Just – keep away.' Panic burned the pit of his stomach.

'Let me explain,' Maidment spluttered, his eyes red with tears. 'Tell you... about it all.'

'I'm not going to do anything to you.' Alan's words were funnelled through tight, identikit lips. 'There's no threat. No danger.'

'Thank you,' Maidment whimpered. 'Thank you.' He gave a sob and diffidently held out his hand. Alan did not shake it.

'Go back.' Alan pointed. 'Go back and sit down.'

Hangdog, Maidment obeyed, trudging to the table and worming onto the chair, as if afraid of damaging himself. He sat with his hands folded, Buddha-like, staring at Alan. 'I appreciate how difficult it is for you,' he said. 'I understand. All you've gone through. The amount you've suffered.'

Alan smiled, not meaning to smile. 'Help me to understand,' he said evenly, nudging closer to Maidment. 'I need you to tell me about it.'

Maidment looked shrunken. 'I... don't think I can help you.'

'That's all I want from you. The reason. Then I'll leave you alone.'

'But you see, that's why it's so terrible,' babbled Maidment. 'All so dreadful. You coming here to me. The years you've waited, getting yourself into the system, positioning yourself like this. All waste, all waste.'

'The why.'

'I'm not your killer, Mr Edwards.'

Silence. Alan heard the music of the Millennium hijinks,

now underway in the park. He stepped closer. 'I have to know,' Alan told him quietly. 'Talk to me about it.'

Maidment swallowed hard, running his fingers through his thinning blonde hair. 'The man who did those… ' Maidment hunted for the right word. '… those bestial things to your family, he's still out there. I'm not him. He's still free.'

Maidment sounded so utterly sincere that Alan almost wanted to believe him. Prison psychologists had concluded that Maidment suffered from the familiar syndrome of prisoners who, unable to accept the heinous nature of their crimes, convinced themselves of their innocence. All Alan required was a simple admission. He doubted if Maidment could ever explain exactly why he had murdered, he would never really know.

Alan stood over Maidment, who looked up with intense sympathy. He spoke gently, treating Alan with the benign sensitivity of someone who had been damaged. 'It would be easy for me to make something up. Satisfy you by admitting something that wasn't true. But I have too much respect for you and what you've endured.' He opened his hands and stared ruefully down at his palms, examining their lifelines. 'I feel for you, I really do.'

'You murdered them, Maidment.' It was the first time Alan had spoken the name he had held in his head for so many years and a shudder drove through him. 'Let me hear you say it.'

Maidment firmly shook his head. 'I'm sorry. I did nothing.'

'You took photographs of them after you shot them. Polaroids!'

'No, sir. I could never do anything like that.'

'You can tell me,' Alan throttled, trying to quell his anger. 'Say it. What difference does it make? You'll never see me again.'

Maidment looked up at Alan, his eyes glazing over, realising that he was about to die. He was perfectly calm, almost serene, a peacefulness haloing him. 'It's no good,' he whispered with finality. 'Just kill me.'

'Just?'

Alan killed him then, quite quickly, with the fearsome precision his training had equipped him. The hard edge of his right hand struck Maidment's neck. He heard the neck break upon the first blow, then hit him twice more as Maidment's head lolled forward, as if dropping from the blade of a guillotine. His face crashed upon the table, and he lay there, his pupils glassy and bulbous, arms spread-eagled, his fat fingers twitching as the death rattle morsed briefly from his throat. A moth fluttered around the dead man's blonde hair, his moist scalp shining underneath. Blood ran from his eyes and nostrils, oozed from his lips, seeping across the papers trapped beneath his chin, the pages covered with his ornately cumbersome handwriting.

Alan let out a shout, an ugly blast, staring at the body in open-mouthed astonishment. A chill gripped him. Bile spurted into his throat and he retched, coughing until his lungs ached. His face and neck slicked with sweat, he staggered, convulsing. His head felt ready to burst. Backing from the table, he hugged himself, teeth chattering. The cell seemed to collapse, the light eclipsing, walls and ceiling sagging. Racked by the shakes, his body quaking, turmoil fermented through him. Gradually he calmed, face ashen, his movements weak and robotic, perspiration dripping from his chin.

Inhaling thickly, filling his sore lungs with the fuggy air, he stole to the door, and stabbed the lighted exit button with his thumb. The cell door drew obediently back. Outside the corridor was empty. Alan looked sheepishly round at Maidment's slumped body, its head twisted to one side. A thin sheet of darkness seemed to settle like coal dust over the disfigured form.

Walking swiftly, with an unhurried gait. Looking straight ahead as he beat a direct line through the maze of corridors and walkways, past the monitor bank with its one inactive screen, conscious of the occasional pacing warder and the blurred laughter of Millennium sprees. Out of the high-security wing, moving through the overcrowded cellblocks occupied by non-priority cons, fielding the bellicose merriment of staff and prisoners. Heading straight for the administration block and the foyer area beyond. His right hand throbbed, the pain darting through the muscles of his arm. Black blood congealed under the nails and his fingers felt broken and crushed.

He faced no threat of imminent seizure. There were no waiting cops and he saw a clear pathway of escape, aware only of a few curious glances, a sympathetic grimace, a jokey voice: 'One of them take a swing at you?' Alan touched the scab of dried blood on his upper lip.

In the locker room, he removed his cap and tunic, packed them away in his locker, pulled on a jumper and his raincoat already planted there. He cleaned his upper lip with a dampened tissue and marched to the exit area.

The system processed him through the security gate and he strode confidently through the prison's outer precincts, now swathed in darkness. A non-smoker for twenty years, Alan crossed to a corner tobacconist's, bought a packet of cigarettes and, sitting on a park bench whilst the Millennium jamboree swirled, chain-smoked all the cigarettes in well under an hour.

❐

He should have left the area, taken flight as he had planned, but he hung around, waiting to see what happened, just as murderers are meant to. Sitting in the park whilst the party histrionics reverberated, he watched the prison, wondering why it was taking so long for the police to arrive.

A large TV screen had been erected in the park, relaying worldwide news coverage of Millennium extravaganzas. Although nearly two hours still remained, crowds gathered impatiently around the screen awaiting the arrival of midnight. Wearied by the rowdy jubilation, Alan left the park. He found himself walking with reluctant inevitability back towards the prison, irresistibly drawn to its familiar estate.

It had all seemed too simple, too easy. No blaring klaxons, no marauding boys in blue, no unexpected mishaps. He had walked into the prison, killed Maidment, and walked out. All his anxieties had proved groundless, and success achieved with aplomb. Yet he felt a vague dissatisfaction. He would have valued greater opposition, some challenge, a testing of tenacity. Everything had been too predictable.

There was an emptiness in the pit of his stomach as he reached the prison, a place where he no longer belonged. He felt flat, despondent. It was over, done with, and he was at a loss, as if facing unemployment. He wondered what he was going to do with his days.

Once more the spectator at the edges of things, hidden within the prison's lugubrious shadows, he pondered the flat of which he was still technically the tenant. The severe yellow beam of the light bulb glowed like a beacon in the lounge. No-one lurked in the darkness of the rooms. Silhouettes refused to pirouette across the windows of his mind. The shadows were only shadows. He had simply left the light on.

He rationalised his need to return there, to his womb. The light irritated him, offended the perfectionist he had become, nagged at his proclivity for neat and tidy ends. He would have to go up and turn off that light. In any case, the flat was the safest place to be, his only available refuge. Soon detectives would discover who Alan Douglas Shaw really was and the manhunt would be on. No one would know to look for him there.

A thin wind sliced the back of his neck as he negotiated the street through the wayward streams of tipsy drivers. Sirens keened incessantly as fireworks entrailed against the night sky to the wild yells of the crowds. Leaves scuttling like dead crabs across his path, he climbed the rooming house steps, insusceptible to illusory prying eyes, freed of the notion of supposed lookouts, insensitive to the laconic jeers of his own invention. He entered the rooming house boldly through its front door.

Messages were left on the hall table, none for him. The hallway and stairs, rooms and passageways lay in slow-ticking silence, chambers of treacle-dark dust, awaiting the return of life to their tomblike deoccupancy. It was a ghost house. No melancholy music played hazily behind walls, no lights spilled from under doors. Even the loners were out tonight.

Alan climbed the stairs, running the limp knuckle of his

injured hand along the banister-rail, another shadow amongst the shadows in the eerie gloom. Out of breath, he paused on the third landing, gathering himself. Moonlight glazed softly over him, nosing in from the skylight as he climbed the final two flights. A narrow shred of light lipped from under the front door of his flat. He fingered away sweat from his forehead and unlocked the door.

Violet patterns of reflected firework trajectories criss-crossed the walls. Alan turned on all lights, letting them blaze out through the rooms. Nobody had been there, nothing had been disturbed. He went to the lounge window and looked out at the prison. The police were there at last. Turret lights flashing, several squad cars were parked inside the main gates. A smattering of uniformed cops stood around the vehicles, smoking and talking with studied nonchalance, carrying that weathered yet blasé air of men used to trouble. A discordant symphony of banshees announced the arrival of more police mobiles. Plainclothes detectives and scenes-of-crime specialists strutted self-importantly into the building.

Watching the proceedings below, Alan found himself thinking about Emma and his old life, the water-coloured enclosures of the past. Maybe he would have woman friends again, find someone else to love, although he doubted it. He was conscious of how lucky he had been with Emma and the children, as if blessed in some way, that the misfortunes afflicting others somehow passed them by. Little disrupted the still pond of their lives. It had been too perfect, all set ready to fall. He knew he didn't want to resurrect Ben Edwards. The man belonged to Emma, to another time and place.

A little before midnight an ambulance drew into the prison grounds. Maidment's corpse, zipped in a plastic body bag, was carried out on a stretcher and lifted into the back of the ambulance. As the vehicle screeched off bearing the body through congested streets, Alan came to appreciate the irony of how dependent he had become on Maidment. The overkill files of encyclopaedic research lying in the office beyond had become Alan's whole life, all that mattered to him. Now that was at an end. Maidment's death had consigned Alan to redundancy.

A grain of doubt concerning his victim's guilt festered. He would probably never know for sure, given Maidment's brave denials. Yet even if Alan had killed an innocent man, he would now pay his dues. His future had evolved with sudden clarity. Tomorrow, on New Century's Day, he proposed to surrender himself to the police. There was a pleasing symmetry to entering the twenty-first century a murderer, in assuming the mantle of the convicted killer. A Lifer. That would be his new role, ready-made for him. Alan didn't want to begin all over again, give birth to another Pimpernel, become the eternal fugitive, always in hiding like a war criminal or a witness under protection. Warder turned prisoner, he would exchange his current cell for a real one. He needed those four walls and time.

The church tower clock struck twelve. Bells pealed out across the city. People hugged, kissed, shook hands, jumped with joy, danced, made music, laughed, wept, leapt into fountains, drank champagne, had sex, cheered, roared and screamed in a cacophony of ear-splitting tumult. Oblivious to the fracas, Alan heard none of it, saw none of it.

He watched the prison.

NIGHT CALL
Richard T. Chizmar

December 31
6:03 pm

The first thing I noticed when I pulled over to the curb was Frank Logan's bald head shining in the outdoor Christmas lights. Even with all the commotion and camera flashes and all the people moving around, his head stuck out like the beacon from a lighthouse. He spotted me right away and made a big show of looking at his wristwatch. I grinned and showed him both my middle fingers.

Frank Logan was my partner. Had been for the past eight years; ever since I made detective. He was a good man. A first-rate cop.

He stood there in the doorway and watched me get out of my car and walk up the front sidewalk. I got close enough and he said, 'Nice of you to show up.'

I shrugged my shoulders. 'Traffic was bad.'

'Yeah, I know. Only been here a couple minutes myself.'

'So what's with the suit?' I asked. He was all decked out – a black, three-piece. It wasn't very wrinkled, and he actually looked pretty good. His tie was bright red and covered with tiny white reindeer, and it wasn't stained. Even his shoes looked shined. All this was new territory for Frank.

'Tonight was Susan's dinner party. Over at the Hilton.'

'Oh, shit. She pissed you had to leave?'

'You know it.'

Right then I glanced over his shoulder at the front door. 'Hey, is that what I think it is?'

'Uh-huh.'

'Jesus.'

'This guy's one sick son-of-a-bitch.'

'You're not kidding.'

'Sliced her goddamn ears off –'

'And pinned 'em to the front door,' I said, shaking my head.

'Wait till you see the upstairs bedroom.'

'How come?'

'Because that's where her hands are.'

'Her hands?'

'That's right,' he said, nodding. 'Rest of her's in the kitchen.'

'Jesus.'

'Third one in three weeks, Ben… I think we might have some real trouble here.'

'You're not kidding.'

'You eat dinner yet?'

'What?'

'I didn't have time to eat at the party. You hungry?'

'A little,' I lied.

'How 'bout we finish up here and go grab a pizza?'

'Sounds good to me.'

'Pepperoni and mushroom?'

'Sounds good to me.'

We went inside.

9:47 pm

The rain had changed over to snow about an hour ago. Almost an inch on the ground already. The guy on the radio was promising six-to-eight by morning with plenty of ice on the roadways. The morgue would be a popular place tomorrow.

The Christmas lights had been turned off. Yellow police tape lined the front yard and driveway, fluttered in the night breeze. It was a lonely sound, a lonely place now. The squad cars and news vans had left some time ago. Even the neighbours had disappeared – gone back inside to their parties, their television sets, their nice warm beds.

Inside the two-storey brick colonial, every light in the house was burning bright. The cleanup crew was on the clock and earning overtime. Three single mothers from up north in the suburbs. Over the past year, I'd gotten to know them pretty well. Frieda, Sandra and Lorraine – all in their early forties. Hard-working and friendly women. I liked them very much. Friends since high school, they'd quit their jobs and formed their own company early last year after watching a television program about a similar business venture in Chicago. Ask any of the three and they'll tell you: it's ugly work, real ugly – some days nothing but blood, urine and human waste, and the smell's enough to kill you – but it sure beats making minimum wage and having your ass grabbed every day by a bunch of smug lawyers. Sure, the hours may stink, but the pay more than makes up for the inconvenience. And it's simple work, really. First thing: turn on all the lights. Especially at night. Then, if necessary, start upstairs and work your way down. Keep your mind focused on something else – anything else – and scrub everything as clean as possible. Spray it all down with disinfectant. And, last thing before you lock the front door, set up the air-fresheners. Typical job takes between two and six hours, depending on the mess and the number of victims. Longer if they have to call someone in to move furniture or pull up the carpet.

Tonight's victim – Mandy Frymann, a 37 year old middle school teacher, 5'2", 125 pounds, brown hair, brown eyes – was already making her way downtown. Zippered tight inside a shiny black body bag. The thing was: this particular bag was designed for a male victim and it was too long to properly secure a 5'2" female, so the coroner's assistant was forced to improvise. He folded the bottom of the bag up over her feet until it practically reached above her knees and then he weighted the extra flap in place with both of her severed hands, both of her ears, and her right foot – each sealed tight inside heavy duty plastic evidence bags. This was not proper transfer procedure, but the assistant didn't much give a damn. He was supposed to be home by seven, and he was late for a party.

9:54pm
'You got cheese in your moustache,' I said.
  'Huh?'

I pointed to my own mouth. 'In your moustache. Cheese.'

'Oh, thanks.'

He located the string of mozzarella and popped it into his mouth. Raised his eyebrows at me. I pretended to be disgusted.

We were sitting across from each other in a booth near the front window of Bontempo Brothers, Frank's favourite pizzeria. He loved this place – with its clean red tablecloths and authentic Italian music on the sound system – always talked about buying a joint just like it when he retired. He wanted me to invest when the time came; that way we could stay partners, he said. Frank was full of crazy ideas.

'Something wrong with you tonight?' I asked, after a few minutes of silence. 'You been kinda quiet.'

He shook his head. 'Just tired I guess.'

'You know we'll find this guy, Frank. You know how it is with the violent ones. He'll get messy, make a mistake and we'll–'

'I'm fine, I tell you.'

We stared at each other for a moment, both of us trying to look convincing.

I looked away first, watched a young couple cross the snow-covered street, holding hands. They turned the corner and I looked back at Frank; he'd been watching them too. There was something in his eyes I didn't recognise.

'Come on, Frank. You don't think I'd know if something was bothering you.'

'Jesus Christ, you're a pest. You know that? A goddamn pest.'

'That's right,' I said, reaching across the table and poking him in the forearm. 'I'm a pest and sometimes you're worse than a goddamn woman. Now tell me the truth.'

He took a sip of his soda and shrugged. 'There's nothing to tell.'

I pointed at him. 'You… are… a… liar'

He pointed back. 'And… you… are… an… asshole.'

I shoved the tip of a slice of pizza in my mouth and flicked him the bird.

We sat there in silence, watching the rest of the pizza get cold.

About a minute later, he spilled it, just like I knew he would.

He said it very quietly. 'Susan wants a divorce. She told me tonight.'

'Jesus, Frank.'

'She's serious, too. You shoulda heard her. She swears she's not seeing anyone else. She's not even thinking of anyone else. She just doesn't love me anymore. Said she doesn't even know me anymore.'

'Ah, hell, I'm sorry.'

He nodded his head sadly. 'Me too.'

'Maybe she'll change her mind. Maybe she's just pissed off, because of you missing the party and all.'

'I don't think so, Ben. I really don't think so.'

He locked his hands together, rested his chin on them, and stared out the window. He looked like he was praying and maybe he was.

'So what'd you say to her?' I asked.

He kept looking out the window at the falling snow. 'What could I say? I told her we would have to talk about it in the morning. That there was a lot we needed to talk about.'

'And?'

'She said the time for talking had come and gone. That it was time to move on. She said her mind was made up.'

'Jesus, Frank. She really said that?'

He looked at me and nodded. He was close to tears. 'She really said that.'

'Damn, I'm sorry, Frank.'

'You already said that.'

I opened my mouth to say something else, and that's when our pagers went off.

10:19 pm

'You believe in any of this Millennium bullshit?'

'You obviously don't,' I said.

We were heading north on 95 but moving slow because of

the storm. The snow was coming down harder now. Bigger flakes and wet. It was sticking to everything.

'How do you know I don't believe?'

'You said Millennium *bullshit*. If you think it's bullshit, then you obviously don't believe in it.'

'I didn't mean it that way. Jesus, Ben, sometimes you're a pain in the ass.'

'What did you mean then?'

'Okay, we're about to hit a new century. Not a new decade but a century. I realise that's pretty damn significant. A big deal even. But now we've got nutcases running loose all over the damn place. Even more so than usual. And why? Just because of the damn calendar. Turn on the television and what do you see? Stories about psycho cult members offing themselves so that they can be transported to another planet. Little kids walking into schools with machine guns in their book bags and blowing their friends away. Murderers and rapists all over the fucking place. Serial killings on the rise. And why? Because a voice told them to do it, because the end of the world is coming, because Judgment Day is upon us all. Jesus Christ, what a bunch of shit.'

Frank got like this once in a while – all red-faced and stuttering and pissed off at the world. A heart attack just waiting to happen. And when he did, it was best to just sit there and listen and not open your mouth. Maybe nod your head once every couple minutes to show that you understood.

'And then when the news is over, you get the goddamn commercials. Fortune tellers, mind readers, psychic healers, mystic forgivers. You tell me, Ben, what the fuck's a mystic forgiver?'

I nodded my head and tried not to laugh.

'And people trying to sell you goddamn everything. What does some crystal you wear around your neck have to do with the year 2000? What the hell can you do with 60 different types of organic herbs? I'd like to shove those herbs up their asses is what I'd like to do…'

I steered onto Exit 23, our tyres cutting fresh tracks in the deep snow, and turned right at the first stoplight. A bunch of kids were having a snowball fight on the front lawn of an elementary school. There had to be at least twenty of them out there.

About a mile up the road, I turned left and we were there. Squad cars and flashing red lights everywhere. Couple of ambulances. One drove right past us when we pulled to the curb.

'Looks like a goddamn traffic accident,' Frank said. 'What'd they call us out here for?'

'Let's check it out.' I turned the car off and got out. Took a half-dozen steps and wished for a warmer jacket. Maybe a scarf. In the police lights, the falling snow was the colour of blood.

It was a working class neighbourhood. Small houses built forty, fifty years ago, narrow front yards – run down and neglected now, peeling paint and cracked driveways. Even the snow couldn't make it look pretty.

There were two cars sitting in the middle of the street. Connected nose to nose by twisted metal. The smaller car was missing a windshield. Frank was right; it looked like a head-on collision.

I looked around. None of the folks involved in the accident appeared to be still at the scene.

I spotted Harvey Weidemann standing next to the other ambulance and walked over. Frank stayed behind, talking to one of the uniforms on the scene.

Harvey used to work city five, six years ago, but then he got married and moved out to the country. Wife's orders. They were going to have kids and she didn't want to raise a family on her own. Smart lady. Harvey's a big man. Real big – six-six and more than two-fifty. These days, most of it's fat, but not all of it. He's still pretty impressive to look at.

'Hey, Harv. What's going on?'

He looked up from his notebook and smiled warmly.

'Christ, look what the cat dragged in.'

We shook hands. The bastard was wearing leather gloves. And a scarf.

He glanced over my shoulder, squinted in the falling snow

and flashing lights. 'And, hey, there's your better half. And wearing a goddamn suit. Never thought I'd see the day.' He shook his head, pointed at the cars in the middle of the street. They were quickly disappearing beneath the snow. 'You believe this shit?'

'What's going on?' I asked.

He smiled again. A big fat grinning pumpkin. 'You're not gonna believe it.'

'Try me.'

'Red Cavalier is Marcus and Joanna Firestone. Husband and wife. Live up the street on Hanson. According to their statement they'd been drinking all day, since before noon.'

He walked over and patted the hood of the other automobile – the one missing a windshield – a dark-coloured Toyota. 'This one is Freddie Jenkins. Next door neighbour to Marcus and Joanna Firestone. The three of them started partying together before lunch. Nothing too serious – beer and a couple of joints. Then a few friends come over and things really start cooking. New Year's Eve comes a little early, if you know what I mean. Seems that sometime around three or four, Marcus catches Freddie making time with his old lady in the upstairs bathroom. Right on the fucking sink. Only he doesn't say anything at the time. Doesn't let on that he knows.

'Around seven, the party gets even bigger and moves across the street to another neighbour's house. But before heading over, Marcus and Joanna drive over to Luskin's Liquor Mart for a beer run. They get their beer and on the way home, they start arguing. Marcus comes clean with her about what he's seen, even starts crying while he's driving. Now get this: the old lady gets pissed off. You believe that shit? She gets royally pissed off. Starts screaming at him about not trusting her and spying on her and bullshit like that. Starts beating on him while he's driving.

'Anyway, while they're weaving up the street, already drunk and stoned off their minds, here comes their neighbour Freddie Jenkins cruising in the opposite direction.'

I rolled my eyes and whispered, 'Oh, shit.'

Harvey's smile got wider and he held up a finger and said, 'It gets better. So Marcus sees Freddie coming his way and with his wife's fingernails digging into his neck and her screaming in his ear *YOU DON'T TRUST ME!*, the poor guy does what comes natural. He fucking loses it. He backhands his wife until she shuts up, crashes head-first into Freddie's Toyota, grabs a gun from under his front seat, jumps out of the car and onto the hood of Freddie's car, kicks in the windshield, pulls Freddie out and gut-shoots him right then and there. Then he does the wife.'

I shook my head. 'Jesus.'

'When the first car got to the scene, the officers found Marcus sitting on the trunk of his car, drinking a Budweiser. They said he was just sitting there, waiting, and he wasn't wearing a shirt; they found it in the front seat of his car, draped over the steering wheel, soaked in blood. Freddie Jenkins was laying on the road, already dead, and Joanna was still in the front seat. She got it in the head... twice. She was a mess. Paramedics said she's eighty-twenty.'

Harvey wasn't smiling anymore.

'Marcus wanted to give a statement right away, so they let him do it. He was crying the whole damn time. They finally took him downtown 'bout a half-hour ago. The poor son-of-a-bitch. I felt sorry for him. I really did.'

'You're not kidding.'

I thanked Harvey and told him it was good to see him. I took a few steps and turned and asked about his wife.

'We're divorced,' he said. 'Two years ago. She got the kids.'

I told him I was sorry and found Frank waiting by the car.

We got out of there.

11:57pm

'Weird couple of calls, huh?'

Frank looked at me and raised his eyebrows. 'Hey, it's the Millennium, remember?'

I couldn't help but smile at the smartass.

'Not really so weird anyway,' he said. 'Not so much out of the ordinary.'

I nodded. 'You're right. Just kinda felt that way tonight is all.'

We were sitting at the end of the bar in the Brass Horse Saloon. Best cream of crab soup in the city. And the prettiest waitresses too. None of that mattered tonight, though. It was a mad house – New Year's Eve and all.

Frank had wanted to go someplace quieter. But I thought it might do us some good to be around people for awhile. Normal, everyday, regular-joe, happy, non-homicidal people.

Of course, when we pulled up, there was a fist fight in the parking lot. Two big guys fighting over a woman.

I finished my drink and looked over at my partner. 'You gonna be all right?'

'Susan, you mean.'

I nodded my head.

'I don't know.' He shrugged his shoulders. 'I really don't know.'

People around us starting counting.

'You know, you need a place to stay for awhile, you always got me.'

He looked up from his drink and I saw the fear in his eyes. It was the wrong thing for me to say and the look on his face made my fucking heart ache. I turned away and ordered another round, but the waitress didn't hear me.

'Frank, I didn't mean –'

The place erupted then. Streamers and confetti and annoying little party horns. Hugging and kissing and yelling.

A man I had never seen before in my life slapped me on the shoulder and gave me a thumbs-up. A very fat redhead kissed Frank on the cheek, then moved over and did the same to the man sitting behind him. A couple of college kids jumped up on the bar and started dancing.

Frank and I just sat there and looked at each other, both of us thinking the same thing.

After a few minutes of this, Frank leaned over and raised his voice above the crowd. 'Hey, great idea, coming here. Thanks for cheering me up, partner.'

I showed him my middle finger and said, 'Happy New Year, Frank. Happy fucking New Year.'

He smiled and raised his glass.

My glass was empty but I raised it anyway.

PHANTOM LOVER

Maxim Jakubowski

I had a history, a bad habit of always wanting what I couldn't have. This time it was her.

You know how it is. You know how it goes, sometimes: the sad ending is already in the sights of your periscope, but you forge ahead regardless. Just in case. Hope against hope and all that.

It was the summer of 1997. Don't ask me about the weather, I can't recall it well, it was neither too hot or too cold, that's all I remember of it. Because of the time we spent naked in alien rooms, I suppose. Just once I had seen her shiver and passed over my over-large grey T-shirt as shelter from the momentary chill. I still wear that T-shirt from time to time; brings back memories. Of the colour of her bare flesh. The concealed shape of her drunken body.

I was on a job. As it is, meeting her was wrong. Very wrong.

But then the rules of this private eye game are ill-defined. Even more so if you're British. We can't carry guns like the ones in America and all the books and movies. Takes some of the glamour away already.

I do my best, though. I don't do adultery, debt research or repossessions. My field's more refined: industrial espionage, corporate shenanigans. Pays well, limited risks. Quiet and unspectacular, just my style, I reckoned.

That's how I first came across her.

A customer called the agency. Labour had come in a few weeks before and were threatening the privatised utilities with the windfall tax. Basically, the agency is me. And a few freelancers. And lotsa names in a computer database. People who could be bribed. British Telecom engineers, book-keepers for stockbroking firms, disenchanted clerks with City banks, underpaid and exploited staff in the despatch departments and postrooms of large corporations. The indispensable human tools of the trade in my business.

One of the larger utilities was mounting some form of legal defence against the government plan. But their counterplotting was somehow making it into the national press. As soon as something was discussed at boardroom level it soon arrived in print on the financial pages of one of the large national newspapers. Inconvenient. You can't play chess when your opponent always knows your likely response to his movements. I was hired by phone by a Mr Jones in Corporate Planning. Money no object. Find out who was leaking the minutes of the secret meetings, and stop them.

Piece of cake.

The annoying columns were penned by the business correspondent of the newspaper. One I used to read once, but had recently given up on. I soon had a tap on his South London mews house telephone and 24 hour surveillance in operation. He operated from his Canary Wharf newsroom; unfortunately, because of the other year's IRA bombing in the vicinity I couldn't get access to the paper's offices and his phone there. Not to worry. I would just have to be patient and more thorough than usual.

Motive was quickly revealed: the guy's wife was a member of the local Labour constituency. Bloody idealists. So now it was just a question of pinpointing who at the utilities was passing him the information. At first I assumed it was also a local party activist, passing information to the press for what he or she thought were all the right reasons. So I left a couple of freelancers to keep a close eye on the Canary Wharf and City jaunts of the damn journo, and decided to concentrate on the South London connection personally.

And met her. The wife. Callie.

And my problems began.

And the joy.

Turns out I was on the wrong trail, anyway. The division at the utilities that had called on my snooping services didn't know what another division on another floor was up to... It seems that they were aware there was no legal chance in hell of reversing the government's new tax, even if they had spent months and mountains in cash taking their case to the European courts or wherever, so they had leaked the stuff to the newspaper themselves to put the frighteners on the politicians in the hope of discouraging the Exchequer to set the windfall tax too high. Manipulating the media, and my business correspondent target was just the patsy they had unwittingly used. He was fairly new to the job, an arrival from TV and radio who didn't realise he was being manipulated. Probably thought all along he was God's answer to investigative journalism. I never did like him anyway.

But I didn't know all that then and also thought I was doing a damn good job. Did I say patsy?

Early bright late May morning, parked fifty yards from the couple's semidetached, I munched on a chocolate biscuit in lieu of breakfast, aware that this job was playing havoc with my expanding waistline. Mark, the journalist, had left half an hour ago for Canary Wharf, and a reliable acolyte had followed him. I'd planned to keep on the wife's trail. Already knew quite a bit about her. Second generation Irish, Epsom grammar school and Cambridge, a second in English, a few dead end jobs on regional newspapers and now a reader in the drama department for one of the new television cable channels; married eight years, in the chapel of the Cambridge college where they had both been undergraduates. No children. Canvassed for the local branch of the party. Must have had her first orgasm in months on the night Labour won and they fucked whilst blinding drunk. On paper, a common type. Somehow, I hadn't summoned a mental picture of her, wasn't really expecting anything surprising. She was just a pawn in another very ordinary case.

The house's front door opened.

I was blinded.

Within a week, I had contrived to meet her at a launch party for a balti curry cookery book in a central London art gallery. Her voice, the way the thin material of her blue dress hung over her shoulders, her dark eyes peering inside me as we spoke inconsequential gossip, it all made the longing reach unthought of agony.

Within two weeks, we were in bed together.

I had crossed the line.

Cookie, my old mentor, had always warned me never to mix business with pleasure, get personally involved in a case. But all the wise precepts were quickly forgotten as her lips engulfed my vile meat in a kiss of fire, unabashed by the fact I had just retreated momentarily from the wet furnace of her innards and was still dripping with her juices.

On the first hotel bed, it was lust. Extraordinary. Venting the frustrations of our respective lives. Reinventing the lovemaking that our respective partners no longer sought with the same intensity as before. Drinking at the tap of life all over again. Reminding ourselves that our bodies still held untold beauty that was elsewhere being taken for granted or perused for growing imperfections.

Oh, my Callie.

Crossing the thin line. She had never been unfaithful before. Accidents hadn't happened. I had. Opportunities. Not very often. One-night stands. The job made it easy. But none of the affairs had lasted long; enjoyable distractions on the journey to middle-age. She was younger, the thought had sometimes occurred, there had been other men making passes, she was pretty in her unconventional way, but it had never been the right time or place, she supposed.

But when I asked for details of her nearly past adventures, she was always reticent and invariably changed the subject quickly. And I had more immediate priorities. Mapping the pale colour of her skin until the morning came when we would have to go our own way. Using her shocking pink lipstick to enhance the blood-engorged colour of her private parts before I licked them clean. Manoeuvring her body into impossible contortions and positions to make my thrusts ever deeper until she screamed loudly, scaring me, 'No, it's okay, it's pleasure, not pain. More, more!' Tracing the bumpy texture of her cunt walls with the probing tip of my tongue. Inserting my fingers past the resistance of the invisible muscles protecting the heart of her moon-shaped arse.

Think of hardcore pornography and add unthought of perverse trimmings and we did it.

She brought out the worst and the best in me.

And vice versa.

'Do you know? I've never done it that way...'

'We can try it, I suppose.'

'I'm not sure it's even possible.'

'No harm in trying.'

'I'll be careful.'

'I know you will.'

And as we sunk in free fall to the very depths of uncontrollable lust, my heart broke. Just like that. One moment we were fucking without abandon, our wetness mingling, our bodies intimately joined in at least three different areas, blissfully unaware of the world outside the pulled calico curtains (we were in her bed; Mark had gone to Oxford for the day: 'Remind me to put the sheets in the washing machine as you leave;' I had parked a few streets away by the Park). I could feel the sweat bucketing down my forehead onto her cheeks, my tongue embedded inside her mouth, my cock growing harder with every forward movement and her insides melting as she jesused away while the pleasure grew within. Just then, I opened my eyes. And looked into hers.

And I walked with the angels as I realised right there and then, that she was the one, the one I had always been looking for without knowing if she even existed. It was love at second-hand sight, no longer lust. I knew, as I fucked her with untold rage, that I had to have her. Not like this, mere copulation, sweat and secretions, but forever. She could belong to Mark no more. I wanted all of her. Sharing was no longer in question, or a mere affair of the flesh.

By now, I knew she wasn't involved in the leak of information from the utilities company, of course. I had reported accordingly to my paymasters and my sidekicks were still tailing her husband, although there was also little evidence of him being in contact with anyone suspicious. At any rate, it was useful to know his whereabouts at all times. Maybe I was secretly hoping he was conducting his own affair somewhere. Would have given me the right impetus to force Callie permanently into my arms. Sadly, he was a boring man and never strayed. Too ambitious and mindful of his career prospects, I assumed, from what Callie had told me of him.

Later that evening, we were having a drink in a pub somewhere along the South Bank, far enough from her home, we thought, to be safe. I couldn't tell her that I was aware Mark was still on his assignment in Finchley where a large theatre chain were opening a new multiplex.

'I love you,' I said.

'I know,' she said, sipping her gin and orange.

'No. I mean, for real, I want us to be together. Leave him. I'll move out, find us a place. We could travel together.'

She knew I was married too. Somehow, I'd have to explain what my job actually was, explain earlier white lies. I was confident I could.

'You're going too fast,' she replied, surprising me. 'We've got to give it time.'

Right then I had the awful feeling we were not going to make it.

That things would not work out.

And it began to kill me inside.

Back home, I carefully composed a letter to her husband, revealing our affair. It was illogical, I knew, but it was a compulsion I could not resist. I slipped the letter into an envelope, and the next day at my office, stuck the letter at the back of a drawer, knowing that one day I would use it as a weapon of vengeance.

We stayed together, so to speak, another three months. Every time we made love, I drew a small star with the letter C in my diary. Looking back at those pages today, it's like a monotonous parade of distracted graffiti strung out between cryptic notes of things to do or telephone numbers, a private milky way leading to my own death by a thousand shards of longing.

The sex became even more frantic, as the despair inside me took a firm hold and her coldness became more apparent every time the subject of our future was broached.

All the time, the ticking bomb inside my desk was on its fatal countdown.

But the sex was good, oh yes, Callie. As if the contact of our skin turned us into incredible two-backed beasts capable of reinventing the flesh like no one had ever done before. With all the energy I was putting into our encounters, I no longer had to worry about my waistline. And sweet Callie bloomed into a sensuous flower of the night, sex vibrating all around her as she walked away to her night train, still full of my seed, her long legs eating up the station concourse, the eyes of every man in the immediate vicinity automatically turning towards her, this creature of sheer lust. Mine.

One day. Summer coming to an end.

Another pub somewhere in the no man's land that separated both of us from our real lives and relationships.

'Joe?'

'Yes?'

'It's still going too fast… I need some time to think. I don't want us hurting any one, you know.'

'What do you mean?'

I had carefully not raised the subject of our getting permanently together for a few weeks now, hoping she would come naturally to the idea.

'I think of you too often. It's not good. It's affecting my work. I just don't know how to act when Mark's around. We don't talk much any more. He's going to suspect something soon…'

'So what?'

'We must spend some time apart.'

'No.'

'A few months maybe. Then we'll see how we feel about each other.'

I knew all too well this was a recipe for disaster.

We negotiated. I pleaded. The time apart, its length, remained unsaid. I begged. We agreed on a final fuck the next evening. Sentimentally, I even asked her to wear the same outfit she had on the first time we met. Well, if this was to be the last time…

That afternoon, I posted the letter.

It was after the final postal pick-up from that particular letter box. Mark wouldn't get it until the morning after next. Or later if the mail room at his newspaper was slow in distributing things.

Which left me one evening to make love to her so well, so badly that she would change her mind and stay with me forever. I had to find the imagination, the words to sway her. Usually, I work well against deadlines. A sad gamble, I realise now.

She never appeared for our clandestine assignment.

There was no answer from her phone. They had no answer machine, but even if they had I wasn't in a position to leave a message.

A few days went by without news from her.

Puzzled, saddened, I tried to phone her at work. Her private line was dead. I hesitated, then decided to phone Mark at the newspaper.

'Did you get my letter?'

He sounded genuinely puzzled.

'What letter? Who are you?'

He must have thought I was some mad man, some crazy guy with a bad grudge against business journalists.

Not only had my letter not reached him, but he wasn't even married, let alone living with any woman right now.

'Whoever you are, you've got the wrong man, mate…' he concluded.

I slammed the phone down before he did.

Felt cold sweat all over.

I phoned directory enquiries to get the number of the cable television company where she worked. How could she have pretended she was married to Mark? It made no sense at all.

Made the reservations she harboured throughout our affair meaningless.

The woman on the switchboard swore blind they had no one called Callie working there. Whether under her married name or her maiden one. Sensing my increasing desperation, she even checked through the list of all the freelancers who occasionally used a desk at the company.

'No. I'm absolutely certain. She does not work here,' she assured me.

'Are you positive?' I asked again. 'It is so important.'

'There ain't that many of us here, you see. I know every one. Nobody answers your description. Are you sure you're not confusing. There are a lot of independent TV companies in the area?'

I had often accompanied her in the morning to the building, seen her from afar walk through the building's portals.

I spent the day being a dedicated private eye. Checking things I should have investigated before. Local property registers: the South London mews house I had first seen her leaving, luminous, was in Mark's name only. Caught a cab to Somerset House to check again on the damn marriage certificate where I'd learned about the Cambridge college chapel. Yes, it was there: eight years ago, maiden name Callie Edwin. Collected my thoughts. Then visited another room in the large official building. And found the divorce papers: Mark and Callie had separated four years ago.

The hole in the pit of my stomach began twisting its spear through my heart. Was her name even Callie?

Who was she?

A million questions whirled frantically through my brain.

But the main one was why?

Why, Callie?

I went home late, torn apart by conflicting emotions. My wife was still awake. Angry, inquisitorial. She had received a letter in the mail that morning accusing me of having an affair. She had repeatedly phoned me throughout the day, but it was always engaged, and in my mixed-up state I hadn't bothered to answer her messages.

'Who sent you the letter?' I asked.

'That's not the point,' she answered. 'Is it true?'

'Who wrote the damn letter?' I shouted back at her.

'So it is true,' she remarked.

'Who?' I asked her again.

'Someone called Callie,' she said.

'Yes, it's true,' I admitted. I didn't have the energy to argue or fight.

My whole world had just been shattered into lots of small, desolate pieces and I just had no answers.

In the days that followed I could not summon the will to lie or apologise and my marriage collapsed, while I still desperately followed every conceivable lead that might lead me to the invisible Callie, her motives and her warm body again. I was in denial. Couldn't accept the unexpected and puzzling rejection. Hitchcock stories surely didn't happen to real people. I tried to recall every conversation we ever had, to remember any name that might have been mentioned by her in passing, any clue to her identity or someone who might be aware of her or even her whereabouts. And all these memories could not help invoking back every little thing we had done, the curve of her breasts, the colour of her lips, the feel of her tongue on my trembling skin, how her throat turned pink as pleasure took hold of her senses, her moans, her sighs, her soft, gentle, almost shy voice when she whispered my name with such awful delicacy as we lay entwined in bed. Constant torture it was. But it got me nowhere.

Not only had she disappeared from the face of London, but there was no evidence she had even existed.

Apart from the deep tattoo she had carved in my errant soul.

Visions of her kept me awake at night for months on end. Fleeting visions of other women in the street recalled a lock of hair, a swish of material, the simile of a smile, but of course it was never her. Just a pale imitation, a fuzzy piece of the overall puzzle that Callie had become.

Time passed.

I still couldn't forget her. Kept on wondering whether she would have disappeared if I had not posted the damn letter. But knew, deep inside, that the scenario had already been written the moment I met her, and nothing I had done would have changed the outcome.

I was a mess.

Single life didn't suit me and there was no way my wife would have me back; she sensed that I had given my heart to Callie and would not tolerate its absence if we resumed our relationship.

For months I haunted the places we had been together. The pubs, the restaurants, I even stayed a few times in the same hotels for a night, always insisting on the room we had originally occupied. And invariably jerked off, screaming her name out loud as I came over the starched sheets or the bed cover, evoking mental images of her body, her sex, her royal rump. Talk about sad!

I tracked the real Callie down, once Mark's wife. She now lived in Brixton with an Irish loft extension builder. She had long, straight, brown hair and round glasses, prettyish face but bad legs. There was no resemblance. But then I had to try every possibility.

By now – I still kept watching him on a regular basis – Mark was shacked up in the South London mews semidetached with a small redhead, who also worked in Canary Wharf. I had actually witnessed their meeting over the lunch break in a sandwich bar. Mr Cupid, that's me.

The windfall tax was passed and the official side of the Callie case came to an end. By then, office A had found out about office B's plans and I was called in and my services dispensed with, with minor apologies and a reasonable cheque for my efforts.

My nights were still empty with the despair of longing and the image of her face at rest on a shared pillow began to lose its intensity, its focus. But still I grieved inside. Badly. On the anniversary of our first fuck, I wrote her a postcard I never sent. Another on the next Valentine's Day. On what she had told me was her birthday. There were still people out there looking for traces of her, who had her description, paid by me. But nothing ever came up. I lost myself in work. Expanded the agency, and finally agreed we should now take on adultery cases. Why have scruples any longer? Business boomed.

Two years had gone by. The pain still buried like a tumour in my previously unfelt depths. Trying to grow old gracefully. I enjoyed an affair with one of our new operatives, Lucy, a small curvaceous auburn-haired young woman who broached no sentimentality and preferred a no-strings attached relationship. She was good for me, uncomplicated, defiantly cheerful. What she didn't know was that most times I had to conjure up the ghost of Callie to stay hard when making love to her. But I suppose you wouldn't call that being unfaithful, technically speaking. Just a sex aid. Even took a holiday with her. Rented a white stucco villa in Southern Portugal where we shared our time fucking nonchalantly and eating too much. Which only served to remind me that I had never managed to go anywhere with Callie further than a few coastal furtive dirty weekend uninspiring hotels, and hadn't seen her on a beach, by the pool or even in a swimming costume.

Time, like a slow, slow river.

August 1999. Waiting for a train at Paddington Station, I was browsing through the newsstand and spotted a Paul Klee postcard. The second anniversary of our first time together was just a few days away, evoking balmy sensations of my fingers slipping through her curls and the oh so tender softness of her uncovered, shivering breasts. I bought the card. Wrote 'I miss you still' on the back, and then lacking an address as usual buried it in my pocket, there to gather oblivion again, until the next absurd celebration of her continuing absence.

Missing her was an understatement.

Every day and every night.

Still.

Always.

The station's loudspeaker system announced a fifteen minute delay on the arrival of the Cardiff train. I had to sign for some documents a junior clerk was bringing up to London from a Bristol solicitor. I backtracked to the newsstand, searching for a magazine to kill the time, but none caught my attention.

Moved over to the book racks.

At first, it was the cover illustration that I noticed. A photographic close-up of a woman's leg (thigh?), the constricted flesh bursting through the fishnet patterns of a stocking. An image that struck a responsive chord inside my dormant libido.

'The Man Who Didn't Understand Women' by Katherine Blackheath.

I seldom read women's fiction, but the back cover blurb intrigued me. Something about a man and a woman, London, anonymous hotel rooms, three months of forbidden passion.

Standing at the centre of the station concourse, I began reading.

I finished the book at two the following morning. I'd cancelled an evening with Lucy earlier.

It was all there.

Our story.

With subtle changes: did I really never smile? I was no longer a private eye but merely an insurance investigator. But then I had never revealed my occupation to Callie; I had indicated I was a freelance journalist. It wasn't Eastbourne, but Brighton, and there was no mention of a husband but I now had two children... Wholesale chunks of conversations we had had, in our usual pub, in bed, were accurately evoked. The fateful letter I had written. She even described the sounds I would make when I came, the words I would say, those she would herself whisper. The rituals of undressing and kissing. And the woman in the book was also called Callie.

I can't say I was shocked. Surprised, maybe. It was strange to see myself in print like that. Or at any rate a character who I could recognise as me. Possibly angry that she should steal our story in this way.

Towards the end of the novel after the two lovers had badly betrayed each other, they both travelled a lot, enjoying rather sordid adventures. Mine, I didn't mind. Hers, I winced at the thought that she might actually have fucked all these other men, it was so realistic. Difficult to know where the fiction and the reality took divergent paths. She wrote well, Callie, or was it

Katherine did. I could sense the emotions, the feelings oozing from the pages as the narrative developed.

But nowhere was there an explanation for her actions, her disappearing act, all the obvious preparations she would have had to undertake to fool me in the way she did about her very existence. And neither was there a reason why the character in her novel did what she did to me, to him, the somewhat passive, seemingly spineless male protagonist.

Because she thought she loved him, she wrote somewhere in the book.

Which made the whole affair no easier to understand.

The novel ended with a melodramatic shoot-out straight out of a hardboiled noir movie, in which most of the characters, including the two of us, perished. Gave things a sense of closure, but felt all wrong, though.

I was tired. It was dark outside. I was puzzled. I was hungry.

Another mystery confronted me now: The Curious Case of Katherine Blackheath. Or The Detective Who Always Drank Coca-Cola.

The next morning I contacted the publicity department of the book's publishers in an attempt to obtain information about the novel's author. They promised something in the mail. All I received was a flimsy press release, which clumsily summarised the plot and promised oodles of promotion and reviews. About Callie, all it said was she lived in New York.

When we were together, my unfulfilled fantasy had been to take her to America. I couldn't quite picture her amongst the Manhattan hustle and bustle.

I tried to get more specific details through a junior in the publicity department, but there was nothing of substance to be had. The manuscript had been bought from a literary agent, through his British counterpart, and the author had been unwilling to provide any biographical details, let alone a photograph.

Within a week, I landed at Kennedy.

As my cab raced down Van Wyck Expressway towards the inevitable traffic gridlock beyond the Midtown tunnel, I wondered what to do next.

I'd never operated in a foreign country. The rules were different.

Here, private dicks used guns.

My hotel on West 44th Street was undergoing renovation and Polish builders tramped up and down the corridors, peppering the lift and lobby with white dust. The television set in the room wasn't working. I called out for a Chinese meal. By the time the food arrived, it was lukewarm and under spiced. By now I had jotted down on a pad my course of action. The art of detecting is to be methodical, organised and, most of all, patient. But I'd never been a patient person. Maybe that had been my undoing with sweet Callie?

Call the New York agent. Arrange an appointment. Have some bogus business cards printed up to present some sort of front. I'd brought over an assortment of glossy British magazines with some of the bylines I'd be borrowing for the occasion. I was confident few, if any, of the journalists involved would be known here. Small risk involved, really. Change travellers cheques for lower denomination dollar bills. For transport, tips and bribes where necessary. Tomorrow, contact the local agency with whom my outfit had sometimes collaborated on the technicalities of past cases involving transatlantic connections. Visit the *New York Times* cuttings library to assemble American reviews of the book which might provide information to the author's whereabouts, in the likely absence of interviews. Determine how regulated British residents were. Was she here on a visitor's visa or did she have a Green Card? Government offices were a weak link where the right amount of money spread around might earn me some valuable information.

That would do to begin with.

If, as I expected, this failed, the second angle of attack would involve more illegal methods to trace financial records at the publishers or the literary agency. This was problematic, though, as I still had no precise indication of her real name.

The biggest risk would involve breaking into her agent's offices to check their records .

Not something I was looking forward to.

But, if it came to that, I knew I would. I could sense it in the air, Callie was in Manhattan. Probably no more than a mile or two away. I had to find her. I would find her.

September 29th 1999
Finally managed a meeting with her agent, a perky preppy twerp with regulation red braces and an insincere smile. No, Miss Blackheath is quite adamant that she wishes to retain her privacy. Did you know we've a Hollywood option for the book? Gwyneth Paltrow is being lined up. Personally I'd have gone for Anne Heche, you know, but she's a hard sell for romantic stories now, of course. If it were up to me I'd love her to consent to an interview. Would help sales. The absent author lark has its drawbacks, you see. He relented slightly, assuring me he would contact her and strongly recommend she agree to seeing me. Absolutely loved the magazine I was pretending to write for. Really. But that's all he could do. He did have this other client, an ex-stripper and dominatrix who lived in Alphabet City and now penned very erotic books. Great angle. Wouldn't a feature on her be great? She wouldn't mind being photographed in the nude, you see. He would get in touch, one way or the other when Katherine Blackheath responded to my request. No, he didn't know how long it would take.

I tried to squeeze some more information out of him. Background stuff for my piece. How had he come to represent her? In fact it was another agent who had since departed from the agency and he had only just taken over her affairs. Had never actually met her. Loved the book. So funny. I noted the previous agent's name. He'd moved to Los Angeles as a reader for a film company.

In her novel, Callie's character had decamped to California and become involved in the making of hardcore porno films. Jotting things down on automatic pilot, in the agent's office with its panoramic views of downtown Manhattan, I recalled the feel of her lips, in London rooms, caressing the dangling sack of my balls, teasing my rigid stem, before tenderly devouring me whole.

I don't think I can really tell you more, the agent said, rising from his padded chair. On the way out, I smiled broadly at one of the young women at a nearby desk. Asked if she was his assistant. No, just an intern. I smiled again. English accents are popular here. A possible future contact?

October 12th 1999

I know it's you, the letter said. Do not try and find me, I implore you, if you have any decency left in your body. Let me be.

Who cares about decency? What the fuck does it have to do with us? I must see you, Callie, or whatever your name really is or was, or is now, Katherine. Please, I answered, sending the letter care of the agency.

At night in my hotel room, I read her few lines a thousand times over. Smelled the paper, desperately attempting to retrieve even a trace of her scent. Two years ago, I had mentally catalogued every one of her fragrances, from the bitter sweet smell of her breath on awakening in strange, sordid hotel rooms, which she always tried to obliterate with mints, to the pungent aroma of her under-arm perspiration following our exaggerated sexual exertions, to the unique perfumes of her inner secretions which I would greedily suck from her as she spread herself open for me.

I still love you madly, I wrote her with a distinct lack of originality. And whatever I have done wrong, I beg for your forgiveness. I must see you. At least, let's talk. It kills me that I don't know the answers.

October 24th 1999

No. I swore it was over, Joe, and nothing you could say or write could make me change my mind now.

Stop stalking me. It doesn't suit you. At all.

It will soon be the year 2000. Can't you understand once and for all that I have rejected you and call an end to this sorry episode?

Do not write again. I will not answer any more.

She signed the letter Katherine Blackheath. It was just addressed to Joe. Not even Dear Joe.

How definitive she could be in her vindictiveness.

And, no, I didn't understand women.

Her words both pained and angered me. I swear we shall meet again before the bloody year 2000. Just wait and see.

November 2nd 1999

I'm seeing Stevie for drinks tonight. She's the young woman with the kind smile back at Callie's literary agency. Exploring another avenue.

Have given out almost five hundred bucks among various contacts I've been given at the immigration offices to track Katherine Blackheath down. None of them asked questions. They took the money and made vague promises.

Now, I wait.

November 3rd 1999

Stevie allowed me to kiss her briefly, as we reached the door to the flat she shared with two other ex-Bennington graduates in a Lexington Street brownstone.

I'd laid on the charm like a real hypocrite, never even hinting at the reason for my attentions.

We're eating out tomorrow night.

Her freckles make her look even younger than she is.

November 8th 1999

Stevie and I are now sleeping together. The first night was good; I didn't even have to pretend she was Callie to maintain my erection.

We went to the Hamptons for the weekend. I hired a car.

She talks too much. But then maybe I'm too quiet, and it balances out in the order of things.

But London nights are, so quickly, back in my mind again, as I wish Stevie's fingers might move a little further, a bit harder, differently, as we make love between crispy white sheets and she catches her breath in spasms under the weight of my body.

November 14th 1999

A month and a half to the Millennium. All the papers and TV news (the hotel have finally put my set right) and chat shows are already interminably rambling on the parties and celebrations on New Year's Eve. Times Square will be a killer.

Six weeks left to locate her.

It will be strange seeing her again. I know there's no point in rehearsing a speech or something, I'd forget it in her incredible presence anyway. I'll have to overcome her initial anger, of course.

She's not here on a Green Card. I have managed to determine that. Expensively. Next Sunday, I intend to ask Stevie an important favour.

November 20th 1999

No, not there, Stevie screamed as we fucked. I'm sorry, I told her, but I know she didn't believe me.

But I AM sorry. She's just the wrong person at the wrong time. I'm too rough because she's not the woman my whole body screams for in an act of madness. I don't like hurting people.

She's agreed to look up the Katherine Blackheath file some time next week, when she gets an opportunity to get into the agent's office during a lunch break. Probably Wednesday as he's booked for lunch at the Metropole Hotel for a meeting with some Bertelsmann top brass.

November 26th 1999

Stevie's provided me with an address. On Varick Street. In the Village. Must have passed the building on countless occasions.

Stevie has also said it would be better if we didn't see each other anymore. She knows I have used her.

November 28th 1999

It's a small three-storey building. There's an intercom by the front door; there are no names on two of the bells. I tried all of them. None answered. This was in the morning. Same again in the afternoon. Maybe she's working during the day. Has to make a living. I returned in the evening and the building was still empty. I lurked outside until three in the morning. Couldn't stand it any longer. Felt like a fool. Major calibre idiot. Freezing. I gave up for the day and returned to the hotel uptown.

This weekend, I'll go to Varick Street again.

December 2nd 1999

They are already spreading decorations throughout the island in preparation for the festivities. Twinkling coloured light bulbs adorn the trees around Union Square. I'm the one who's anything but cheerful.

I've finally made contact with the other two occupants of her building in the Village. They know little of her. Very quiet. Keeps to herself. Hasn't been seen around for a few weeks. The merchant banker from the top floor thought he remembered her catching a cab, holding a suitcase. Maybe a trip to the West Coast because of the film rights to the novel, I wondered?

I try her bell every two days.

Surely she'll be back for Christmas?

December 5th 1999

She misses Thanksgiving in New York.

Well, she ain't a Yank, is she?

December 10th 1999

Callie has returned.

But I managed to miss her.

She knew I'd been, though.

There was an envelope with my name hastily scrawled on it sellotaped to the bell.

How dare you follow me the way you do, Callie said. Just go away. I can't stand it any more, Joe.

She had vacated the apartment the same morning. I contacted the letting agent and visited the premises, maybe hoping she had left something, papers that might provide me with a clue to where she decamped to.

This was the bed in which she had slept.

No, I think it's too small for me, I told the realtor.

I was back to square one.

And needing her was eating me up inside like a cancer.

December 20th 1999

At last, I'm no longer running around in ever diminishing circles. I'm back on the trail. Through her erstwhile agent who had moved to L.A. I discovered that she had accepted to dine on New Year's Eve at the 42nd St Brewery that now overlooked Times Square with some studio executives who were developing her novel.

I tried to make a booking there, but it had been sold out for months for such a momentous evening. No doubt, for the view rather than the food.

December 29th 1999

My final contact in Immigration at last provided me with an address. Varick Street. A bit late in the day. I already knew she had left no forwarding address.

The *New York Post* kindly outlined the crowd control measures being put into operation for the Times Square Millennium Party on New Year's Eve.

I knew from one of the waiters that her booking was for 10.30.

The only access to the Brewery would be down 42nd Street, coming from 5th Avenue.

December 31st 1999

I await the year 2000 standing in front of the Fun City sex shop. Its neon lights turn my skin a sickly shade of pink. The window end-of-century sale advertises six hour all-anal gang bang tapes for only $9.99, but tall blondes with shaven snatches and extreme amateur debuts go for $12.99. A few yards further down, there's a security cordon of cops who check people's passes to Times Square venues.

Everything around sounds too loud.

Artificially joyful.

The sky is clear of stars.

10.15. Here she comes, sashaying down, her long legs like metronomes, her strawberry blonde hair shorter than I remembered, walking too fast as usual, her eyes full of sadness peering ahead in a myopic trance.

The crowd of revellers parts slightly as she moves nearer.

She sees me.

Not a sign of emotion.

My heart beats like the onset of a major symphony.

She approaches.

Glares at me.

'Hi,' I say.

She stays silent.

'We were bound to meet eventually,' I clumsily say, by way of excuse.

'I told you not to,' she finally answers.

The crowds whiz by on their way to the party of all parties.

'I had to see you.'

'Why?'

'Answers.'

'You know it's over. It can never be the same again.'

'You owe me some explanations.'

'No, I don't.'

'You just disappeared…' I mumble.

'You can't take rejection, can you?' she says.

'You're right. It's physical, mental, whatever, I just can't accept there's not even a diamond of hope you might listen to me again, remember the way we felt…'

'The way *you* felt.'

'Please, Callie.'

'It's Katherine, now.'

'Please.'

'No, Joe. Life is not like fiction, there are no second chances.'

'So why did you write the book?'

'A way of finally putting it all behind me, I suppose.'

I see her lips, I look into her eyes, I can feel the warmth of her body just a few inches away from me, in the cold air her breath smokes away from her mouth. Is this really the way it ends?

'Walk away now,' she asks me.

'No.'

Her features stay blank as her hand moves to the small black handbag and pulls out a small silvery gun. I don't even recognise the model.

'You wouldn't,' I say.

And move closer to her, to the familiar pale skin now shielded by winter clothes. The gun is now all that separates us.

'I would,' my sweet Callie says, a vision of terrible pain taking control of her face.

'So do it,' I order her.

She shoots me in the heart. The bang of the small gun is surprisingly unloud.

As the century recedes slowly, I see the cops over there move towards her in slow motion, their own weapons drawn.

Everything blurs around us. We are imprisoned in a pocket of time.

Callie raises her hands as the cops approach her.

'The guy was stalking me,' she says.

THE SILENT SERVER

A (Short) Detective Christy Kennedy Mystery

Paul Charles

'Aye, Sir,' began DS James Irvine in his best Sean Connery voice, which just happened to be his genuine accent. 'The body's through here.'

'Can you believe this place?' Kennedy said, his fingers flexing wildly as he found something, anything, to create his traditional distraction from the imminent viewing of a corpse.

In this particular instance the Detective Inspector was referring to a house. This remarkable house was built, not *from* trees but around one: a proud chestnut, to be exact. Someone had obviously decided that rather than go to the expense of cutting it down and then removing the roots, it would be better to leave the tree standing. So it had remained, saved from the indignity of becoming several chairs, a couple of tables or an entire floor, giving the mews house its centre (and talking-point), creating the most unique home this side of the Swiss Family Robinson's tree top.

'I've never been in a tree house before,' Irvine replied with amusement, as he looked around the four storey (including basement) mews house. He was decked out in his finest tweeds and two-tone brogues.

'It's quite incredible what they can do with space, or the lack of it,' Kennedy added observing the narrowness of the stairwell.

The Camden architect responsible for this project had obviously been inspired by something – punk hair styles by the look of the place – and he, and/or she, was clearly into light in a big way. Ninety-percent of the building front was constructed

using glass, which served to light the narrow stairwell and illu-
minate the large growth within.

Kennedy followed his Detective Sergeant down the stair
well – there wasn't even enough room for them to go down two
abreast – away from the light and into the deathly darkness of
the basement.

Kennedy, and the rest of the world, was on the threshold of
a new Millennium, minutes away from it and he was about to
investigate his first crime of the big 2000. Kennedy could think
of better, much better, ways of crossing the great divide and all
of them involved ann rea in one manner or other.

If it hadn't been for a nosy neighbour complaining about
hearing noises in the (supposedly) empty tree house, Kennedy
would have been a couple of chilled glasses of white wine the
better by this point in the evening.

Kennedy and ann rea had loosely planned to go to the Big
Bop at the Royal Albert Hall but then at the last moment they
had decided that they didn't want to be led into the next thousand years. Kennedy was trying hard not to make a big thing
about the new Millennium; the media, on the other hand, had
been on about absolutely nothing else for years.

When he examined his lack of enthusiasm for the big celebrations Kennedy kept returning to his own mortality. How
many years into the 2000's would he last? Say he even managed
to make it to the year 2030; by which time he'd be seventy-four
– old for a human, ancient for a London policeman but merely
a fly swat on mankind's windscreen, all the same.

A disturbed neighbour, a Mr Ray Martins, was hovering
around in the hallway just outside a large glass door which led,
Kennedy assumed, into the basement. Martins was in his mid-
thirties, medium height (five foot, seven inches), medium build
(eleven stone, four pounds), short dyed-blond hair. The
Detective Inspector wouldn't have been surprised if Medium
had been his middle name.

Martins had called the police because, 'They'd gone away
for the celebrations, she to Islington and he was supposedly
staying with friends in Wimbledon. The famous Tree House

was meant to be empty but I could have swore I heard these noises early this evening, about 7.45, so I figured there must be burglars in there. And that's not on, is it, on December 31st 1999? So I rang the Old Bill, didn't I?'

The 'Old Bill' at North Bridge House, Parkway, Camden Town dispatched WPC Anne Coles and PC Tony Essex to investigate. They used the keys and alarm code left with Martins to gain admission and were just about to leave when Coles thought they'd better check out the basement. They did so and found the co-keyholder, Mr Barry Griffin in exactly the same position Kennedy now saw him.

Mr Barry Griffin was 31- years-old, although he looked to be in his early forties. (Martins seemed to take great pleasure in imparting this information to Kennedy; did the neighbour think it made him look younger? the detective wondered.) He was overweight, but not fat and his shoulder length grey hair was sprawled out in a halo around his skull as he lay lifeless on the polished wooden floor. Slightly to his right and towering over him was a black wooden table ably supported by shiny chrome legs. As Kennedy knelt down he saw a distorted reflection of the corpse in the table leg closest to the body. Strangely, Griffin's right hand was in his light brown corduroy trouser pocket. The left hand was extended at right angles to the torso showing off the sleeve of his blue shirt. His waistcoat matched his trousers. His feet were covered with black flip-flops over black socks, so close in shade it was hard to figure where the flip-flops stopped and the socks took over.

◗

The first look at Griffin blew Kennedy's original theory out of the water. He had thought that Griffin, who'd not meant to be at home, had been for some reason or other. He'd simply and inconveniently disturbed the burglars. If, as was usually the case, the crime was a means of creating money for buying drugs, then the intruders would not have thought twice about attacking, and possibly even killing, the home owner. But there were no obvious marks on Griffin's person to indicate that such a struggle had taken place. Even so, the blueness of Griffin's shirt collar drew sharp attention to a ring made up of red, purple, yellow, blue and black bruising which seemed to circumnavigate the victim's throat just between his north and south chins.

The pathologist, Dr Leonard Taylor, greeted Kennedy with one of his well-rehearsed stage entrances, 'Well, old chap, not long dead if you ask me. Cheated the Millennium, didn't he? But only just, I would reckon.'

Kennedy brought Martins back into the room to effect a positive ID and all he said was, 'Are those her finger marks around Barry's neck?' as though he was seeing them for the first time. Surely he must have seen them when Coles and Essex discovered the body, thought Kennedy to himself. He determined to check on that when he'd a moment alone with Coles, but deemed it unimportant for now...

Kennedy nodded to Irvine to take the witness out of the room, they could talk more later. Then he would find out all the gossip, he was sure, about this 'her'.

In one corner of the basement, close to the cooking area was a dumb waiter. Handy, Kennedy thought, especially considering the narrowness of the stairwell. He guessed that the dining room would be at least one, if not two floors up. The basement was incredibly clean, more like a kitchen in one of the Magnet showrooms. Not a speck of dirt was visible to the naked eye. Most of the fixtures and fittings were either black or shiny chrome, including – Kennedy noted – all in a row, a large black pepper grinder, a white water purifier and electric kettle. It was as though the pepper grinder was a soldier guarding the important tea-making instruments.

The black electric kettle was plugged into a timer which in turn was plugged into one of two thirteen-amp wall sockets. This was at the extreme right hand side of the preparation deck. Just to the left of the kettle, water purifier and their guard was the hot plate of the cooker and to the right of that was a white sink and matching draining board and then, at the other end of the draining board, a white microwave oven. Kennedy studied the electric kettle and timer, evidently the occupants liked to return home from work to a freshly boiled kettle, water ready for a cup of coffee. Kennedy had decided that this was most positively a coffee drinking house and not a tea drinking establishment like his own. Perhaps, the timer was set for first thing in the AM to send them out into the cold Camden winter air with a hot coffee. Kennedy's curiosity got the better of him and he elected to find out which. The timer was set for 16.00 hours. Four o'clock in the afternoon. That was a strange time; surely a bit early in the day to get home from work, even for Camden people.

Kennedy put on a pair of the SOCO gloves and wandered over to the dumb waiter, his perfectly-polished black leather shoes creaking on the floor boards as he did so. He pressed the button marked *one*. Nothing happened. But when he pressed the button marked *two* the doors of the dumb waiter shut automatically and it crunched into action as the motor spun the wheel which wound a steel cable on to its drum. There were no additional buttons so Kennedy assumed (correctly) that the dining room was on the ground floor.

Now, with the dumb waiter stationary on the ground floor, Kennedy took the opportunity to peer into the darkness beyond the recently created hole in the wall. He borrowed a pocket torch from WPC Coles, noticing she was wearing more make up than usual. Kennedy found himself staring at her involuntarily, she blushed slightly and smiled at him. Now wasn't a good time for him to tell her that the penny had just dropped, as he realised she was still hoping to be able to make the midnight celebrations. The waiter wasn't the only dumb thing in the room, DI Kennedy thought. He used the torch to peer into the lift shaft. He could see the untreated red brick to the right, left and rear of the shaft and at the foot of the well he could see the lift motor and its mechanism. The motor was drawing its power from a thirteen amp-plug on the wall on the left hand side of the hatch.

◻

'So, whose fingermarks on his neck were you referring to?' Kennedy said, by now back in the dinning room with Martins.

'Well, his wife, Tamsin, of course. They are forever at each other's throats,' Martins replied confidently.

'Oh yeah?' Kennedy ventured, the information seemingly too good to be true.

'The marriage is, in cliché language, but a sham. It's over. They've had no time for each other for ages and in fact both now have other relationships. Well, that is if what I've seen going on is anything to go by,' Martins offered, all the time moving from foot to foot. Kennedy couldn't work out if Martins was nervous or was just feeling the cold, being dressed only in tartan slippers, no socks, blue jogging trousers and a grey sweat shirt. His nose was quite red, but Kennedy put that down to pre-Millennium liquid refreshments rather than to winter coldness. He had dyed blond hair, short back and sides with the give away brown eyebrows (bushy) and dark five o'clock shadow.

'Have you any idea where the wife, Tamsin, is?' Kennedy inquired not feeling the cold but nonetheless not feeling warm enough to remove his Crombie coat which swung about his body lightly, as he moved around. The black Crombie highlighted, in flashes, Kennedy's red waistcoat, buttoned up over a white shirt, top button done up but with no tie. Kennedy followed his question to Martins with a quick swish through his ear-length brown hair. The hair fell back into the exact same shape following the interference of his gloved fingers. He'd forgotten he was still wearing the gloves and the sensation was not exactly as disturbing as someone scraping glass with their fingernails but it wasn't pleasant either.

At that precise moment a Rover, old style, dark blue with real leather seats and wooden internal fittings, screeched to a halt out in the mews and a woman as irate as a rat trapped in a milk bottle ran through the open front door.

'What's going on here? Has there been a fire?' And then on spying Martins, 'What are *you* doing here?'

She wore a large mustard buttonless and beltless coat which was wrapped around and held tight about her waist with one hand while the other tossed the car and door keys a fair distance on to the hall table. The bunch of keys landed on one of the unopened envelopes and slid across the table past the flower pot and just missed falling to the floor by about ten millimetres.

'Raymond, what's been happening here? What's going on?'

'It's Barry, Tamsin, he's...' and Martins stopped dead in his vocal tracks as he stared over to Kennedy. His eyes were screaming at the detective to break the bad news to the wife of the house.

'Ah, look, Mrs Griffin...'

'Tamsin Peters, please. I prefer you used my maiden name.'

'Sorry, Ms Peters, I'm afraid I've some bad news for you, it's about your husband.' Kennedy continued staring directly into her brown eyes looking for something, anything. But whatever it was he was searching for, he couldn't find.

'Your husband has been found dead,' Kennedy said gently but firmly.

'Dead, dead? Where is he? What was it, his heart? Was it a heart attack? Is he at the hospital?' Tamsin Peters, nee Griffin, replied guardedly. Either she was on shock automatic or well versed in dealing with personal traumas.

'No, not his heart. He's in the basement. Ah, you shouldn't go down there without...' Kennedy began as she forced her way past him, basement bound. The wife was seemingly speechless as she ran down to the basement-cum-kitchen. She held the fingers of her right hand over her mouth as she sat down on one of the four chairs placed around the table. Again they had black wooden seats and backs, with chrome legs and arms matching the table.

'God, what happened? Did he hang himself?' she gasped through her fingers still covering her mouth. Fingers which in this position showed off, to great effect, blood red varnish upon her finger nails. Blood red was also the colour she used for her lipstick and it looked as though she had recently 'freshened it up.' Tamsin had longish black hair, down below her shoulders with a parting in the middle, a style made famous in the Sixties by Cathy MacGowan. She was good looking in a way other men's wives or girlfriends sometimes are. Attractive but not so attractive you wished you were dating them yourself. But she dressed well, took good care of herself and was probably more of a head-turner at thirty paces.

'No, not unless someone got here before us and cut him down and tidied the place up. He was exactly like this when we found him,' Kennedy answered, considering the woman before him carefully. He removed the plastic gloves and shoved them in his coat pocket. He lifted his right hand to stroke the side of his clean-shaven face.

'Was there a note or anything found in his pockets?' the wife asked, surprisingly composed, Kennedy assessed, for a recent widow.

'No,' Irvine replied as he had been responsible for the search of the body. A search which strangely enough had produced zero pocket contents, no little bits of stones or bits of pen tops, no sweet wrappings. Not even a dead match or pocket fluff, the kind which always seems to gather in the bottom of most pockets, making it harder to extract change for papers, and such, as speedily as you would like.

'I need to ask you some questions,' Kennedy started tentatively, his fingers flexing like Billy the Kid about to draw. 'But we can leave them until later. Is there anyone we can call to be with you?'

'No, no I'm fine, thank you. I have somewhere I can go, a friend. But I'd like to answer your questions first, now if you don't mind. I'd like to talk with you before the gossips get their spokes in,' Tamsin Peters answered, looking in the general direction of Martins who had followed them down the stairs.

'Let's go upstairs shall we?' Kennedy said. Never mind the widow's feelings, he didn't feel particularly comfortable questioning the corpse's wife a few feet from where Barry Griffin lay, his spirits ebbing away to somewhere. If indeed spirits existed in the first place and they had in fact anywhere to go in the second place. It never got any easier for Kennedy; this dealing with dead bodies. He wasn't squeamish or anything like that. It was just every time he came into contact with a dead person, someone recently robbed of life, and in Kennedy's line of work it was not unusual for the victims to be robbed of their most precious gift violently, he felt an overwhelming sense of sadness. He wondered often, every time he saw a corpse in fact, whether this sadness was what drove him on with such determination to find the perpetrator of the crime.

He could remember vividly when he was young, about eleven, and living in Portrush in Northern Ireland, being taken in to see his dead grandmother. And there were a bunch of people all sitting around saying, 'Doesn't she look well?' The young, and now the older, Christy Kennedy felt that was such a bizarre thing to say. His grandmother was dead for heaven's sake, how on earth could you describe her as looking well? Kennedy supposed it was just at wakes people felt a need to say something, anything, to try to comfort the relatives. So they would say things like, 'Ah, she'd a good innings, didn't she?'

Well, thought Kennedy, Barry Griffin hadn't had a particular good innings had he? At least the detective's grandmother lived to the ripe old age of 'three score and ten' as the minister had reported during her funeral service. Mr Griffin, on the other hand had been cut off in his prime. Kennedy stole one last look at the corpse before exiting the basement. This time the sadness he felt was mixed with emotions of his own mortality because of the speedily approaching Millennium. The line between life and death *is* very narrow, Kennedy thought, such an incredibly thin line to cross and none of us knew where we were going to cross to. Barry Griffin looked like he might be asleep. His life had been stolen from him, yet he looked peaceful. He looked like he had crossed the thin line with somewhere to go. But Kennedy couldn't and wouldn't believe that there was anywhere to go after death. Griffin's tranquil state was, perhaps, a state created by he or she who does, to bring comfort to those left behind.

The one left behind, Ms Tamsin Peters, was certainly behaving liked she needed little or no comfort at all. In fact when they reached the dining room she began the interview. She sat on the opposite side of the table from Kennedy; WPC Coles, under instructions from Kennedy, was off making tea.

'Well, you're going to find all of this out anyway, so I prefer to tell you myself. You've probably been given the gossip's version by Raymond Martins. But you shouldn't set too much store by what he says, he's just a trolley dolly with British Airways. Anyway, there was no love lost between Barry and myself. I mean I never would wish this kind of end to anybody, least of all him,' Peters began as she wrapped her mustard coat tight around her for warmth, perhaps even for some self-comfort, the detective reckoned. He also was surprised at how quick she was dealing with her husband in the past tense. In most cases relatives usually say things like, 'There is no love lost, Oh I'm sorry, I meant there *was* no love lost.' But not Tamsin, she had obviously already counted her husband out.

'What will I find out anyway, Ms Peters? Were you fighting?'

'Yes. Yes all the time!'

'What were the fights about? Other people? Money?' Kennedy prodded her gently.

'Well, mostly about this place really. Oh, I better explain the whole thing to you.' Peters sighed just as the tea arrived. They all helped themselves to milk and sugar from the matching black jug and bowl. Kennedy was the only one out of the three who took sugar. He stirred the tea for a long time waiting for Tamsin Peters to take up the threads of the story again. Following a few sips of the liquid comforter she did exactly that.

'Our marriage was over. History. Gone. I'd met a new man you see. These things happen and when they happen you have to deal with them,' Widow Griffin said as Kennedy blinked just a little bit too obviously. 'Yes, fine, and then he met a new woman, so I suppose we were quits in a way.'

Kennedy didn't bother to state that she'd already broken up the marriage at that point.

'The only difference was that my partner is an American and we wanted to go to America, to upstate New York, a place called Woodstock.' Kennedy guessed that Peters thought she saw a look a recognition flick in his eyes, as indeed she had.

'Yes, indeed, the name, but not the location, of the famous rock festival. So I needed a quick divorce from Barry so that Burt and I – Burt Lee that is – could marry and I could then secure a spouse visa to stay in the States. Well Barry was prepared to oblige in the quickie divorce but only if I was prepared to sign over my share in this house.'

Aha, thought Kennedy.

'Barry's main claim was that I'd have somewhere to live, with Burt, but Barry needed and wanted to continue living here. Quite simply he didn't want to sell the place in order to pay me off. He claimed he'd be able to find nothing in Camden Town for his half. I told him I didn't care if he had to go and live in the hostel in Arlington Road but I wanted my share. I mean we bought the place nine years ago for £95,000. Of course we did a lot of work on it and I figured that with all this work and the uniqueness of the building, it would be worth about £450,000. In fact I had an estate agent come and value it and he said we'd probably get about half a million pounds for it. Now my share works out at about four hundred thousand dollars, so I'm not going to leave a little nest egg like that behind now, am I?'

It was a rhetorical question and Kennedy did not retort. Instead he excused himself. Dr Taylor was making to leave and Kennedy believed (correctly) that the good Doctor had some more information for him.

'Yes, I'm quite convinced that death did occur by strangulation, old chap, and I'd guess between four thirty and five this afternoon. Oh yes, there was also a large bump on the back of his head, caused – I'd say – by a knock from a blunt object.'

'But he definitely didn't die from it, did he, the bump that is?' Kennedy inquired.

'No, positively not, although it would probably have knocked him out.'

'Is there any way of telling at what time he'd received the knock on the head?'

'No, sorry. The only thing I can tell you with a degree of certainty is that it occurred before he died. Quite a bit before I would guess because the bruising is well formed and the bump is quite large, so it had to have a chance to form before the heart stopped pumping blood,' the Doctor surmised.

'Would you hazard a guess as to how long before he died? Please, it's quite important,' Kennedy inquired looking Dr Taylor straight in his baby blues.

'It would be a guess, Christy, and nothing more than a guess at this stage but let's say for arguments sake that it happened a minimum of one and a half hours before he died. I'll know more when I open him up of course.'

'Yes of course, Doctor, I'll look forward to your report. But as usual you've been of great help,' Kennedy said as he stood on the chilly doorstep shaking hands with the Doctor and wishing him all the best for the next thousand years. Kennedy then returned to his interview with Ms Tamsin Peters.

❒

Perhaps the tea was taking effect, but upon Kennedy's return the widow seemed more content, more composed. The way she was behaving was weird, the detective felt. As in totally weird.

Yes, she and her husband were no longer together spiritually or physically but they had shared a life together. Kennedy imagined that some of the time must have been good for them to have bothered getting married in the first place.

But then marriage didn't mean all it used to in the time of Kennedy's parents. When they married, in 1948, they were choosing their partners for life. Pure and simple as that. The commitment they made on their wedding day was to stay with each other until death separated them. Trial separations, splitting up or a divorce were never available options.

They would work their way through their problems as and when they arose. This pledge to making their marriage work *made* their marriage work.

But Mr and Mrs Griffin were a different kettle of fish entirely. Although in a way death was the reason they had been separated. Their boat had hit the stormy seas of life and instead of fighting to steer it through the troubled waters they had selfishly deserted the boat and jumped overboard, each for themselves and swam separately to the safety of the nearest dry land leaving their boat, or marriage, to shatter to pieces on the rocks.

Now one of them was dead and, for Kennedy, the strange thing was the behaviour of the survivor. She seemed more concerned about her looks than about her dead husband. A death is a death and no matter the feelings between them, surely Tamsin Peters should be showing some remorse. They must have made love after all. How could you once have shared life's most intimate magic with someone and not grieve their passing in some way?

The Detective Inspector had a hunch, a long shot he knew, and if it didn't work out correctly, the repercussions from Superintendent Thomas Castle would be severe. However, if Kennedy's hunch paid off, the rewards would be very satisfying, hewould have saved a lot of precious police time and, consequently, Castle's budget. The way the Superintendent hoarded the funds made you think that all the Camden CID budget came out of Castle's personal account. This of course was impossible since Castle was a man with short hands and deep pockets.

'Mrs Tamsin Griffin,' Kennedy announced, choosing to address the widow by her official legal title, 'I am arresting you for the murder of your husband, Mr Barry Griffin. I must caution you that you don't have to say anything but it may harm your defence if you say something later in court you did not say. Anything you do say will be taken down and can be used in evidence against you.'

Kennedy couldn't work out who was in the greater shock. Peters or WPC Coles. At least Coles had the subtlety not to show it *too* much.

'What? What on earth are you on about?' Tamsin Peters smiled, first at Kennedy and on finding no solace in his eyes, turned her attention to the WPC, who appeared to be equally unforgiving.

Kennedy decided that he needed to continue on now ruthlessly, strike with his advantage for whatever it was worth.

'I will show you, if you care to accompany me back down to the basement, exactly how you murdered your husband.'

'But I wasn't here, I was with friends all afternoon in Ellington Street in Islington. I can get some of them on the phone if you wish?' Peters pleaded.

Kennedy allowed himself a moment of satisfaction.

If Peters had said anything other than the words she just spoken, then he would have been worried. Anything else, like simply pleading her innocence, that 'she didn't do it', then Kennedy would have felt the shadow of Castle towering over him.

But to evoke an alibi so quickly and so precisely was exactly what he wanted. It was Kennedy's logic that people mostly, at least those connected with crime, have an alibi only if they need one. And if they needed one that badly, well... Kennedy didn't want to go putting the cart before the horse, that was all for later.

At this point Taylor had instructed the SOC team to bag the body and remove it to the morgue in St Pancras All Saint's Hospital so that he could carry out the PM, hopefully quickly enough so as not to interfere with his Millennium celebrations. The portly doctor was having a few of his theatrical friends over to his place in Belsize Village to see in the New Year, and more, with a bang.

Two police officers had great difficulty in carrying the body bag and contents up the narrow curving stairwell. Kennedy, Coles, Irvine and their number one (and only) suspect waited until the body was through the front door before they proceeded in line to the basement. They sat around the table and Peters took a pen out from her inside pocket and started to fidget with it.

'Before we start I wonder if my WPC could borrow your car keys, I noticed you placed them on the table,' Kennedy said.

Maybe Peters thought he wanted the Rover moved so that they could let the vehicle carrying her dead husband through, or perhaps she didn't care, but either way she said, 'Fine.'

Kennedy nodded to Coles to follow him and as they reached

the door to the stairwell he put his arm around her shoulder and whispered something through a fragrance as fresh as Donegal coastal winds. He obviously was giving Coles some instructions but neither Irvine nor Peters could hear the details as Kennedy and Coles' backs were to them and Kennedy was speaking in a very soft lilt.

Coles gone, Kennedy put on his gloves again and crossed the room to the preparation area where the electric kettle and purifier were situated. Kennedy removed the timer from the wall and fiddled with it a bit, appearing to reset it. He then moved to the dumb waiter and pressed the button marked *one* and the lift returned from the first floor to the basement, the doors automatically opening as it reached its resting place. Kennedy pressed the button marked *two* and the doors closed again and the lift moved upwards towards the ground floor again. When it was but a few feet on its heavenward journey Kennedy reached into the hole in the wall the lift's departure had just created. He removed the thirteen amp plug from its socket. As he did this they all could hear the motor grind to a halt.

Next, Kennedy placed the timer in the thirteen amp socket the lift motor plug had just vacated and he in turn placed the very same plug into the timer.

He now returned to the table and waited in silence. Not one of the trio spoke. The only sound was the sound from the second hand of the clock on the wall as it edged its way to the year 2000. Eighty-three of these ticks could have been counted before WPC Coles returned to the basement. She was carefully carrying a ten foot piece of nylon rope in a ring made with her thumb and forefinger.

'It was exactly where you predicted, sir, in the boot of Mrs Griffin's car,' Coles confidently announced.

Peters visibly sank an inch or two into her chair. Kennedy wasn't sure if this was from the WPC addressing her incorrectly or from the appearance of the rope. He assumed it had a lot to do with the rope.

Kennedy carefully took the rope from Coles and returned to

the open hatch of the dumb waiter. He reached up to the under-side of the mobile portion of the lift and threaded the rope through the iron hook the steel cable was attached to, he tied the rope to this hook. He then removed his Crombie coat and tied the other end of the rope to the eye on the inside collar. He dropped the coat to the floor where it lay on a heap close to the open mouth of the lift.

The Detective Inspector returned to the table and took his seat. Again they waited in silence, this time, though, Peters echoed the ticks of the clock by tapping her pen on the table in time. It took one hundred such ticks before the timer activated itself releasing electricity, via the thirteen-amp plug, to the lift motor which charged into action and continued its interrupted journey towards the ground floor. The rope and Kennedy's Crombie coat followed.

'Great, excellent. So Camden's CID know how to make a timer and lift work and how to pull a coat up from the floor. I can sleep easier now knowing that my taxes are well spent,' Peters half shouted, trying hard to force some laughter into her voice.

'Well, yes, Ms Peters, it is as simple as that. In order to achieve your alibi you hit your husband over the head with the pepper grinder as he sat down here in the basement reading a newspaper, having a cup of tea, or whatever. At two-thirty this afternoon you knocked him unconscious but didn't kill him. That came later. You fixed the rope around his neck and the other end to the underside of the lift. You set the timer to acti-vate at a time, four o'clock, when you would be over in Ellington Street in Islington entertaining your alibi. The lift sprang into action just as it did just now. As the lift climbed upwards, the rope pulling against the dead weight of your unconscious husband tightened, eventually raising him from the floor, just as far as the hatch, and strangled him,' Kennedy offered in his quiet voice to the captive audience. He let all of this sink in before he continued.

'Your motive? Simply to rid yourself of your husband and head off to Woodstock, a newly married woman eight hundred thousand dollars the richer.'

Peters made to say something but Kennedy refused to allow her to speak, 'You needn't plead your innocence. The rope the WPC found in the boot of the car was the one used for your crime. I bet we'll find rope hair fragments about the body and on the underside of the dumb waiter.'

'I was about to say, that's not how it happened,' Peters began with such conviction that Kennedy's heart sank, 'I didn't want to do anything as gross as hitting him on the head with the pepper grinder. At least you didn't suggest I was a washer woman and hit him over the head with a rolling pin. No, I spiked his drink with a couple of two milligram Rohypnol tablets, you know, Roofies? The date rape drug. I was able to buy, through a friend of Burt's, three of them for a tenner, would you believe. I thought it was quite ironic to use the drug men use to have power over women back on them. I figured this would put Barry in a comatose state and allow me to carry out the plan you've just described,' Tamsin boasted. The members of Camden CID listened, some in disbelief, as she continued.

'But the pills turned out to be very effective on Barry. Maybe he'd too much to drink or whatever but he literally fell unconscious in front of my eyes, collapsed out of his chair and banged his head on the table leg on the way down to the ground. He was a total dead weight and proved very difficult to manoeuvre over to the lift and even harder to pull back over to the table afterwards. If only that nosy parker next door hadn't disturbed me tidying up. He came in and wandered around, but he didn't come down here. Then he left, I figured he'd gone back to his house to ring for you guys, so I had to get out quick and didn't manage to do the job properly. But if I had more time I would have disposed of the rope and covered up my tracks a bit better. Then you guys wouldn't have found the body 'til after the Millennium. Then the neighbours from across the mews rang me at Burt's telling me there was a big fuss going on at my house and I thought it would appear natural if I rushed over.'

The widow sighed at this point and put her head in her hands. Her shame not from killing her husband but for being found out.

Irvine and Coles were speechless. A case for the *Guinness Book of Records*. Mrs Griffin, nee Peters, would be booked by the ever reliable custody sergeant, Tim Flynn, and in the cells within eight hours of committing her crime.

The members of Camden CID were now free to party all night, through the 2000 year barrier, knowing that those unlucky enough to be on duty first thing tomorrow morning, would be starting off a new day, week, month, year, decade, century and Millennium with a clean slate, thanks to Detective Inspector Christy Kennedy.

Kennedy's sole resolution? To play as the first music of the new Millennium the Beatles', 'Tomorrow Never Knows', not because it was his favourite Beatles song but because it caught his mood...

BEAUTY WITH CRUELTY

David Bowker

There are approximately nine hundred hereditary peers in Britain, but only one of them hunts members of her own class for pleasure. This thought brought a faint smirk to my face as I reached the end of Francis Rachel street. I was now facing Victoria's silver clock tower, a modest structure that, for want of any genuine tourist attractions, all guides to the Seychelles are obliged to mention. A full minute passed before I deemed it safe to cross the road – drivers in this part of the world rarely give signals or wait for pedestrians. Then I walked up Albert Street, towards the Roman Catholic Cathedral.

I've never been ashamed of my noble origins. Why apologise for that which is beyond your control? It's just that I've always believed that one human life should not be valued over another. Or that those who behave without honour, regardless of their wealth and station, should escape unpunished.

My name is India St Just. I became a Countess when my brother Josh, the eleventh Earl of Penwith, was killed in action, although I don't bother with the title unless I need to intimidate tradespeople or want a good restaurant table. Lord Lucan, the man I'd been searching for, disappeared on November 7th, 1974, when I was seven years old. At the time, not understanding, I thought the roguishly handsome man on the cover of every newspaper looked witty and rather sexy and must therefore be innocent of the crime of which he stood accused. Now, a quarter of a century later, it seemed as if the world viewed the absent Earl with a similar child-like indulgence. Guilty or not, Lucan had escaped, he was either old and decrepit or already dead, but above all he had been one hell of a character. Besides, it had all happened long ago. What did it matter anymore?

The seventh Earl of Lucan was guilty. That fact was beyond question. But the world had always found his legendary elusiveness more interesting than the murder he had committed. His face appeared in advertisements, in comedy programmes, as the visual joke in the background. (And guess who's propping up the bar? Why, it's your friend and mine, Lucky Lucan.) He would always be remembered for vanishing off the face of the earth, not for taking the life of an innocent woman. Lucan, the disappearing peer. Good luck to him.

I took a rather different view. I had time on my hands and money to burn. And after talking to the Earl's surviving friends, who still wondered, as they had always wondered, why a good man had been driven into hiding by the death of a servant, a mere nanny, I was fired with the necessary venom.

This was why, on the 31st of December, 1999, I found myself on Mahé, the largest island in the Seychelles. I, or rather the Trust that represents me, had received a tip-off from a most unlikely quarter. A priest from the village of Cascade, learning of my crusade, had written to us in connection with the disappearance of a prostitute. Officially, there were no prostitutes in the Seychelles.

Officially, there were no dishonest police officers or corrupt bureaucrats on the islands, either. In any event, the priest's communication had been promising enough to bring me halfway across the world in an overcrowded Boeing 767.

Normally, I travelled in luxury. If the only available airlines could not provide that luxury, I made my own arrangements. But it had been important to arrive in the Seychelles without fuss or ceremony. If Lucan was living here, then he would undoubtedly have powerful and influential friends. (A strange fact about this man: he always inspired affection and loyalty wherever he went.)

The heat and humidity were oppressive. I was pouring with sweat as I climbed the steps to the Cathedral of the Immaculate Conception, despite the lightness of my white Workers for Freedom dress.

When I reached the arched entrance the Cathedral clock, Le Clocher, began to sound the hour. It was noon. A few minutes later, the bell would chime again, for the benefit of those who failed to hear it the first time. In the tropics, people tend to move and act slowly in order to economise on energy. If you want something, you often have to ask twice.

The Cathedral was only marginally cooler than the street outside. My contact was waiting for me by the altar, a small black man with a round, child-like face. He was about forty, and he grinned as I approached, unable to disguise his wonder and admiration. And who can blame him?

'Countess St Just?'

He gave my name its French pronunciation. I promptly corrected him. 'St Just. To rhyme with "faint lust".'

Father Germain blushed. I had never seen a black person blush before. Bowing his head, he clasped my right hand in both of his. 'You look just as in your photograph.'

I drew back in mock-indignation. 'You mean I look like a photograph in *Hello* magazine?'

It amused me that an unauthorised telephoto lens shot of myself should have appeared in a publication that was normally dedicated to 'exclusive pictures of the Right Honourable Humphrey Staines, his wife Tilly and their beautiful new daughter, Olympia.' (This next to a photograph of a rich, sun-tanned fifty-year-old sod, his blonde, vapid, twenty-eight-year-old handmaiden and a baby fresh from the roof of Notre Dame Cathedral.)

The Priest looked puzzled. 'I mean you look just as young. And beautiful.'

'Who did you expect? Miss Marple?'

He laughed uncertainly. Perhaps he was unsettled by my brash manner. Perhaps he'd simply never heard of Miss Marple. He said: 'Did you come alone?'

'Of course.' I didn't particularly care for his question, so felt no compunction about lying.

The priest bowed his head and reapplied his hands to mine. His palms were hot and wet. 'Your grace, I am overwhelmed that you have travelled all this way to see me.'

I extricated my hand from his grasp and surreptitiously wiped it on the hip of my dress. 'I came for selfish reasons, Father. And please – although I have a title, I prefer not to use it. My friends call me India.'

'Yes.' Father David Germain smiled as he raised his eyes to heaven. 'We are all equal in the sight of God.'

I said: 'Don't believe in God.' The priest reacted as if he had been slapped. 'Don't believe we're all equal, either.'

We sat down, directly before the cross of Christ. Feeling the priest's discomfort, I sighed. 'I'm sorry, Father. I didn't mean to be rude. It was a long flight. I didn't get much sleep.'

'No. It is I who should apologise.' His English was slow and precise, with a mild Creole accent. 'It is a fault of mine, I know… to confuse goodness with Christianity.'

Flicking my hair away from my eyes, I resisted the urge to make matters worse by denying my alleged goodness. 'Please. Just tell me what I need to know. We don't have a great deal of time.'

Once again, hurt flickered in Germain's eyes. Men can be such babies… I clasped his arm to reassure him. Hesitantly, he began. 'Her name was Simone Savy. She was nineteen years of age.'

'Was?'

'I would like to believe that Simone is still alive. But I cannot believe this, for two reasons. Firstly, Simone was a kind-hearted girl. She would not have absented herself from her family, leaving them sick with worry, without giving some sign of her whereabouts.

'Secondly, I have prayed and prayed to God that if Simone is alive, he should send me a sign of some kind. I have received no such sign. I trust in my redeemer, so must conclude that Simone is not living.'

I nodded cautiously. So far, I was not favourably impressed by the man's powers of deduction.

'I have known Simone Savy since she was a small child,' resumed the priest. 'A very bright girl, that nobody bothered with. She had many brothers and sisters. The mother and father never worked or helped themselves and expected others to feed them. Not bad people, just shiftless. You know the sort I mean.'

I smiled and nodded. 'In England we have a family called the Windsors who behave in much the same way.'

The priest ignored the pleasantry. 'I will be honest with you,' he stated proudly. 'I am Seychellois. I love the place of my birth. But certain things about our life here are difficult to defend. Here, most people are of mixed race. But some are almost exclusively of European origin, and, well, there exists a most definite hierarchy, with the palest skinned people taking high government posts and enjoying the best of everything, the Asian people coming second, and...'

He hesitated. I completed his sentence for him. 'The blackest people coming last. And I take it that Simone Savy is as black as you are?'

Father Germain drew back slightly, once again shocked by my lack of tact. 'She is of mainly African blood, yes.'

'And was she beautiful?'

'Yes. Her beauty was the cause of all her joys – and all of her woes. She was noticed, when she was still quite young. A man called Gilbert Lazare – a son of the devil – picked her up after school one day and offered to act as her "business manager". Lazare is well-connected, and you can guess what kind of business he is involved in...'

I sighed wearily. If only sinners could be more original. 'So despite Simone's unfortunate skin-tone, the whites in high government posts still managed to find a use for her.'

'You are most astute, my lady.'

'No, Father. Just cynical.'

'Simone had no illusions about herself. She was a sinner, and she knew it. But I ask you to contemplate the enormous temptation posed by wealth and influence, to a woman who would otherwise have had nothing.' The Seychellois clenched both fists and shook them for emphasis. 'Nothing! Just think. Suddenly, Simone found that she was able to support her entire family with her immoral earnings. She bought herself a fine house, down the shore from the President's weekend home. She was genuinely happy with her lot. Until three months ago, when she came to me in a state of great distress.

'She had suffered a terrible ordeal on an island called Oubliette. Have you heard of a British man called Ashley Moore?'

'No.'

'Ashley Moore is the richest man in the Seychelles. He owns Oubliette. He hired Simone for the weekend. She was made to do disgusting things.'

'What sort of things?'

He frowned in disapproval. 'Please. Surely I don't have to go into detail.'

'You mean you don't know?'

Father Germain glared back defiantly. 'I did not ask. But I know Simone. She would not have lied to me. I saw the bruises on her face. The burns upon her wrists and ankles, where the cords with which they bound her...' He shook his head, unable to finish his sentence.

Le Clocher chimed again. We waited in silence until the soulful voice of the great bell had died away. Then the priest resumed his account. 'Simone told me that Ashley Moore took no part in her humiliation. Most of the abuse was either inflicted by or at the instruction of another man. A tall Englishman in late middle age.' Father Germain had been gazing up at the altar. With these words, he turned to fix me with his moist, soulful eyes. 'Simone heard Moore call the old man by name. One name only. He called him "Lucky".'

I felt a warm surge of excitement which was immediately replaced by doubt. Lucan had never been interested in women. His main passions had always been gambling and money. Nor was it likely that a man in his late sixties had suddenly developed a taste for debauchery. 'And why didn't Simone go to the police… show them her bruises?'

The priest laughed good-naturedly. 'Have you any idea what the police are like on these islands? Even if they had believed her, what do you imagine they would have done about it? Ashley Moore is well connected. Simone was a whore. When she came back from Oubliette, she was a nervous wreck. But Gilbert Lazare assured her that she had been a resounding success, that her services on Oubliette would be required again, and that any failure to indulge such prestigious clients might prove dangerous for her family's well-being.'

'He threatened her.'

'Of course. Isn't that how all pimps operate? But Simone was proud. She refused to comply. Two weeks later, she went missing.'

'What about her family?'

'They live. Praise be to God.'

'And you think that Simone was killed by her pimp?'

'No. Lazare is a wicked man, but I do not believe he is a murderer. Simone was killed by someone from Oubliette. I believe this with all my heart.'

'And you think she died because she'd seen – and heard – too much?'

The priest nodded vigorously. 'Most of all, because she could not be trusted to remain silent. Since her disappearance, I have been unable to think of anything else. I am sure that because of what Simone knew, because she dared to say "enough", she was murdered. There will be no justice for her, the world will never know or care that she existed, because she was a lowly person. But our Lord Jesus Christ cared about the lowly, and so do I, which is why, in Simone's name, I am offering you the Englishman that you have been searching for…'

'Tell me something: how do you know all this?'

Father Germain's eyes filled with tears. 'I was Simone's confessor.'

I nodded slowly. The priest took out a handkerchief and wiped his eyes. During the ensuing silence, he noticed the Chinese Dragon tattooed on my left shoulder. His eyes widened.

'This Lucan,' he said at last. 'What was his crime?'

I told him what I knew, being no more than most people knew: that Richard John Bingham, the seventh Earl of Lucan, went missing from his Belgravia flat on the same night that Sandra Rivett, his children's nanny, was bludgeoned to death with a length of lead piping. Lucan had been living apart from his estranged wife at the time, and had been attempting to win custody of their children.

In short, Lady Lucan was not his favourite person. The police and the inquest jury shared the view that Lucan had murdered Sandra Rivett by accident, mistaking her for his wife. Then, realising his error, he had tried to strangle Lady Lucan, lost heart at the last moment and fled.

Some of Lucan's friends had attempted to promote the theory that Lucan, as a man of honour, would have committed suicide rather than live with the shame of his crime. The only flaw in this argument was that a man of honour would not have clubbed a defenceless woman to death.

Three years ago, I attended a dinner party thrown by my Uncle Jack. Among the guests was Perry Schmidt, a wealthy financier, formerly one of Lucan's closest friends. After downing more than his fair share of Calvados, Schmidt had started bragging about how easy it had been to make a fortune in the early seventies. One of the guests had asked how close Schmidt had been to Lucan before his disappearance. Schmidt had silenced the table by replying that their relationship had only really blossomed *since* the Earl's disappearance. Despite the curiosity of his fellow diners, the smug financier had conceded no further information.

When the guests had gone home, I quizzed my uncle.

Unable to shed further light on the matter, he owned up to being greatly surprised by Schmidt's outburst. I was sufficiently intrigued to read everything I could find pertaining to the case. And when I saw a photograph of the murdered nanny, my interest became an obsession. Because although the world had heard of Lord Lucan, the name Sandra Eleanor Rivett meant nothing to anyone besides her family and friends.

I have only ever seen one photograph of Sandra Rivett; the same snapshot that appears in all those books with titles like: *Lucan: Living or Dead?* In this photograph, Mrs Rivett looks like the kind of woman with whom one could easily pass an enjoyable evening. She has a wide smile. There is a distinctly humorous gleam in her eyes. She appears to be wearing a typical seventies wig: long, straight, shoulder length hair that curls upwards at the ends. In this photograph – and I promise you that I'm not being remotely sentimental – Sandra Rivett looks like a very nice woman indeed.

Add to this the knowledge that the victim was five feet two inches tall, a foot smaller than her killer. Had Mrs Rivett survived, the blows that dented her skull would have left her badly brain damaged. The actual cause of death had been suffocation, caused by internal bleeding. Blood from the lining of her battered skull had quickly filled her throat and lungs. Only coughing would have prolonged her life, and the comatose, as a rule, do not cough.

I related all of this to Father Germain, who listened with quiet respect. When I had finished, he smiled. 'So both of us, in our own ways, keep faith with the dead.'

'I'm sure the dead are past caring,' I said flippantly. 'But I won't stop until I've found Lucan. I think he's a callous bastard and I'm going to make him pay for what he did.' I stretched my arms and yawned. 'Now, how do I get to Oubliette?'

Father Germain wiped his eyes with his sleeve and smiled like a small boy whose mother has told him to be brave.

'Tonight there is a grand Millennium ball at Ashley Moore's home. Only the most wealthy and influential people on the islands have been invited. Several boats have been chartered to ferry the guests to the ball. I know the captain of one of them. A South African gentleman. His name is Oliver Raphaely. His boat is *La Belle Marie*. Oliver is a good man, a very good friend of mine. Tell him that I sent you, and he will overlook your lack of an invitation. Be at the jetty for sundown.'

We rose and shook hands.

'I will pray for your safety.' He removed a slim prayer-book from his jacket, opened it and passed me a small crumpled pass-port-sized snap. It was a photograph of a spectacularly attrac-tive black girl with huge eyes, a wide sharply-defined jaw and a long, graceful neck. 'It is not very recent, but that is her. That is Simone.'

'Can I keep it?'

'But of course… if it will help you.'

I thanked him, and walked away, leaving Germain standing alone at the altar. I didn't look back in case he waved.

❏

A ten year old Mercedes was waiting on the road below. The driver honked the horn as I approached. The door opened. I peered in to see an overweight forty-year-old man smiling up at me. His name was Christopher John Bromley. The quality of Bromley's smile was largely dependent on whether or not he was wearing his false tooth. He had a gap in his teeth, for which he sometimes wore a denture. Today, his denture was out. Today was a bad smile day.

As I stepped into the car, I opened a new pack of Gitanes and lit one. Bromley tutted, right on cue. To annoy him, I blew a lungful of smoke in his general direction. He sighed, rolled down his window, and took the winding south-west road, towards Barbarons.

'This the best car they had?'

He grunted in affirmation, then cast another baleful glance at my cigarette.

'You're smoking like a beagle,' he said. It was one of Bromley's favourite jokes, a reference to a scandal that I was too young to remember; an experiment to determine the effect of tobacco smoke on the lungs of chain-smoking dogs. Not surprisingly, the effect of cigarette smoke on these unfortunate animals was nausea, illness and death.

'You're smelling like one,' I answered indifferently, gazing out of the window as we sped across the island. The Mercedes clung to the extravagant bends with impressive ease. The light was intense, so that everything from passing cars to the washing hanging outside the wooden shacks looked as if it had been digitally enhanced. The blossoms of the flame trees, the hibiscus and the begonias burned vividly in the afternoon shade.

'Nice island,' I commented.

Bromley sniffed. 'May look it on the surface. But you can smell the corruption underneath. This whole place reminds me of a beautiful cradle with a really ugly baby in it.'

I laughed rudely.

'What's funny?'

'That must be just about the worst analogy I've ever heard in my life.'

Unruffled, he said: 'You've obviously never read anything by Jeffrey Archer.' After a silence, he asked what I'd learned in the cathedral. I told him. When I'd finished, he made an odd groaning sound in his throat.

'What's the matter now?'

Bromley shook his head, hardly knowing where to begin. 'You've got no idea, have you? What if he's lying to you?'

'He's a priest.'

'What if he's a lying priest?'

'Lucan's here. I feel it.'

Bromley snorted sceptically.

I had never quite known how to treat the man who had been acting as my aide for the past eighteen months. He had a permanent limp, earned in the Falklands, where he'd served in the same SAS squadron as my brother. Looking at Bromley now, with his untrimmed moustache and his considerable paunch, I found it incredible that he'd ever been part of the British Army's most prestigious regiment. As a human being, Bromley was immensely likable but as a personal assistant, he left much to be desired. He was rude, he was insubordinate, and he was forever finding fault with his employer's thought processes.

He said: 'I just hope you know what you're doing. That's all.'

'What are you talking about?'

'This obsession of yours. If it's upper class criminals you're after, England's full of 'em. What did we have to come all this way for?'

It was a perfectly reasonable question, for which I had no ready answer.

At Barbarons, we checked into Le Meridien, a modest establishment without a casino. But the hotel was quiet and unobtrusive, and no-one would expect a rich woman to be staying there. In the long, open-plan lobby, a porter offered to carry our cases. Bromley, inexplicably, insisted on carrying them himself. There was a brief dispute, which Bromley won by picking up the cases and walking off. We were booked into neighbouring suites, facing the pool.

'Be ready by about six,' I reminded him.

'What for?'

'I need a lift to the marina.'

'Why can't you drive there yourself?'

'Because I want *you* to drive me.'

'I'm too bloody hot to run about after you.'

Bromley unlocked the door to his room and pushed his bag inside. As he returned to remove his key from the lock, I nodded at my own case. 'What about this?'

I unlocked the door and Bromley, grumbling, bundled the suitcase inside. 'What did your last servant die of?'

'He didn't die. I sacked him.'

I left Bromley swearing under his breath and entered my suite. It lacked grandeur but was perfectly adequate, apart from the rather tacky plastic swordfish on the wall above the bed. At least the air conditioning worked. I undressed and took a long, cool shower. After drying myself, I lay on the bed and closed my eyes. In moments, I fell into a deep, untroubled sleep.

❒

I awoke shortly after five, feeling dizzy and disorientated. I drank some mineral water and took another shower to revive myself. Still dripping, I opened my case and laid out a black gown on the bed. Then I ordered a pot of strong coffee and a well-done fillet steak from room service. When the meal arrived, I ate slowly, chewing each mouthful to pulp in order to extract as much energy from my food as possible.

Then I rinsed my face and hands and dressed. (I never wear make up or perfume and consider jewellery to be vulgar in the extreme.) Tonight, I was wearing a black silk hooded creation by Issey Miyake. Carefully, I lifted the hood over my hair. The effect was dramatic. I looked like a first class bitch.

❐

La Belle Marie was waiting at the marina, a gleaming white passenger cruiser with a blue dolphin painted on its side. The boat was full of middle-aged men with overhanging midriffs and bored second wives who shopped but didn't eat. I approached the small, powerfully built islander who was standing on the jetty, clipboard in hand, collecting the passengers' tickets and crossing their names off a list. His only greeting was a sharp upwards tilt of the head.

I said: 'Father Germain sent me.'

The ticket collector shrugged arrogantly. 'Ticket.'

'Could I speak to Mr Raphaely?'

With an exaggerated show of reluctance, the Seychellois turned and whistled to someone on board the vessel. A sandy haired man, dressed entirely in white, made his way through the chattering throng on deck and leaned over the boat rail. Oliver Raphaely was in his early fifties. He had the snub nose, the broiled lobster complexion and the mean, narrow eyes that I associate with the most bigoted breed of Afrikaaner. The hard eyes narrowed further at the sight of me, but my obvious wealth forced him to exercise caution. 'Mademoiselle?'

I told him that Father Germain had sent me.

With this, the South African's suspicions evaporated. 'Yes, yes, of course.' He nodded vigorously and waved me aboard. The Seychellois guarding the deck grinned and bowed as I embarked, as if he'd secretly been rooting for me all along.

I sat astern, slightly removed from the local socialites. I lit a cigarette and gazed out to sea. A few moments later, Raphaely approached, carrying a pink bottle and an empty glass. Without consulting me, he filled the glass and held it out to me.

'No thank you,' I said, peering at the label on the bottle. 'Never touch the stuff.'

'You don't drink champagne?'

'Well, yes. But that isn't champagne. It's sparkling wine.'

He grimaced. His shoulders stiffened. 'You know, my lady, that is not very polite. *Debrett's Correct Form* advises that it is always better to tell a white lie than to hurt someone's feelings.'

'Fuck Debrett.'

Raphaely exhaled noisily, then laughed. Shaking his head in good-humoured despair, he walked away. A small black boy who ought to have been home in bed loosed the mooring rope and climbed aboard. The engine rattled and roared into life. Then *La Belle Marie* slowly pulled away from the jetty.

The white boat slewed pleasantly through the calm waters, setting a north-westerly course. As we left port, I looked back towards Mahé. The island was a long fertile hump, teeming with vegetable and criminal life.

I thought about Roger Jowett, one of the main reasons I had leapt at this chance to escape England. Jowett was a married man that I'd been enjoying a casual affair with. Unfortunately, the affair had only been casual on my side. On Boxing Day, without consulting me, he left his wife and children and turned up on my doorstep. I gave him a brandy and a mince pie and was then forced to admit that although I had enjoyed sex with Roger, I had no wish to share my life with him. Undeterred, he had subjected me to hourly phone calls and thrice-daily flowers. After such virulent persecution, my current escapade seemed like a rest-cure.

I glanced up to see that Raphaely had returned. He now brandished an ice bucket containing a bottle of Moet & Chandon. 'Is this good enough?' he inquired sweetly.

It wasn't, but I didn't have the heart to snub the man twice. I smiled sweetly and nodded. Almost gratefully, Raphaely filled the glass and passed it to me. His face suddenly became serious. 'You know, it is not too late to change your mind. You could stay on the boat at Oubliette. We would return you to Mahé, and no one would be any the wiser.'

'Is Oubliette such a dangerous place?'

He leant towards me, and in a low voice said: 'For you, *yes*.'

'Meaning?'

'Only this, Mademoiselle.' He patted my arm lightly. 'That those who look for trouble usually find it.'

Then Raphaely joined his guests, who were gathering to toast the last sunset of the twentieth century.

❒

Oubliette is a small heart-shaped island to the north of La Digue. Tonight, it was a heart that glittered. A thousand tiny fires lined the shore. Red, white and green lights, the colours of the Seychellois flag. Sega music pulsed out across the water, beckoning *La Belle Marie* and its passengers. The bright lanterns on the long jetty caught the prow of a gleaming white yacht. *La Belle Marie* moored between the yacht and a fishing boat. Two servants in evening dress helped the illustrious passengers ashore. Raphaely leaned against the rail, moodily watching me disembark. 'Good luck,' he shouted after me. I gave him a cool nod of thanks and walked on.

Although the sun had set, the heat and humidity were still murderous. I followed the other guests up a twisting flight of carved stone steps. As we climbed, I glanced back at the ocean and saw the lights of several boats drawing in from all directions. Hordes of birds shrieked and clattered in the trees above and around us. Finally, a white colonial-style house came into view, large but unobtrusive, perfectly in sympathy with the dimensions of the island. A five-piece sega band were playing on a verandah at the side of the Moore residence. Most of the guests stood on the floodlit lawns and gardens surrounding the house. So far, no one had plucked up the courage to dance.

I suddenly felt extraordinarily out of place. For me, this was a novel sensation. Normally, I'm at home wherever I invite myself. Here, however, I knew no one. Yet everyone seemed to be aware of me. Wherever I walked, the elegant guests turned their heads to whisper and stare.

I entered a huge baronial style dining room and wandered over to the buffet table. With the help of an attentive caterer, who explained what all the unfamiliar dishes contained, I filled a plate with sliced yam, curried beans, breadfruit and raw red snapper, seasoned with nutmeg and ginger. An elegantly dressed man in his sixties was standing a few yards to my left, leering with anticipation of the night's promise as he poured wine into the ever-empty glass of a young, melon-breasted blonde. The man's hair was jet-black and the shape of an onion-seller's beret. I turned my back on the President and his unfortunate toupee and stepped out into the sweltering night.

I ate alone, perched on the wall of an ornamental fountain. Behind my back, a swordfish spewed pink foam from its bronze jaws. The food was delicious; particularly the raw snapper, which I guessed had been caught that afternoon.

For the next two hours I wandered alone through the party guests, until a tall, blandly handsome opportunist cornered me by the bar and asked me to dance. I didn't want to dance so we talked, while the band, improbably, sang: 'Sega-sega, gotta sega, if you wanna be loved.'

My would-be suitor, a New Zealander, enthused about the Country and Western club he was about to launch in Mahé.

'Have you any idea how big Country music is here? Makes no difference that it's recorded by North American rednecks. The blacks here love it. Really love it.'

When the Country & Western Kiwi returned to the bar to fetch cocktails, I escaped. I walked to the tip of the lawn and sat alone on a wooden bench, flanked by two old naval cannons that kept eternal watch over the horizon. Between the land and the sky, I sensed rather than saw the black curved immensity of the Indian ocean. I guessed that in daylight, this would be a wonderful place to sit and to dream, watching the sunlight glittering on the waves, feeling the island vibrate with life.

I heard a faint sound behind me. I turned and saw the silhouette of a woman. She had her back to the house, so I could not see her face. 'Countess India?' The voice was soft and young.

'Yes. Who is it?'

'Would you come with me, please?'

I felt a sharp pang of disquiet. She turned and walked down the sloping lawn. I picked up my bag and caught up with her. She was Seychellois, tall and bejewelled, a diamond necklace accentuating her long Modigliani neck. When she turned to smile at me, I swore under my breath. It was Simone Savy.

'Simone?'

She nodded and gave me a limp handshake that was worthy of a fashion model. 'Enchanté.'

'So you're alive? And quite well?' The young woman shrugged apologetically. I stared at her for a long time before speaking again. 'I met Father Germain today. He seemed to think you were in some kind of trouble.'

Simone nodded. 'Yes. Father Germain told us you were coming.'

A prickling coldness rose from the nape of my neck to the crown of my head. 'What did you say?'

'He said you were coming. Didn't you want to meet John?'

I mumbled idiotically.

'John Bingham? I thought you wanted to meet him?'

I nodded slowly. So Bromley had been right. What a bloody fool I'd been. Cheerfully, Simone took me by the arm. 'Come on. Let me take you to him.'

She led me through the garden and across the south lawn to an open French window. Then into a candlelit drawing room that smelled of pipe tobacco and old timber. The room was empty apart from two startled adulterers on the sofa, their limbs unravelling hastily as we stepped through to the wide hallway beyond.

'The house, it is like a ship, yes?' smiled Simone Savy, as we climbed a narrow staircase. As if to prove her point, we passed an exquisitely framed map, allegedly charted by Captain

Nicolas Morphey in 1756. We ascended three flights before emerging onto a spacious balcony under the apex of the sweeping roof.

There was a cheap picnic table on the balcony, where four men were quietly playing cards. Oil lamps hung from the ceiling. The players were drinking cognac. The stillness of the gamblers and the golden glow on their faces made the scene resemble a painting by Goya.

Simone Savy cleared her throat to announce my presence, then departed. One of the men leapt to his feet and beamed at me. He was lean, in his late fifties, with an impressive shock of white hair. He wore white slacks and a pink silk shirt with a bow tie.

'Countess Penwith? I'm Ashley Moore. I'd like to welcome you to my island.'

Warily, I shook his hand. Grinning boyishly, Moore added: 'But I don't believe you came here to see me. I think you're rather more interested in this reprobate...'

On cue, the man at the end of the table got to his feet. He towered above me, just as he'd towered above the woman he bludgeoned to death. He was dressed informally in chinos and a short-sleeved tropical island shirt. The belly that had only begun to swell over his waistband in the seventies was now enormous, but then so were his arms, chest and slightly rounded shoulders. He was grossly overweight.

The stranger's face was hidden behind a neatly-trimmed greying Edwardian beard that partially masked the sagging jowls, but there was no mistaking that snub nose with its wide, porcine nostrils or the dark narrow eyes with their sardonic, uncompromising stare. But for its corpulence, the face might have been impressive. The hair had thinned considerably and was oiled back across a peeling scalp that was tanned to the colour of mahogany. Whatever Richard John Bingham had been doing for the past twenty-six years, he had clearly not been hiding in a darkened room.

Lucan extended his hand in greeting. It was a crude and powerful machine tool of a hand, wider than it was long, with short, fleshy nicotine-stained fingers. I glared accusingly at the proffered extremity until its owner withdrew it. 'You've got time to take a brandy with us, have you?' Lucan smiled, half-mockingly, the implication being that if he had anything to do with it, I was going nowhere.

With rapid, nervous movements, Ashley Moore grabbed a glass and filled it with brandy. 'Your health, my dear,' he said without irony as he passed the glass to me. This time, when Moore spoke, I detected the faint lilt of a Dublin accent.

'I'd heard you'd had a road accident,' I said to Lucan. 'Heard you were in a wheelchair.'

'Yes. I heard that too,' he drawled lethargically. 'Extraordinary, isn't it? I also heard that I was a resident guest in a Mozambique Hotel. And that I was frightened of running and on the verge of giving myself up.'

Lucan threw back his head and cackled delightedly. My enquiries had led me to believe that Lucan was quiet and reflective by nature, but the man at my side was repellently loud. If he wasn't drunk, then two and a half decades of hiding had indeed taken their toll. I examined the defiant old face. Disappointingly, I felt no anger or hatred. Lucan was arrogant, but no more arrogant than most of the people I grew up with.

'What's this about?' I demanded.

Lucan sniffed and looked away, as if the question was too tedious to answer.

Ashley Moore introduced me to the two other gamblers. I guessed the identity of the first man before Moore had opened his mouth. The stranger was in his forties, dressed rather theatrically in a black silk shirt and leather waistcoat. He looked like a cowardly, self-indulgent gunfighter. The colour of his clothes matched his oiled hair and his dark, drug-shadowed eyes.

'Meet Gilbert Lazare,' said Moore. 'Gilbert, this lady is an English Countess.'

I felt that I had met Lazare before – too many times. Every conceivable sin and human weakness seemed to have been etched into his complacent, leering face. Lazare also offered me his hand. I declined to take it. Ignoring the snub – such a man could not afford to be sensitive – Lazare said: 'Thank you, thank you, whoever you are.' He jerked a thumb in Lucan's direction, then waved at the cards on the table. 'This bastard is one hell of a Bridge player. One more rubber and he'd have cleaned me out.'

'All right, Lazare,' said Lucan wearily, his voice and manner broadcasting his disdain for the pimp.

The fourth man was something of an unknown quantity. He was about fifty, short and wide, with a head of ginger stubble and the flat, broad nose of a pugilist. He was the only man at the table who neglected to stand in my presence. 'This is Viscount Willis. Perhaps you know him?'

'We've never met. But I'm aware of his reputation,' I said, studying the Viscount's square, unyielding face. 'In his youth he tried to introduce neo-fascism to the Home Counties. He failed, mainly because neo-fascism was already thriving there. On Sundays he chases foxes. During the week, he chases small boys.'

Willis gave the barest nod of assent, but the hint of a smile at the corners of his thin mouth revealed he would rather have a bad name than no name at all.

'You ride with the Berkshire Hunt, I believe. Do you know what "Berkshire Hunt" means in cockney rhyming slang?'

Willis didn't react. Moore and Lazare waited a moment to allow the insult to sink in, then laughed raucously. Lazare pointed at Willis with puerile glee. 'She has you there! Admit it! She has you!'

'Shut up!' snapped Lucan with surprising aggression. All four men fell silent. 'This isn't a bloody game, damn you!'

Remembering his manners, Moore pulled up a chair for me, seating me between himself and Lucan. Then he gathered up the playing cards and placed them in a neat silver box. Lucan opened a packet of Marlboro with his thumbnail and offered one to me. I hesitated, then accepted, my eyes never once leaving his face.

'Thought you smoked Peter Stuyvesant International,' I commented.

'My, my. She *has* been doing her homework.' Lucan shook his head. 'Haven't seen a packet of Stuyvesant for years. Do they still make 'em?'

I shrugged.

With an odd show of servility, Ashley Moore leapt to his feet and produced a golden lighter. As Debrett would have recommended, he held the naked flame out for me, then Lucan. Narrowing his eyes, Lucan inhaled deeply and snorted smoke out through both nostrils. Abruptly, he smashed a hand down hard on the back of his neck and outstretched his palm to inspect the minute bloody corpse of a dead mosquito.

Then he inclined his head to one side and with a hint of indignation said: 'You ask me what this is about. Well, my dear Countess, I might very well ask you the same question. I've been arsing around in the tropics for the best part of a quarter of a century. Not having a particularly good time, if the truth be told. Getting tired of hiding, tired of the heat and the constant jabber of wogs.'

He saw the contempt on my face and tutted mildly. 'Oh, lor'. I can't even say "wog" without her looking daggers at me. Perhaps I shouldn't expect anything less from a woman called "India".'

Willis and Lazare laughed appreciatively. Ashley Moore merely looked uncomfortable.

I drained my brandy glass. Confidently, Lucan refilled the glass, spilling a large amount of spirit on the table. 'Point is, dear lady, things were working out pretty reasonably for me. No one but you could remember what I'd been accused of. It'd been a long time. The police couldn't care bloody less about me. I thought it was time to go back home, spend time with my children. Friends said: "You're safe now, Johnny. Come back to us, no one's looking for you, come back and grow old here." Then what happens? You come along, rich little vigilante, opening old wounds, reawakening bad memories.'

My eyes blazed. 'Like the memory of Sandra Rivett?'

Lucan affected infinite weariness. 'Oh, what about her?'

'She's the reason I'm here.'

Lucan and Lazare snorted with amusement. 'No, *no*, my dear Madam,' scoffed Lucan. 'Don't flatter yourself. You're here because your life is so empty that you've got nothing better to do with your time. You're here because we *wanted* you here.'

Willis nodded darkly. I felt the blood rushing to my face. Carefully, I placed my brandy glass on the table. 'Go on.'

Wearily, Lucan explained. 'Willis here sees you as a threat. Not just to me personally, but to the fabric of bloody society in general.' (Lazare sniggered like a schoolboy.) 'Viscount Willis represents the members of an elite organisation, whose esteemed members take exception to you and your methods.'

I smiled. 'You're referring, of course, to the Conservative Party?'

For the first time, Lucan allowed the enmity that he felt for me to show in his eyes. 'I believe you've been offering a substantial reward for information leading to my arrest.'

'I wouldn't call a hundred thousand "substantial". But then, you've never really been "lucky" with money, have you, Bingham?'

'At least I know who my friends are,' retorted Lucan sharply. 'You haven't the faintest idea how bloody stupid you've been, have you? Just look at you: a vain and spoilt little girl in an expensive party dress.'

'Look at you: a beach-ball with a stupid face drawn on it.'

Bingham's complexion darkened. The insult had struck home. 'Don't you realise you've been tricked?' he spluttered.

'Say it, don't spray it,' I advised.

For some reason, I didn't see the blow coming. My head snapped back as Lucan's huge hand swiped me across the face. The silence around the table intensified. I sniffed and put my hand to my nose. Blood. Quietly, Moore passed me a clean white handkerchief.

I knew then that they planned to kill me.

'Was that really necessary?' wondered Moore.

'Yes,' barked Lucan. 'Someone should have done that a long time ago.' He took a long ruminative drag of his cigarette. 'What was I saying?'

'That I'd been tricked.'

'Oh yes. Old Willis here knew of your reputation and pointed out that nothing gets you more hot under the collar than the idea of wicked rich people using and abusing decent poor people. So between us, we concocted the heart-rending story of a humble black whore who'd been maltreated by wicked white men. And you fell for it. Hook, line and sinker.'

Finding Lucan's fondness for clichés as irritating as this proof of my gullibility, I scanned the faces around the table, saw the relish in the fixed smiles of Willis and Lazare. Moore avoided my eyes. A movement below caught my attention. I looked down. A bright green gecko was sitting in the bag at my feet. The small lizard, its eyes round and coal-black, sat stark and motionless, poised between my hairbrush and my CS gas spray. I looked up to see if Lucan had noticed the reptile. But he only had eyes for me.

In the garden below, the irritating sega music stopped abruptly. There was a polite ripple of applause.

Lucan smiled with satisfaction and stretched his arms languidly. 'You see, *India*, the main reason that I've been free for so long is that I've always been blessed with bloody good friends. Whereas, I hear that by comparison, your social life is a little on the quiet side.'

Lucan nodded grimly to Ashley Moore, who yanked a bell rope dangling from the ceiling. Moments later, a tall black manservant arrived, carrying a silver tray covered with a square of blue silk. The man placed the tray before Moore, then left. Moore turned anxious eyes to Lucan.

'All righty,' said Lucan. 'Let's spell out the rules of the game. You're a bolshy rich girl who, incidentally, is far too pretty to be playing the crusader.'

I fluttered my eyelids. '*Gosh*. Do you really think so?' He paused to contemplate my insolence. Then he hit me again. 'I don't know whether you're congenitally stupid or just mentally ill. But it appears you came here without any back-up. It's not as if you can kidnap me and take me back to England. What were you planning to do? Stare me to death?'

I said nothing, simply carried on staring. Lucan glanced down at my left hand, in which my unsmoked cigarette was burning. 'Look at you. You're shaking like a leaf.'

Decisively, I got to my feet and headed for the door. Demonstrating the speed and grace of a large and dangerous animal, Willis leapt out of his chair to bar my way.

'Sit down,' Lucan warned me. Willis puffed out his chest like a bouncer at a cheap nightclub. I glanced at Moore, who closed his eyes and nodded regretfully to show that my cooperation was indeed required. I sat down.

Moore removed the silk cover from the tray to reveal a gleaming revolver. I was raised with firearms. I recognised the weapon instantly. 'I believe you can shoot a little?' said Lucan, picking up the weapon and weighing it in the palm of his hand.

I said nothing, but experienced a powerful sense of déjà-vu. I'd seen all this before, in a dream. Not the kind of dream I'd wish upon anyone.

'Hardly surprising,' continued Lucan. 'You're a country girl. Seen one of these before?'

'Yes,' I admitted. 'It's a classic. A Smith & Wesson Centennial Airweight.'

Lucan whistled softly. He was impressed. So impressed that he aimed the revolver at my right eye. 'Very good. Go on.'

Struggling to keep my voice steady, I said: 'No stopping power, but at this range, you could kill me with no trouble at all.'

Ashley Moore got to his feet. 'All right. This has gone far enough.'

Lucan said: 'Dear me. Don't tell me you're welching on a bet, Ashers?'

Moore hesitated, then shook his head.

'Then bloody well sit down.'

Moore complied. I looked at the unhappy millionaire, saw that his brow and upper lip were damp with sweat. At that moment, even though my life was threatened, I felt an odd twinge of sympathy for the owner of Oubliette Island.

I said: 'What bet?'

Lucan studied me dispassionately. 'Moore thinks I wouldn't have the nerve to kill you. What do you think?'

Smirking, Lucan aimed the gun over my shoulder and fired. I turned to see a hanging basket filled with bright orchids explode into colourful fragments. A cloud of soil burst into the air, rattling as it scattered over the bare floorboards. Willis and Moore jumped slightly as the gun boomed. Lazare gasped, then emitted a shrill nervous laugh. Only Lucan remained calm and unmoved. There was an eerie smile on his face. The smile was almost sexual.

He pointed the gun at me. The muscles above his trigger finger twitched. I knew that this was the moment. There would be no more talk. I glanced down. That beautiful bright green lizard was still calmly sitting in my bag. I grabbed the strap of the bag with my right hand. Lucan saw me do it. His face split into a hideous grin. Perhaps he thought I was about to hit him with my handbag.

Without releasing the strap, I gently swung my bag towards my enemy. As I'd hoped, the lizard took to the air and landed on Lucan, clinging to his chest and hanging there, petrified. Despite his years in the tropics, Lucan reacted as most people would have done. He looked down, saw the gecko and gave a violent shudder of revulsion.

Lowering his left hand, the hand that held the gun, he tried to brush the creature away, but it darted over his shoulder and was gone before he could touch it. I released the bag and seizing his left wrist, stubbed my cigarette out on his enormous knuckles. Hissing through his teeth, he dropped the weapon. I caught it as it fell. Then I aimed the gun at Lord Lucan's large, startled face and squeezed the trigger.

What happened next was shocking and grotesque. Half of Lucan's face separated from his head in a solid mass and sprang sideways across the floor. Instantly, I and the men around the table were drenched in his blood. A split-second later, the sound of the shot cracked painfully in our ears. The injured man emitted a sound that was somewhere between a splutter and a sigh before lurching backwards in his chair. Then the chair and the body of the seventh Earl of Lucan crashed violently to the floor.

There were two seconds of utter silence before the band on the lawn below began to play another insanely cheerful refrain. Lucan murmured something. Although I'd blown the roof of his mouth away, he was trying to speak. It seemed cruel to leave him like that, half-dead and suffering. So, as Debrett would have recommended, I stood over him and shot him once through the heart. Despite his bulk, his body bounced three inches into the air, then lay still.

Moore's Irish accent became comically pronounced as he said 'Jaysus, Jaysus' over and over again. Lazare was cowed into terrified silence. Willis snarled and leapt at me. I tried to shoot but the gun jammed. Or perhaps I'd run out of ammunition. There was no time to debate the issue. I blocked a blow from the Viscount's right fist with my left forearm. Simultaneously, I smashed the revolver into his left temple. He groaned, and clung to me, trying to drag me earthward. Repeatedly, I clubbed Willis in the teeth with the butt of the gun. At last, blood spilling from his open mouth, he released me and adopted a foetal position on the ground, whimpering, his hands covering his face.

I turned to Moore and Lazare, who had fled the table and were now cowering by the balcony. Moore looked as if he was preparing to jump. 'Whoa,' said Lazare, warding me off with the palms of his hands.

I turned my back on them and walked away. On the stairs I met two male servants who had been alerted by the gunfire. Seeing the gun in my hand, they turned and fled. On reaching the lawn, I pushed my way through the dancing guests, none of whom suspected that there was an executioner in their midst. On the path down to the shore, hundreds of crabs scattered before my feet.

Bromley was standing alone on the jetty, drinking a bottle of Sey Beer and looking up at the stars. I almost wept with relief at the sight of him. His expression was grave as he registered my wild appearance: my torn dress and dishevelled hair; the blood spattered over my face and arms. Without comment, he led me to a powerboat with an unsightly brown stain on its side and sang: 'Did you think I would leave you crying, when there's room on my boat for two?'

We climbed aboard. Bromley untied the mooring rope and started the engine. The outboard motor came to life with a loud, dirty roar. Then, with a lurch the boat turned full circle and surged out into the ocean, its bright lamps turning the water to milk. I looked back and saw three men running down the jetty, bellowing threats across the water.

The boat gathered speed and the figures on the spangled shore shrank to nothing. The darkness and the cold black water surrounded us. There was a whizzing sound as three rockets slashed the black, star-rich sky. With a chorus of deafening booms, the rockets exploded, flowering exquisitely into brilliant arcs of red, white and green fire.

It was midnight.

Bromley, still gripping the wheel, turned and shouted something in my face. His voice was drowned by the engine roar, but I managed to read his lips. He had wished me a 'Happy New Century.' Bromley prised the gun out of my stiff, numb fingers and hurled it overboard. With a wink, he pressed a bottle into my hand.

Shivering with cold, I put the bottle to my lips and drank. It was filthy stuff, some illicit local brew, but I was grateful for the warmth it brought to my belly and my soul.

There was a terrific explosion, followed by a loud and rapid volley of minor bangs. Then the dark underbelly of heaven erupted with fire and light as a hail of fireworks streaked upwards from Oubliette, Praslin and La Digue.

I, who until tonight had never taken a human life, had entered the new century as an executioner. This fact was surprising enough. What was even more surprising was that as I pondered the dead man, his ruined face and the two shots that had ended his life, I felt nothing.

Nothing at all.

ABOUT THE AUTHORS

COLIN BATEMAN was born in Northern Ireland in 1962. He worked as a reporter with *The County Down Spectator* for many years until becoming a full time writer in 1996. His novels *Divorcing Jack* and *Cycle of Violence* have recently been filmed. His other novels are *Of Wee Sweetie Mice and Men, Empire State* and *Niagara Falls*.

NICHOLAS BLINCOE is the author of the already classic crime 'n' clubland novels *Acid Casuals* and *Jello Salad*. His latest novel, *Manchester Slingback*, tells the story of two Bowie-boys, running around Manchester in the early 'eighties, high on beauty, amphetamine and betrayal. It is dedicated to Manchester's ex-Chief Constable James Anderton, God's Cop. A collection of his short stories was recently published.

DAVID BOWKER is the author of *The Death Prayer* (soon to be filmed), *The Secret Sexist* and *The Butcher of Glastonbury*. He lives in the Bedfordshire countryside with his best friend and their young son.

MOLLY BROWN's short stories have appeared in numerous magazines and anthologies. Her books include *Virus, Cracker: To Say I Love You*, and *Invitation to a Funeral*. She is also webmistress of an award-winning online tour of Restoration London at http://www.okima.com/

PAUL CHARLES is an agent, manager and promoter in the music business and currently co-owner of Asgard Promotions, one of Europe's leading agencies. He is the author of three novels featuring Detective Inspector Christy Kennedy: *I Love the Sound of Breaking Glass, Last Boat to Camden Town* and *Fountain of Sorrow*. All are published by The Do-Not Press.

RICHARD T. CHIZMAR has published over forty stories in a variety of magazines and anthologies. His first collection, *Midnight Promises*, appeared in 1996 and his first novel is due in 1999. He is also the editor of a number of anthologies, including *The Earth Strikes Back*.

PETER CROWTHER is the author of more than sixty published short stories and the editor of eight anthologies. His novel *Escardy Gap* was published earlier this year. SIMON CONWAY is a former newspaper journalist. His published short fiction includes two other stories written in collaboration with Peter Crowther.

JOHN FOSTER is currently Screenwriter-in-Residence at Bournemouth University. His writing credits include many episodes for TV series such as *Z Cars*, *Softly Softly*, *Juliet Bravo* and *The Bill*, and an award-winning BBC Omnibus film on Raymond Chandler. His screenplay *Letters from a Killer* has recently been filmed starring Patrick Swayze.

ED GORMAN has published a number of novels and three collections of short stories. His latest novels are *The Silver Scream* (Headline), and *Night Kills* and *Cage of Night*, the latter of which was named as one of the ten best crime novels of the year by *Ellery Queen's Mystery Magazine* when it appeared in the US.

JOHN HARVEY is recuperating in the wake of writing *Last Rites*, the last of the ten Nottingham-based Resnick novels. For now, he is concentrating on publishing the first fiction titles from his own Slow Dancer Press and putting the finishing touches to *Bluer Than This*, the second collection of his own poems.

LAUREN HENDERSON was born and bred in London, where, after university, she worked as a journalist for *Marxism Today* and *Lime Lizard*, an indie music magazine. She has published four books to date featuring Sam Jones - *Dead White Female*, *Too Many Blondes*, *The Black Rubber Dress* and *Freeze My Margarita*.

MAXIM JAKUBOWSKI runs the Murder One bookshop and reviews crime fiction for *Time Out* magazine. Crowned 'The King of the Erotic Thriller' by Crime Time, his latest books are *The State of Montana* and *Because She Thought She Loved Me*. He also co-edits the *Fresh Blood* anthologies.

DENNIS LEHANE lives in Boston, Massachusetts, the setting for his four Kenzie and Gennaro novels: *A Drink Before The War*, which won the Shamus Award for best first novel, *Darkness, Take My Hand*, *Sacred* and *Gone Baby Gone*.

IAN RANKIN lives in Edinburgh and is the author of the Inspector Rebus series of novels, the latest of which is *The Hanging Garden*, as well as writing radio plays and award-winning short stories. He has twice won the CWA/Macallan Short Story Dagger and the Gold Dagger in 1997 for *Black and Blue*. The title of this story, *Unknown Pleasures*, is also the title of his all-time favourite rock album.

JASON STARR was born in Brooklyn, New York, in 1966. His noir crime novel *Cold Caller* has been published in the UK, US, Canada, France and Germany. His second novel, *Nothing Personal*, will be published this year. He lives with his wife in New York City.

JERRY SYKES's stories have appeared in a number of magazines and anthologies, including *Cemetery Dance*, *Crime Time*, *Love Kills* and *The Year's 25 Finest Crime and Mystery Stories*. Further stories are due to appear in *Crimewave*, *Shots* and the US collection *Subeterranean Gallery*. Together with his wife Julia he runs the small press, Revolver. He has just completed his first novel.

Also available from The Do-Not Press

Ray Lowry: INK
1 899344 21 7 – Metric demy-quarto paperback original, £9

A unique collection of strips, single frame cartoons and word-play from well-known rock 'n' roll cartoonist Lowry, drawn from a career spanning 30 years of contributions to periodicals as diverse as Oz, The Observer, Punch, The Guardian, The Big Issue, The Times, The Face and NME. Each section is introduced by the author, recognised as one of Britain's most original, trenchant and uncompromising satirists, and many contributions are original and unpublished.

Paul Charles: FOUNTAIN OF SORROW Bloodlines
1 899344 38 1– demy 8vo casebound, £15.00
1 899344 39 X – B-format paperback original, £6.50

Third in the increasingly popular Detective Inspector Christy Kennedy mystery series, set in the fashionable Camden Town and Primrose Hill area of north London. Two men are killed in bizarre circumstances; is there a connection between their deaths and if so, what is it? It's up to DI Kennedy and his team to discover the truth and stop to a dangerous killer. The suspects are many and varied: a traditional jobbing criminal, a successful rock group manager, and the mysterious Miss Black Lipstick, to name but three. As BBC Radio's Talking Music programme avowed: "If you enjoy Morse, you'll enjoy Kennedy."

Jenny Fabian: A CHEMICAL ROMANCE
1 899344 42 X – B-format paperback original, £6.50

Jenny Fabian's first book, Groupie first appeared in 1969 and was republished last year to international acclaim ("Truly great late-20th century art. Buy it." —NME; "A brilliant period document" —Sunday Times). A roman à clef from 1971, A Chemical Romance concerns itself with the infamous celebrity status Groupie bestowed on Fabian. Expected to maintain the sex and drugs lifestyle she had proclaimed 'cool', she flits from bed to mattress to bed, travelling from London to Munich, New York, LA and finally to the hippy enclave of Ibiza, in an attempt to find some kind of meaning to her life. As Time Out said at the time: "Fabian's portraits are lightning silhouettes cut by a master with a very sharp pair of scissors." This is the novel of an exciting and currently much in-vogue era.

Miles Gibson: KINGDOM SWANN
1 899344 34 9 – B-format paperback, £6.50

Kingdom Swann, Victorian master of the epic nude painting turns to photography and finds himself recording the erotic fantasies of a generation through the eye of the camera. A disgraceful tale of murky morals and unbridled matrons in a world of Suffragettes, flying machines and the shadow of war.

"Gibson writes with a nervous versatility that is often very funny and never lacks a life of its own, speaking the language of our times as convincingly as aerosol graffiti" —The Guardian

Miles Gibson: VINEGAR SOUP
1 899344 33 0 – B-format paperback, £6.50
Gilbert Firestone, fat and fifty, works in the kitchen of the Hercules Café and dreams of travel and adventure. When his wife drowns in a pan of soup he abandons the kitchen and takes his family to start a new life in a jungle hotel in Africa. But rain, pygmies and crazy chickens start to turn his dreams into nightmares. And then the enormous Charlotte arrives with her brothel on wheels. An epic romance of true love, travel and food...
"I was tremendously cheered to find a book as original and refreshing as this one. Required reading..." –The Literary Review

Ken Bruen: A WHITE ARREST Bloodlines
1 899344 41 1 – B-format paperback original, £6.50
Galway-born Ken Bruen's most accomplished and darkest crime noir novel to date is a police-procedural, but this is no well-ordered 57th Precinct romp. Centred around the corrupt and seedy worlds of Detective Sergeant Brandt and Chief Inspector Roberts, A White Arrest concerns itself with the search for The Umpire, a cricket-obsessed serial killer that is wiping out the England team. And to add insult to injury a group of vigilantes appear to to doing the police's job for them by stringing up drug-dealers... and the police like it even less than the victims. This first novel in an original and thought provoking new series from the author of whom Books in Ireland said: "If Martin Amis was writing crime novels, this is what he would hope to write."

Maxim Jakubowski: THE STATE OF MONTANA
1 899344 43 8 half-C-format paperback original £5
Despite the title, as the novels opening line proclaims: 'Montana had never been to Montana". An unusual and erotic portrait of a woman from the "King of the erotic thriller" (Crime Time magazine).

Mark Sanderson: AUDACIOUS PERVERSION Bloodlines
1 899344 32 2 – B-format paperback original, £6.50
Martin Rudrum, good-looking, young media-mover, has a massive chip on his shoulder. A chip so large it leads him to commit a series of murders in which the medium very much becomes the message. A fast-moving and intelligent thriller, described by one leading Channel 4 TV producer as "Barbara Pym meets Bret Easton Ellis".

Geno Washington: THE BLOOD BROTHERS
ISBN 1 899344 44 6 – B-format paperback original, £6.50
Set in the recent past, this début adventure novel from celebrated '60s-soul superstar Geno Washington launches a Vietnam Vet into a series of dangerous dering-dos, that propel him from the jungles of South East Asia to the deserts of Mauritania. Told in fast-paced Afro-American LA street style, The Blood Brothers is a swaggering non-stop wham-bam of blood, guts, lust, love, lost friendships and betrayals.

The Do-Not Press
Fiercely Independent Publishing

Keep in touch with what's happening at the cutting edge of independent British publishing.

Join The Do-Not Press Information Service and receive advance information of all our new titles, as well as news of events and launches in your area, and the occasional free gift and special offer.

Simply send your name and address to:
The Do-Not Press (Dept. MT)
PO Box 4215
London
SE23 2QD
or email us: thedonotpress@zoo.co.uk

There is no obligation to purchase and
no salesman will call.

Visit our regularly-updated web site:
http://www.thedonotpress.co.uk

Mail Order

All our titles are available from good bookshops, or (in case of difficulty) direct from The Do-Not Press at the address above. There is no charge for post and packing.

(NB: A postman may call.)